Nola's Worlds

#3

even for a dreamer like me

A BIG THANK YOU TO MY LITTLE BAND OF DREAMERS, ALICIA, GAËL, AND ANNA. AS ALWAYS, A HUGE ACKNOWLEDGEMENT TO MY TRAVELING COMPANIONS, KIM AND MÉLANIE. THE JOURNEY ISN'T OVER YET; HAPPILY, WE'LL SOON SET OFF AGAIN FOR THE LAND OF NOLA BANANA. AND FINALLY, THANK YOU TO ALL OUR READERS FOR THEIR ENTHUSIASTIC RESPONSES, AS WELL AS TO THOSE WHO'VE HAD CONFIDENCE IN US AND HELPED US WITH THIS PROJECT.

THANK YOU TO
MYLÈNE HENRY
NICOLAS PLAMONDON
CÉCILIA RAVIX-ANTONINI

TO MY PÉPÉ ♡

THANK YOU TO CHKLE, JOANY D. LEBLANC, KIRA, AND CALAMITY, WHO HELPED SO MUCH WITH THE COLORING. THANK YOU TO GATE AND MY FAMILY, WHO HAVE SUPPORTED ME IN EVERY SENSE OF THE WORD FROM THE BEGINNING, JUST LIKE KIM AND MATHIEU. ^ ^ AND THANK YOU TO EVERYONE WHO PATIENTLY AWAITED THE RELEASE OF THIS THIRD VOLUME IN THE ADVENTURES OF NOLA. À BIENTÔT UNTIL THE NEXT THANK YOUS. :P

STORY BY MATHIEU MARIOLLE
ART BY MINIKIM
COLORS BY POP
TRANSLATION BY ERICA OLSON JEFFREY AND CAROL KLIO BURRELL

First American edition published in 2010 by Graphic Universe™.
Published by arrangement with MEDIATOON LICENSING — France.

Alta Donna 3 – Même pour une rêveuse comme moi . . .
© DARGAUD BENELUX (DARGAUD-LOMBARD S.A.) 2009, by Mariolle, MiniKim, Pop.
www.dargaud.com

English translation copyright © 2010 by Lerner Publishing Group, Inc.

Graphic Universe™ is a trademark of Lerner Publishing Group, Inc.

Graphic Universe™
A division of Lerner Publishing Group, Inc.
241 First Avenue North
Minneapolis, MN 55401 U.S.A.

Website address: www.lernerbooks.com

The image in this book is used with the permission of:
© iStockphoto.com/Lobke Peers, p. 30.

Library of Congress Cataloging-in-Publication Data

Mariolle, Mathieu.
    Even for a dreamer like me / by Mathieu Mariolle ; illustrated by MiniKim ; colored by Pop. — 1st American ed.
        p. cm. — (Nola's worlds ; #3)
    Summary: Nola learns that the city of Alta Donna is more important than she imagined, and that her storytelling ability is the key to saving her world, the world of stories, and her friends Damiano and Inés.
        ISBN: 978-0-7613-6505-1 (lib. bdg : alk. paper)
    1. Graphic novels. [1. Graphic novels. 2. Imagination—Fiction. 3. Characters in literature—Fiction. 4. Supernatural—Fiction. 5. Ferrets—Fiction.] I. MiniKim, ill. II. Pop, 1978– ill. III. Title.
PZ7.7.M34Eve 2010
741.5'944—dc22   2010015215

Manufactured in the United States of America
1 – DP – 7/15/10

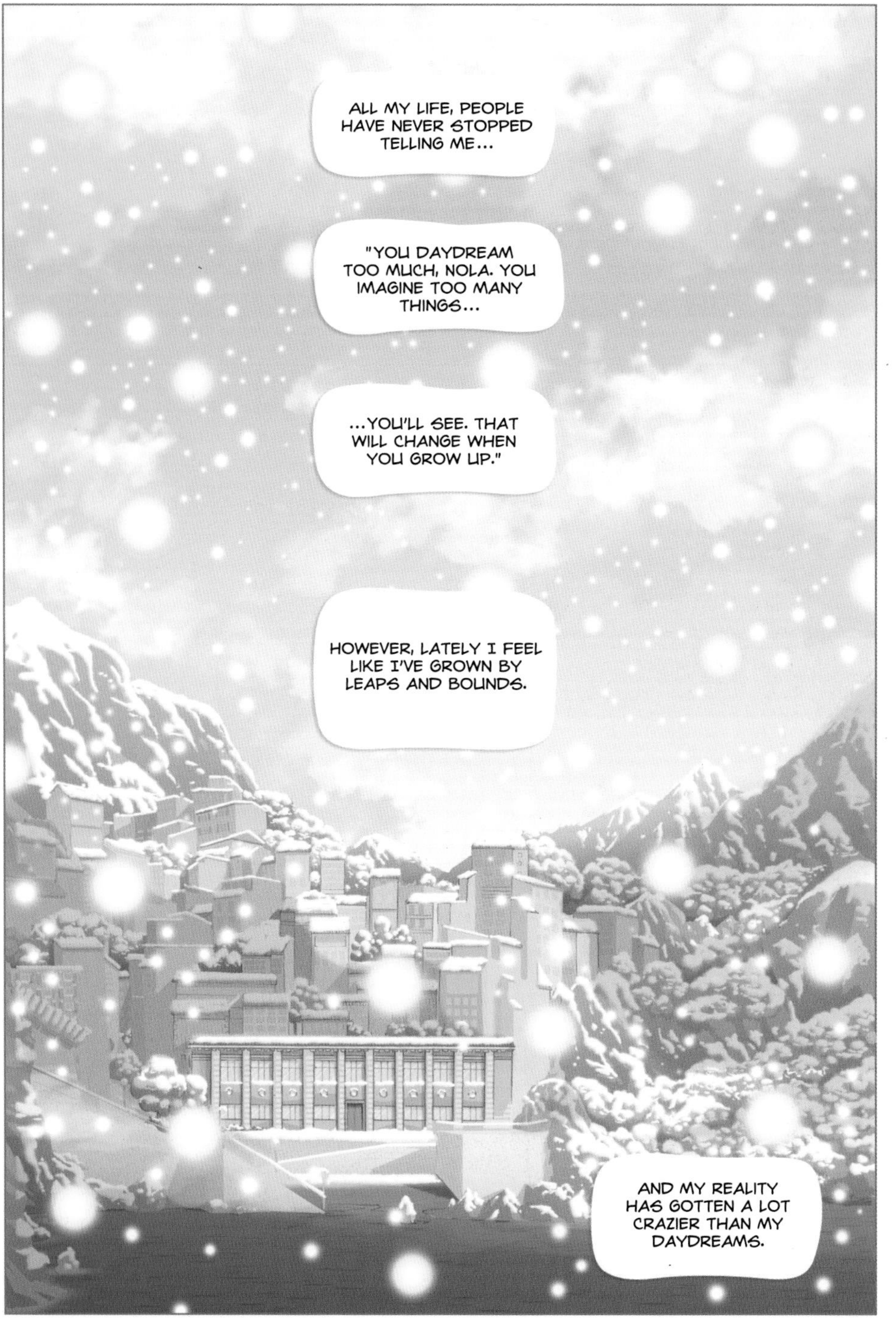
ALL MY LIFE, PEOPLE HAVE NEVER STOPPED TELLING ME...
"YOU DAYDREAM TOO MUCH, NOLA. YOU IMAGINE TOO MANY THINGS...
...YOU'LL SEE. THAT WILL CHANGE WHEN YOU GROW UP."
HOWEVER, LATELY I FEEL LIKE I'VE GROWN BY LEAPS AND BOUNDS.
AND MY REALITY HAS GOTTEN A LOT CRAZIER THAN MY DAYDREAMS.

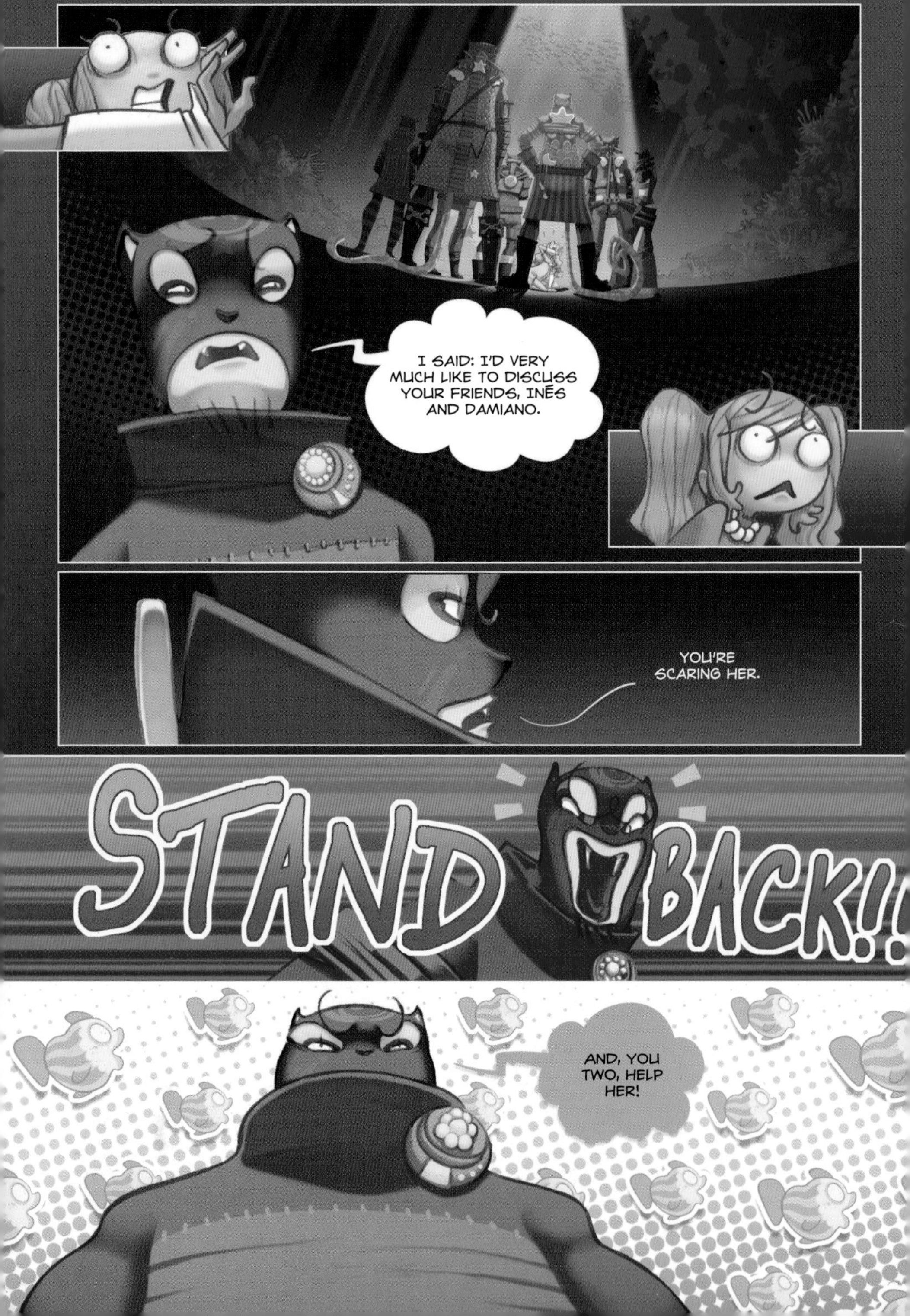
I SAID: I'D VERY MUCH LIKE TO DISCUSS YOUR FRIENDS, INÉS AND DAMIANO.
YOU'RE SCARING HER.
STAND BACK!!
AND, YOU TWO, HELP HER!

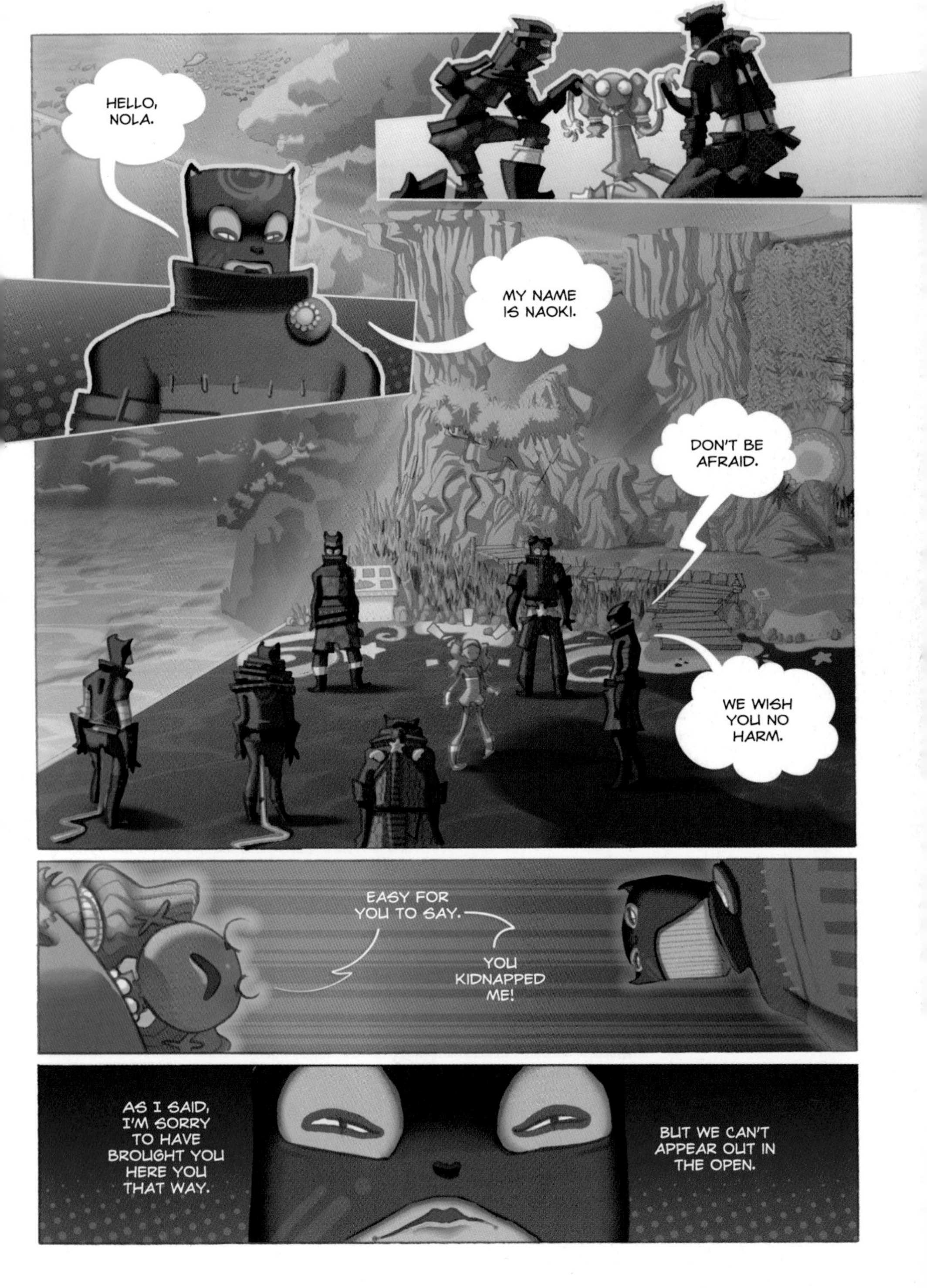

HELLO, NOLA.
MY NAME IS NAOKI.
DON'T BE AFRAID.
WE WISH YOU NO HARM.
EASY FOR YOU TO SAY.
YOU KIDNAPPED ME!
AS I SAID, I'M SORRY TO HAVE BROUGHT YOU HERE YOU THAT WAY.
BUT WE CAN'T APPEAR OUT IN THE OPEN.

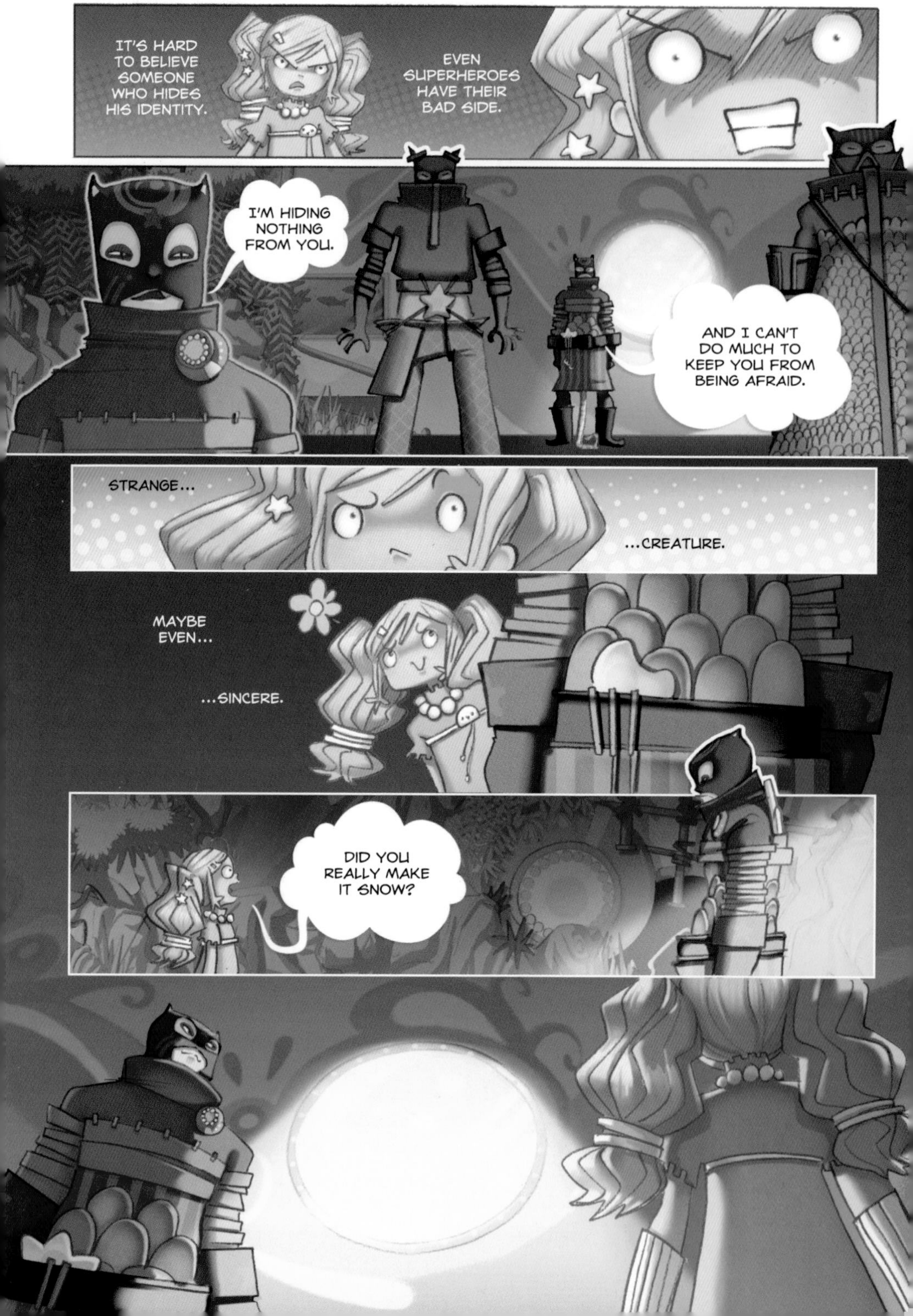
IT'S HARD TO BELIEVE SOMEONE WHO HIDES HIS IDENTITY.
EVEN SUPERHEROES HAVE THEIR BAD SIDE.
I'M HIDING NOTHING FROM YOU.
AND I CAN'T DO MUCH TO KEEP YOU FROM BEING AFRAID.
STRANGE...
...CREATURE.
MAYBE EVEN...
...SINCERE.
DID YOU REALLY MAKE IT SNOW?

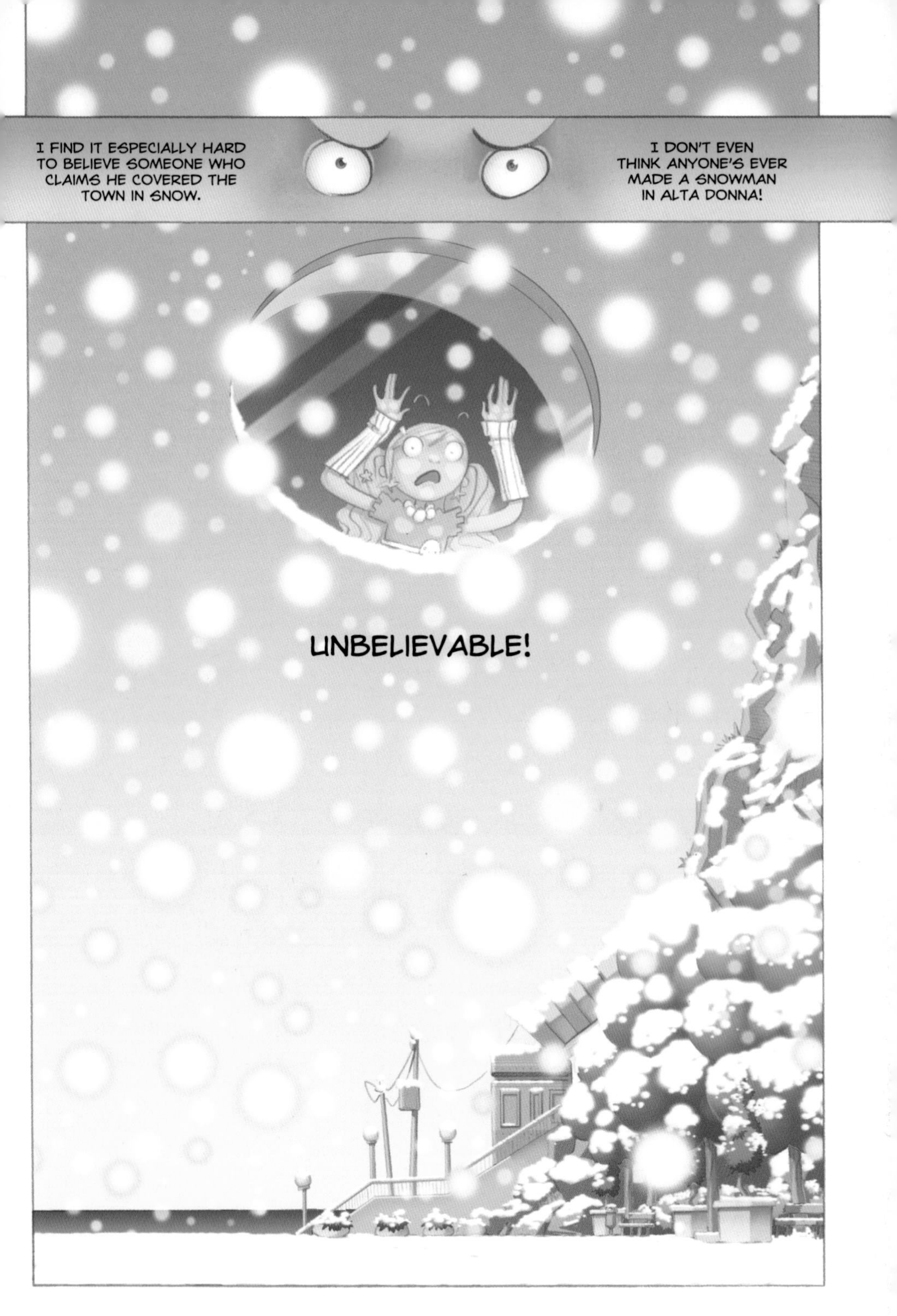
I FIND IT ESPECIALLY HARD TO BELIEVE SOMEONE WHO CLAIMS HE COVERED THE TOWN IN SNOW.
I DON'T EVEN THINK ANYONE'S EVER MADE A SNOWMAN IN ALTA DONNA!
UNBELIEVABLE!

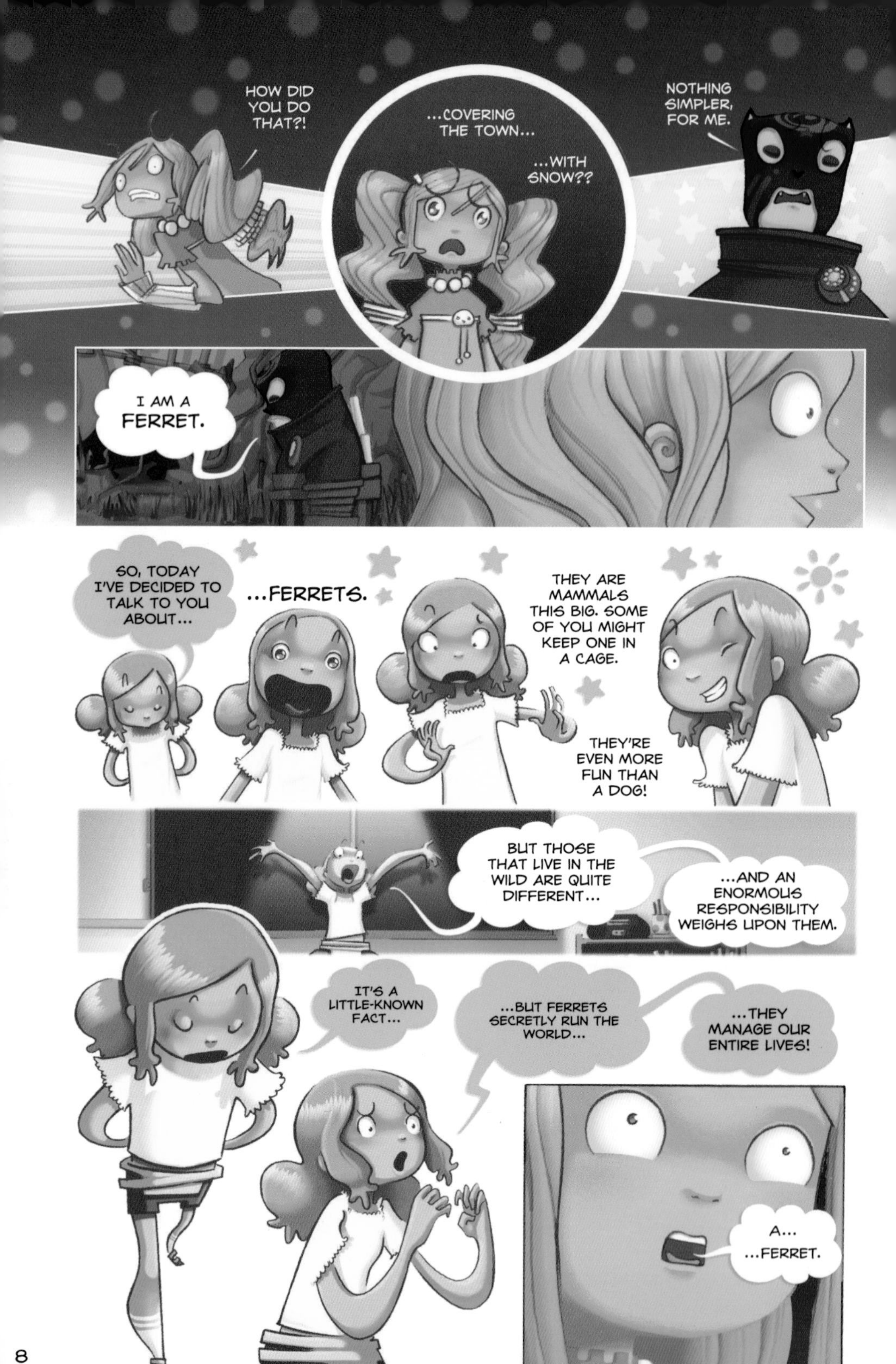
HOW DID YOU DO THAT?!
...COVERING THE TOWN...
...WITH SNOW??
NOTHING SIMPLER, FOR ME.
I AM A FERRET.
SO, TODAY I'VE DECIDED TO TALK TO YOU ABOUT...
...FERRETS.
THEY ARE MAMMALS THIS BIG. SOME OF YOU MIGHT KEEP ONE IN A CAGE.
THEY'RE EVEN MORE FUN THAN A DOG!
BUT THOSE THAT LIVE IN THE WILD ARE QUITE DIFFERENT...
...AND AN ENORMOUS RESPONSIBILITY WEIGHS UPON THEM.
IT'S A LITTLE-KNOWN FACT...
...BUT FERRETS SECRETLY RUN THE WORLD...
...THEY MANAGE OUR ENTIRE LIVES!
A...
...FERRET.

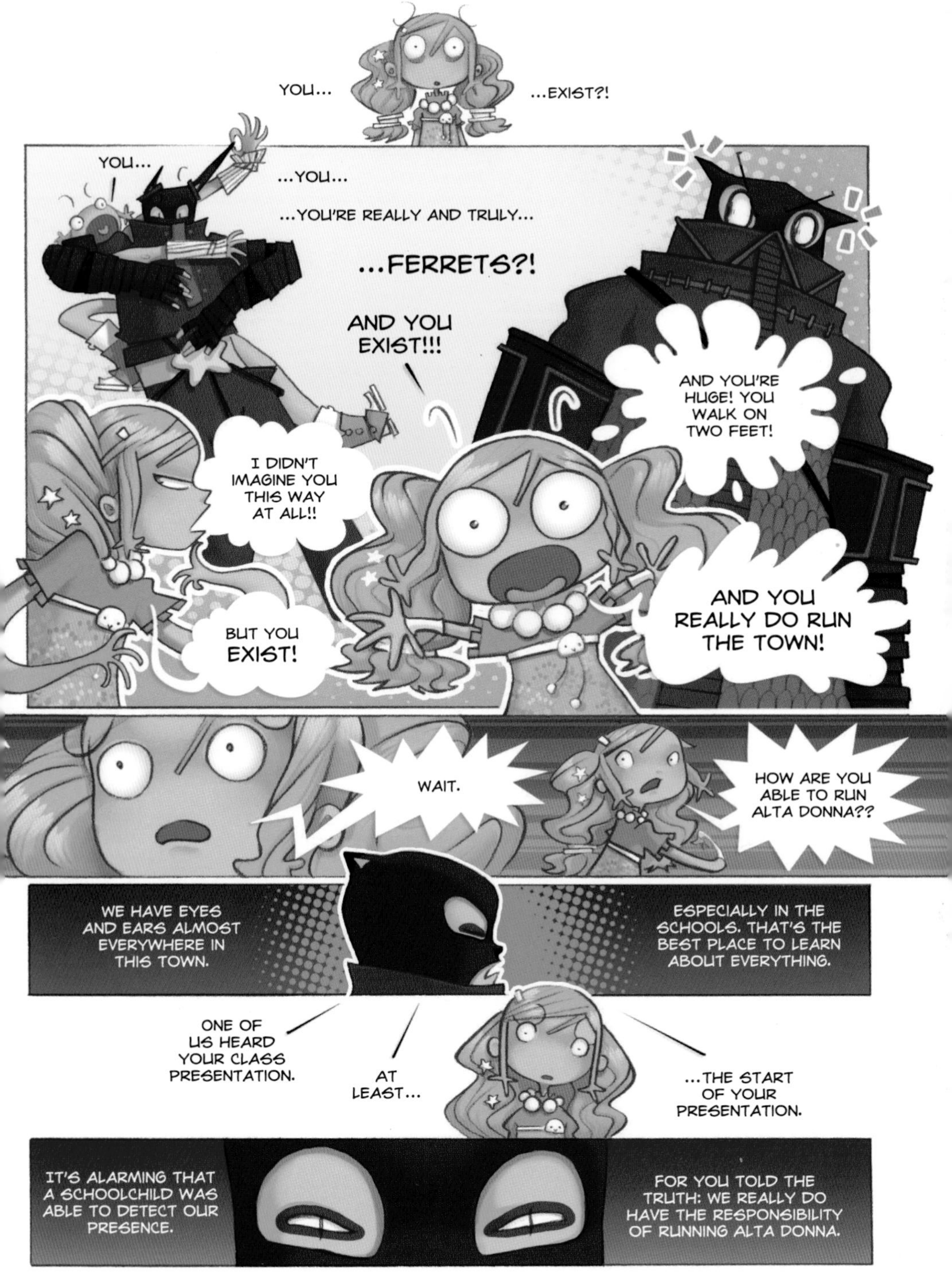
YOU...
...EXIST?!
YOU...
...YOU...
...YOU'RE REALLY AND TRULY...
...FERRETS?!
AND YOU EXIST!!!
AND YOU'RE HUGE! YOU WALK ON TWO FEET!
I DIDN'T IMAGINE YOU THIS WAY AT ALL!!
BUT YOU EXIST!
AND YOU REALLY DO RUN THE TOWN!
WAIT.
HOW ARE YOU ABLE TO RUN ALTA DONNA??
WE HAVE EYES AND EARS ALMOST EVERYWHERE IN THIS TOWN.
ESPECIALLY IN THE SCHOOLS. THAT'S THE BEST PLACE TO LEARN ABOUT EVERYTHING.
ONE OF US HEARD YOUR CLASS PRESENTATION.
AT LEAST...
...THE START OF YOUR PRESENTATION.
IT'S ALARMING THAT A SCHOOLCHILD WAS ABLE TO DETECT OUR PRESENCE.
FOR YOU TOLD THE TRUTH: WE REALLY DO HAVE THE RESPONSIBILITY OF RUNNING ALTA DONNA.

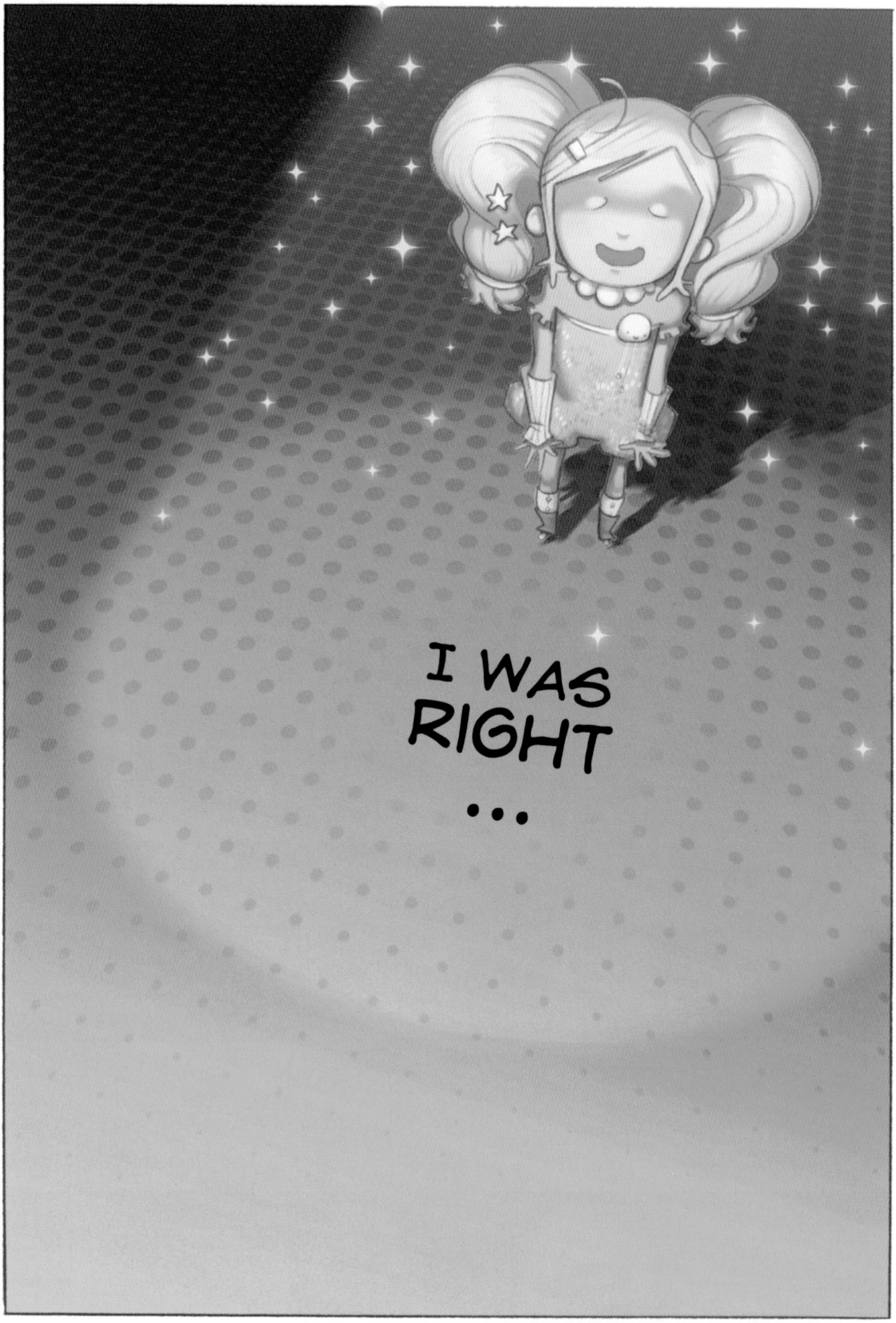
I WAS RIGHT
...

Nola's Worlds #3

even for a dreamer like me

minikim ★ mariolle ★ pop

GRAPHIC UNIVERSE™ · MINNEAPOLIS · NEW YORK · LONDON

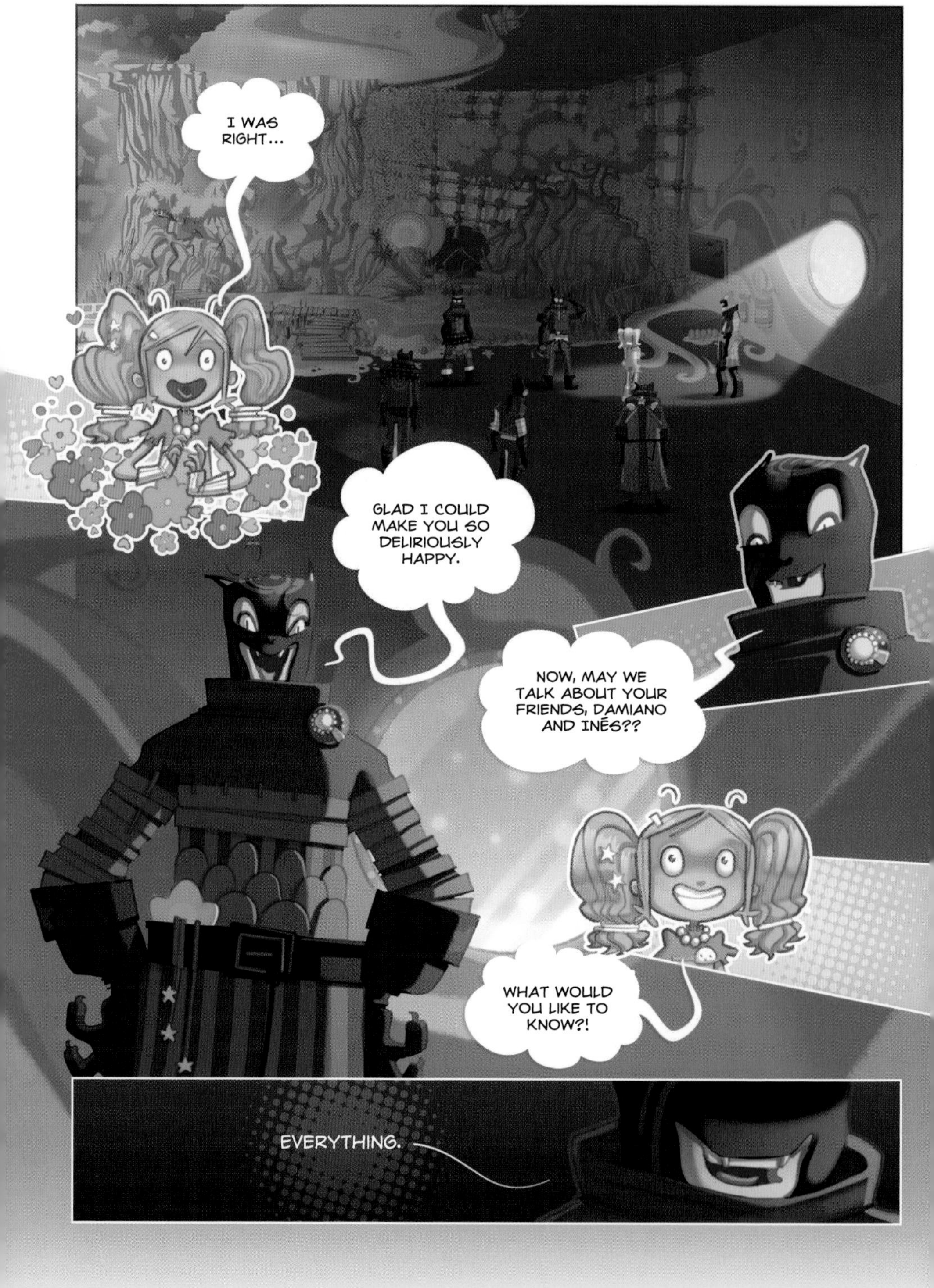
I WAS RIGHT...
GLAD I COULD MAKE YOU SO DELIRIOUSLY HAPPY.
NOW, MAY WE TALK ABOUT YOUR FRIENDS, DAMIANO AND INÉS??
WHAT WOULD YOU LIKE TO KNOW?!
EVERYTHING.

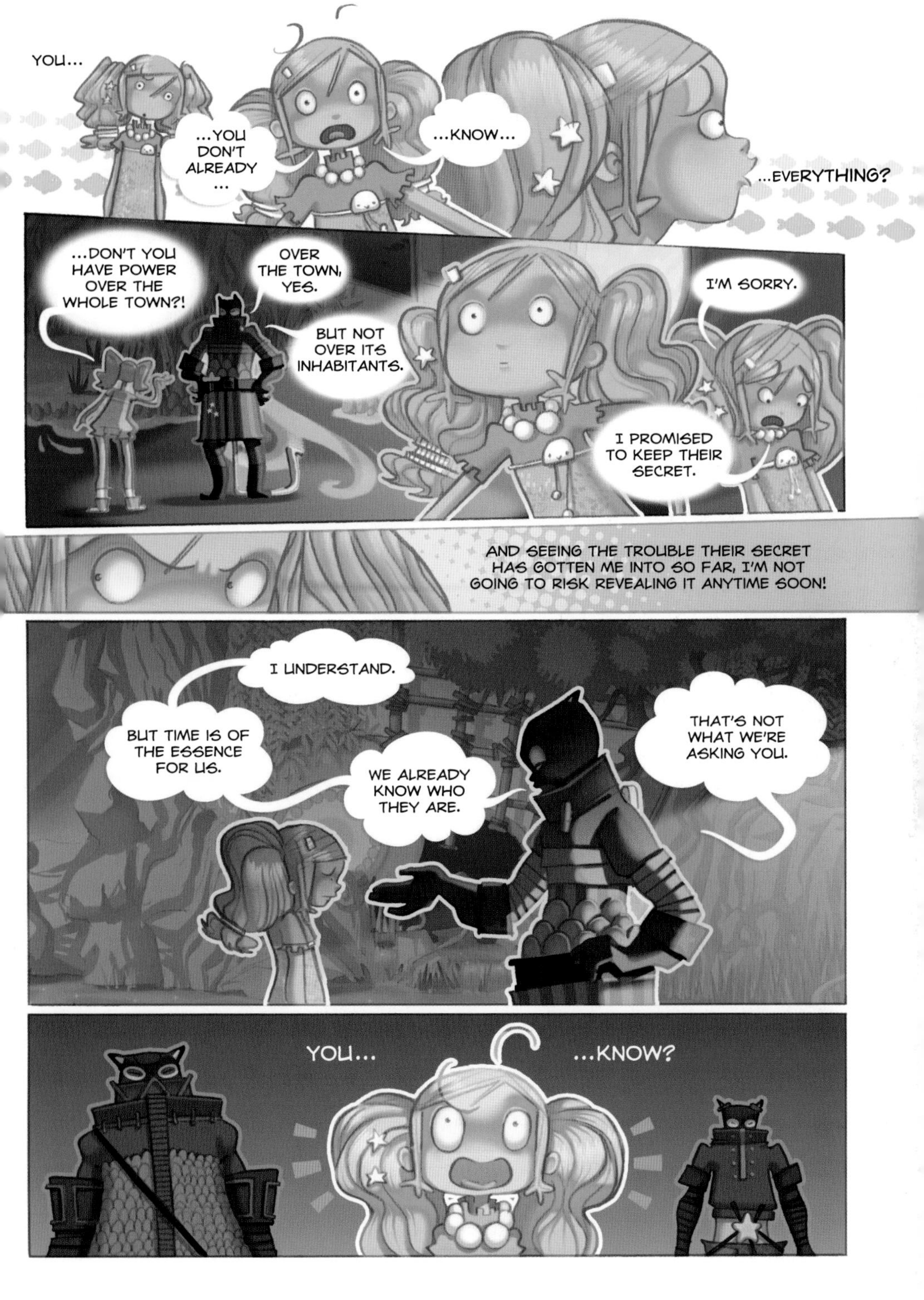
YOU...
...YOU DON'T ALREADY ...
...KNOW...
...EVERYTHING?
...DON'T YOU HAVE POWER OVER THE WHOLE TOWN?!
OVER THE TOWN, YES.
BUT NOT OVER ITS INHABITANTS.
I'M SORRY.
I PROMISED TO KEEP THEIR SECRET.
AND SEEING THE TROUBLE THEIR SECRET HAS GOTTEN ME INTO SO FAR, I'M NOT GOING TO RISK REVEALING IT ANYTIME SOON!
I UNDERSTAND.
BUT TIME IS OF THE ESSENCE FOR US.
WE ALREADY KNOW WHO THEY ARE.
THAT'S NOT WHAT WE'RE ASKING YOU.
YOU...
...KNOW?

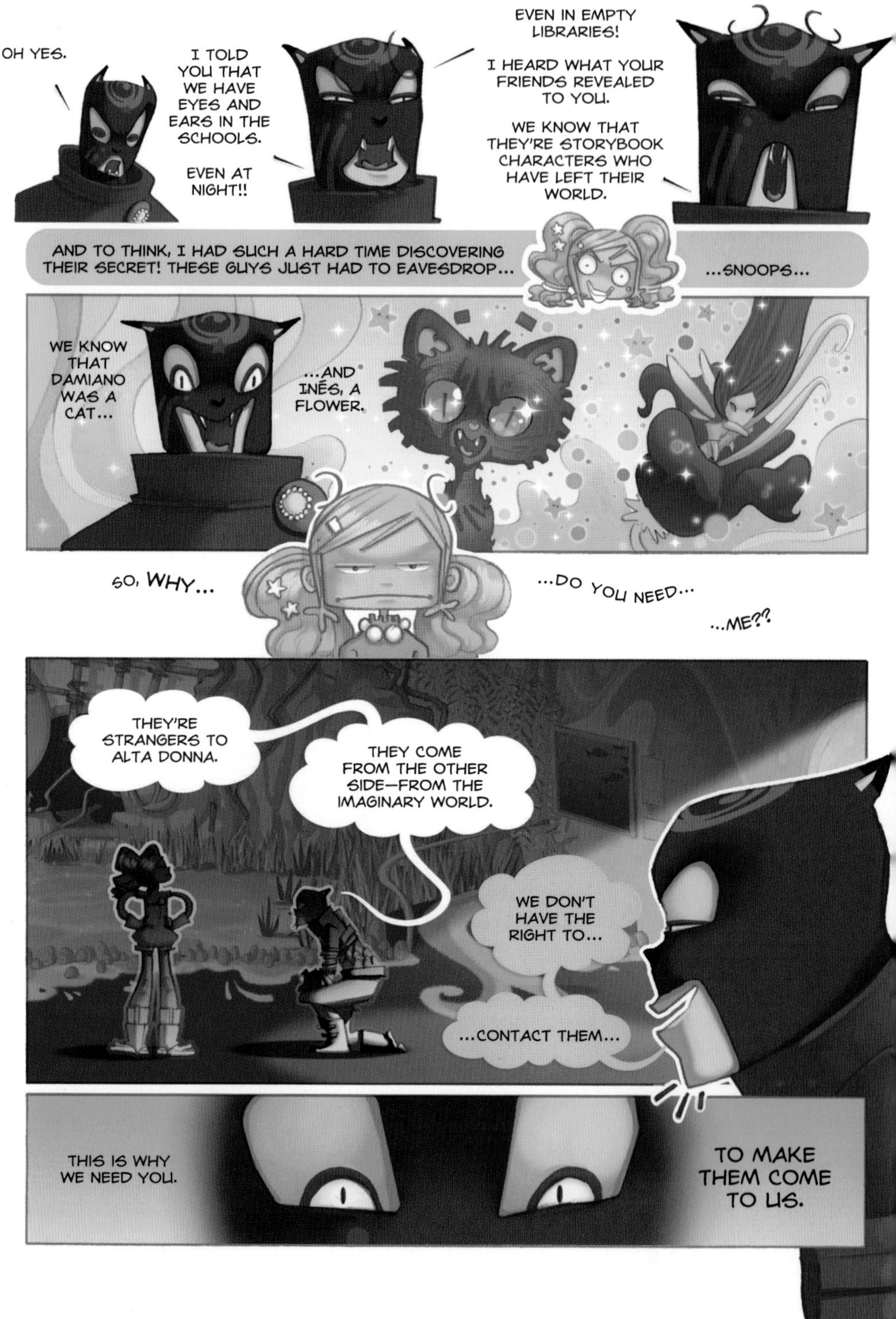
OH YES.
I TOLD YOU THAT WE HAVE EYES AND EARS IN THE SCHOOLS.
EVEN AT NIGHT!!
EVEN IN EMPTY LIBRARIES!
I HEARD WHAT YOUR FRIENDS REVEALED TO YOU.
WE KNOW THAT THEY'RE STORYBOOK CHARACTERS WHO HAVE LEFT THEIR WORLD.
AND TO THINK, I HAD SUCH A HARD TIME DISCOVERING THEIR SECRET! THESE GUYS JUST HAD TO EAVESDROP...
...SNOOPS...
WE KNOW THAT DAMIANO WAS A CAT...
...AND INÉS, A FLOWER.
SO, WHY...
...DO YOU NEED...
...ME??
THEY'RE STRANGERS TO ALTA DONNA.
THEY COME FROM THE OTHER SIDE—FROM THE IMAGINARY WORLD.
WE DON'T HAVE THE RIGHT TO...
...CONTACT THEM...
THIS IS WHY WE NEED YOU.
TO MAKE THEM COME TO US.

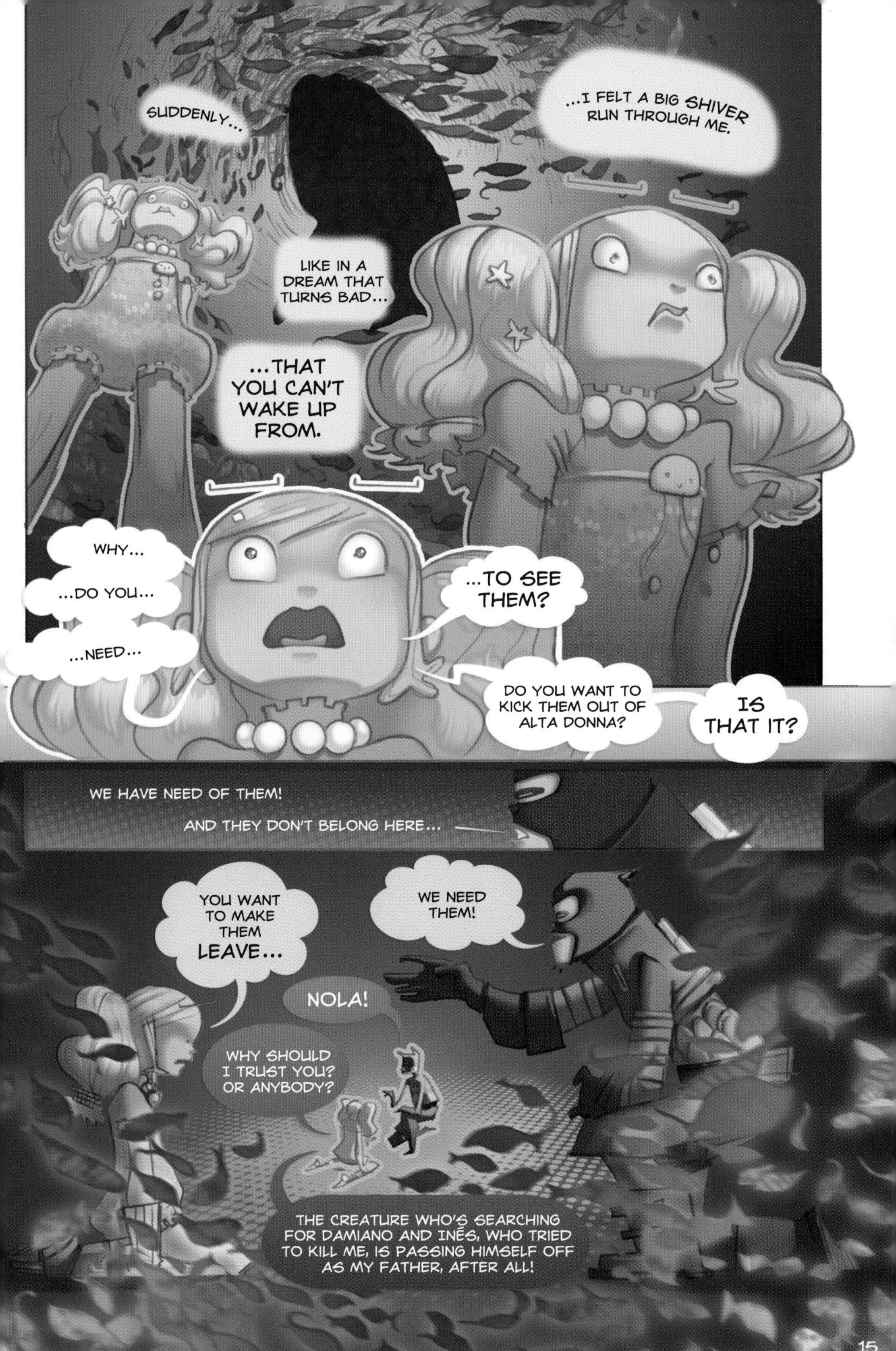
SUDDENLY...
...I FELT A BIG SHIVER RUN THROUGH ME.
LIKE IN A DREAM THAT TURNS BAD...
...THAT YOU CAN'T WAKE UP FROM.
WHY...
...DO YOU...
...NEED...
...TO SEE THEM?
DO YOU WANT TO KICK THEM OUT OF ALTA DONNA?
IS THAT IT?
WE HAVE NEED OF THEM!
AND THEY DON'T BELONG HERE...
YOU WANT TO MAKE THEM LEAVE...
WE NEED THEM!
NOLA!
WHY SHOULD I TRUST YOU? OR ANYBODY?
THE CREATURE WHO'S SEARCHING FOR DAMIANO AND INÈS, WHO TRIED TO KILL ME, IS PASSING HIMSELF OFF AS MY FATHER, AFTER ALL!

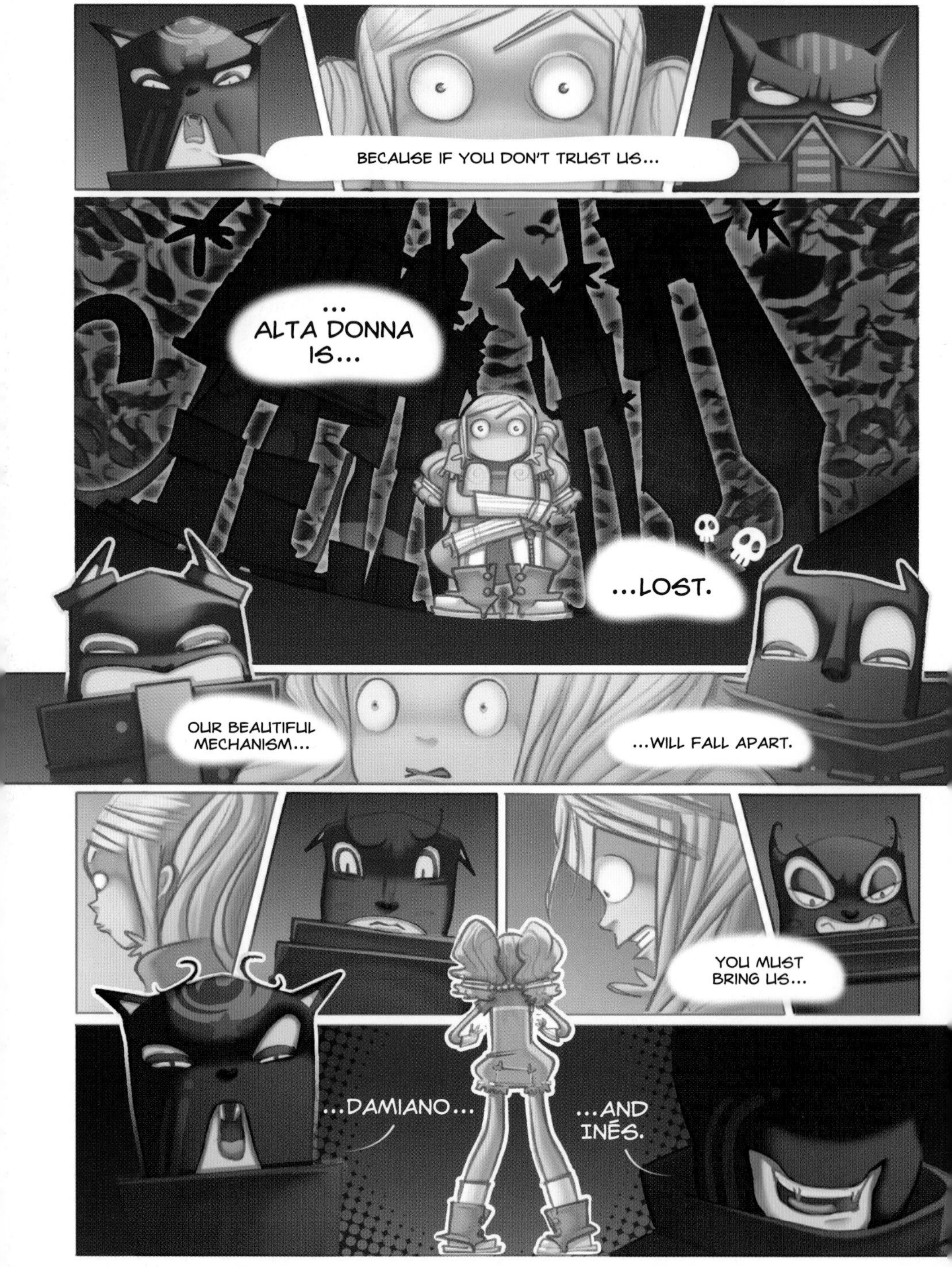
BECAUSE IF YOU DON'T TRUST US...
... ALTA DONNA IS...
...LOST.
OUR BEAUTIFUL MECHANISM...
...WILL FALL APART.
YOU MUST BRING US...
...DAMIANO...
...AND INÉS.

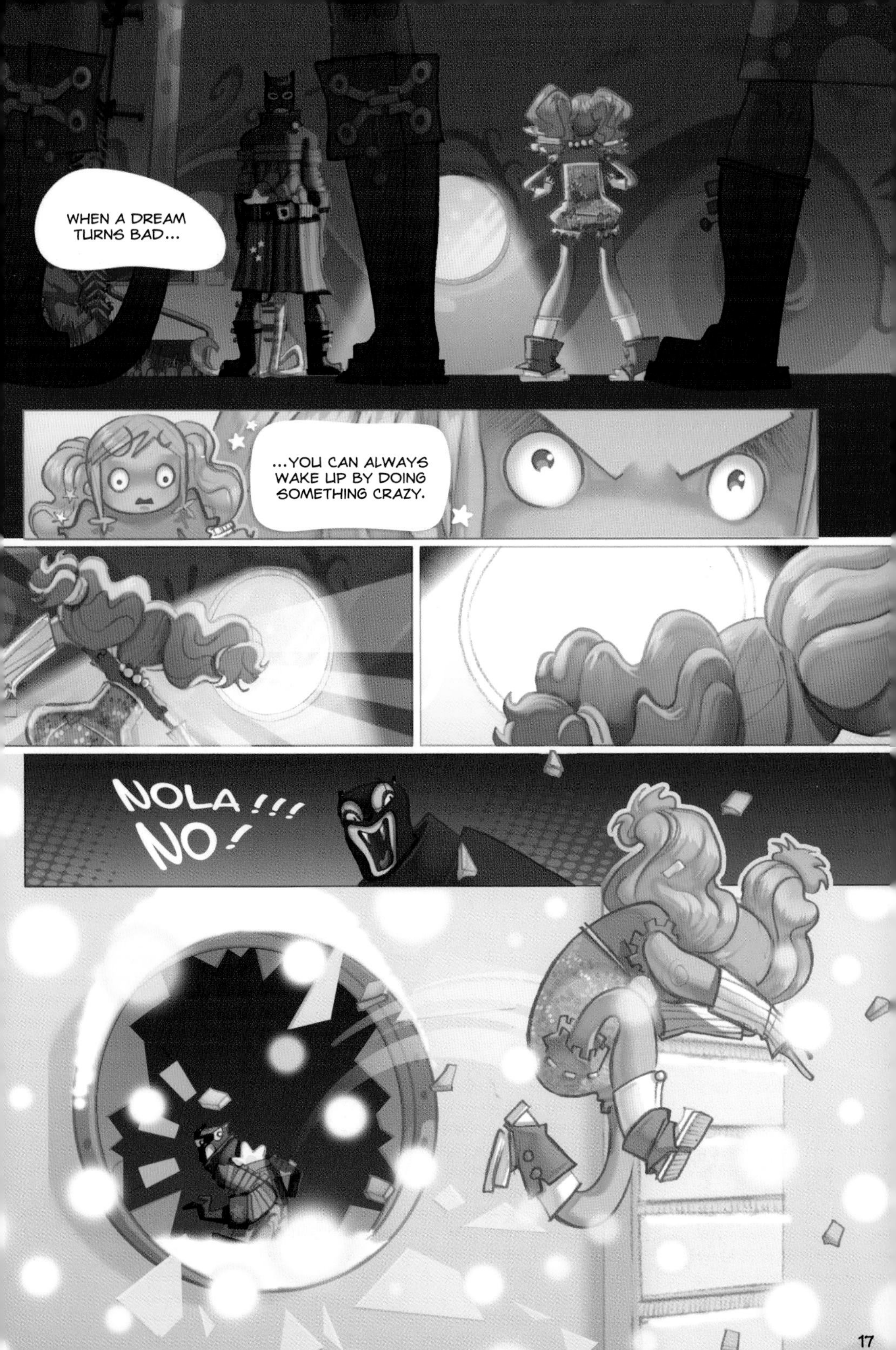
WHEN A DREAM TURNS BAD...
...YOU CAN ALWAYS WAKE UP BY DOING SOMETHING CRAZY.
NOLA!!! NO!

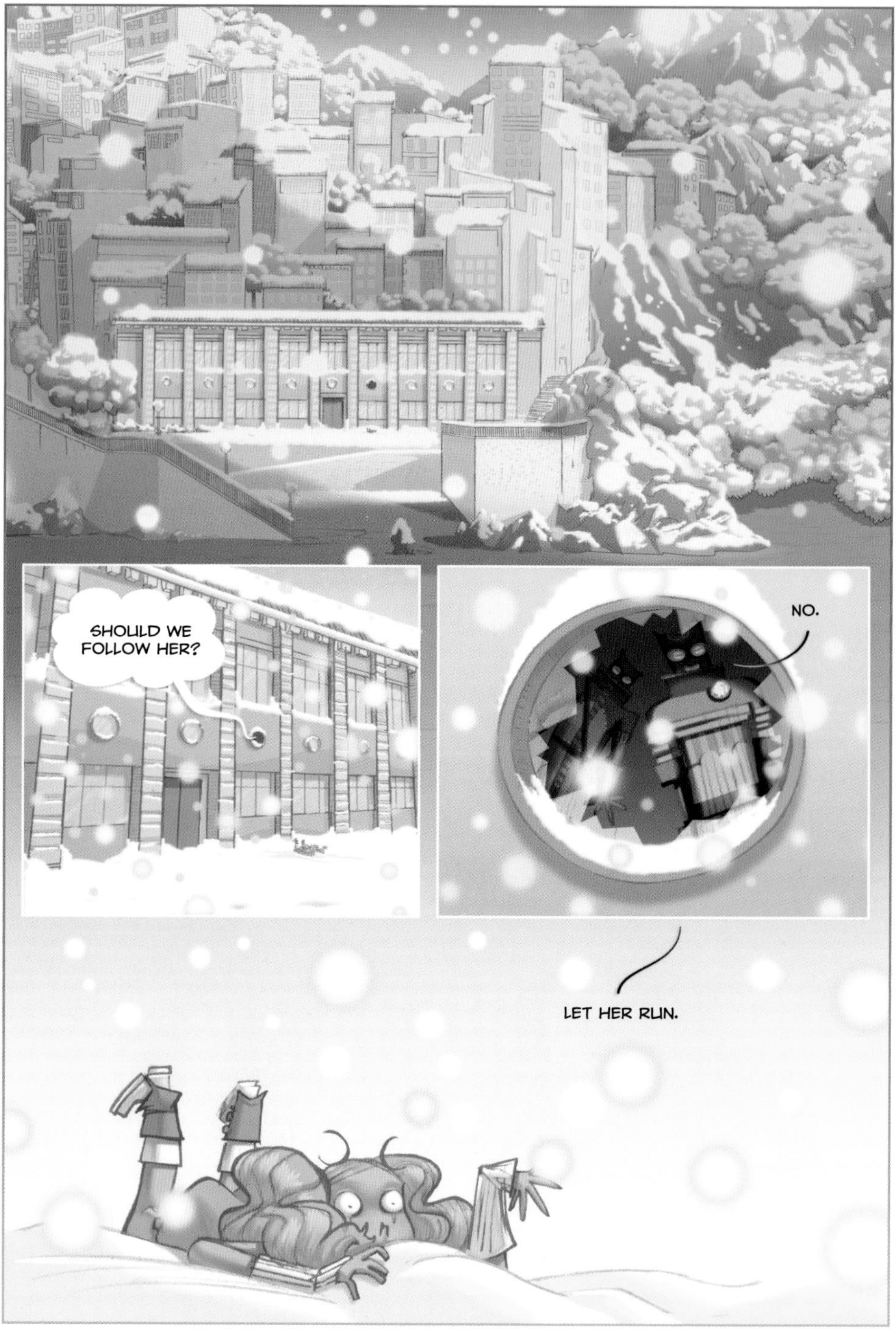
SHOULD WE FOLLOW HER?
NO.
LET HER RUN.

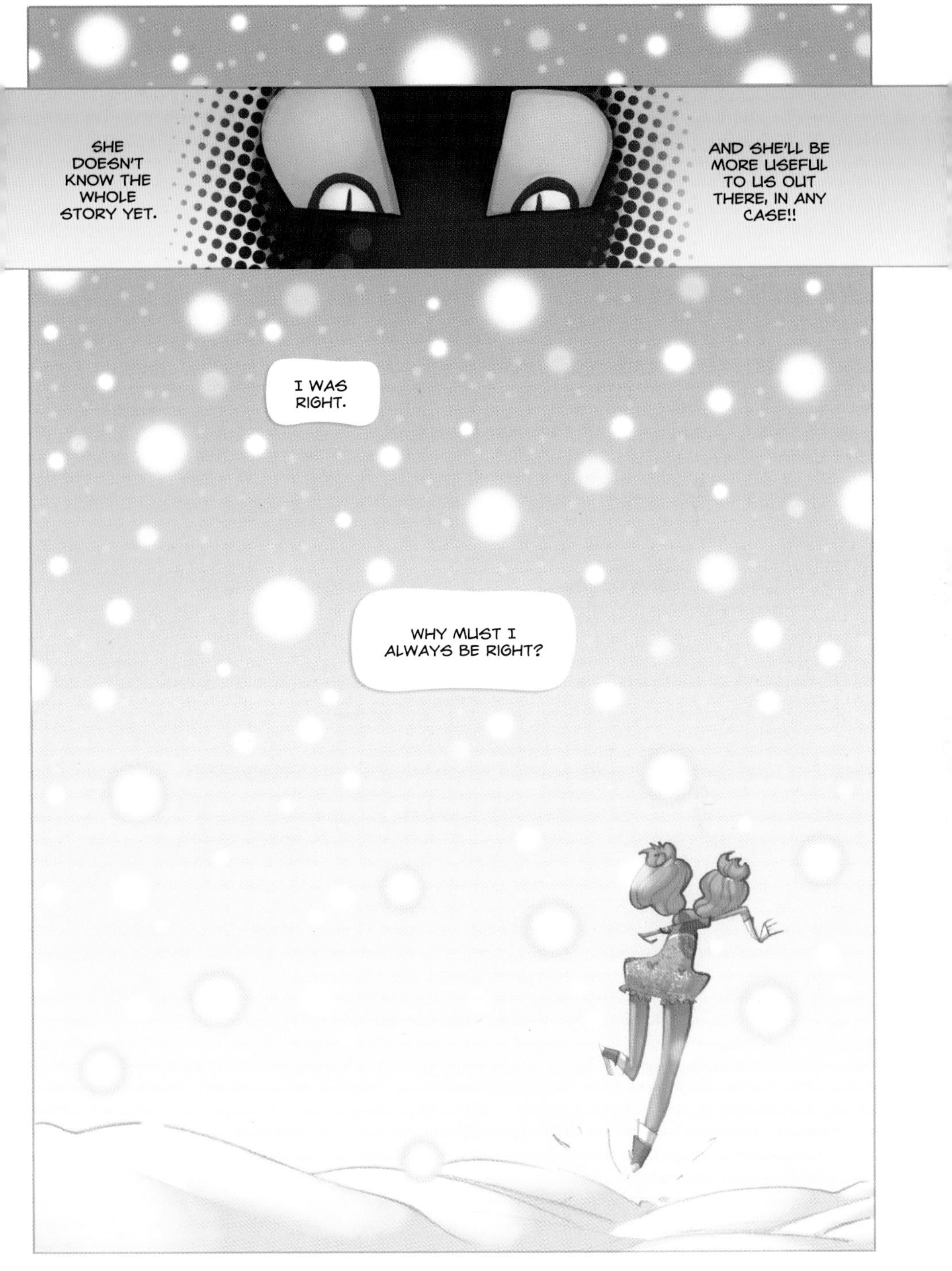
SHE DOESN'T KNOW THE WHOLE STORY YET.
AND SHE'LL BE MORE USEFUL TO US OUT THERE, IN ANY CASE!!
I WAS RIGHT.
WHY MUST I ALWAYS BE RIGHT?

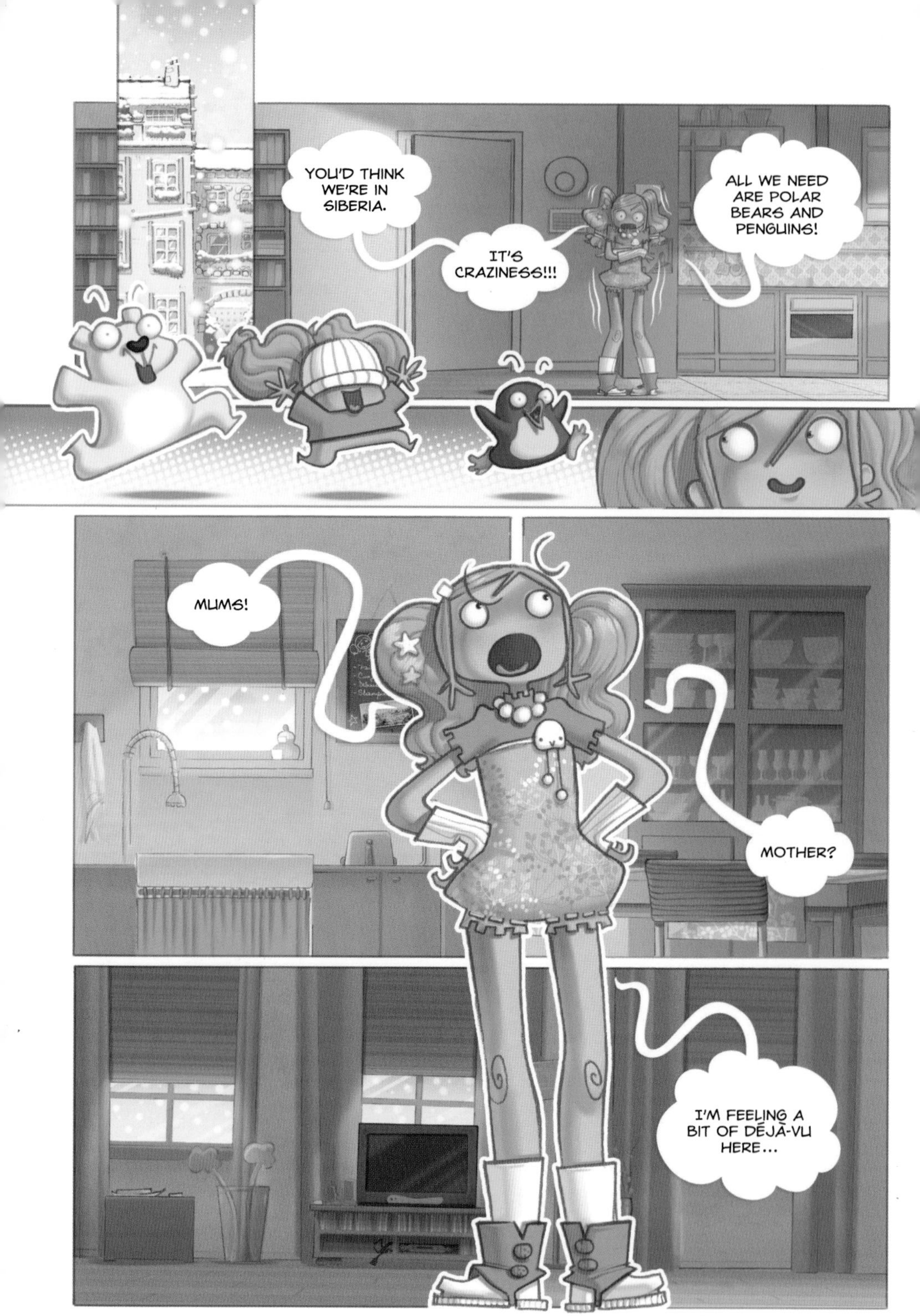
YOU'D THINK WE'RE IN SIBERIA.
IT'S CRAZINESS!!!
ALL WE NEED ARE POLAR BEARS AND PENGUINS!
MUMS!
MOTHER?
I'M FEELING A BIT OF DÉJÀ-VU HERE...

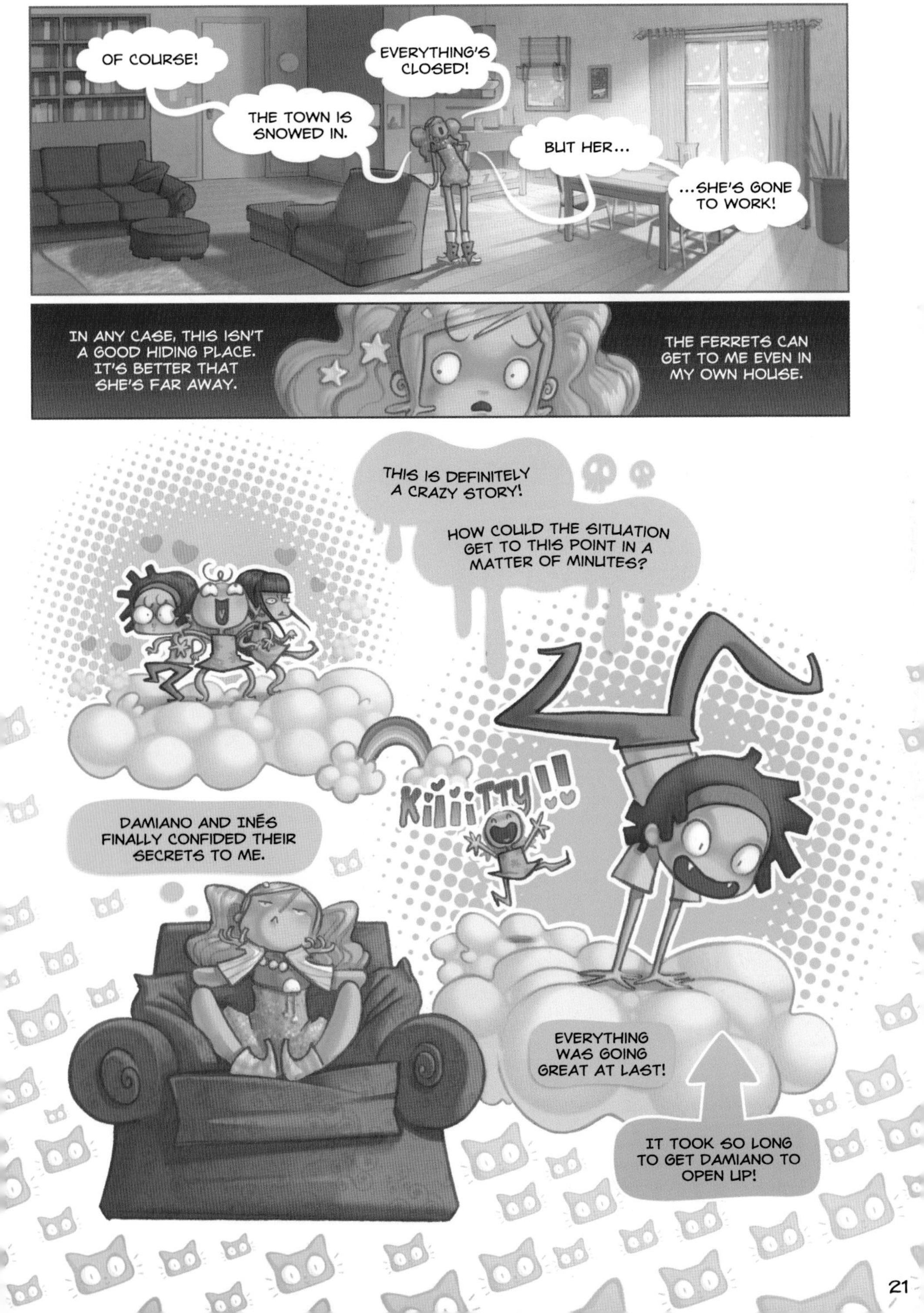

OF COURSE!
THE TOWN IS SNOWED IN.
EVERYTHING'S CLOSED!
BUT HER...
...SHE'S GONE TO WORK!
IN ANY CASE, THIS ISN'T A GOOD HIDING PLACE. IT'S BETTER THAT SHE'S FAR AWAY.
THE FERRETS CAN GET TO ME EVEN IN MY OWN HOUSE.
THIS IS DEFINITELY A CRAZY STORY!
HOW COULD THE SITUATION GET TO THIS POINT IN A MATTER OF MINUTES?
KIIIITTY!!
DAMIANO AND INÉS FINALLY CONFIDED THEIR SECRETS TO ME.
EVERYTHING WAS GOING GREAT AT LAST!
IT TOOK SO LONG TO GET DAMIANO TO OPEN UP!

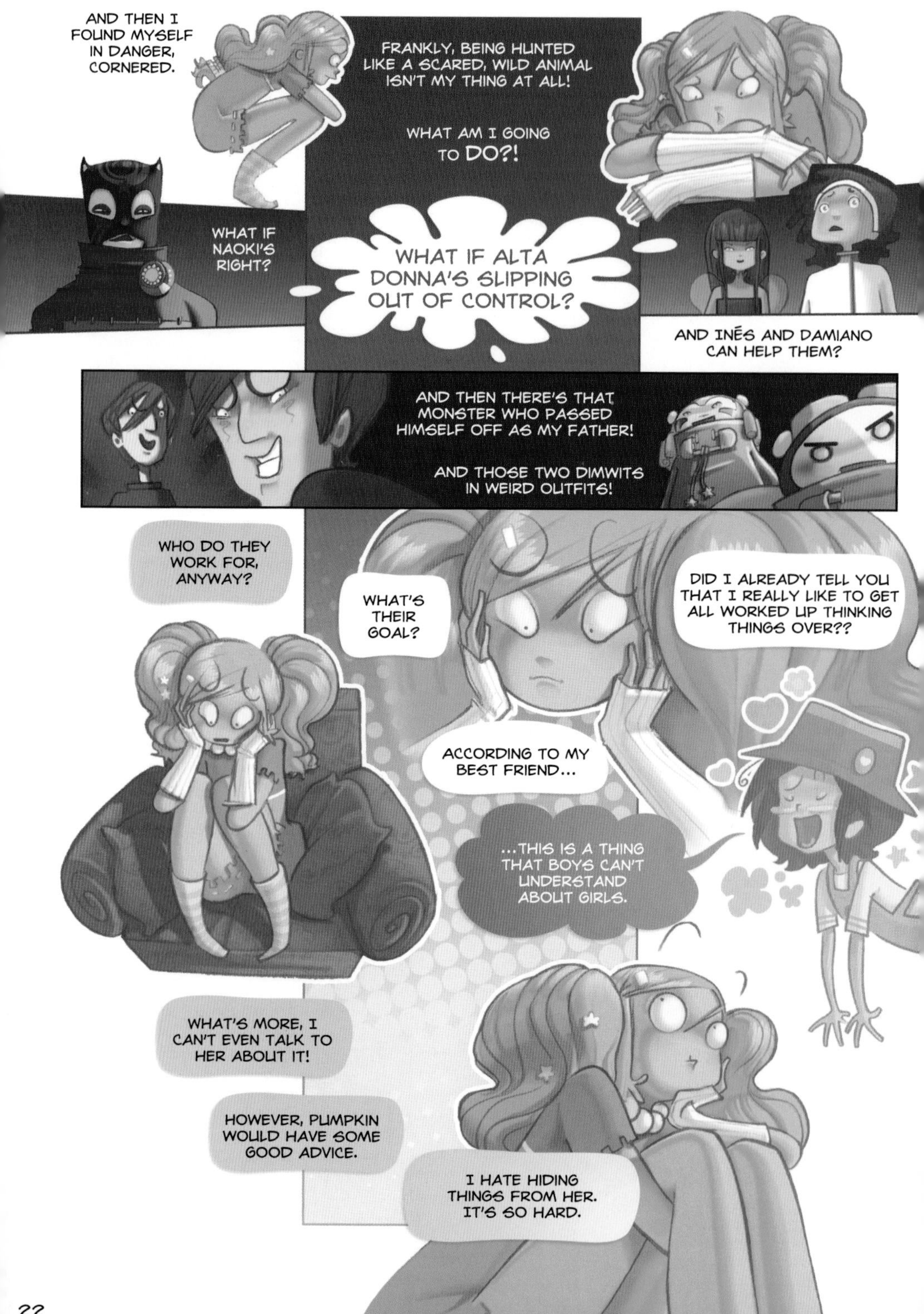

AND THEN I FOUND MYSELF IN DANGER, CORNERED.
FRANKLY, BEING HUNTED LIKE A SCARED, WILD ANIMAL ISN'T MY THING AT ALL!
WHAT AM I GOING TO DO?!
WHAT IF NAOKI'S RIGHT?
WHAT IF ALTA DONNA'S SLIPPING OUT OF CONTROL?
AND INÉS AND DAMIANO CAN HELP THEM?
AND THEN THERE'S THAT MONSTER WHO PASSED HIMSELF OFF AS MY FATHER!
AND THOSE TWO DIMWITS IN WEIRD OUTFITS!
WHO DO THEY WORK FOR, ANYWAY?
WHAT'S THEIR GOAL?
DID I ALREADY TELL YOU THAT I REALLY LIKE TO GET ALL WORKED UP THINKING THINGS OVER??
ACCORDING TO MY BEST FRIEND...
...THIS IS A THING THAT BOYS CAN'T UNDERSTAND ABOUT GIRLS.
WHAT'S MORE, I CAN'T EVEN TALK TO HER ABOUT IT!
HOWEVER, PUMPKIN WOULD HAVE SOME GOOD ADVICE.
I HATE HIDING THINGS FROM HER. IT'S SO HARD.

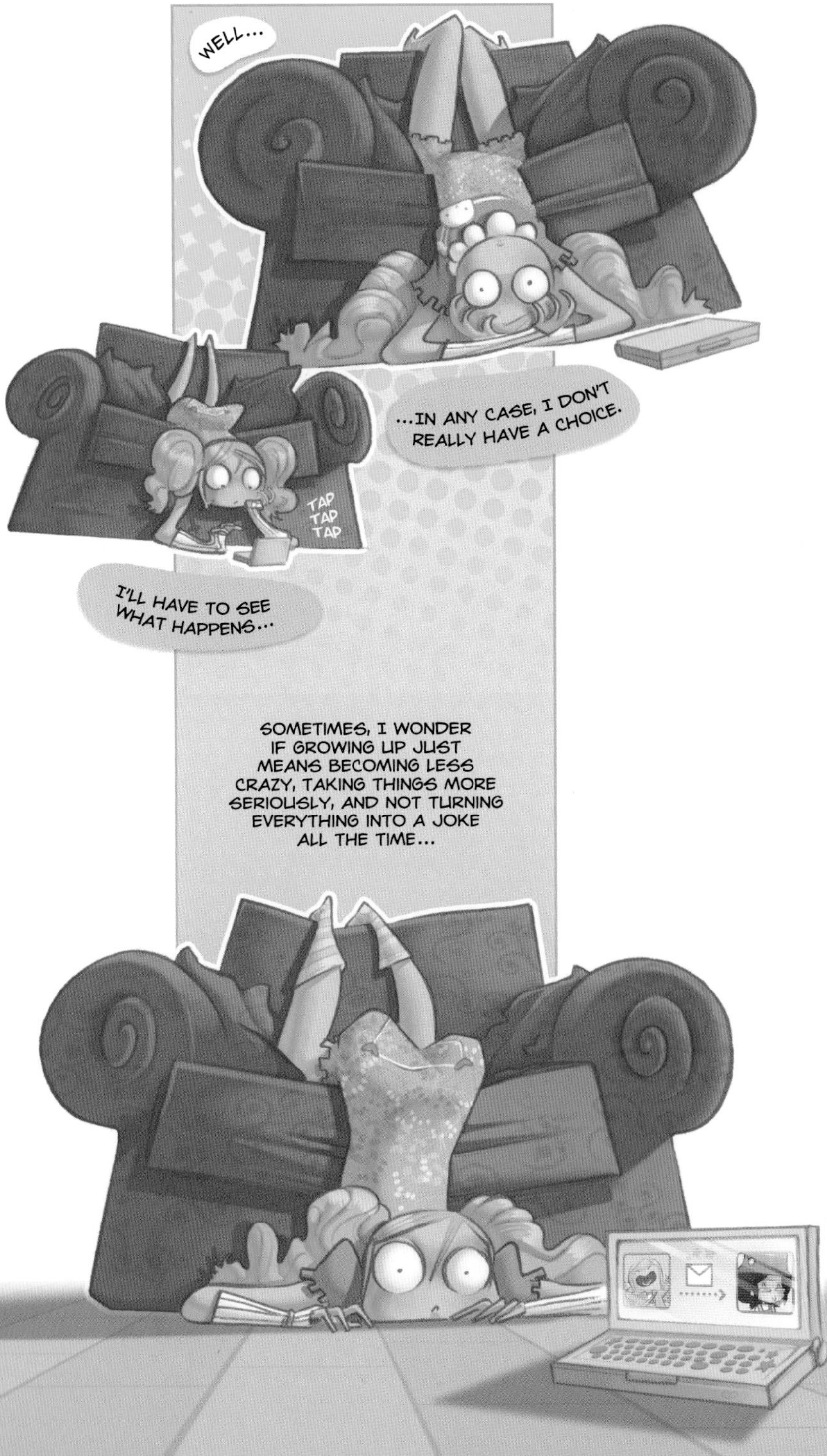
WELL...
...IN ANY CASE, I DON'T REALLY HAVE A CHOICE.
TAP TAP TAP
I'LL HAVE TO SEE WHAT HAPPENS...
SOMETIMES, I WONDER IF GROWING UP JUST MEANS BECOMING LESS CRAZY, TAKING THINGS MORE SERIOUSLY, AND NOT TURNING EVERYTHING INTO A JOKE ALL THE TIME...

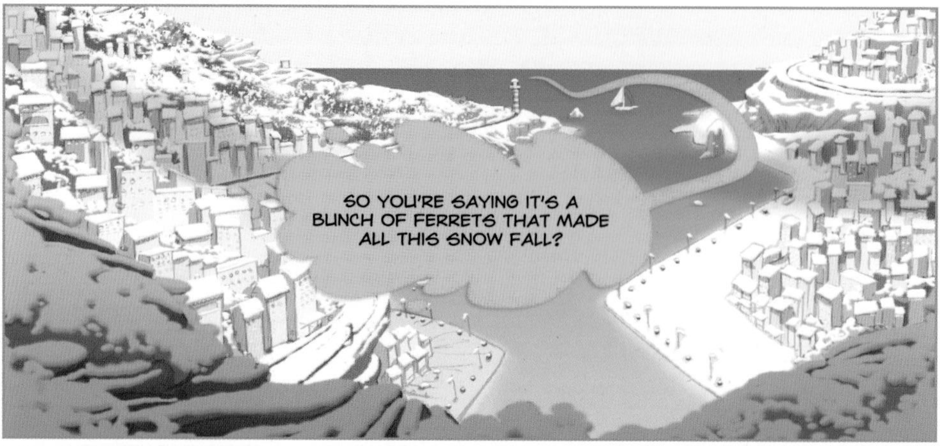
SO YOU'RE SAYING IT'S A BUNCH OF FERRETS THAT MADE ALL THIS SNOW FALL?

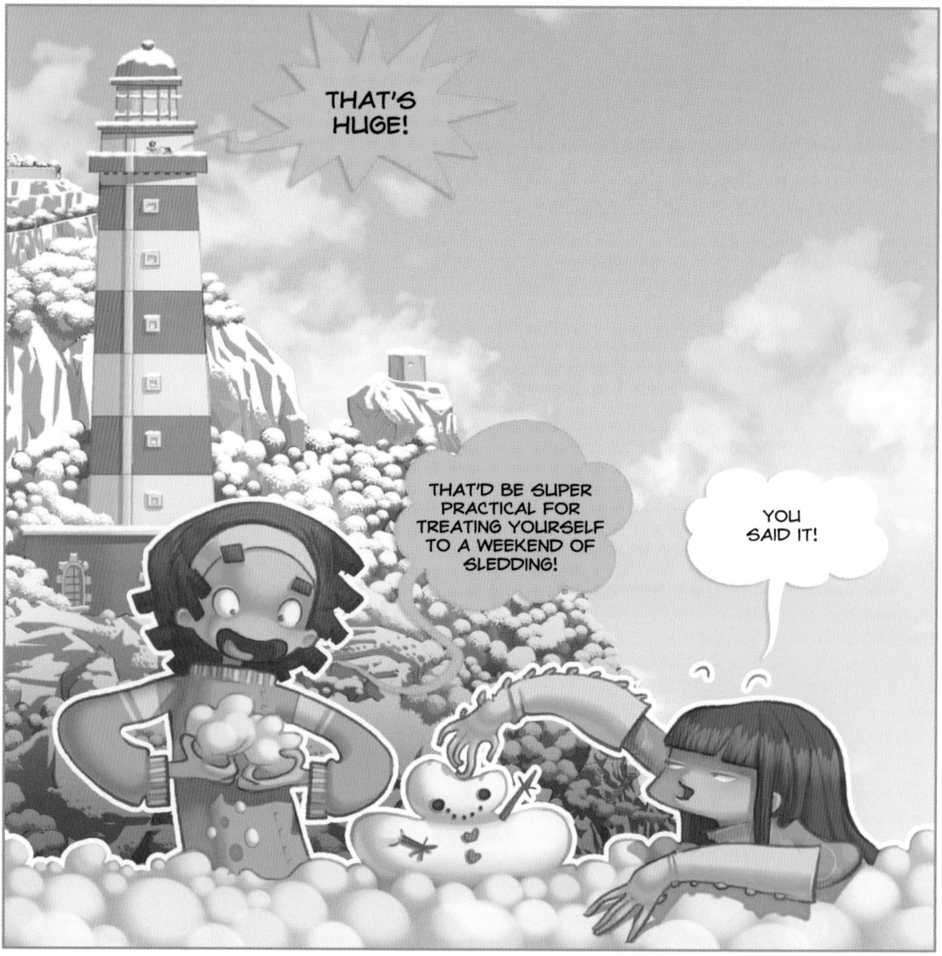
THAT'S HUGE!
THAT'D BE SUPER PRACTICAL FOR TREATING YOURSELF TO A WEEKEND OF SLEDDING!
YOU SAID IT!

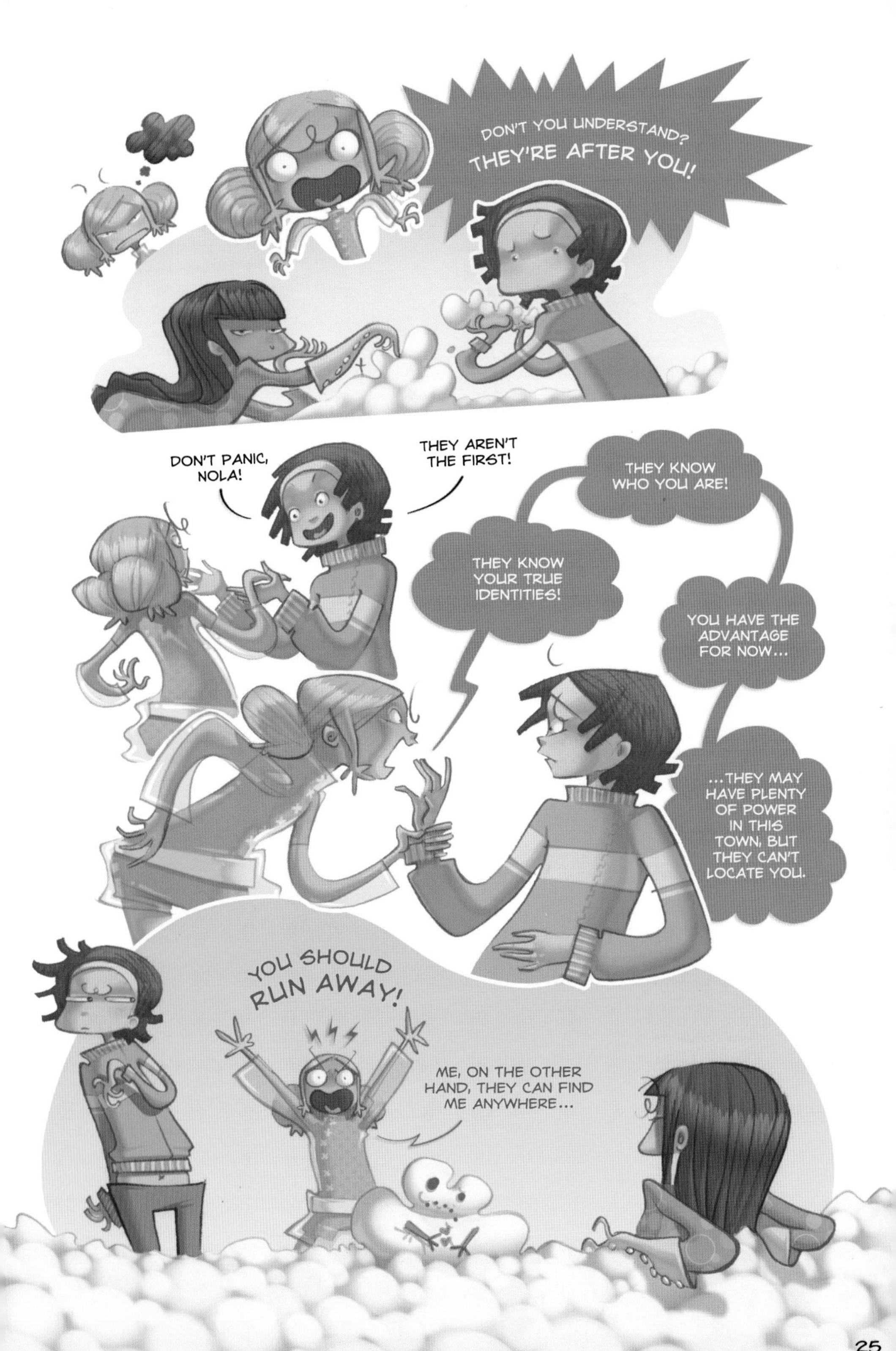
DON'T YOU UNDERSTAND?
THEY'RE AFTER YOU!
DON'T PANIC, NOLA!
THEY AREN'T THE FIRST!
THEY KNOW WHO YOU ARE!
THEY KNOW YOUR TRUE IDENTITIES!
YOU HAVE THE ADVANTAGE FOR NOW...
...THEY MAY HAVE PLENTY OF POWER IN THIS TOWN, BUT THEY CAN'T LOCATE YOU.
YOU SHOULD RUN AWAY!
ME, ON THE OTHER HAND, THEY CAN FIND ME ANYWHERE...

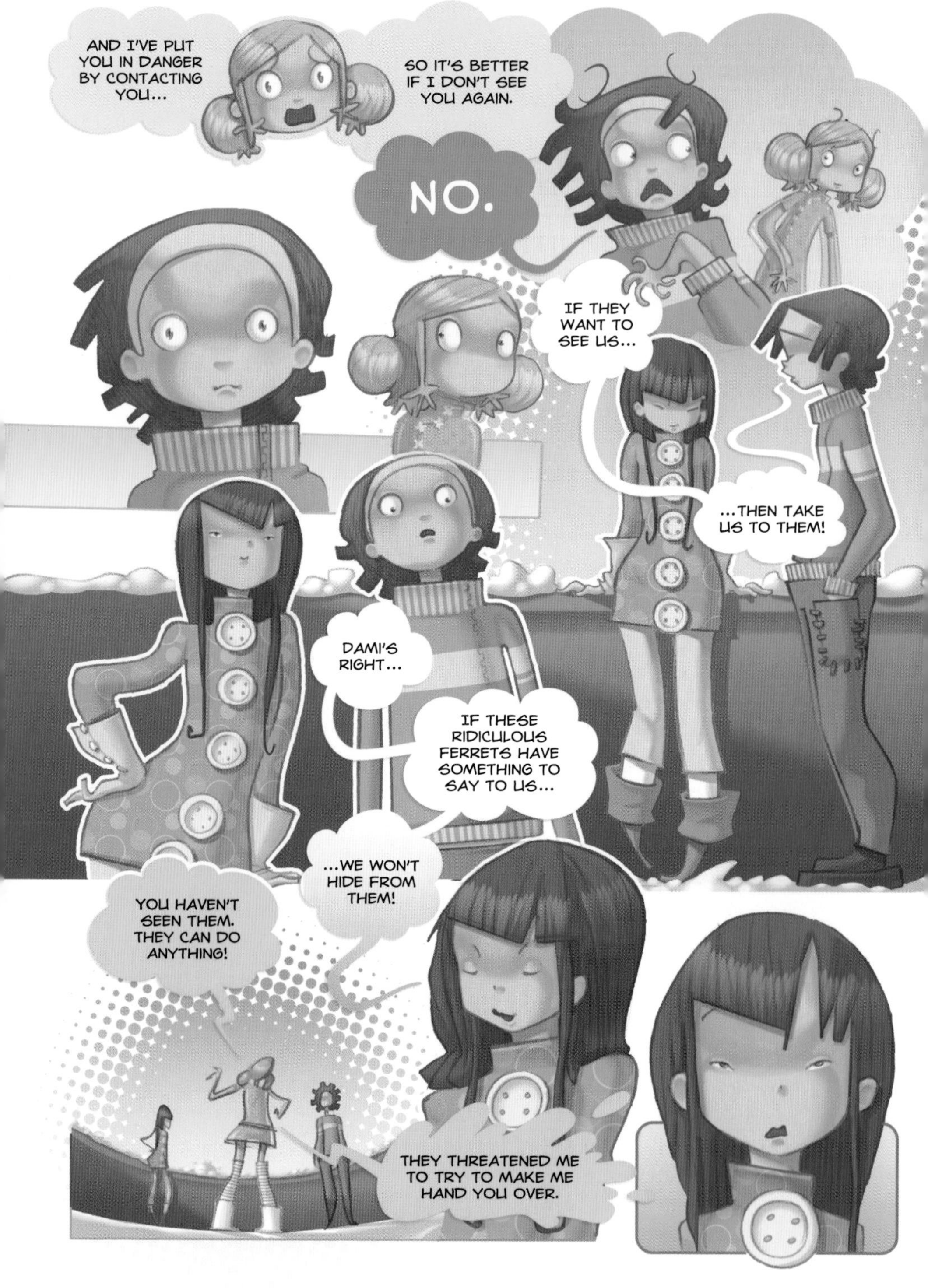
AND I'VE PUT YOU IN DANGER BY CONTACTING YOU...
SO IT'S BETTER IF I DON'T SEE YOU AGAIN.
NO.
IF THEY WANT TO SEE US...
...THEN TAKE US TO THEM!
DAMI'S RIGHT...
IF THESE RIDICULOUS FERRETS HAVE SOMETHING TO SAY TO US...
...WE WON'T HIDE FROM THEM!
YOU HAVEN'T SEEN THEM. THEY CAN DO ANYTHING!
THEY THREATENED ME TO TRY TO MAKE ME HAND YOU OVER.

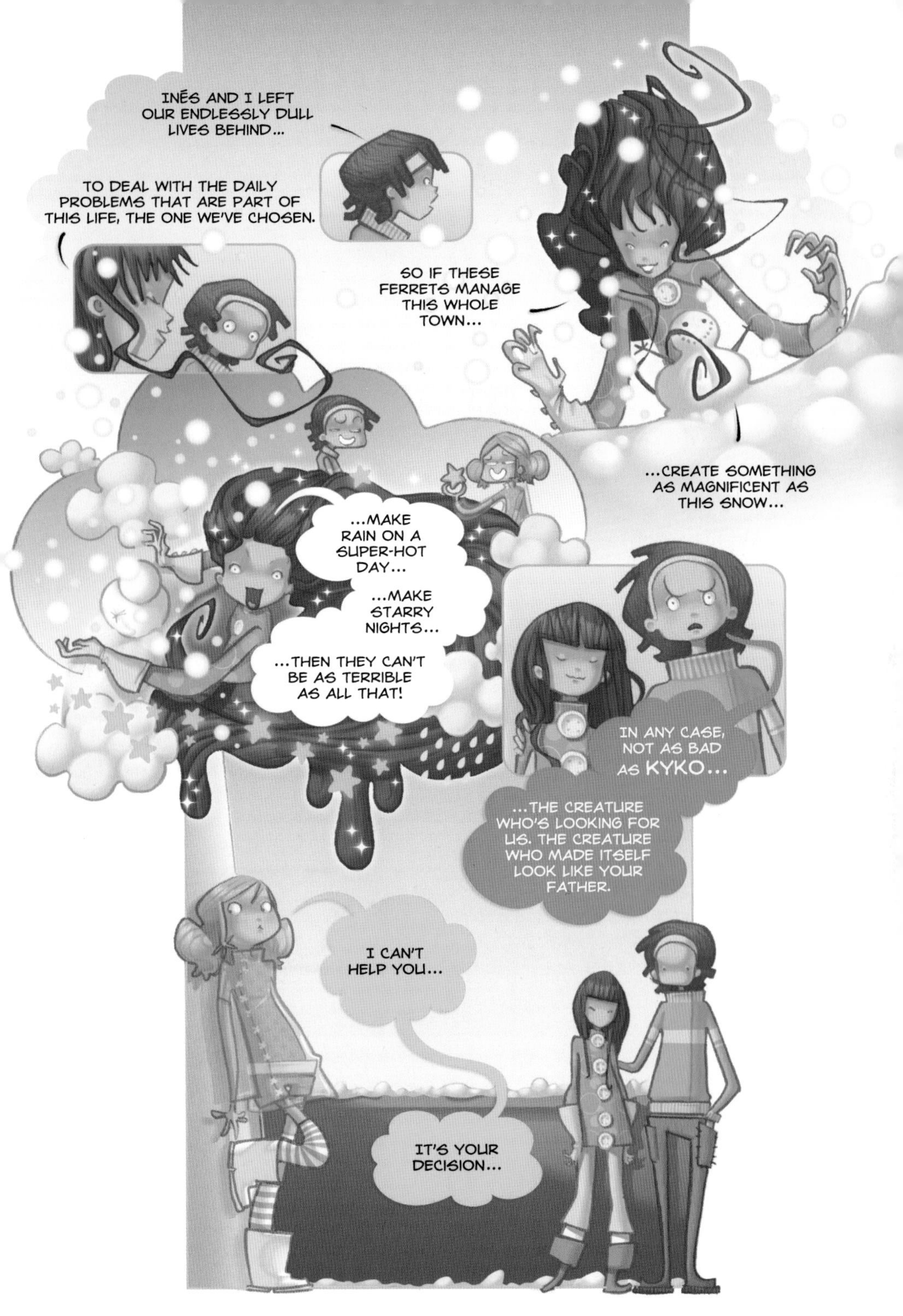
INÉS AND I LEFT OUR ENDLESSLY DULL LIVES BEHIND...
TO DEAL WITH THE DAILY PROBLEMS THAT ARE PART OF THIS LIFE, THE ONE WE'VE CHOSEN.
SO IF THESE FERRETS MANAGE THIS WHOLE TOWN...
...CREATE SOMETHING AS MAGNIFICENT AS THIS SNOW...
...MAKE RAIN ON A SUPER-HOT DAY...
...MAKE STARRY NIGHTS...
...THEN THEY CAN'T BE AS TERRIBLE AS ALL THAT!
IN ANY CASE, NOT AS BAD AS KYKO...
...THE CREATURE WHO'S LOOKING FOR US. THE CREATURE WHO MADE ITSELF LOOK LIKE YOUR FATHER.
I CAN'T HELP YOU...
IT'S YOUR DECISION...

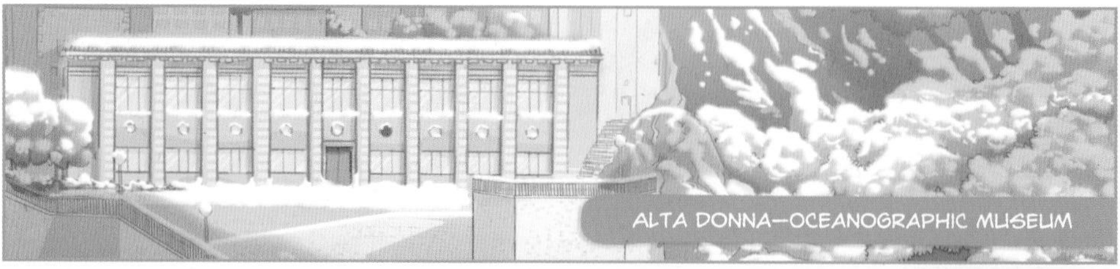
ALTA DONNA—OCEANOGRAPHIC MUSEUM

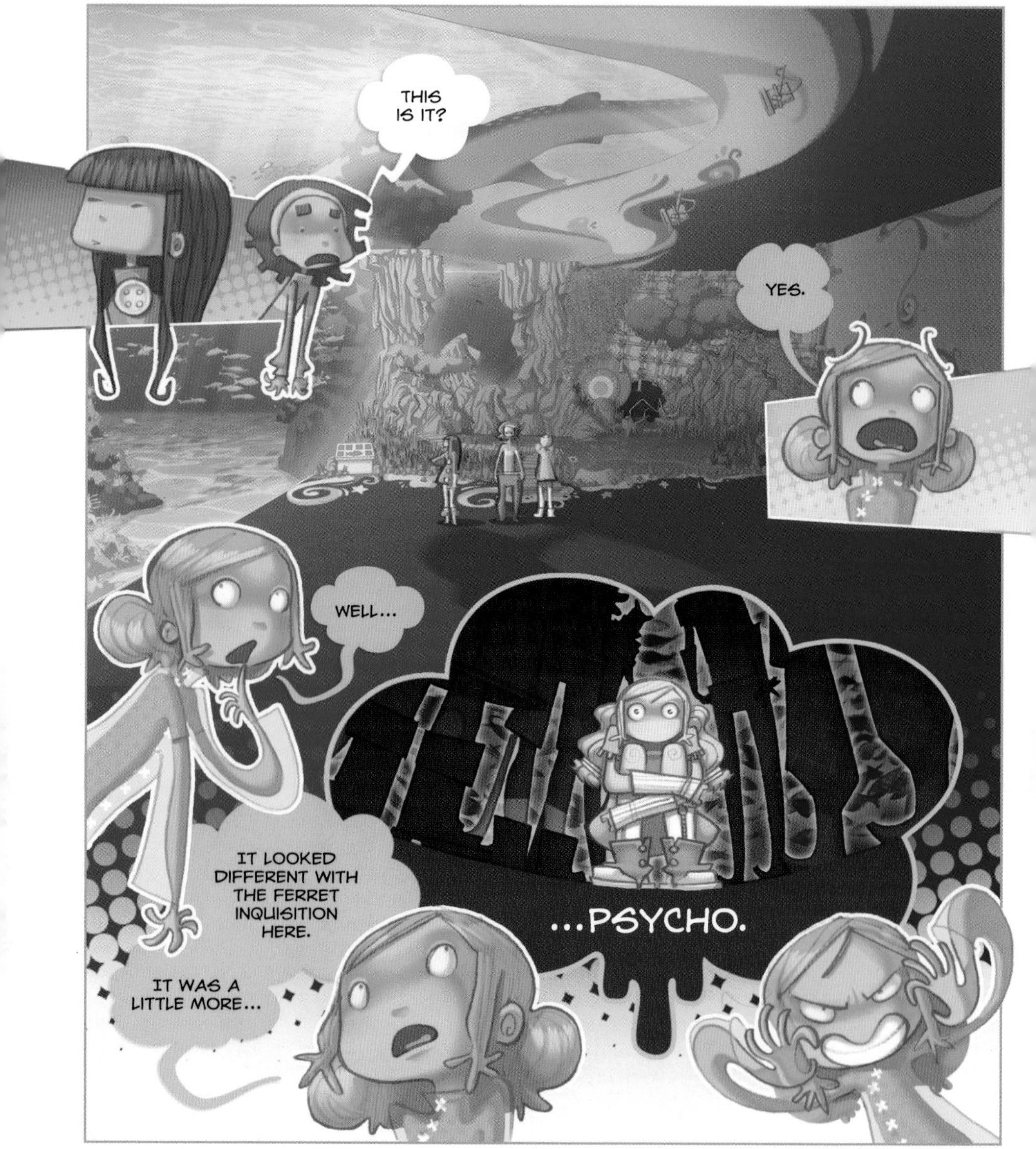
THIS IS IT?
YES.
WELL...
IT LOOKED DIFFERENT WITH THE FERRET INQUISITION HERE.
IT WAS A LITTLE MORE...
...PSYCHO.

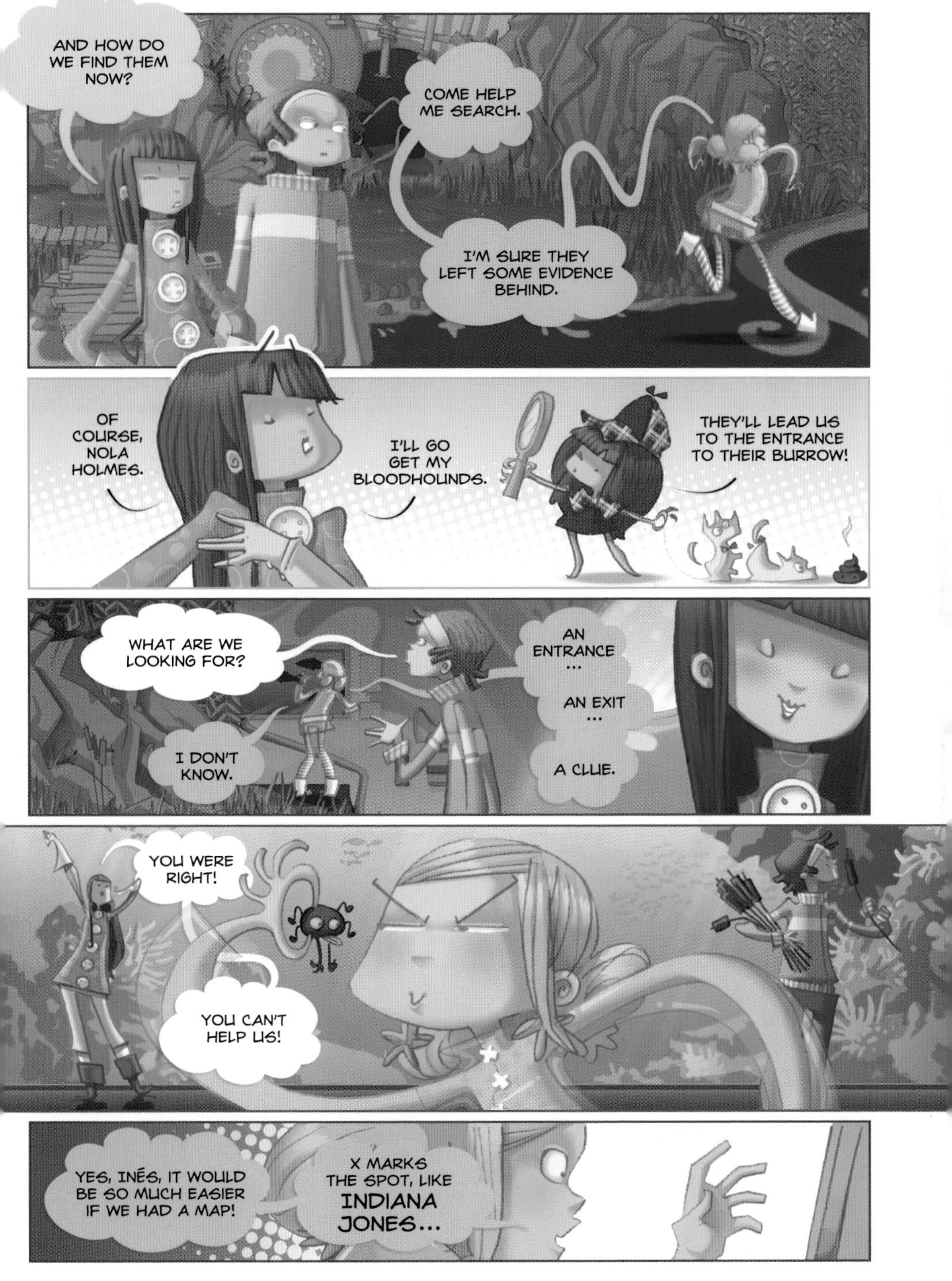
AND HOW DO WE FIND THEM NOW?
COME HELP ME SEARCH.
I'M SURE THEY LEFT SOME EVIDENCE BEHIND.
OF COURSE, NOLA HOLMES.
I'LL GO GET MY BLOODHOUNDS.
THEY'LL LEAD US TO THE ENTRANCE TO THEIR BURROW!
WHAT ARE WE LOOKING FOR?
I DON'T KNOW.
AN ENTRANCE ...
AN EXIT ...
A CLUE.
YOU WERE RIGHT!
YOU CAN'T HELP US!
YES, INÉS, IT WOULD BE SO MUCH EASIER IF WE HAD A MAP!
X MARKS THE SPOT, LIKE **INDIANA JONES**...

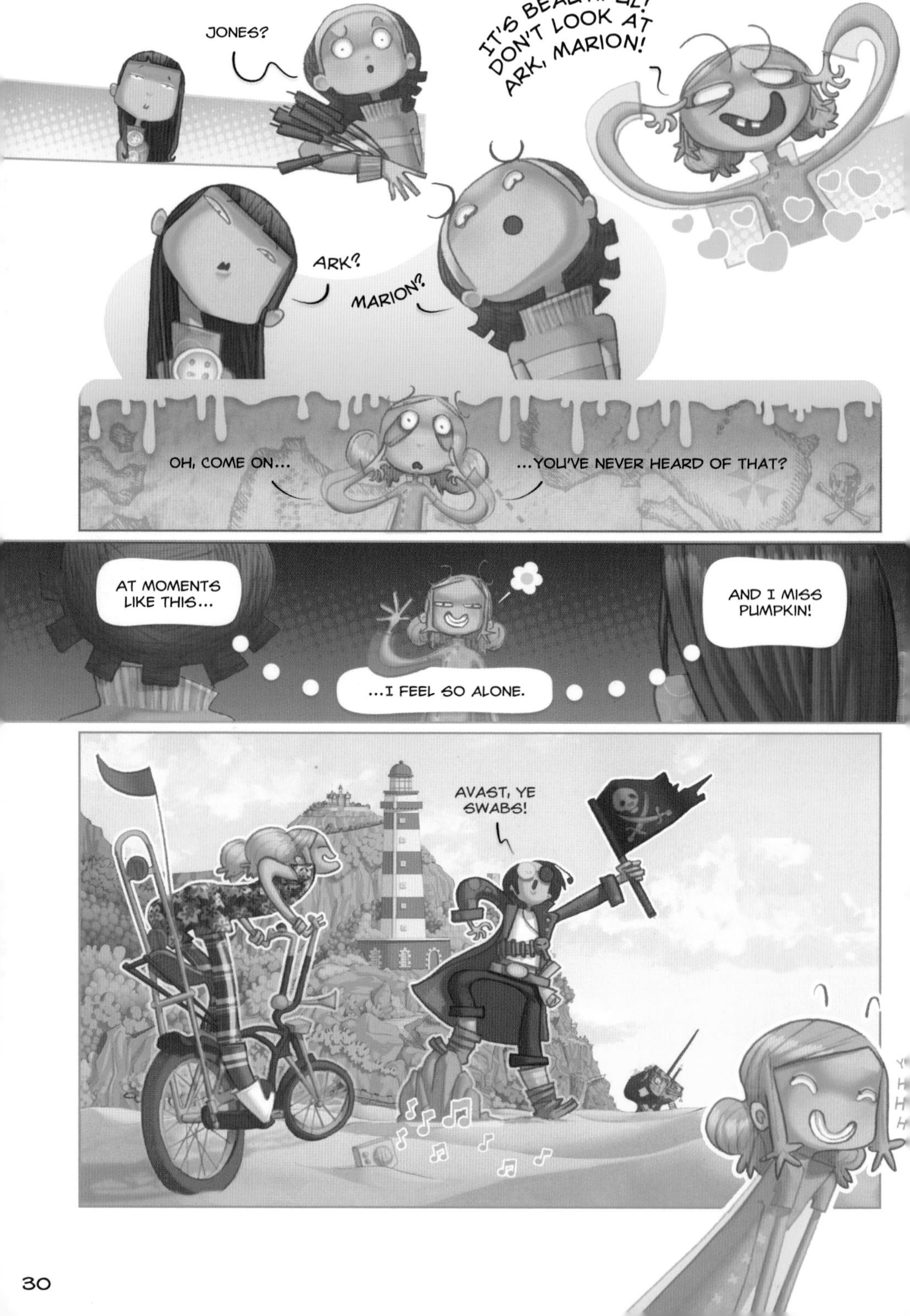
JONES?
IT'S BEAUTIFUL! DON'T LOOK AT ARK, MARION!
ARK?
MARION?
OH, COME ON...
...YOU'VE NEVER HEARD OF THAT?
AT MOMENTS LIKE THIS...
...I FEEL SO ALONE.
AND I MISS PUMPKIN!
AVAST, YE SWABS!

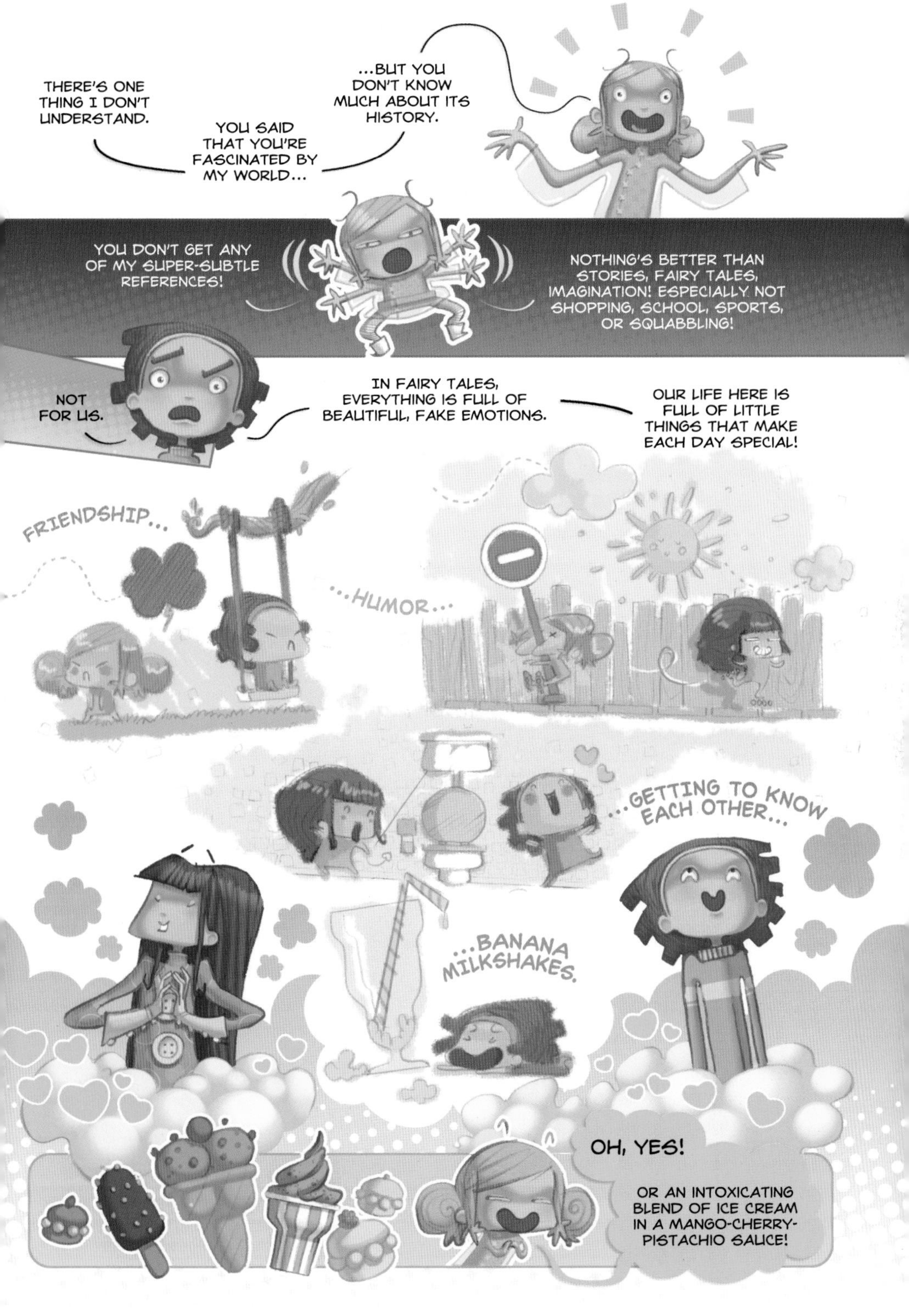
THERE'S ONE THING I DON'T UNDERSTAND.
YOU SAID THAT YOU'RE FASCINATED BY MY WORLD...
...BUT YOU DON'T KNOW MUCH ABOUT ITS HISTORY.
YOU DON'T GET ANY OF MY SUPER-SUBTLE REFERENCES!
NOTHING'S BETTER THAN STORIES, FAIRY TALES, IMAGINATION! ESPECIALLY NOT SHOPPING, SCHOOL, SPORTS, OR SQUABBLING!
NOT FOR US.
IN FAIRY TALES, EVERYTHING IS FULL OF BEAUTIFUL, FAKE EMOTIONS.
OUR LIFE HERE IS FULL OF LITTLE THINGS THAT MAKE EACH DAY SPECIAL!
FRIENDSHIP...
...HUMOR...
...GETTING TO KNOW EACH OTHER...
...BANANA MILKSHAKES.
OH, YES!
OR AN INTOXICATING BLEND OF ICE CREAM IN A MANGO-CHERRY-PISTACHIO SAUCE!

CLIC !

CLIC ?

muste
puto

HEY, WAIT...

...

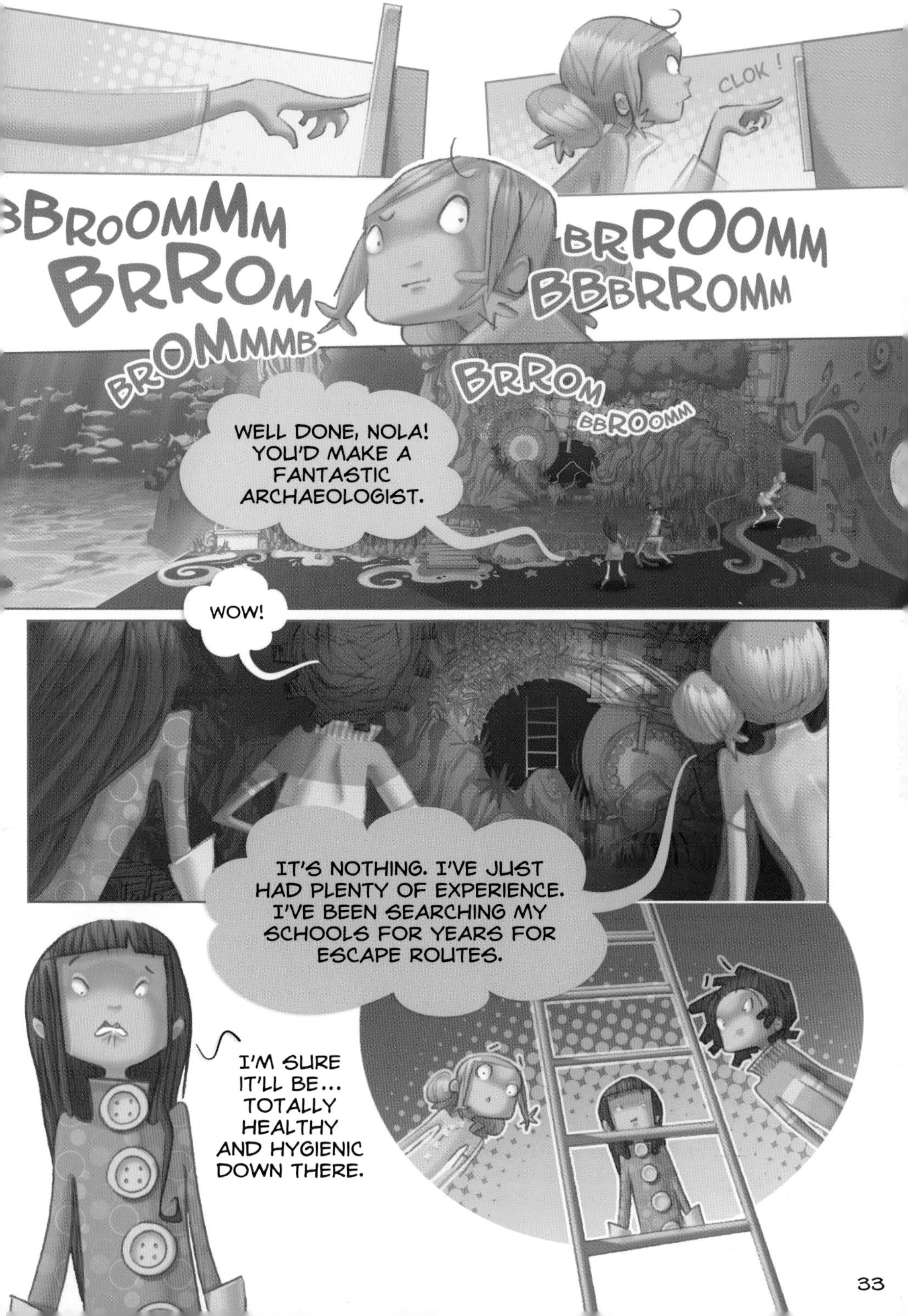
CLOK !
BBROOMMM
BRROM
BROMMMB
BRROOMM
BBBRROMM
BRROM
BBROOMM
WELL DONE, NOLA! YOU'D MAKE A FANTASTIC ARCHAEOLOGIST.
WOW!
IT'S NOTHING. I'VE JUST HAD PLENTY OF EXPERIENCE. I'VE BEEN SEARCHING MY SCHOOLS FOR YEARS FOR ESCAPE ROUTES.
I'M SURE IT'LL BE... TOTALLY HEALTHY AND HYGIENIC DOWN THERE.

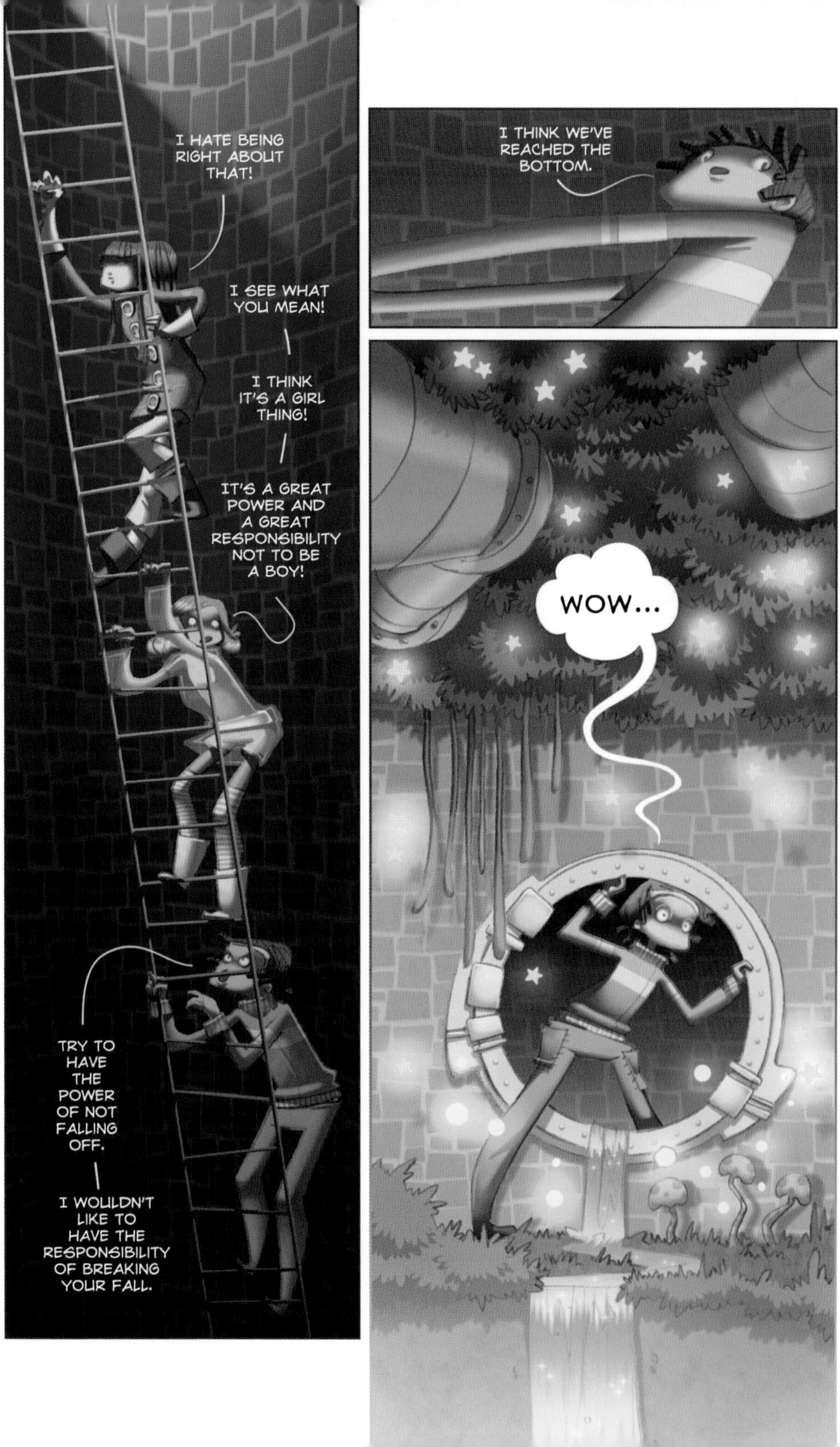

I HATE BEING RIGHT ABOUT THAT!
I SEE WHAT YOU MEAN!
I THINK IT'S A GIRL THING!
IT'S A GREAT POWER AND A GREAT RESPONSIBILITY NOT TO BE A BOY!
TRY TO HAVE THE POWER OF NOT FALLING OFF.
I WOULDN'T LIKE TO HAVE THE RESPONSIBILITY OF BREAKING YOUR FALL.
I THINK WE'VE REACHED THE BOTTOM.
WOW...

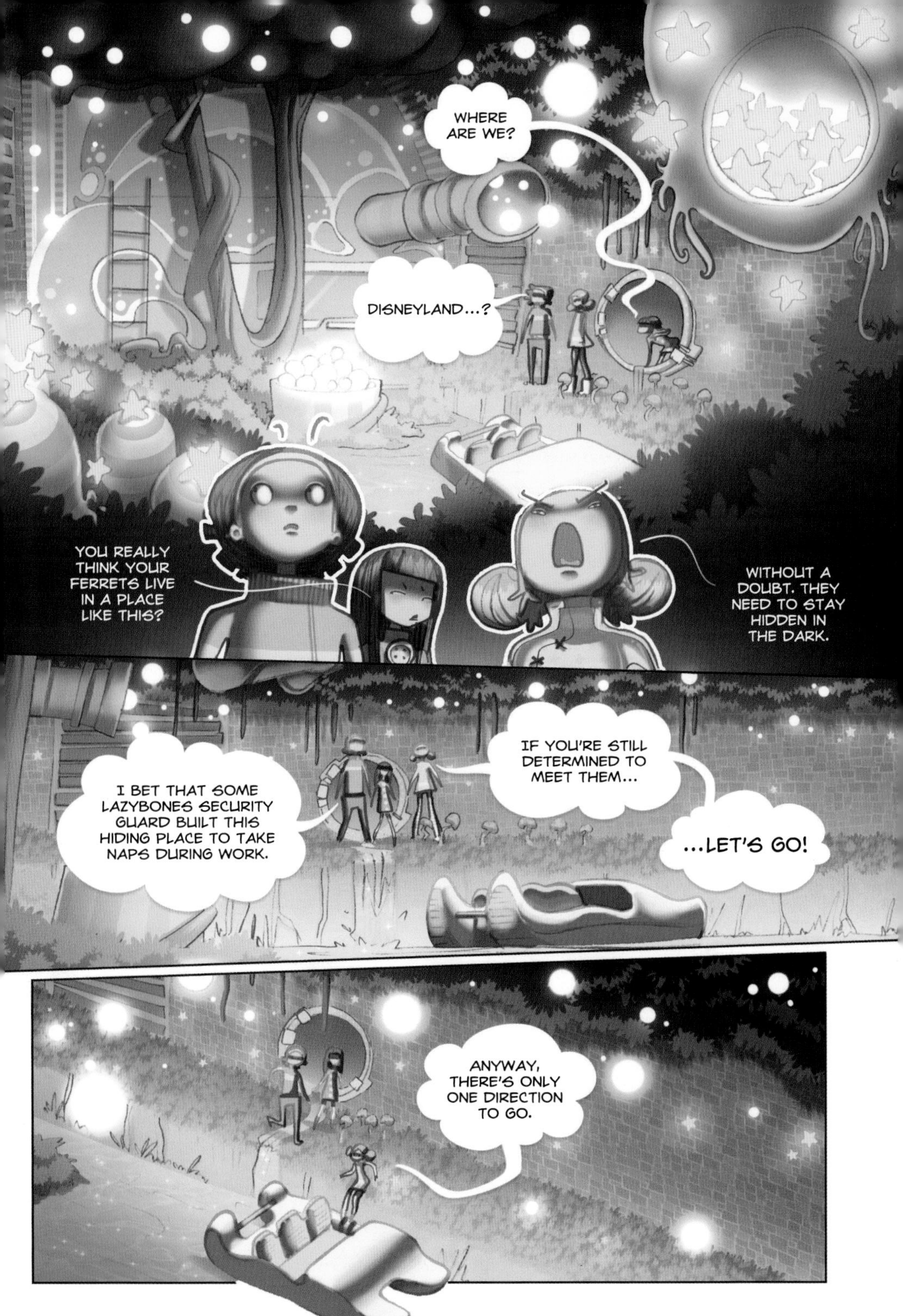

WHERE ARE WE?
DISNEYLAND...?
YOU REALLY THINK YOUR FERRETS LIVE IN A PLACE LIKE THIS?
WITHOUT A DOUBT. THEY NEED TO STAY HIDDEN IN THE DARK.
I BET THAT SOME LAZYBONES SECURITY GUARD BUILT THIS HIDING PLACE TO TAKE NAPS DURING WORK.
IF YOU'RE STILL DETERMINED TO MEET THEM...
...LET'S GO!
ANYWAY, THERE'S ONLY ONE DIRECTION TO GO.

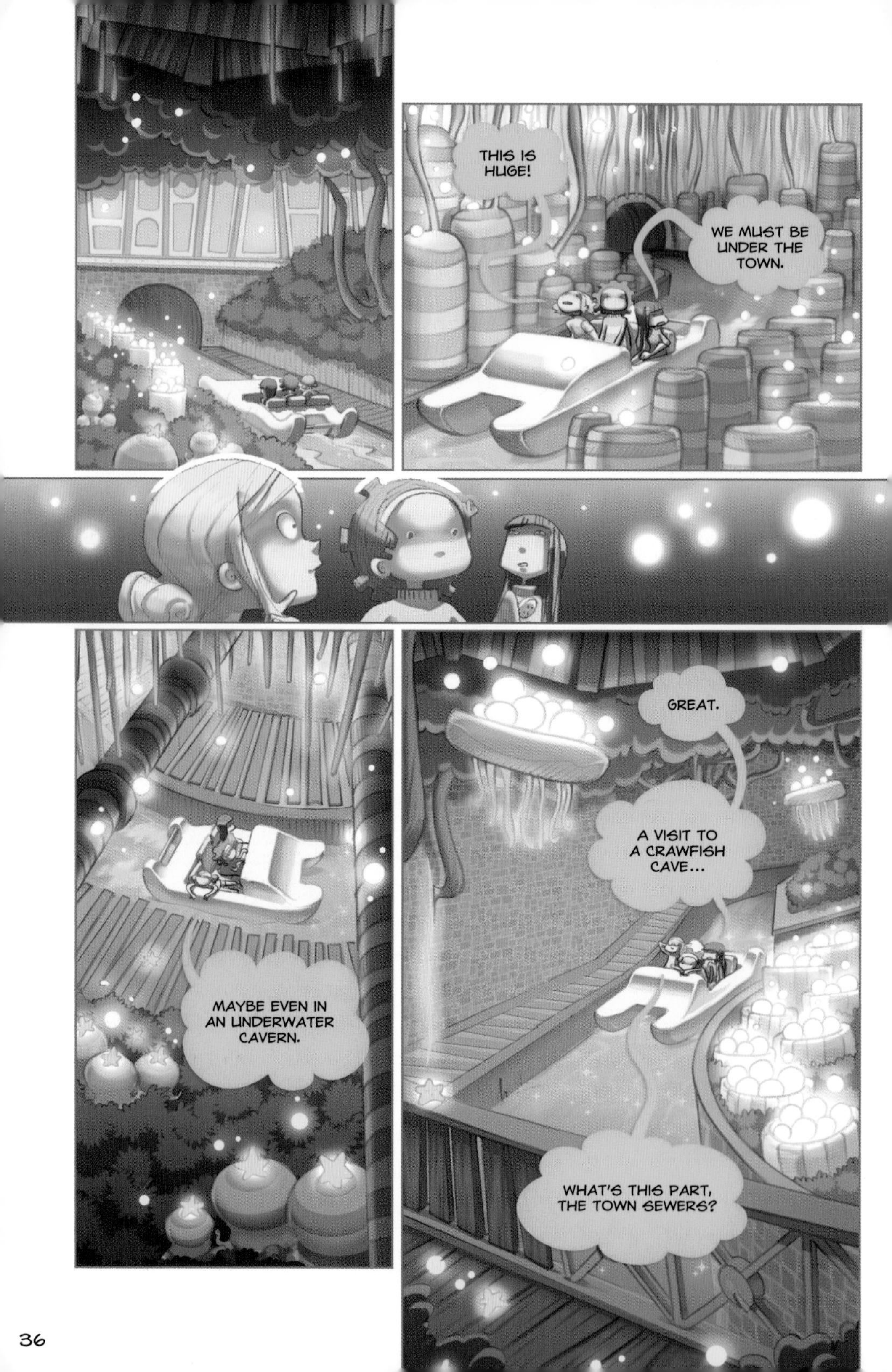
THIS IS HUGE!
WE MUST BE UNDER THE TOWN.
MAYBE EVEN IN AN UNDERWATER CAVERN.
GREAT.
A VISIT TO A CRAWFISH CAVE...
WHAT'S THIS PART, THE TOWN SEWERS?

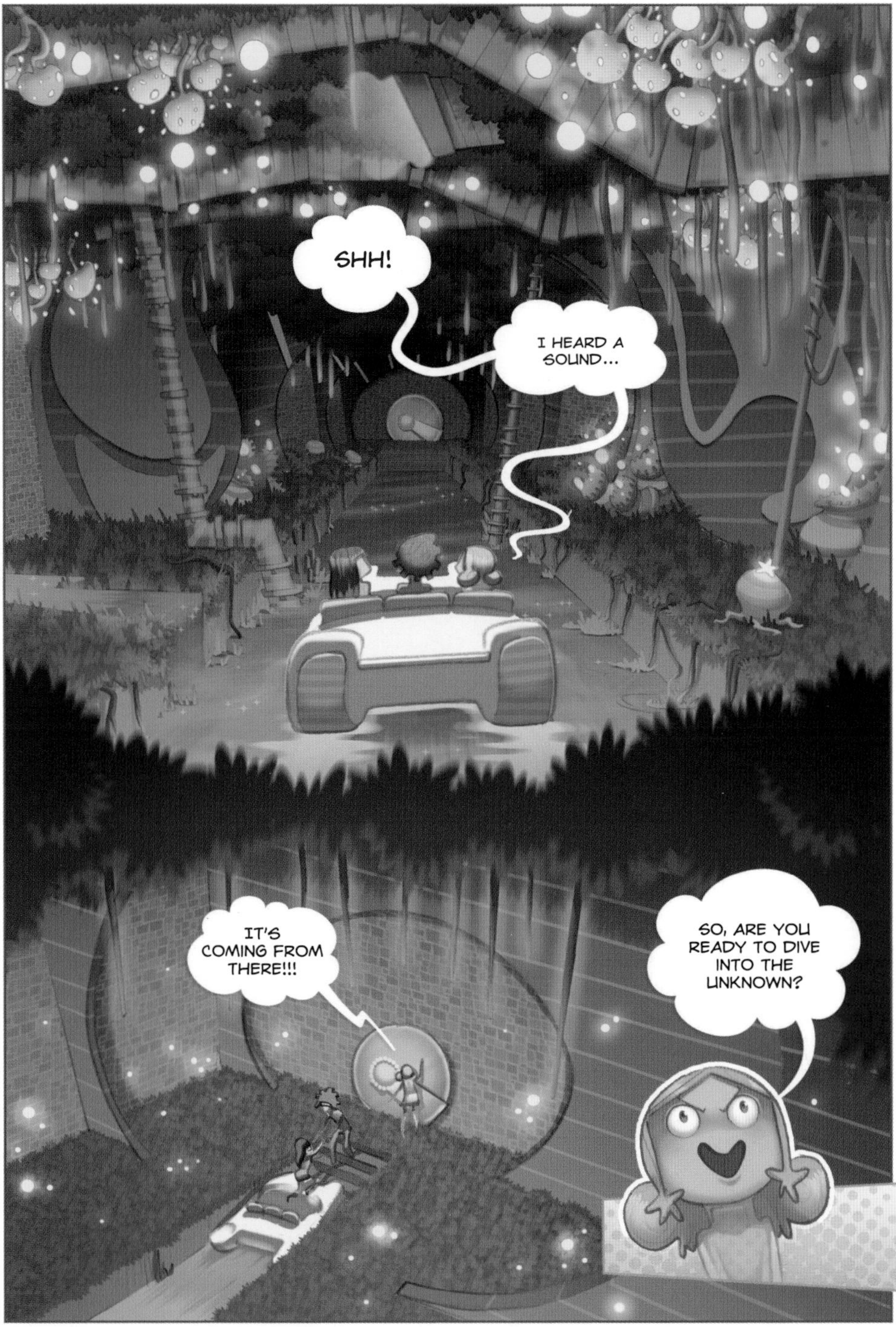
SHH!
I HEARD A SOUND...
IT'S COMING FROM THERE!!!
SO, ARE YOU READY TO DIVE INTO THE UNKNOWN?

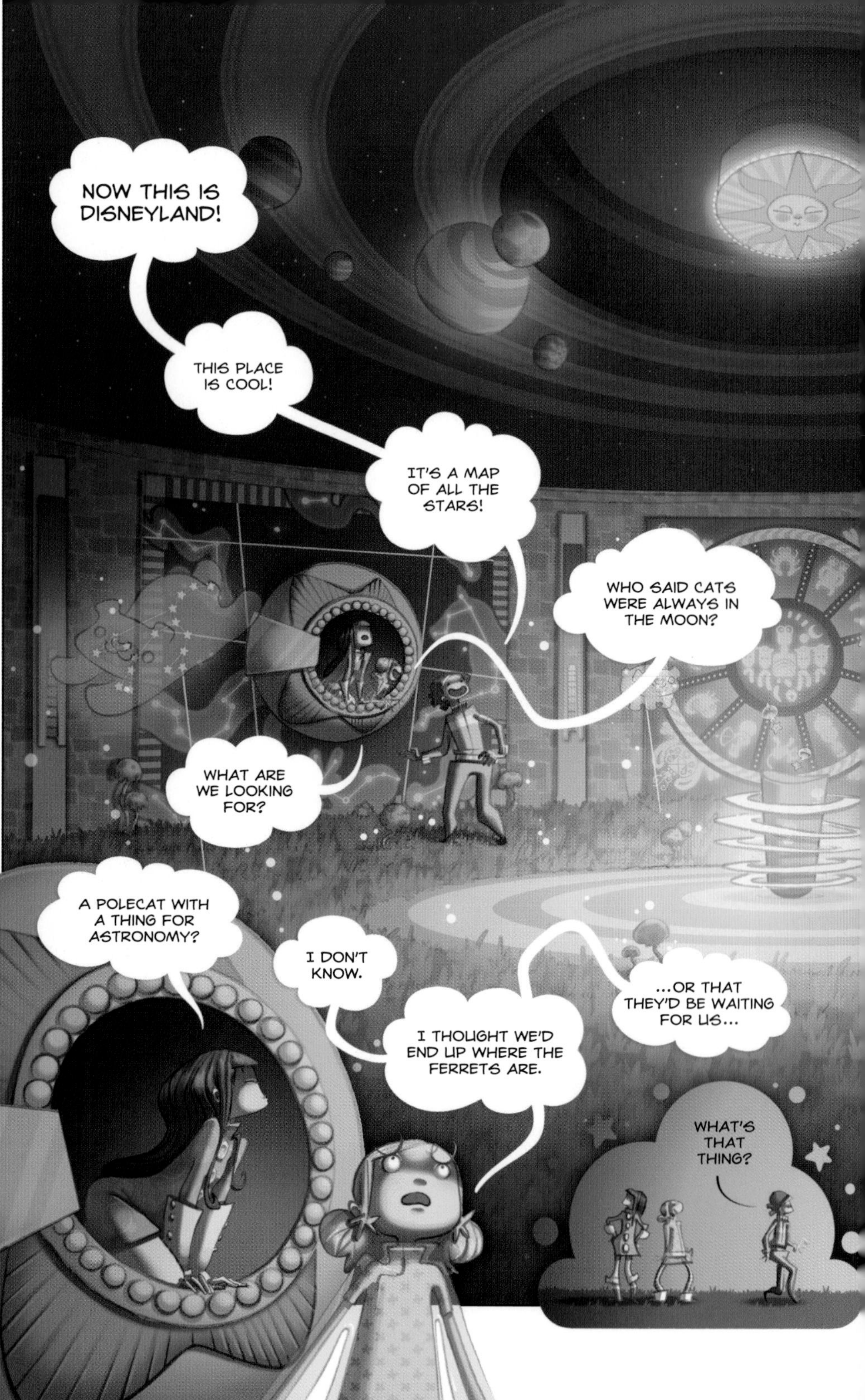
NOW THIS IS DISNEYLAND!
THIS PLACE IS COOL!
IT'S A MAP OF ALL THE STARS!
WHO SAID CATS WERE ALWAYS IN THE MOON?
WHAT ARE WE LOOKING FOR?
A POLECAT WITH A THING FOR ASTRONOMY?
I DON'T KNOW.
I THOUGHT WE'D END UP WHERE THE FERRETS ARE.
...OR THAT THEY'D BE WAITING FOR US...
WHAT'S THAT THING?

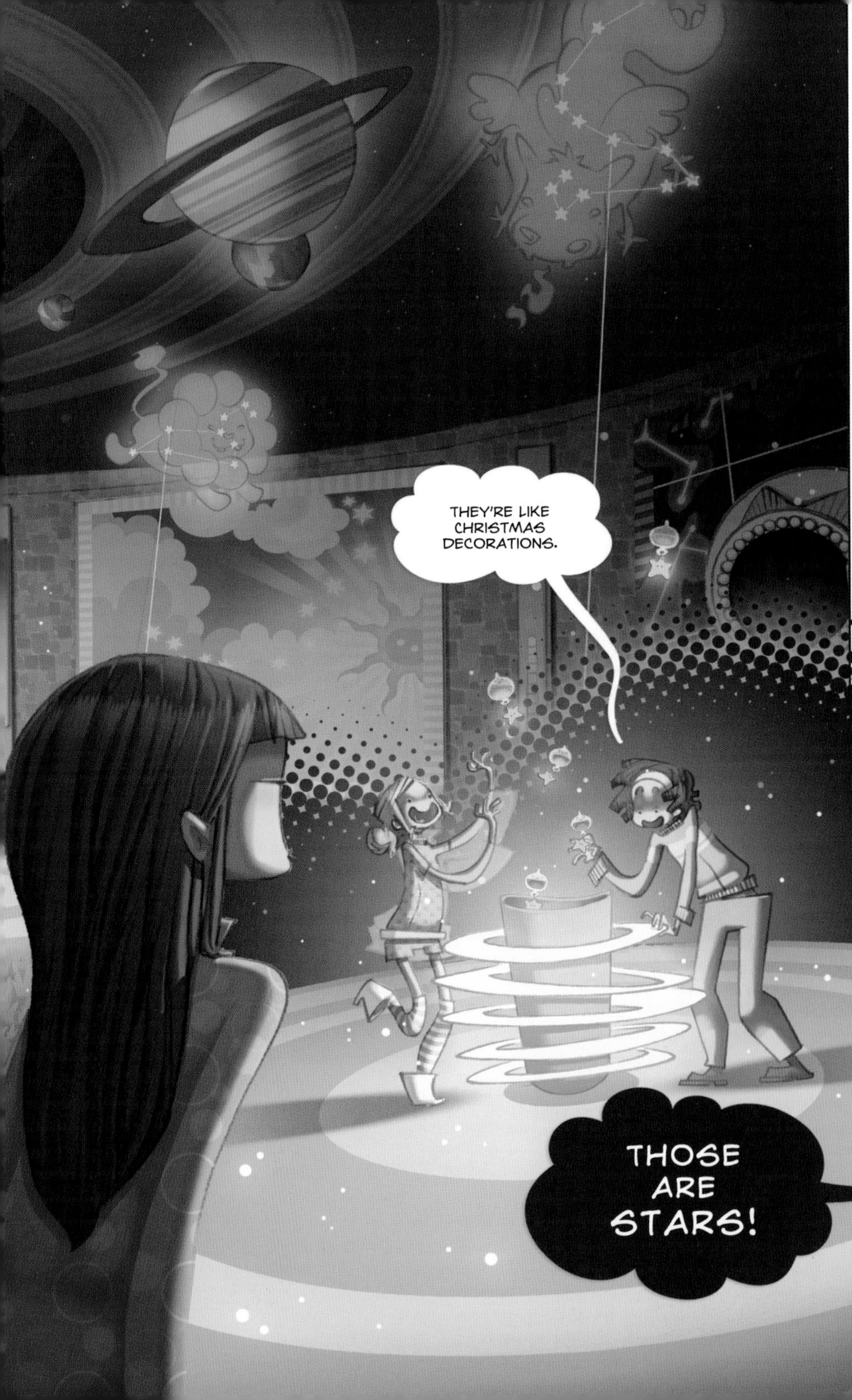
THEY'RE LIKE CHRISTMAS DECORATIONS.
THOSE ARE STARS!

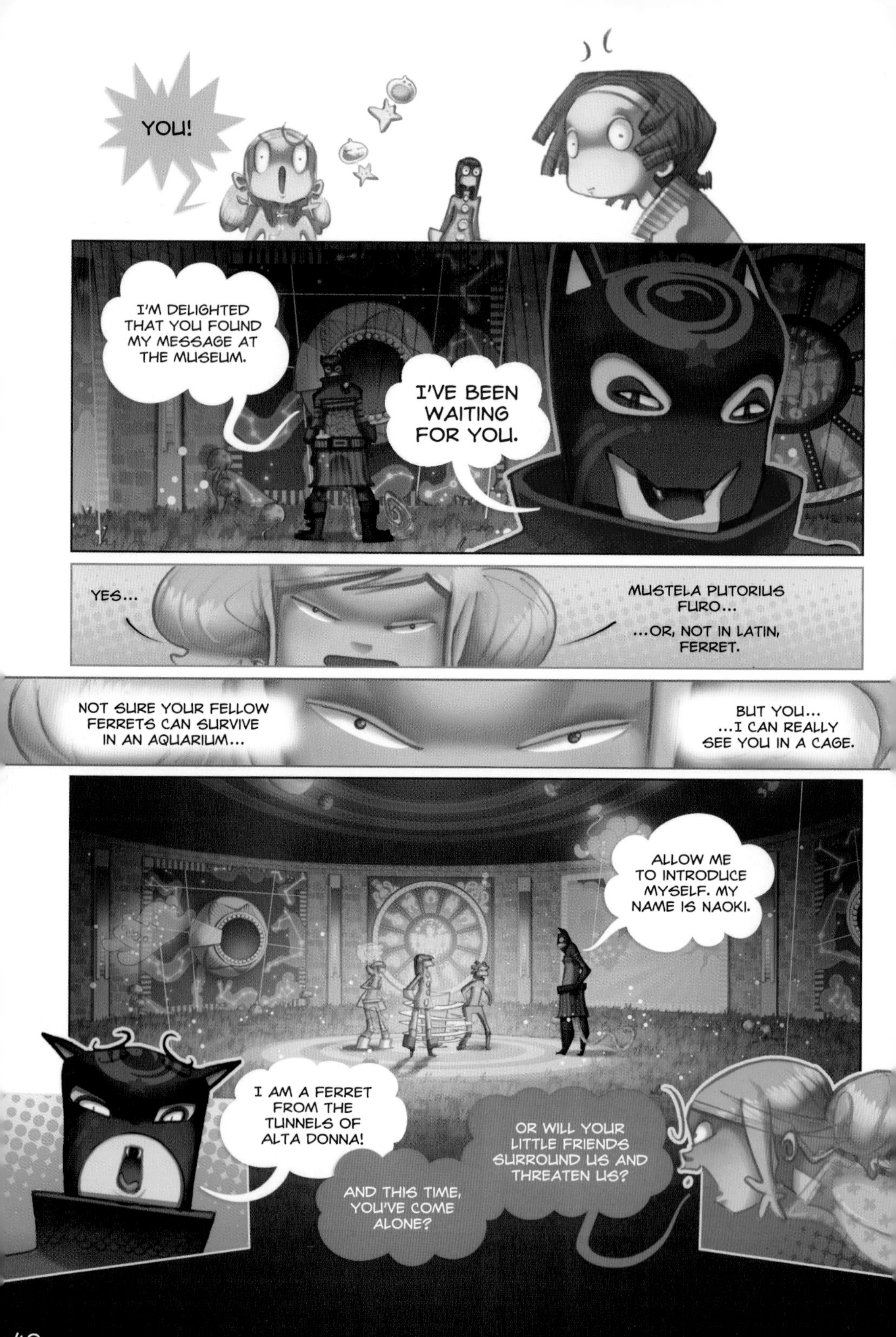
YOU!
I'M DELIGHTED THAT YOU FOUND MY MESSAGE AT THE MUSEUM.
I'VE BEEN WAITING FOR YOU.
YES...
MUSTELA PUTORIUS FURO...
...OR, NOT IN LATIN, FERRET.
NOT SURE YOUR FELLOW FERRETS CAN SURVIVE IN AN AQUARIUM...
BUT YOU...
...I CAN REALLY SEE YOU IN A CAGE.
ALLOW ME TO INTRODUCE MYSELF. MY NAME IS NAOKI.
I AM A FERRET FROM THE TUNNELS OF ALTA DONNA!
AND THIS TIME, YOU'VE COME ALONE?
OR WILL YOUR LITTLE FRIENDS SURROUND US AND THREATEN US?

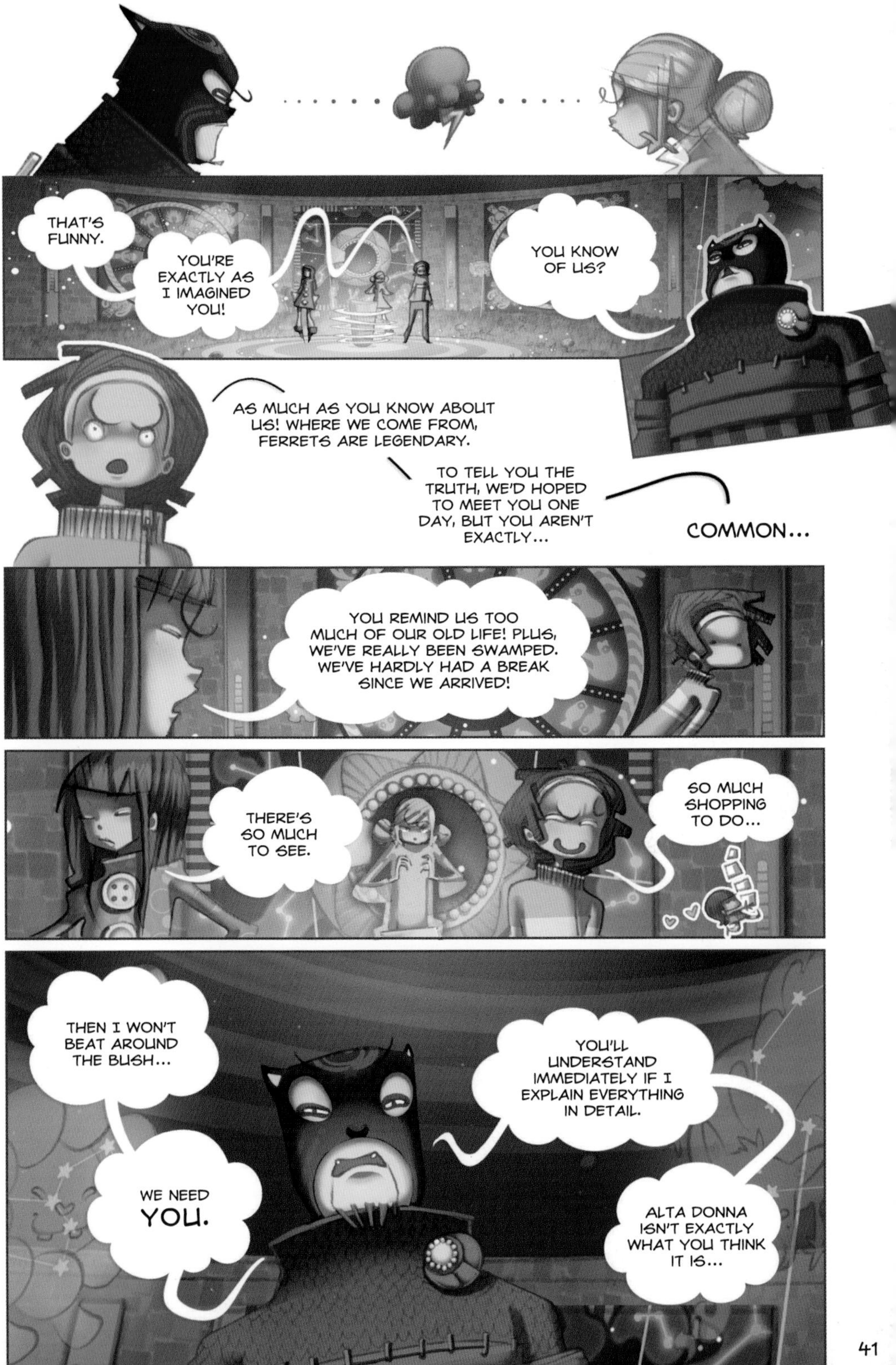
THAT'S FUNNY.
YOU'RE EXACTLY AS I IMAGINED YOU!
YOU KNOW OF US?
AS MUCH AS YOU KNOW ABOUT US! WHERE WE COME FROM, FERRETS ARE LEGENDARY.
TO TELL YOU THE TRUTH, WE'D HOPED TO MEET YOU ONE DAY, BUT YOU AREN'T EXACTLY...
COMMON...
YOU REMIND US TOO MUCH OF OUR OLD LIFE! PLUS, WE'VE REALLY BEEN SWAMPED. WE'VE HARDLY HAD A BREAK SINCE WE ARRIVED!
THERE'S SO MUCH TO SEE.
SO MUCH SHOPPING TO DO...
THEN I WON'T BEAT AROUND THE BUSH...
WE NEED YOU.
YOU'LL UNDERSTAND IMMEDIATELY IF I EXPLAIN EVERYTHING IN DETAIL.
ALTA DONNA ISN'T EXACTLY WHAT YOU THINK IT IS...

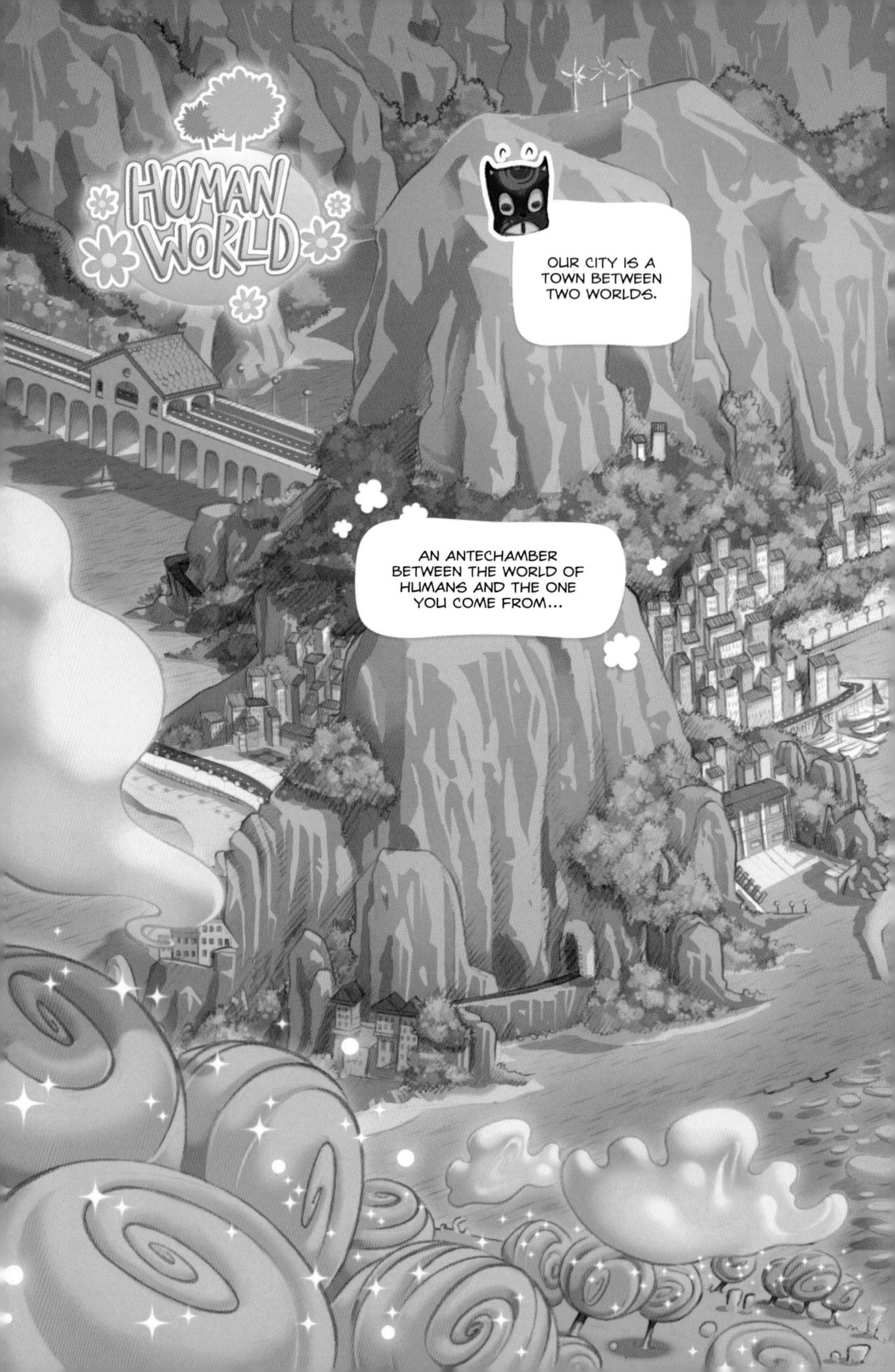
HUMAN WORLD
OUR CITY IS A TOWN BETWEEN TWO WORLDS.
AN ANTECHAMBER BETWEEN THE WORLD OF HUMANS AND THE ONE YOU COME FROM...

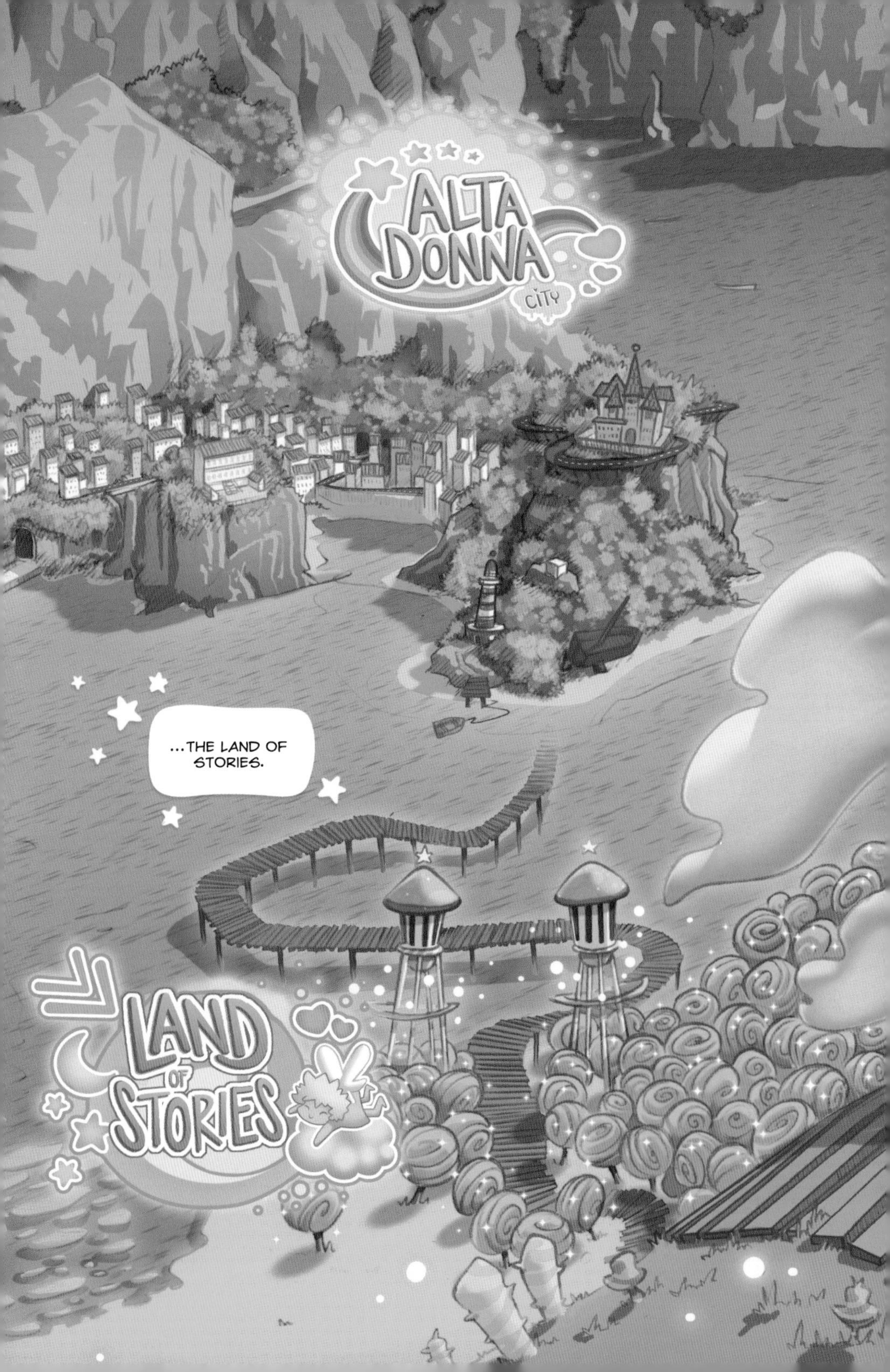
ALTA DONNA CITY
...THE LAND OF STORIES.
LAND OF STORIES

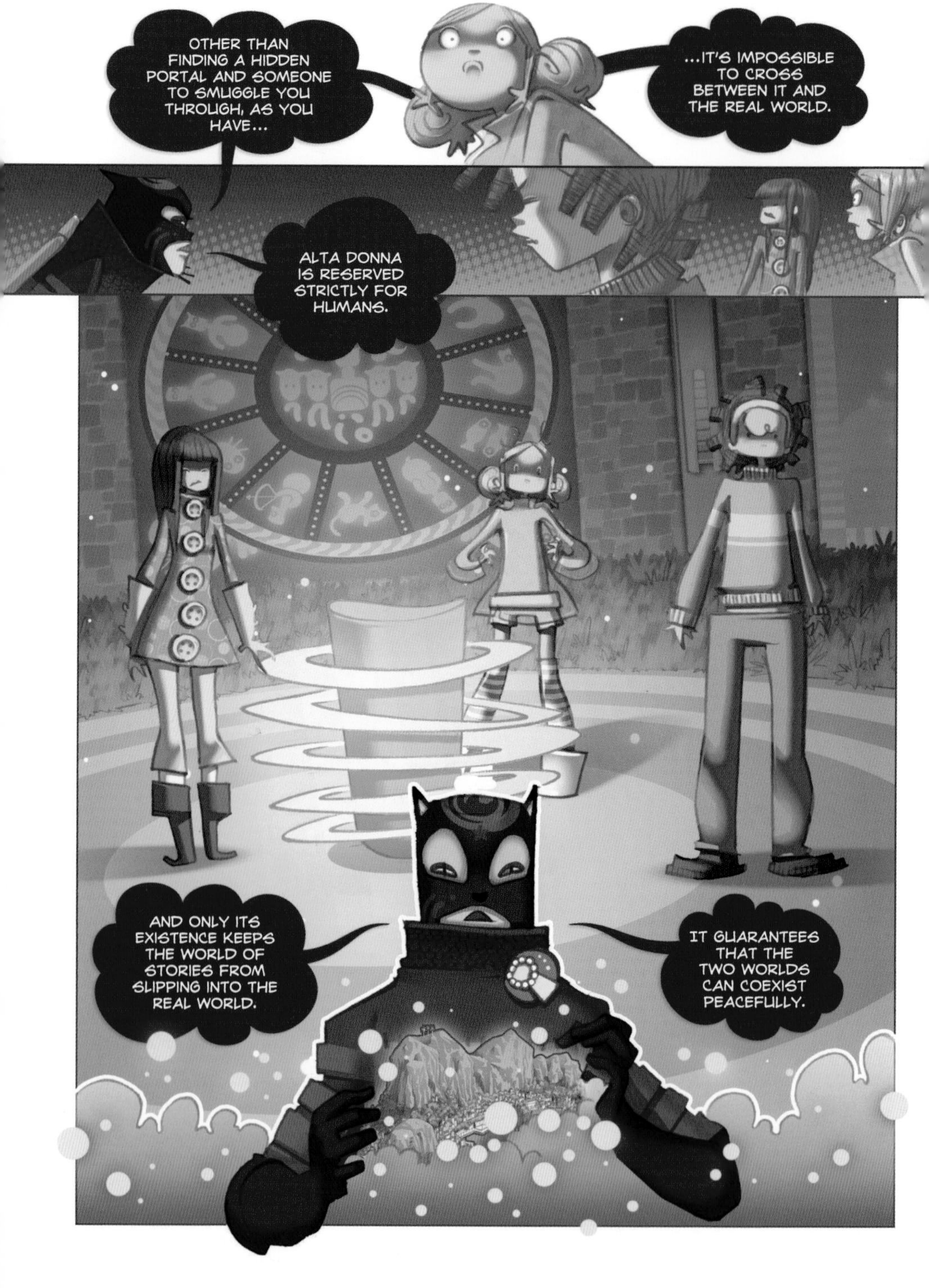
OTHER THAN FINDING A HIDDEN PORTAL AND SOMEONE TO SMUGGLE YOU THROUGH, AS YOU HAVE...
...IT'S IMPOSSIBLE TO CROSS BETWEEN IT AND THE REAL WORLD.
ALTA DONNA IS RESERVED STRICTLY FOR HUMANS.
AND ONLY ITS EXISTENCE KEEPS THE WORLD OF STORIES FROM SLIPPING INTO THE REAL WORLD.
IT GUARANTEES THAT THE TWO WORLDS CAN COEXIST PEACEFULLY.

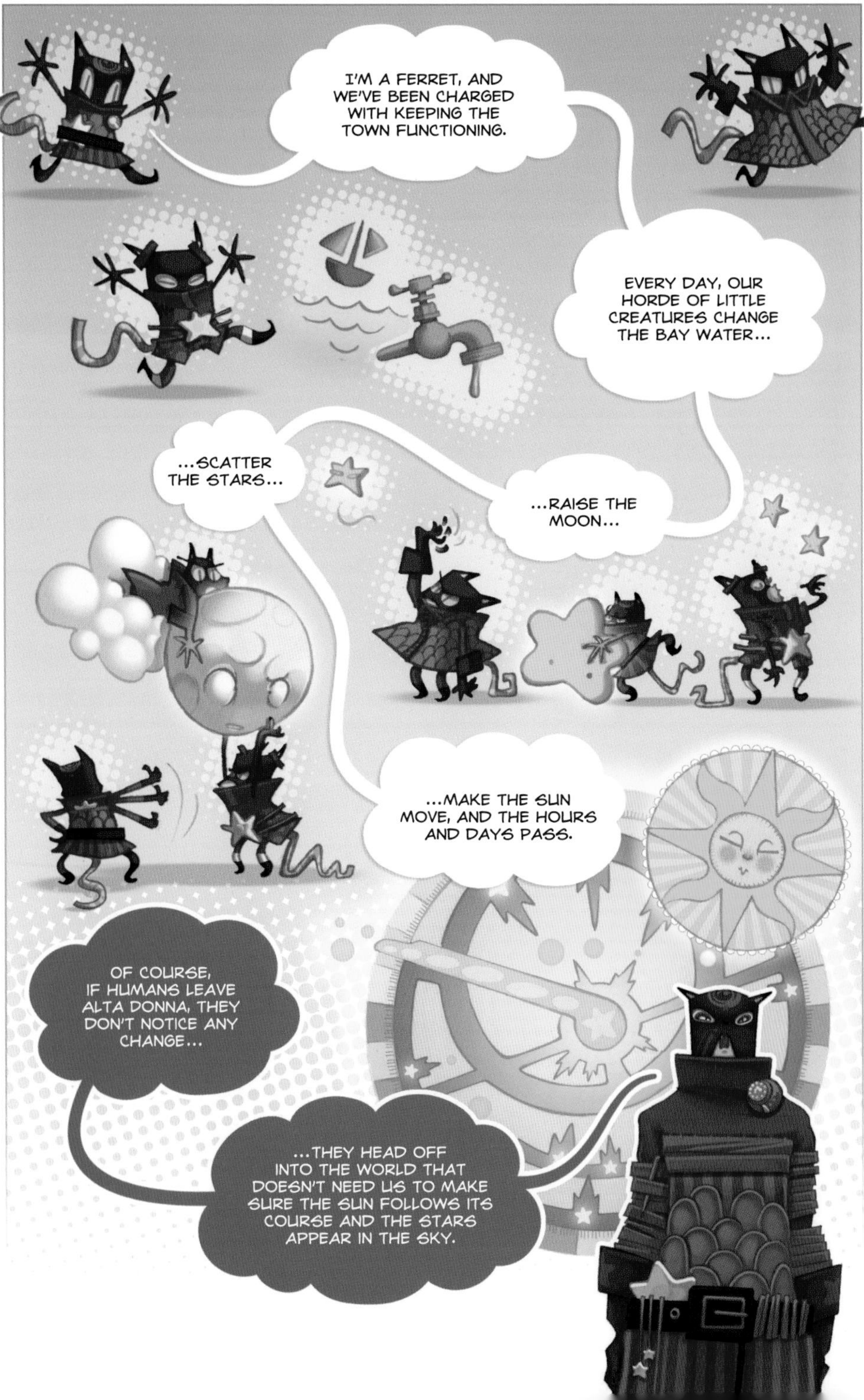
I'M A FERRET, AND WE'VE BEEN CHARGED WITH KEEPING THE TOWN FUNCTIONING.
EVERY DAY, OUR HORDE OF LITTLE CREATURES CHANGE THE BAY WATER...
...RAISE THE MOON...
...SCATTER THE STARS...
...MAKE THE SUN MOVE, AND THE HOURS AND DAYS PASS.
OF COURSE, IF HUMANS LEAVE ALTA DONNA, THEY DON'T NOTICE ANY CHANGE...
...THEY HEAD OFF INTO THE WORLD THAT DOESN'T NEED US TO MAKE SURE THE SUN FOLLOWS ITS COURSE AND THE STARS APPEAR IN THE SKY.

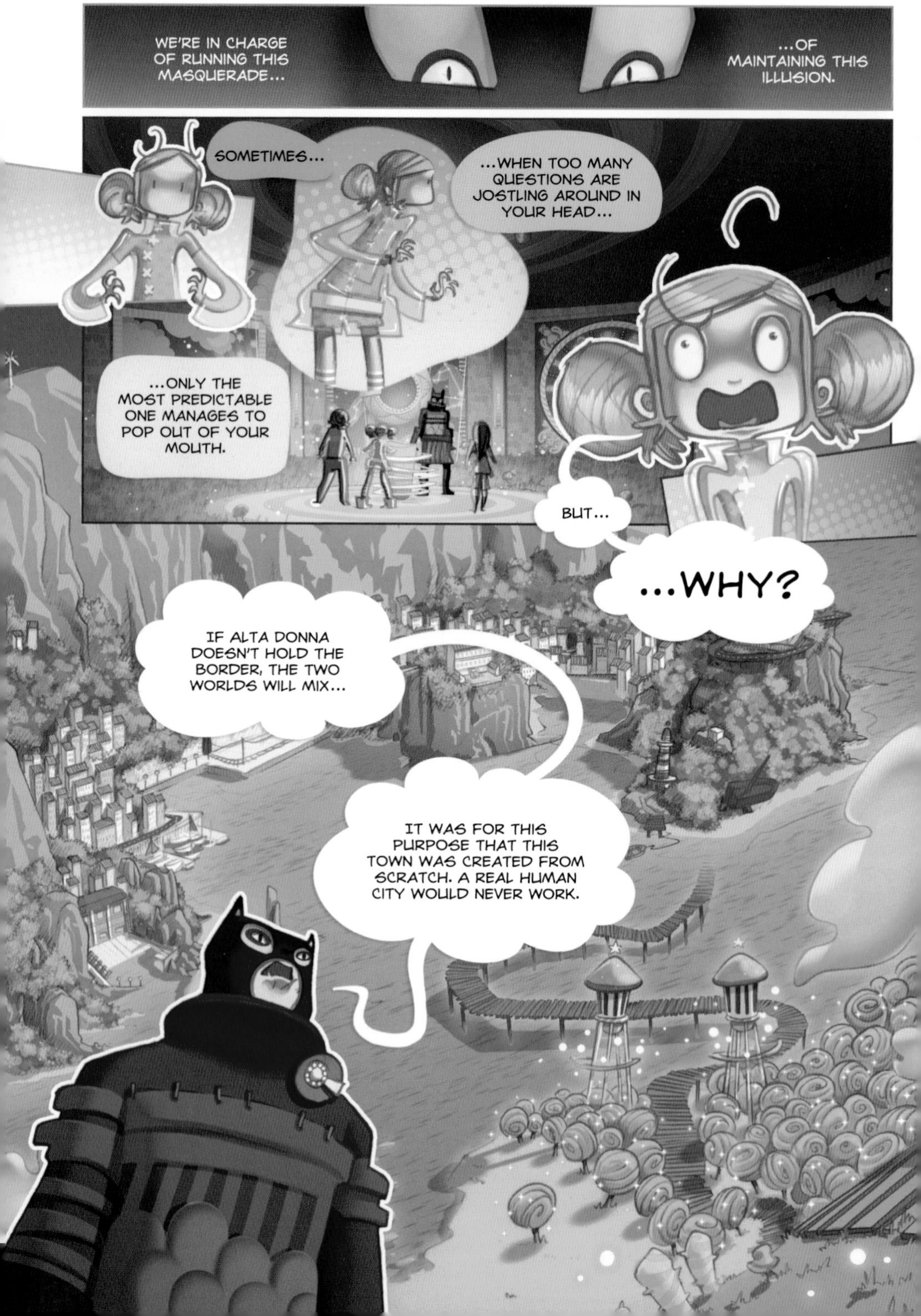
WE'RE IN CHARGE OF RUNNING THIS MASQUERADE...
...OF MAINTAINING THIS ILLUSION.
SOMETIMES...
...WHEN TOO MANY QUESTIONS ARE JOSTLING AROUND IN YOUR HEAD...
...ONLY THE MOST PREDICTABLE ONE MANAGES TO POP OUT OF YOUR MOUTH.
BUT...
...WHY?
IF ALTA DONNA DOESN'T HOLD THE BORDER, THE TWO WORLDS WILL MIX...
IT WAS FOR THIS PURPOSE THAT THIS TOWN WAS CREATED FROM SCRATCH. A REAL HUMAN CITY WOULD NEVER WORK.

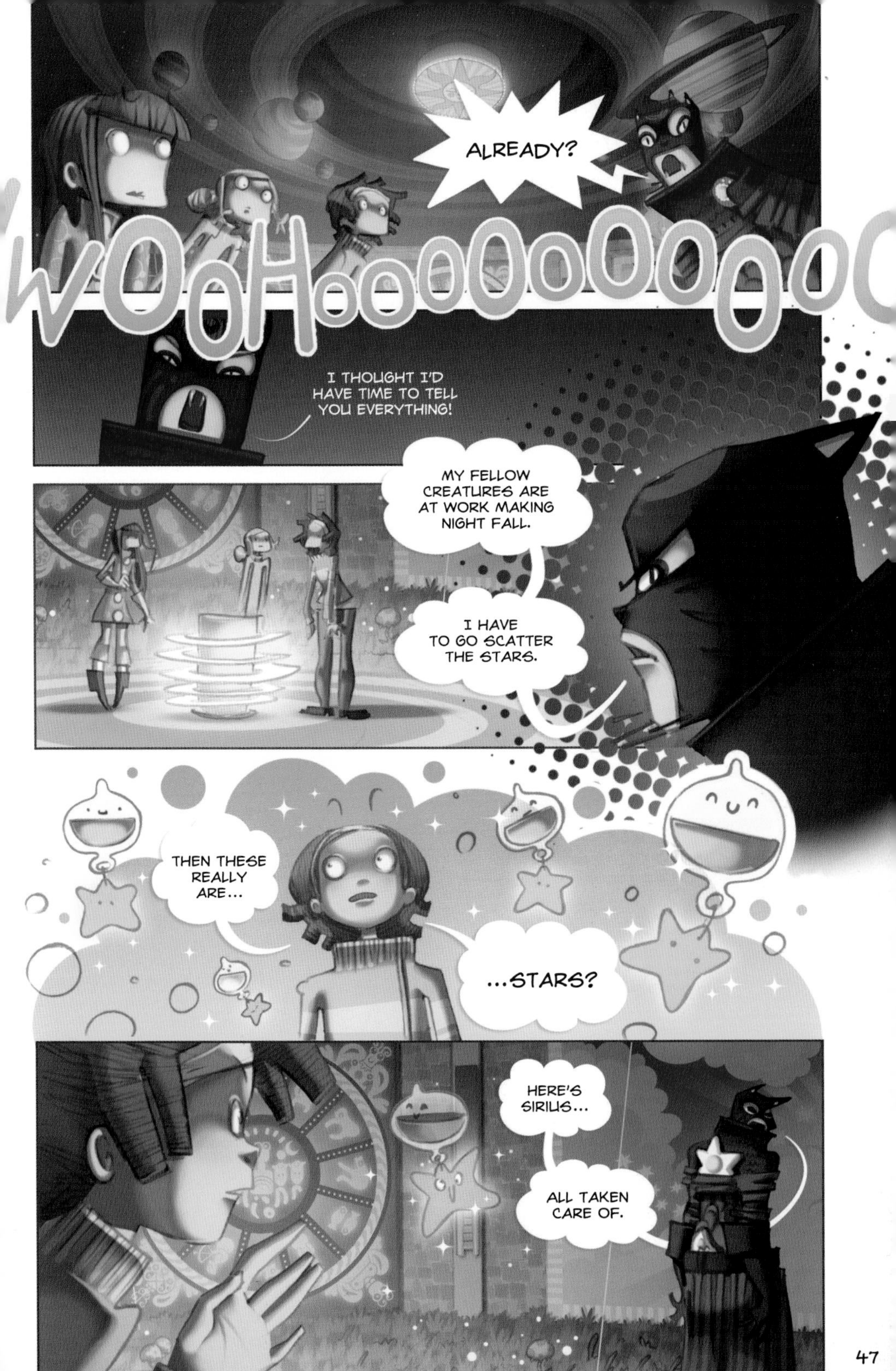

ALREADY?
WOOHOOOOOOOOOOO
I THOUGHT I'D HAVE TIME TO TELL YOU EVERYTHING!
MY FELLOW CREATURES ARE AT WORK MAKING NIGHT FALL.
I HAVE TO GO SCATTER THE STARS.
THEN THESE REALLY ARE...
...STARS?
HERE'S SIRIUS...
ALL TAKEN CARE OF.

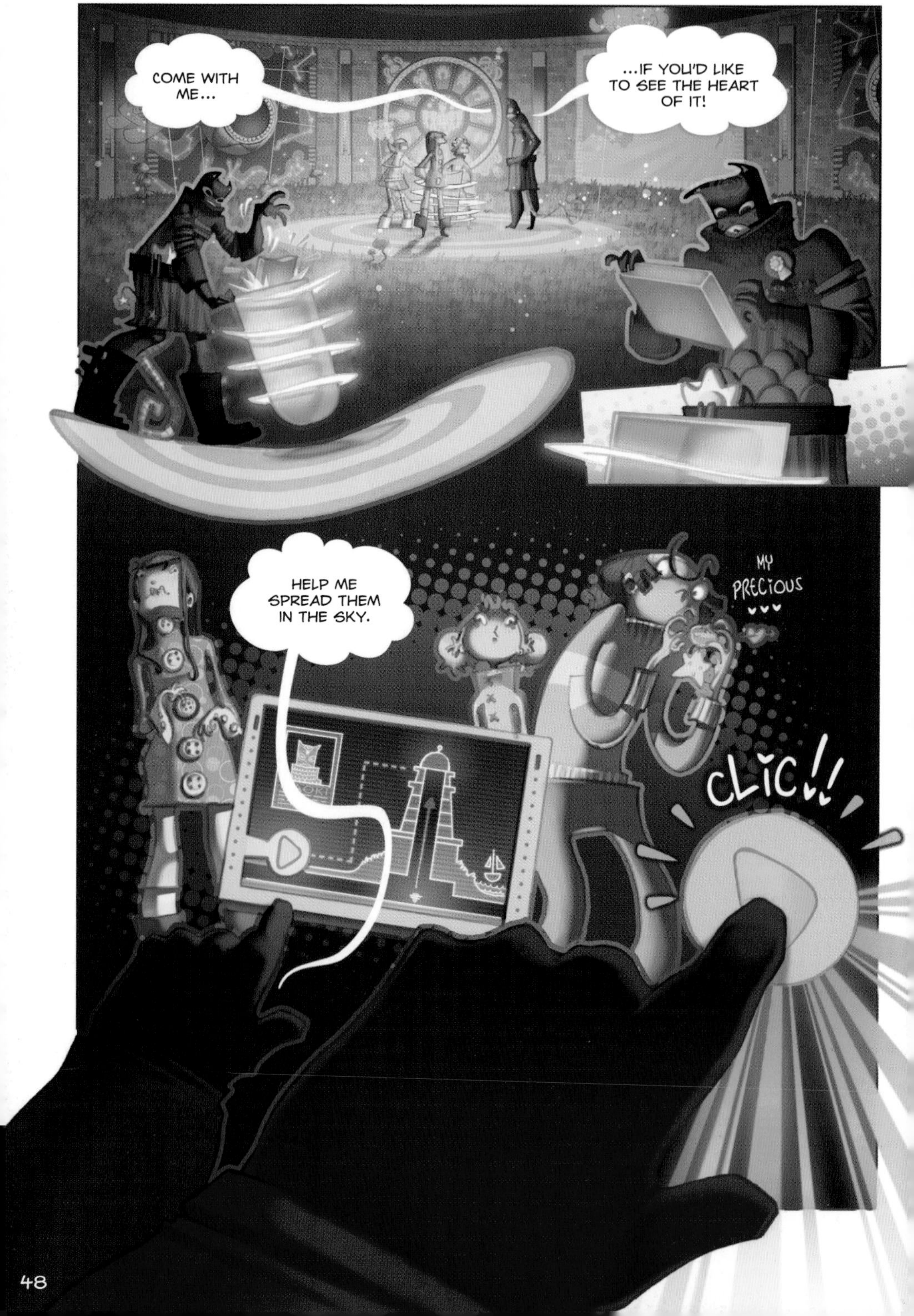
COME WITH ME...
...IF YOU'D LIKE TO SEE THE HEART OF IT!
HELP ME SPREAD THEM IN THE SKY.
MY PRECIOUS
CLIC!!

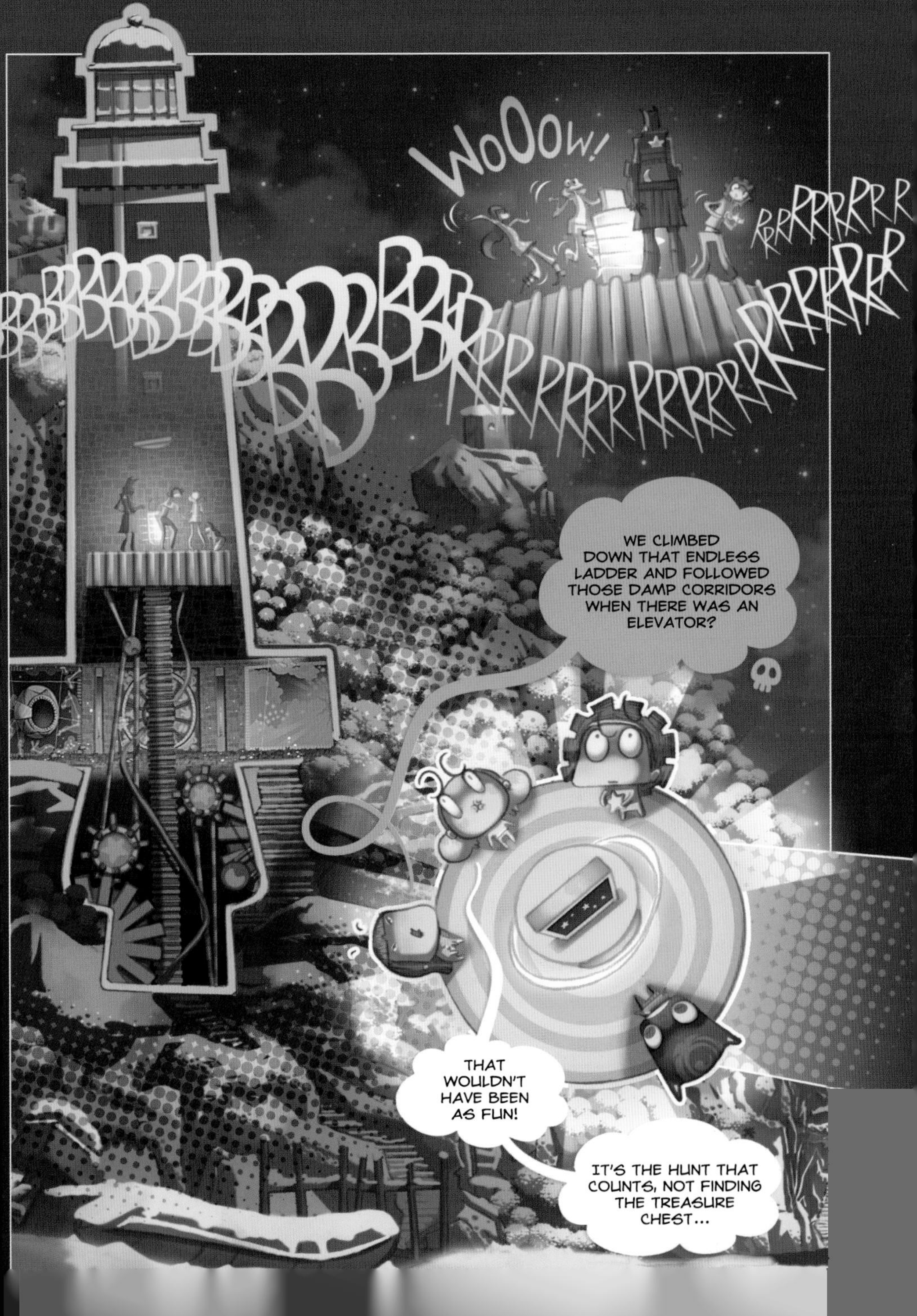
WoOow!
BBBBBBBBBBBBBBBRRRRRRRRRRRRRRRRR
RRRRRRRRR
RRRRRRRRR
WE CLIMBED DOWN THAT ENDLESS LADDER AND FOLLOWED THOSE DAMP CORRIDORS WHEN THERE WAS AN ELEVATOR?
THAT WOULDN'T HAVE BEEN AS FUN!
IT'S THE HUNT THAT COUNTS, NOT FINDING THE TREASURE CHEST...

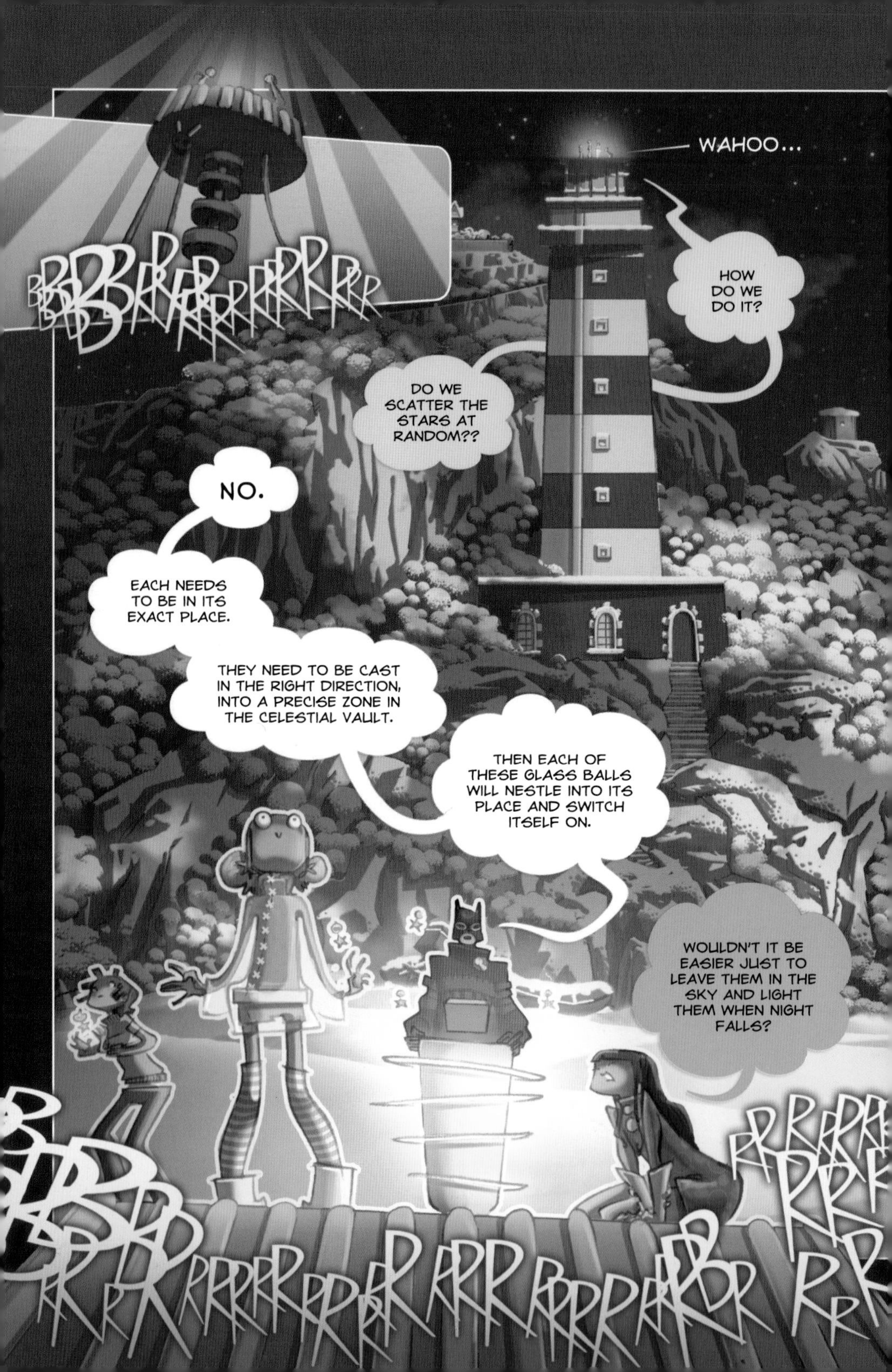
BBBBRRRRRRRRRRRRRRRRR
WAHOO...
HOW DO WE DO IT?
DO WE SCATTER THE STARS AT RANDOM??
NO.
EACH NEEDS TO BE IN ITS EXACT PLACE.
THEY NEED TO BE CAST IN THE RIGHT DIRECTION, INTO A PRECISE ZONE IN THE CELESTIAL VAULT.
THEN EACH OF THESE GLASS BALLS WILL NESTLE INTO ITS PLACE AND SWITCH ITSELF ON.
WOULDN'T IT BE EASIER JUST TO LEAVE THEM IN THE SKY AND LIGHT THEM WHEN NIGHT FALLS?
BBBBRRRRRRRRRRRRRRRRRRRRRRRR

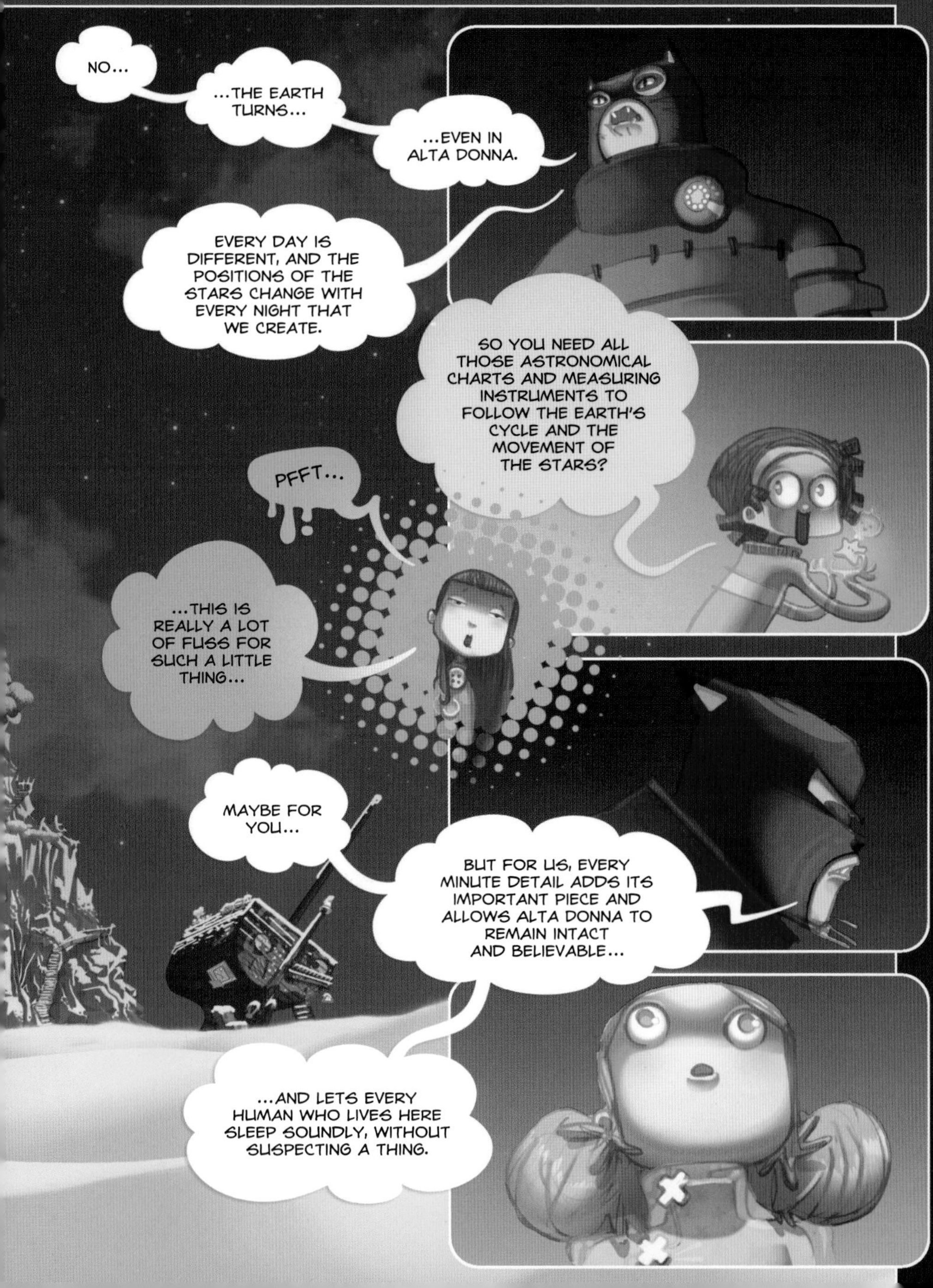
NO...
...THE EARTH TURNS...
...EVEN IN ALTA DONNA.
EVERY DAY IS DIFFERENT, AND THE POSITIONS OF THE STARS CHANGE WITH EVERY NIGHT THAT WE CREATE.
SO YOU NEED ALL THOSE ASTRONOMICAL CHARTS AND MEASURING INSTRUMENTS TO FOLLOW THE EARTH'S CYCLE AND THE MOVEMENT OF THE STARS?
PFFT...
...THIS IS REALLY A LOT OF FUSS FOR SUCH A LITTLE THING...
MAYBE FOR YOU...
BUT FOR US, EVERY MINUTE DETAIL ADDS ITS IMPORTANT PIECE AND ALLOWS ALTA DONNA TO REMAIN INTACT AND BELIEVABLE...
...AND LETS EVERY HUMAN WHO LIVES HERE SLEEP SOUNDLY, WITHOUT SUSPECTING A THING.

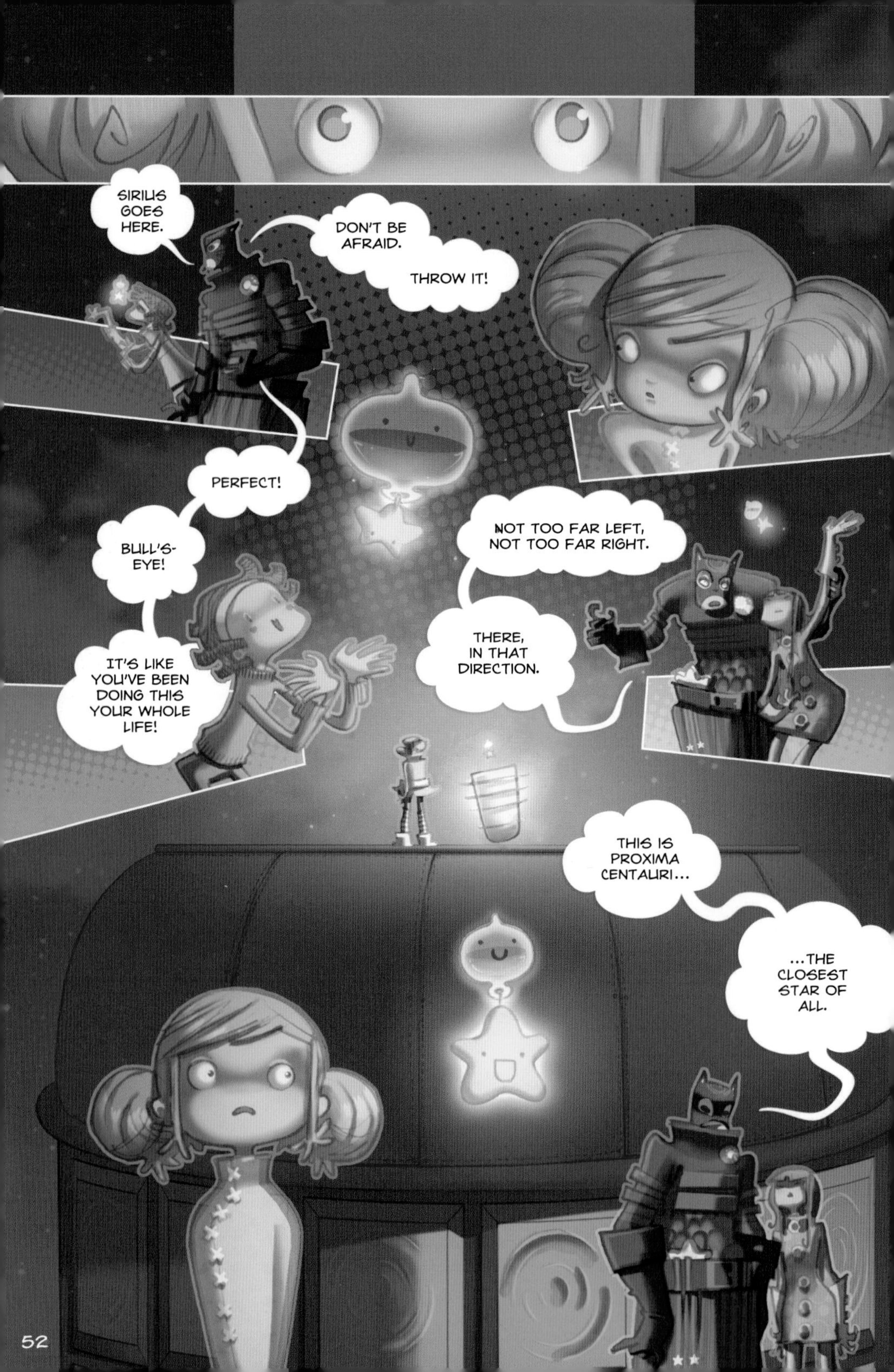
SIRIUS GOES HERE.
DON'T BE AFRAID.
THROW IT!
PERFECT!
BULL'S-EYE!
IT'S LIKE YOU'VE BEEN DOING THIS YOUR WHOLE LIFE!
NOT TOO FAR LEFT, NOT TOO FAR RIGHT.
THERE, IN THAT DIRECTION.
THIS IS PROXIMA CENTAURI...
...THE CLOSEST STAR OF ALL.

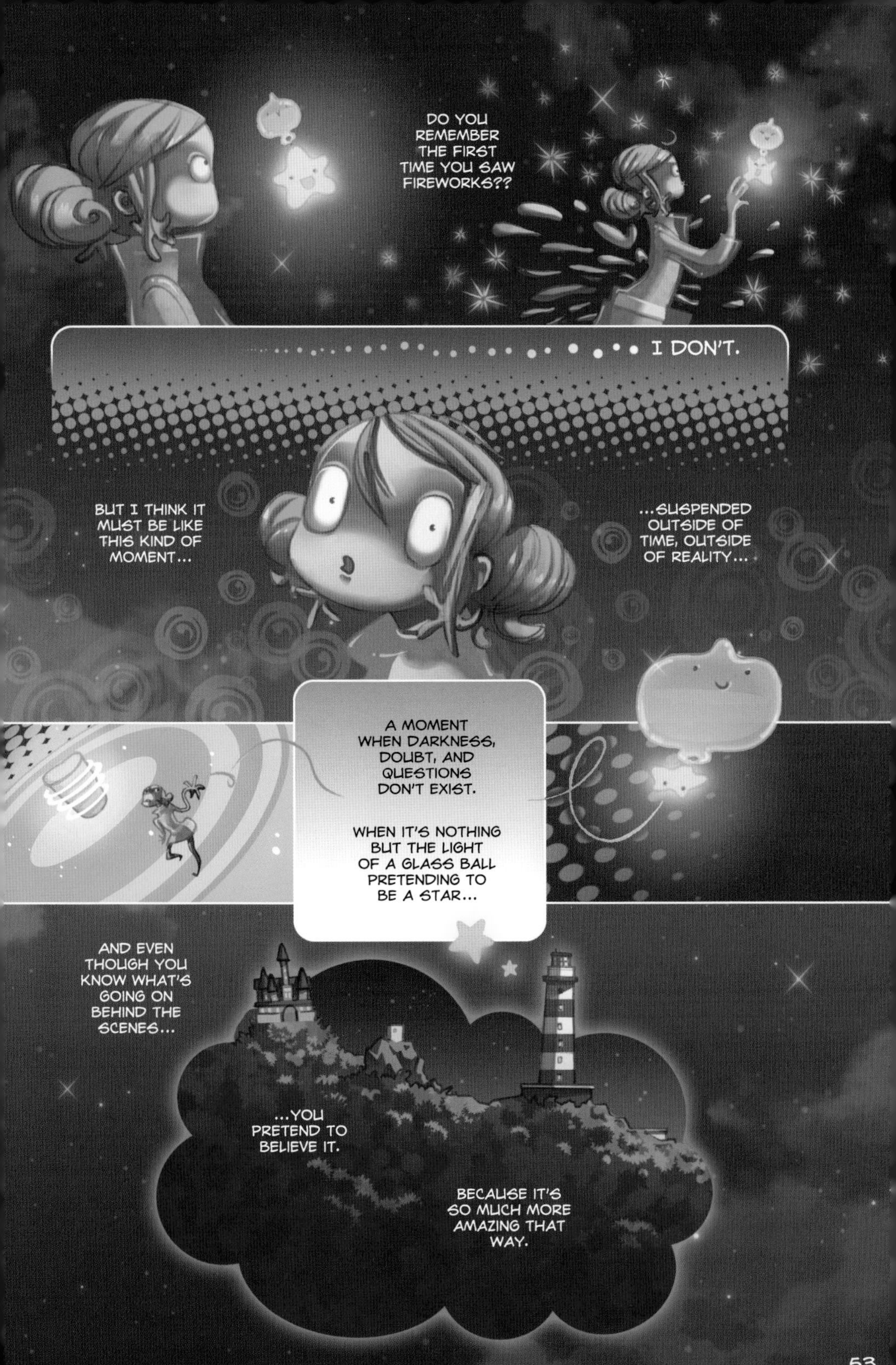
DO YOU REMEMBER THE FIRST TIME YOU SAW FIREWORKS??
I DON'T.
BUT I THINK IT MUST BE LIKE THIS KIND OF MOMENT...
...SUSPENDED OUTSIDE OF TIME, OUTSIDE OF REALITY...
A MOMENT WHEN DARKNESS, DOUBT, AND QUESTIONS DON'T EXIST.
WHEN IT'S NOTHING BUT THE LIGHT OF A GLASS BALL PRETENDING TO BE A STAR...
AND EVEN THOUGH YOU KNOW WHAT'S GOING ON BEHIND THE SCENES...
...YOU PRETEND TO BELIEVE IT.
BECAUSE IT'S SO MUCH MORE AMAZING THAT WAY.

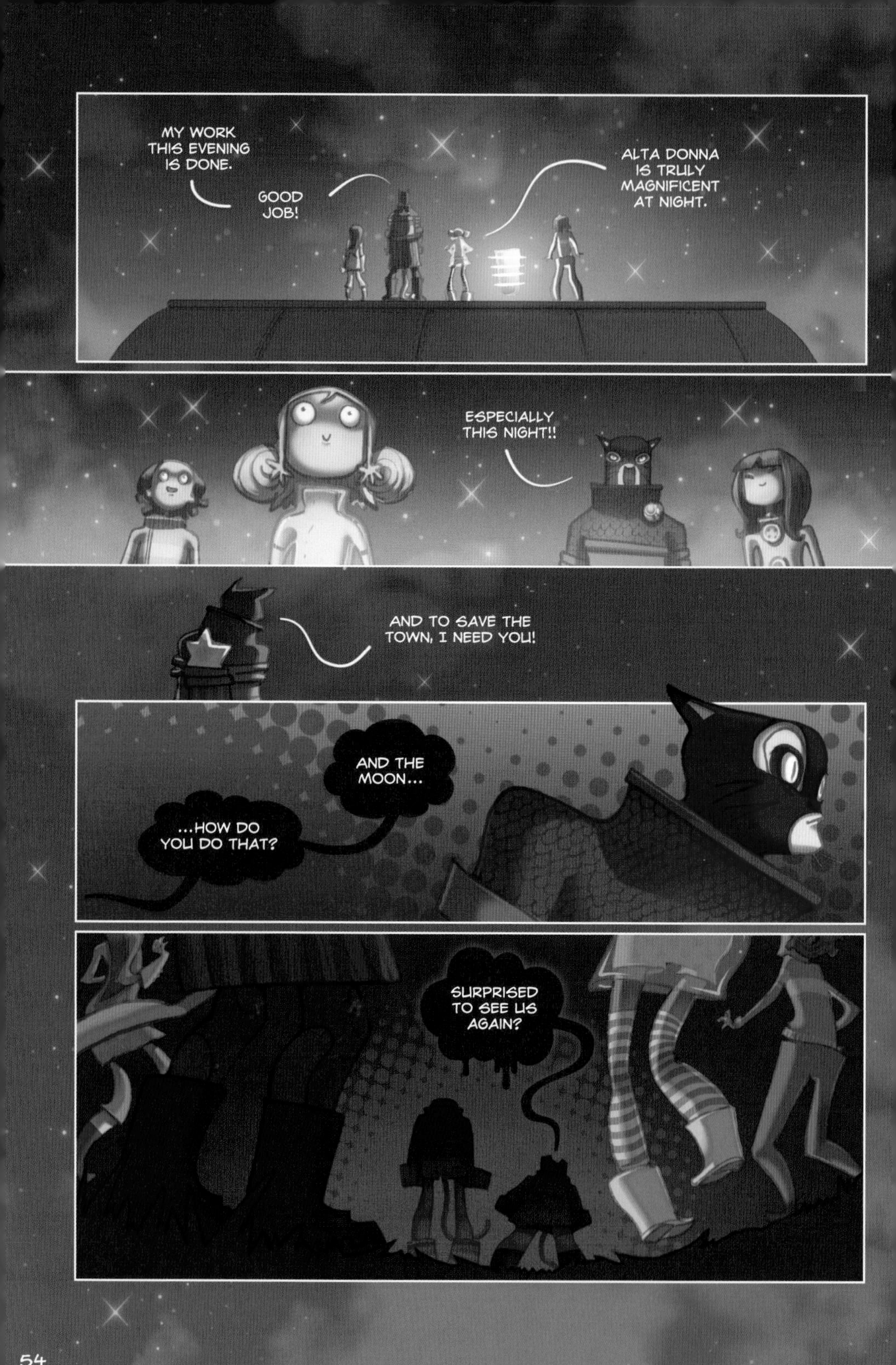

MY WORK THIS EVENING IS DONE.
GOOD JOB!
ALTA DONNA IS TRULY MAGNIFICENT AT NIGHT.
ESPECIALLY THIS NIGHT!!
AND TO SAVE THE TOWN, I NEED YOU!
AND THE MOON...
...HOW DO YOU DO THAT?
SURPRISED TO SEE US AGAIN?

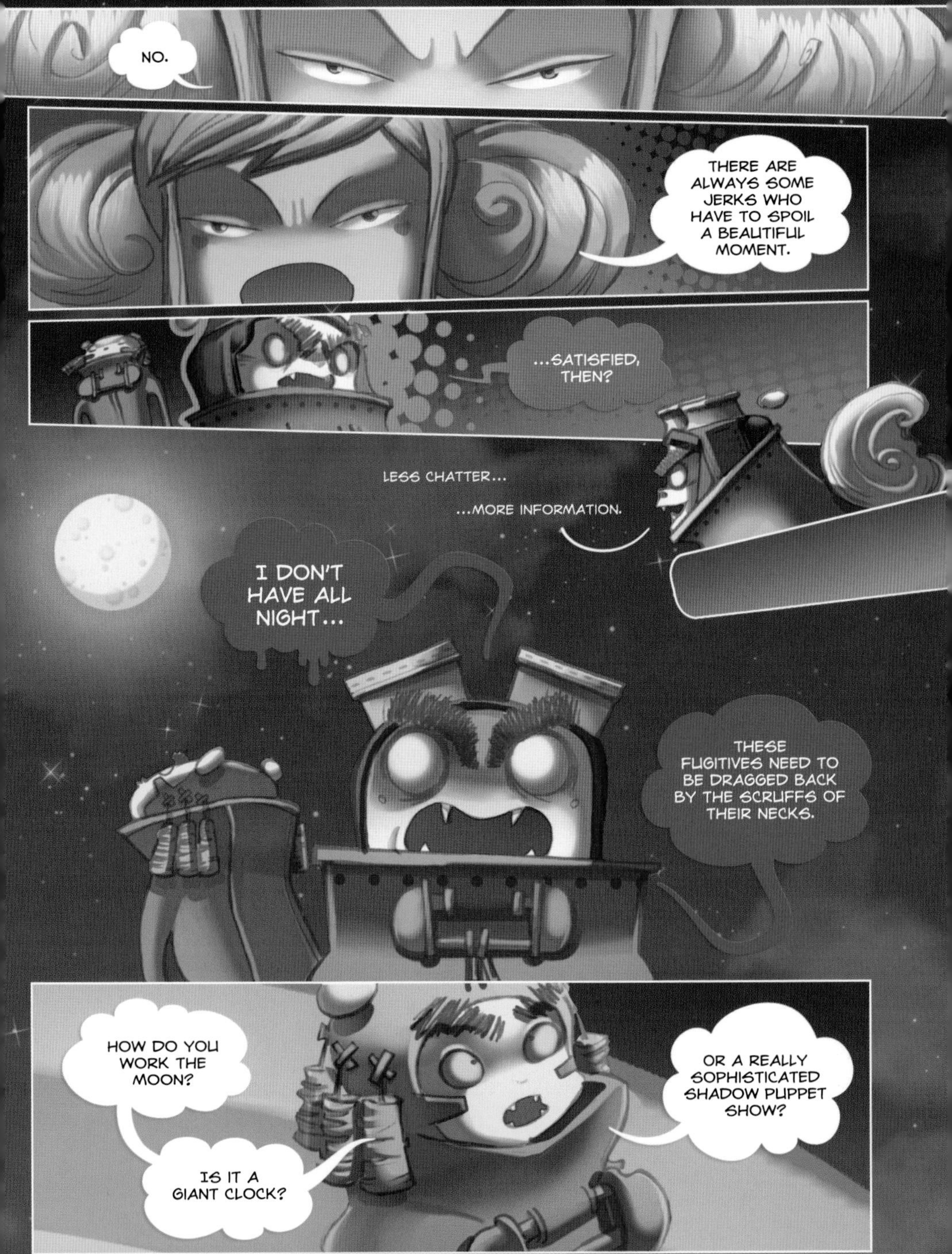
NO.
THERE ARE ALWAYS SOME JERKS WHO HAVE TO SPOIL A BEAUTIFUL MOMENT.
...SATISFIED, THEN?
LESS CHATTER...
...MORE INFORMATION.
I DON'T HAVE ALL NIGHT...
THESE FUGITIVES NEED TO BE DRAGGED BACK BY THE SCRUFFS OF THEIR NECKS.
HOW DO YOU WORK THE MOON?
IS IT A GIANT CLOCK?
OR A REALLY SOPHISTICATED SHADOW PUPPET SHOW?

I COULD TELL YOU...

...BUT THEN I WOULD BE FORCED TO SILENCE YOU...

...FOREVER!

DON'T TAUNT US.

YOU WOULDN'T BE THE FIRST FERRET WHOSE BIG MOUTH GOT HIM IN TROUBLE.

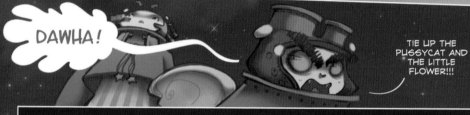

DAWHA!

TIE UP THE PUSSYCAT AND THE LITTLE FLOWER!!!

RIGHT AWAY, DIDDO!

IF WE BRING BACK THE TWO FUGITIVES, SURELY THE BOSS LADY WILL TAKE US BACK.

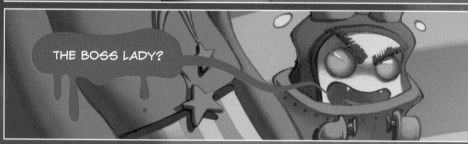

THE BOSS LADY?

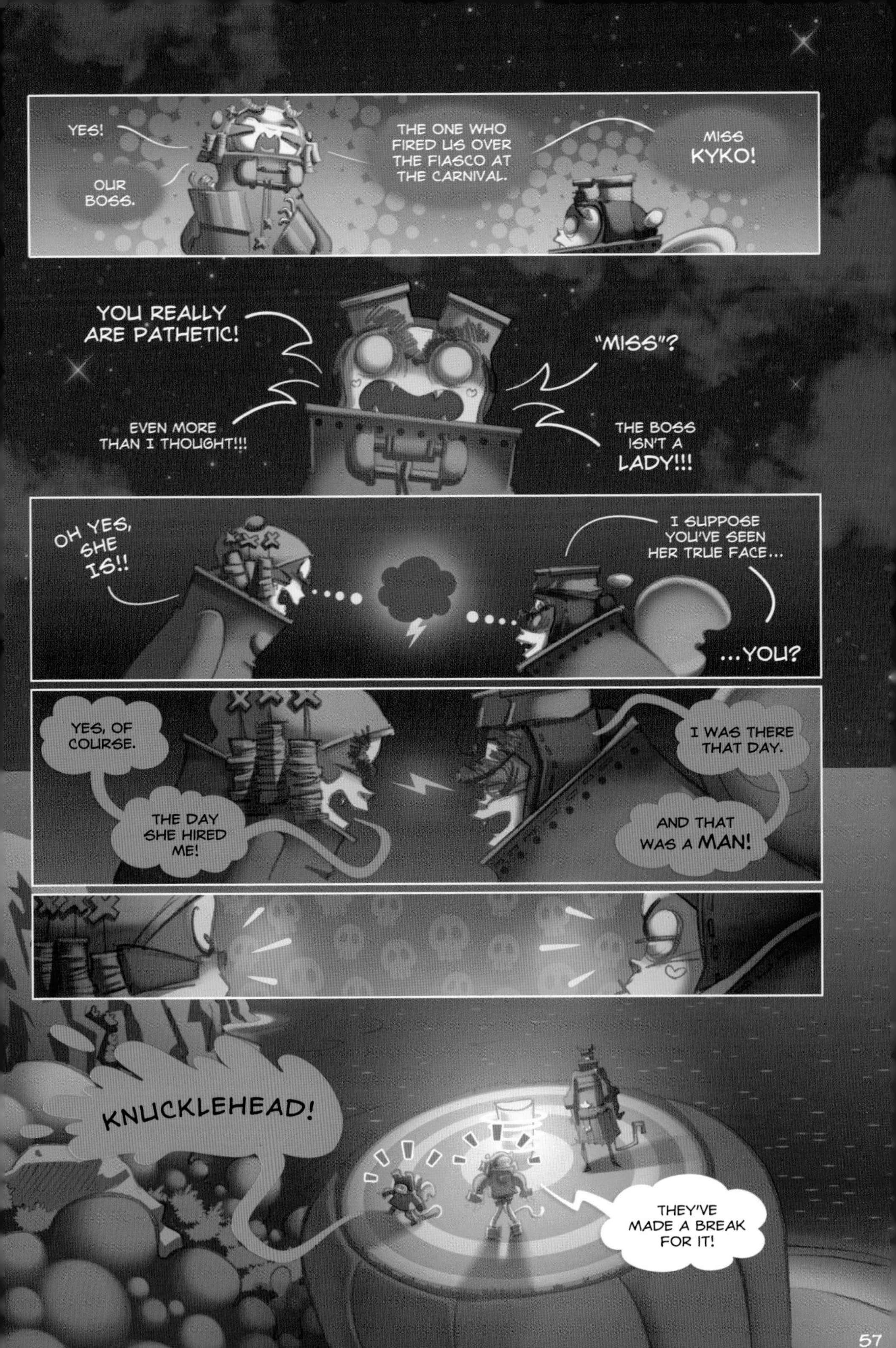
YES!
OUR BOSS.
THE ONE WHO FIRED US OVER THE FIASCO AT THE CARNIVAL.
MISS KYKO!
YOU REALLY ARE PATHETIC!
EVEN MORE THAN I THOUGHT!!!
"MISS"?
THE BOSS ISN'T A LADY!!!
OH YES, SHE IS!!
I SUPPOSE YOU'VE SEEN HER TRUE FACE...
...YOU?
YES, OF COURSE.
THE DAY SHE HIRED ME!
I WAS THERE THAT DAY.
AND THAT WAS A MAN!
KNUCKLEHEAD!
THEY'VE MADE A BREAK FOR IT!

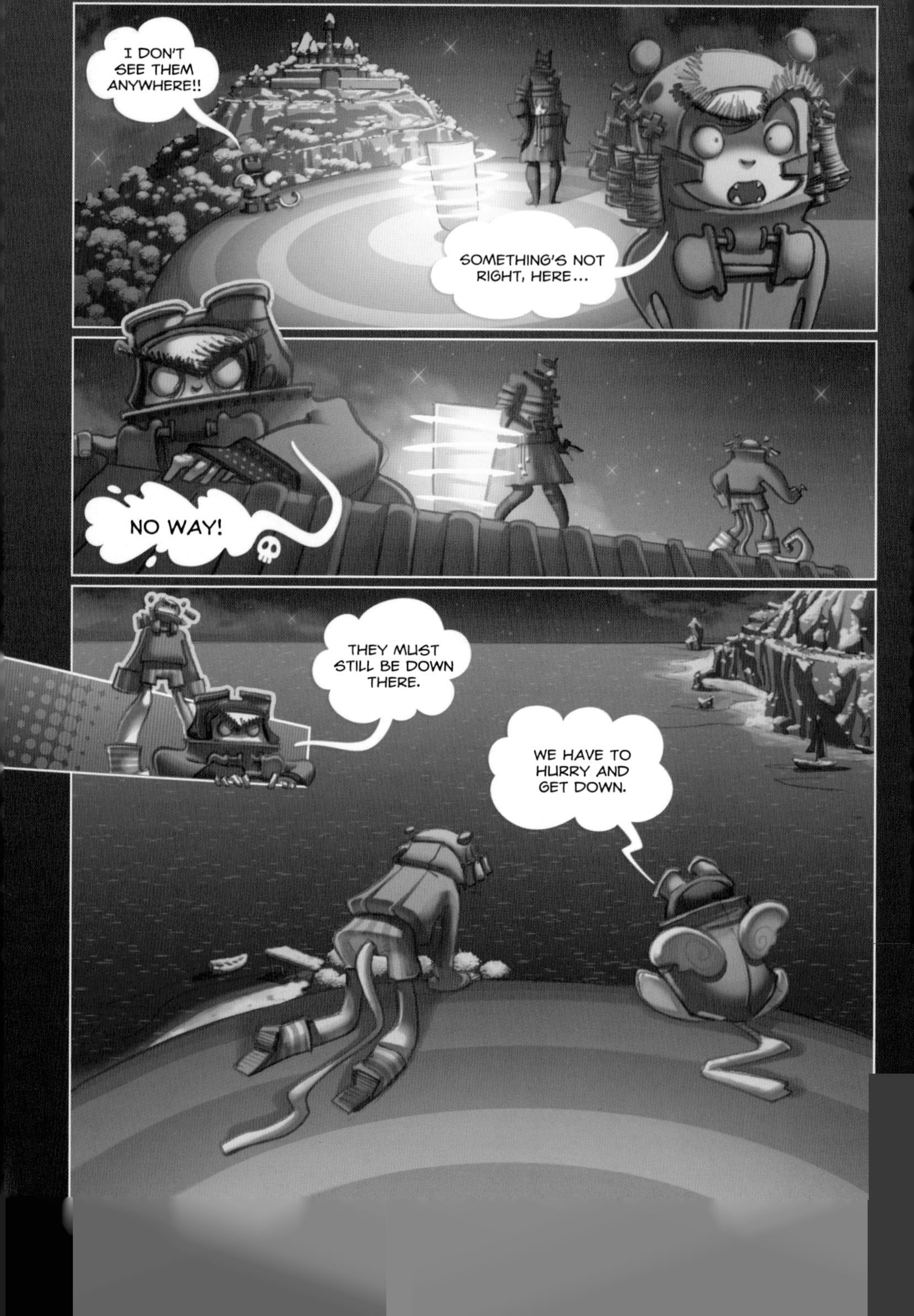
I DON'T SEE THEM ANYWHERE!!
SOMETHING'S NOT RIGHT, HERE...
NO WAY!
THEY MUST STILL BE DOWN THERE.
WE HAVE TO HURRY AND GET DOWN.

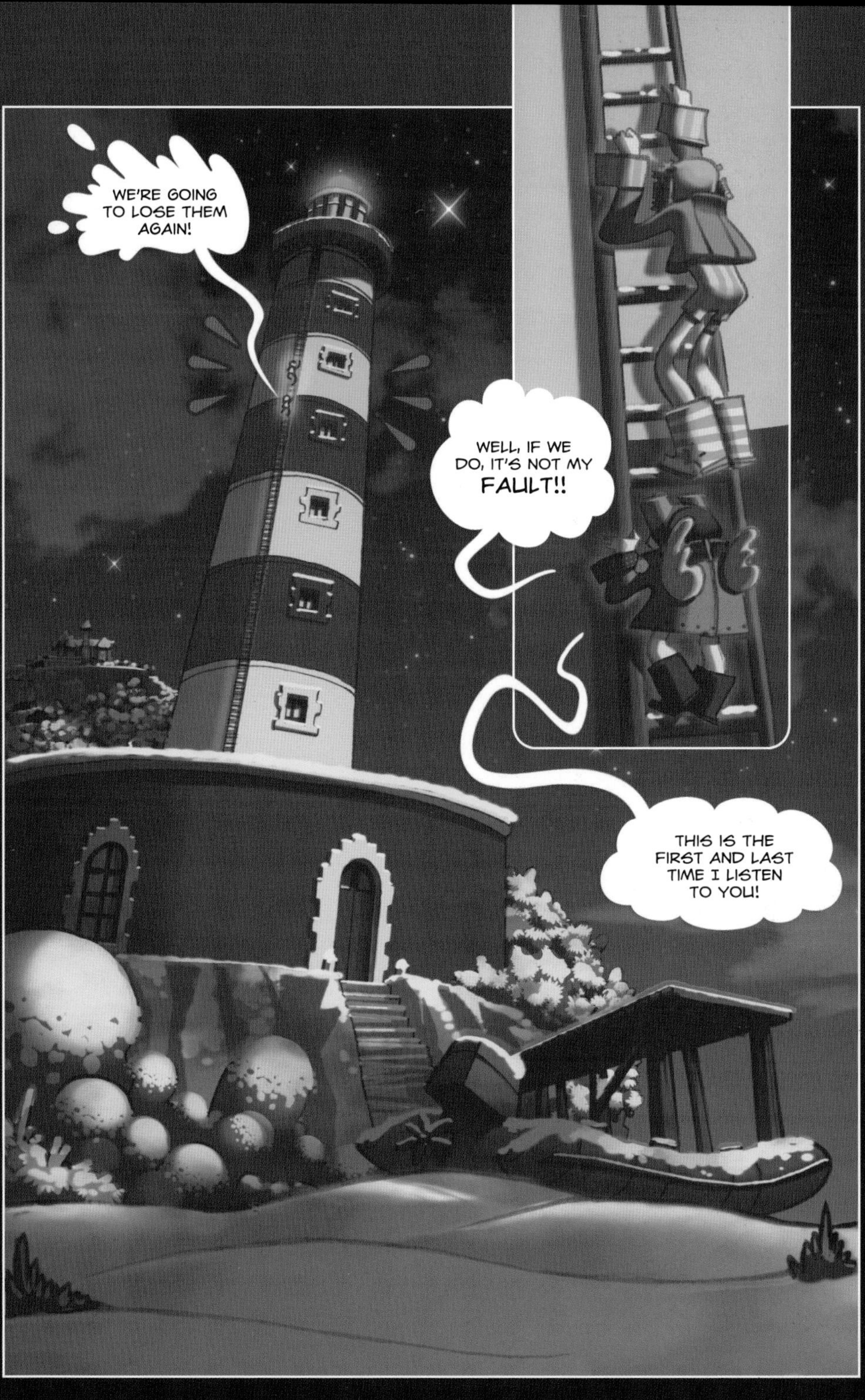
WE'RE GOING TO LOSE THEM AGAIN!
WELL, IF WE DO, IT'S NOT MY FAULT!!
THIS IS THE FIRST AND LAST TIME I LISTEN TO YOU!

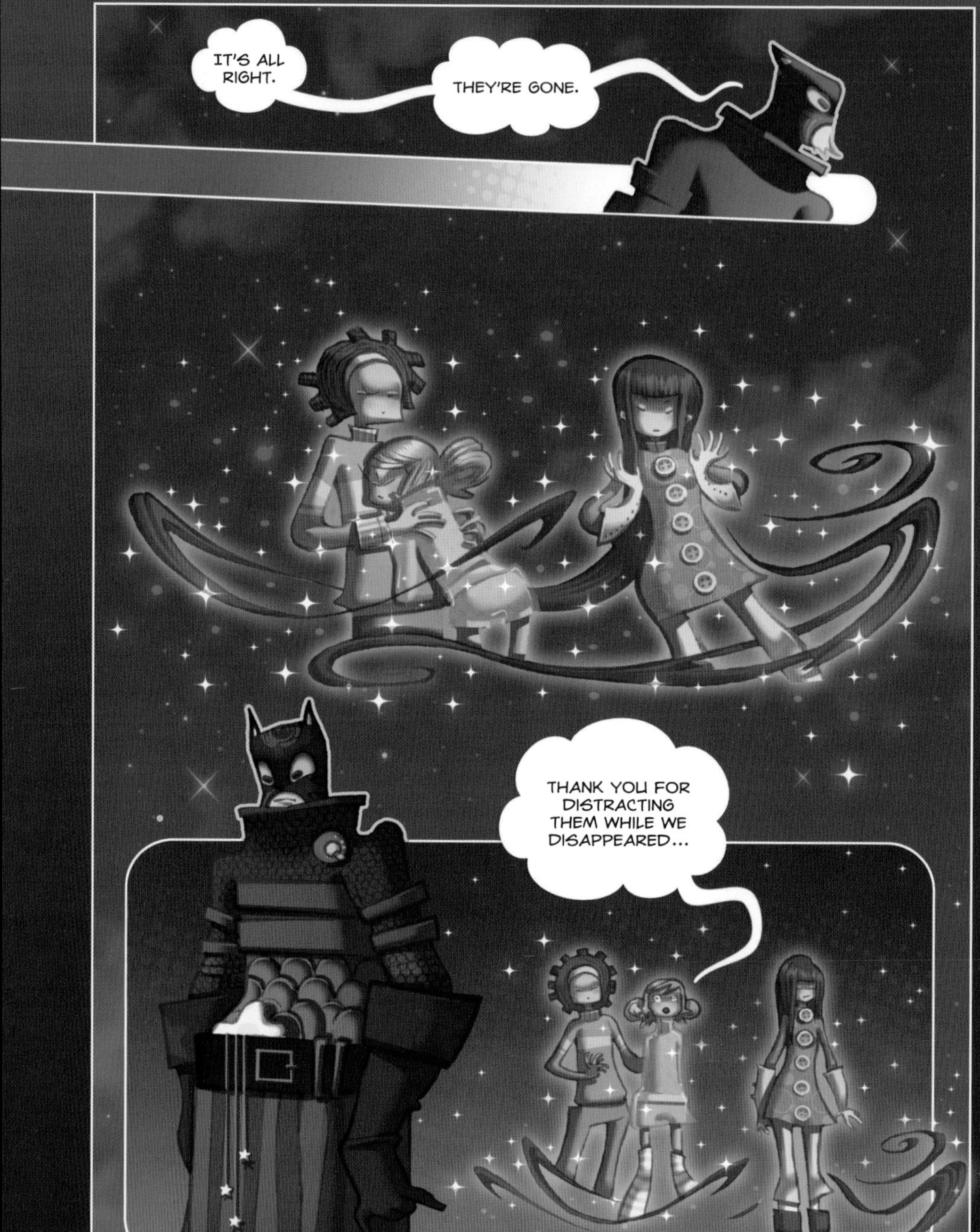
IT'S ALL RIGHT.
THEY'RE GONE.
THANK YOU FOR DISTRACTING THEM WHILE WE DISAPPEARED...

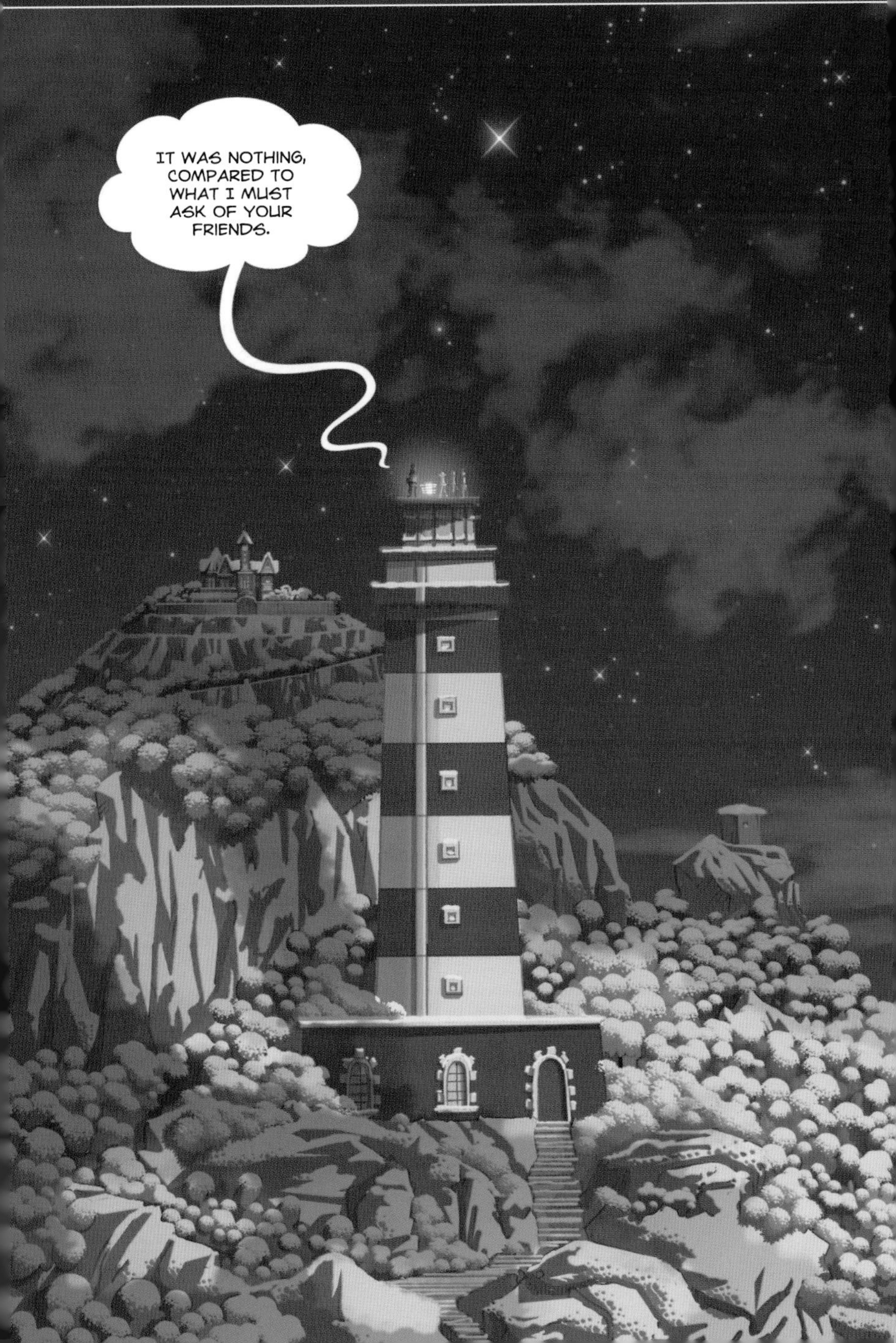
IT WAS NOTHING, COMPARED TO WHAT I MUST ASK OF YOUR FRIENDS.

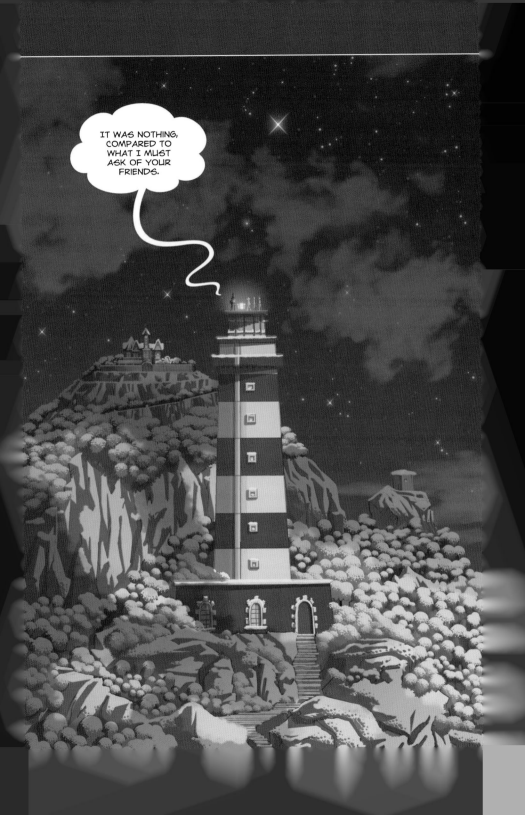

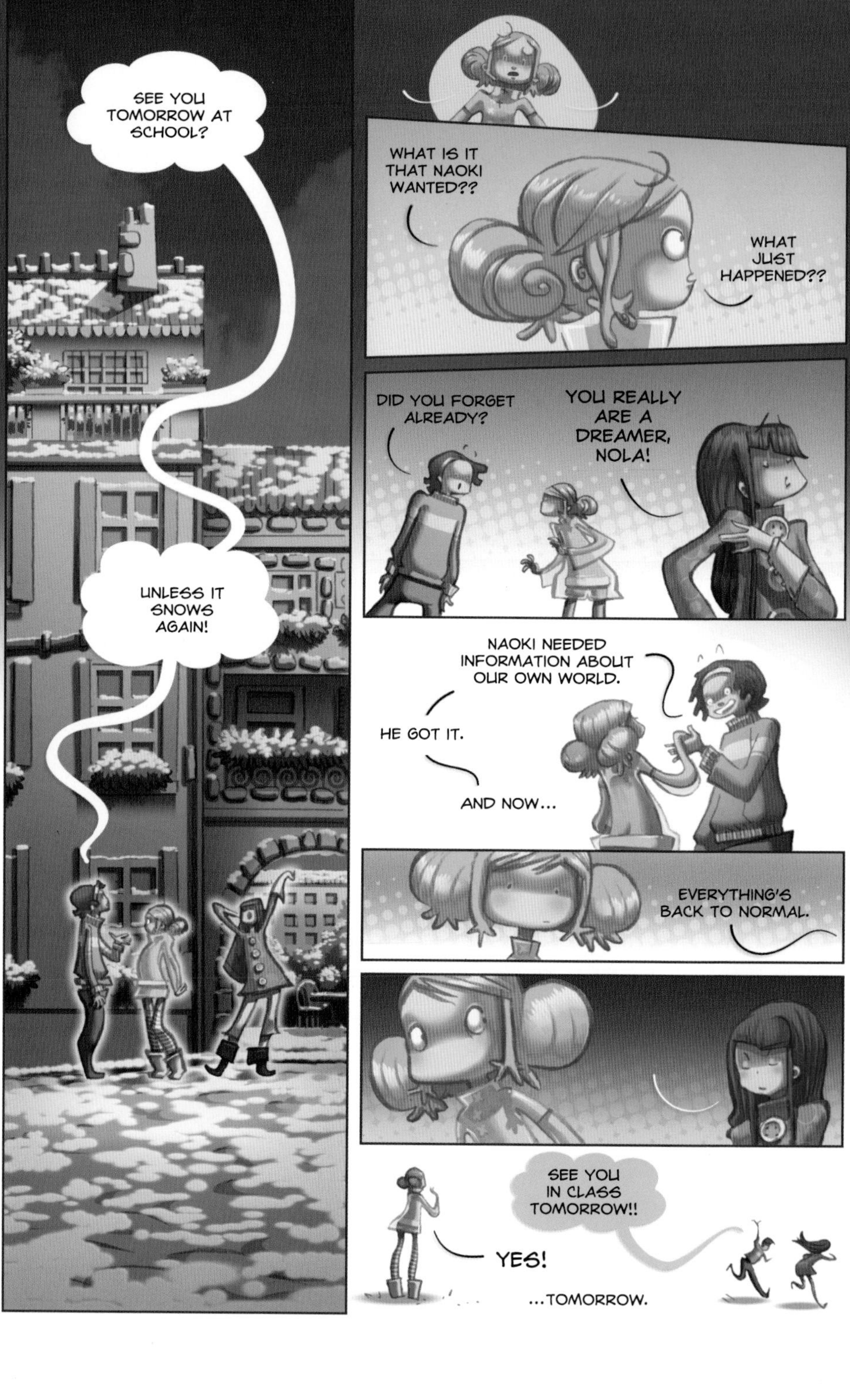
SEE YOU TOMORROW AT SCHOOL?
UNLESS IT SNOWS AGAIN!
WHAT IS IT THAT NAOKI WANTED??
WHAT JUST HAPPENED??
DID YOU FORGET ALREADY?
YOU REALLY ARE A DREAMER, NOLA!
NAOKI NEEDED INFORMATION ABOUT OUR OWN WORLD.
HE GOT IT.
AND NOW...
EVERYTHING'S BACK TO NORMAL.
SEE YOU IN CLASS TOMORROW!!
YES!
...TOMORROW.

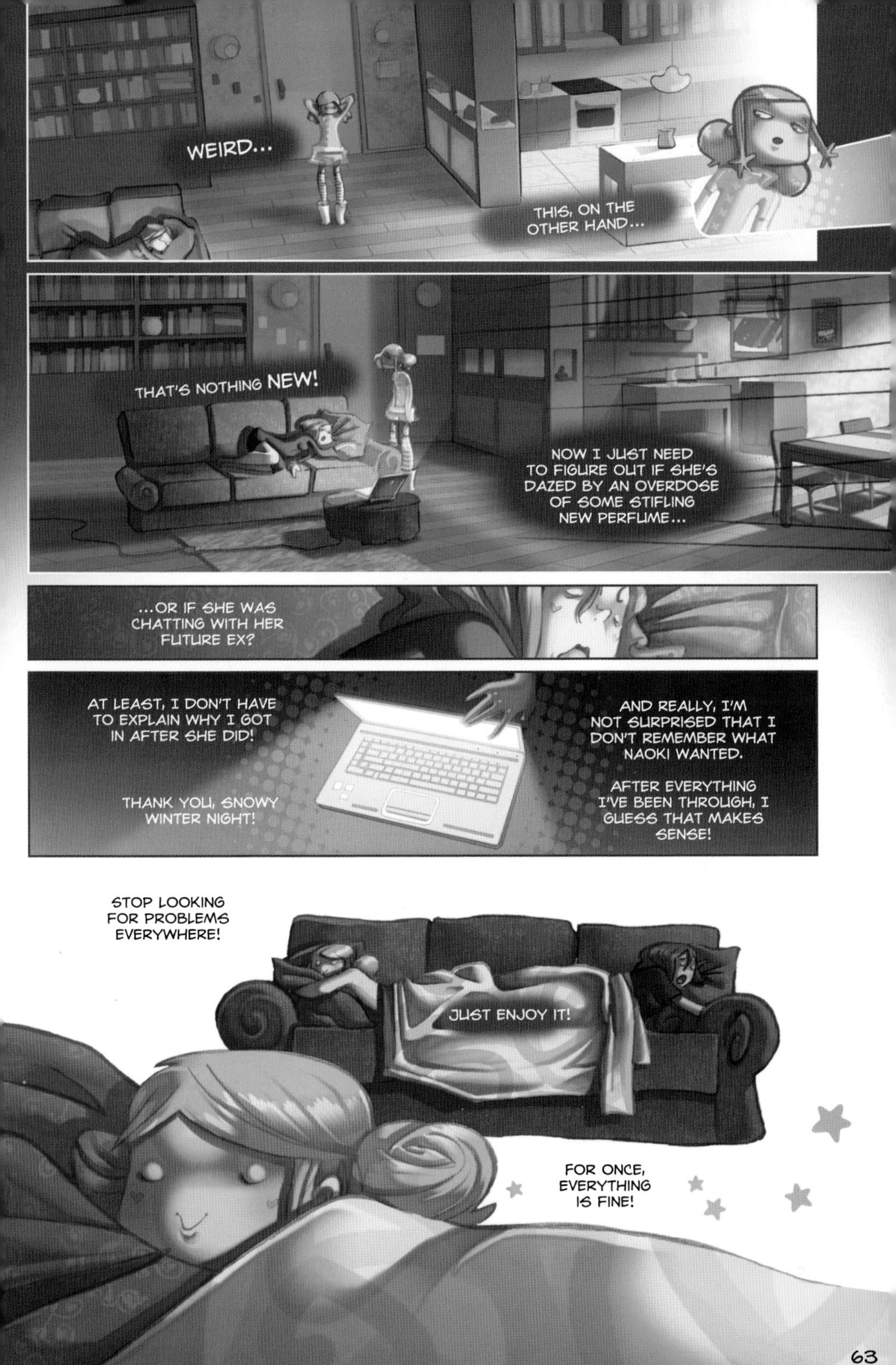

WEIRD...
THIS, ON THE OTHER HAND...
THAT'S NOTHING NEW!
NOW I JUST NEED TO FIGURE OUT IF SHE'S DAZED BY AN OVERDOSE OF SOME STIFLING NEW PERFUME...
...OR IF SHE WAS CHATTING WITH HER FUTURE EX?
AT LEAST, I DON'T HAVE TO EXPLAIN WHY I GOT IN AFTER SHE DID!
THANK YOU, SNOWY WINTER NIGHT!
AND REALLY, I'M NOT SURPRISED THAT I DON'T REMEMBER WHAT NAOKI WANTED.
AFTER EVERYTHING I'VE BEEN THROUGH, I GUESS THAT MAKES SENSE!
STOP LOOKING FOR PROBLEMS EVERYWHERE!
JUST ENJOY IT!
FOR ONCE, EVERYTHING IS FINE!

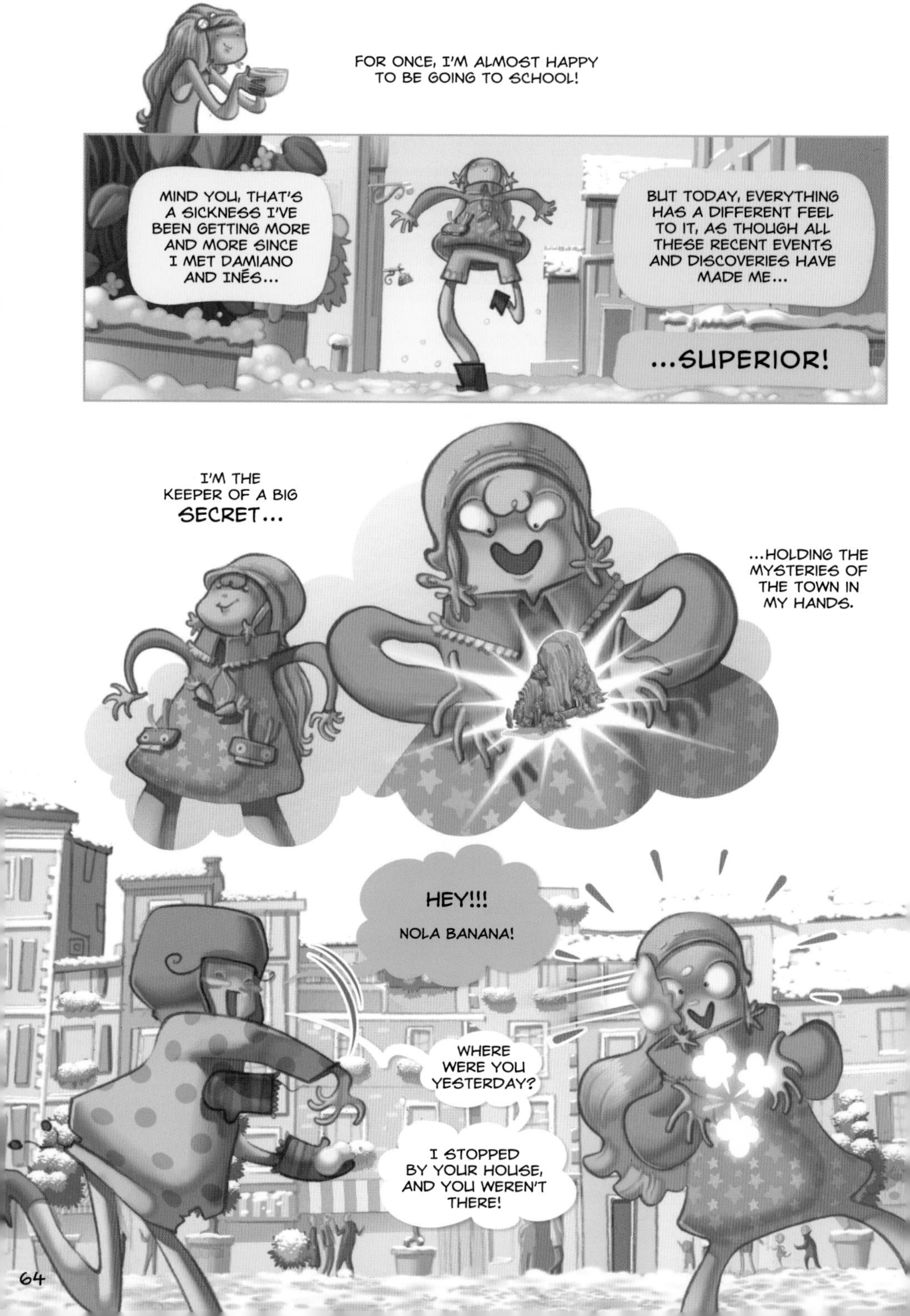
FOR ONCE, I'M ALMOST HAPPY TO BE GOING TO SCHOOL!
MIND YOU, THAT'S A SICKNESS I'VE BEEN GETTING MORE AND MORE SINCE I MET DAMIANO AND INÉS...
BUT TODAY, EVERYTHING HAS A DIFFERENT FEEL TO IT, AS THOUGH ALL THESE RECENT EVENTS AND DISCOVERIES HAVE MADE ME...
...SUPERIOR!
I'M THE KEEPER OF A BIG SECRET...
...HOLDING THE MYSTERIES OF THE TOWN IN MY HANDS.
HEY!!!
NOLA BANANA!
WHERE WERE YOU YESTERDAY?
I STOPPED BY YOUR HOUSE, AND YOU WEREN'T THERE!

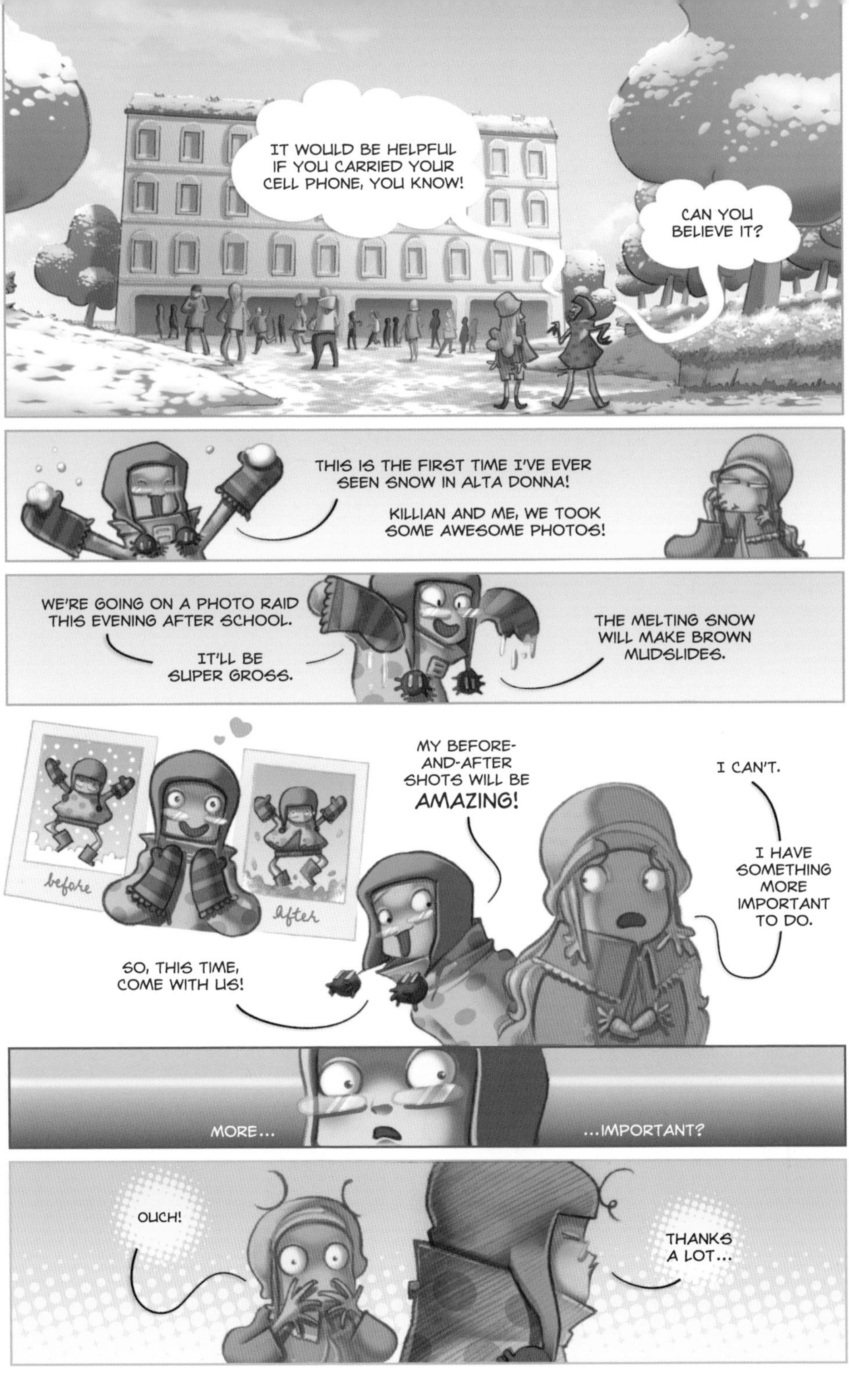
IT WOULD BE HELPFUL IF YOU CARRIED YOUR CELL PHONE, YOU KNOW!
CAN YOU BELIEVE IT?
THIS IS THE FIRST TIME I'VE EVER SEEN SNOW IN ALTA DONNA!
KILLIAN AND ME, WE TOOK SOME AWESOME PHOTOS!
WE'RE GOING ON A PHOTO RAID THIS EVENING AFTER SCHOOL.
IT'LL BE SUPER GROSS.
THE MELTING SNOW WILL MAKE BROWN MUDSLIDES.
before
after
MY BEFORE-AND-AFTER SHOTS WILL BE AMAZING!
SO, THIS TIME, COME WITH US!
I CAN'T.
I HAVE SOMETHING MORE IMPORTANT TO DO.
MORE...
...IMPORTANT?
OUCH!
THANKS A LOT...

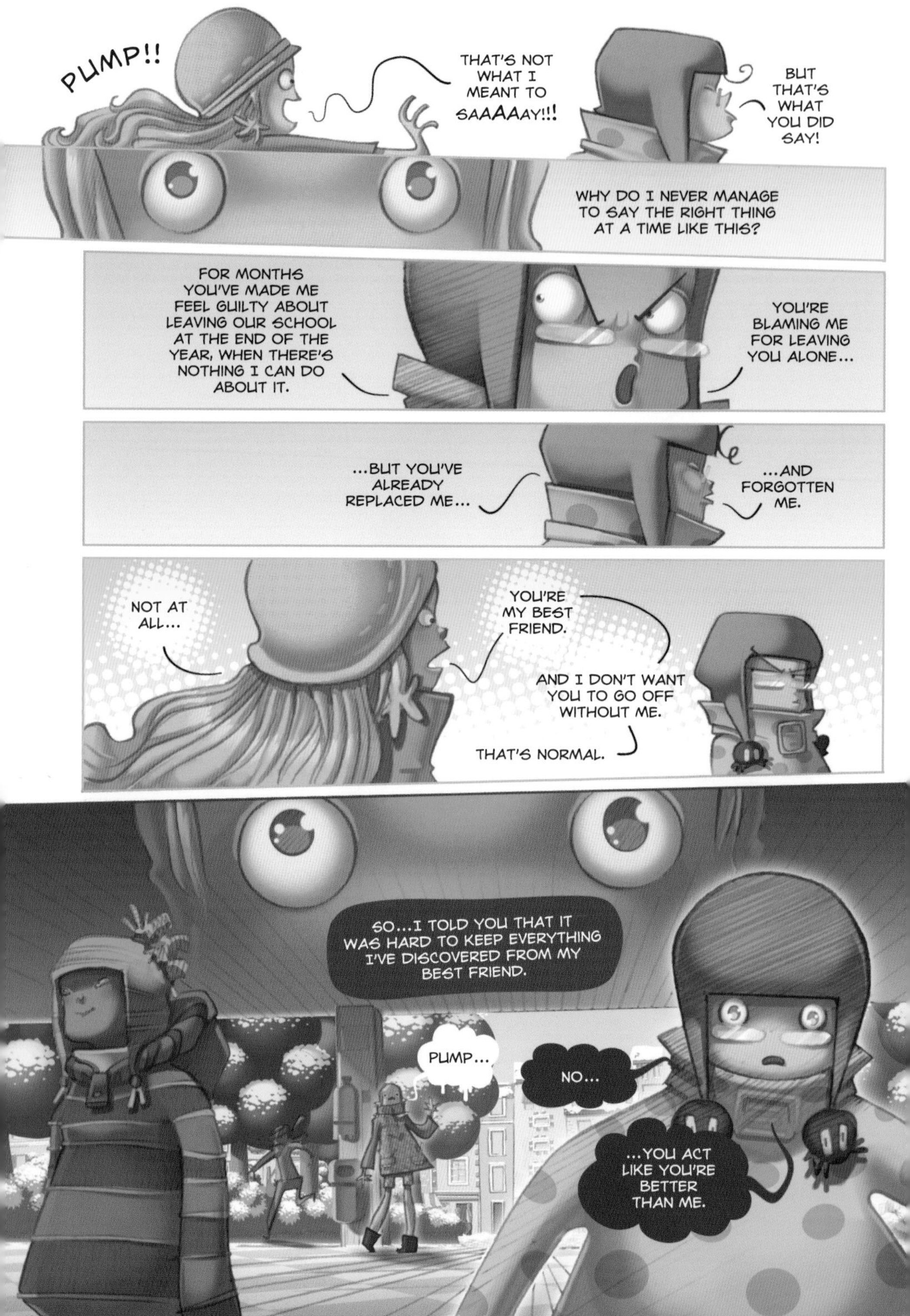
PUMP!!
THAT'S NOT WHAT I MEANT TO SAAAAAAY!!!
BUT THAT'S WHAT YOU DID SAY!
WHY DO I NEVER MANAGE TO SAY THE RIGHT THING AT A TIME LIKE THIS?
FOR MONTHS YOU'VE MADE ME FEEL GUILTY ABOUT LEAVING OUR SCHOOL AT THE END OF THE YEAR, WHEN THERE'S NOTHING I CAN DO ABOUT IT.
YOU'RE BLAMING ME FOR LEAVING YOU ALONE...
...BUT YOU'VE ALREADY REPLACED ME...
...AND FORGOTTEN ME.
NOT AT ALL...
YOU'RE MY BEST FRIEND.
AND I DON'T WANT YOU TO GO OFF WITHOUT ME.
THAT'S NORMAL.
SO...I TOLD YOU THAT IT WAS HARD TO KEEP EVERYTHING I'VE DISCOVERED FROM MY BEST FRIEND.
PUMP...
NO...
...YOU ACT LIKE YOU'RE BETTER THAN ME.

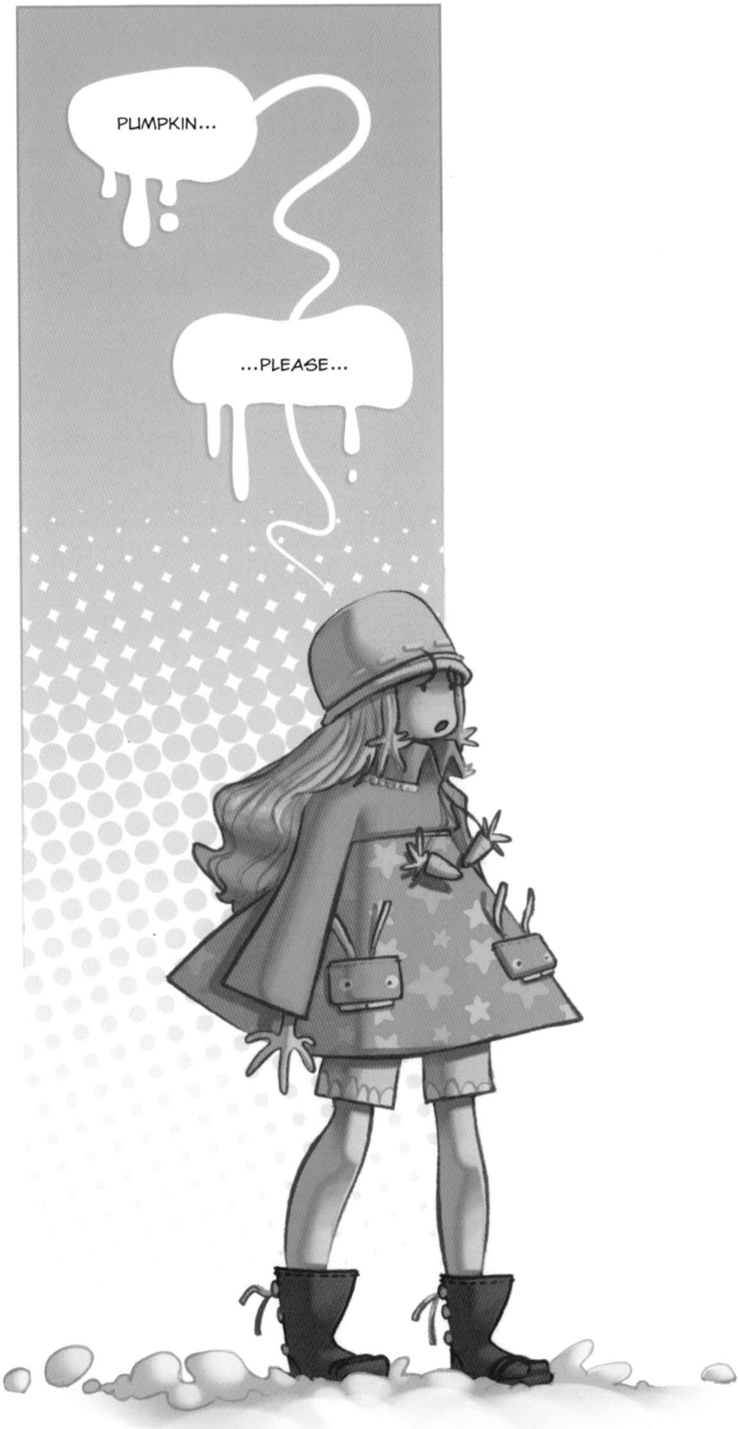
PUMPKIN...
...PLEASE...

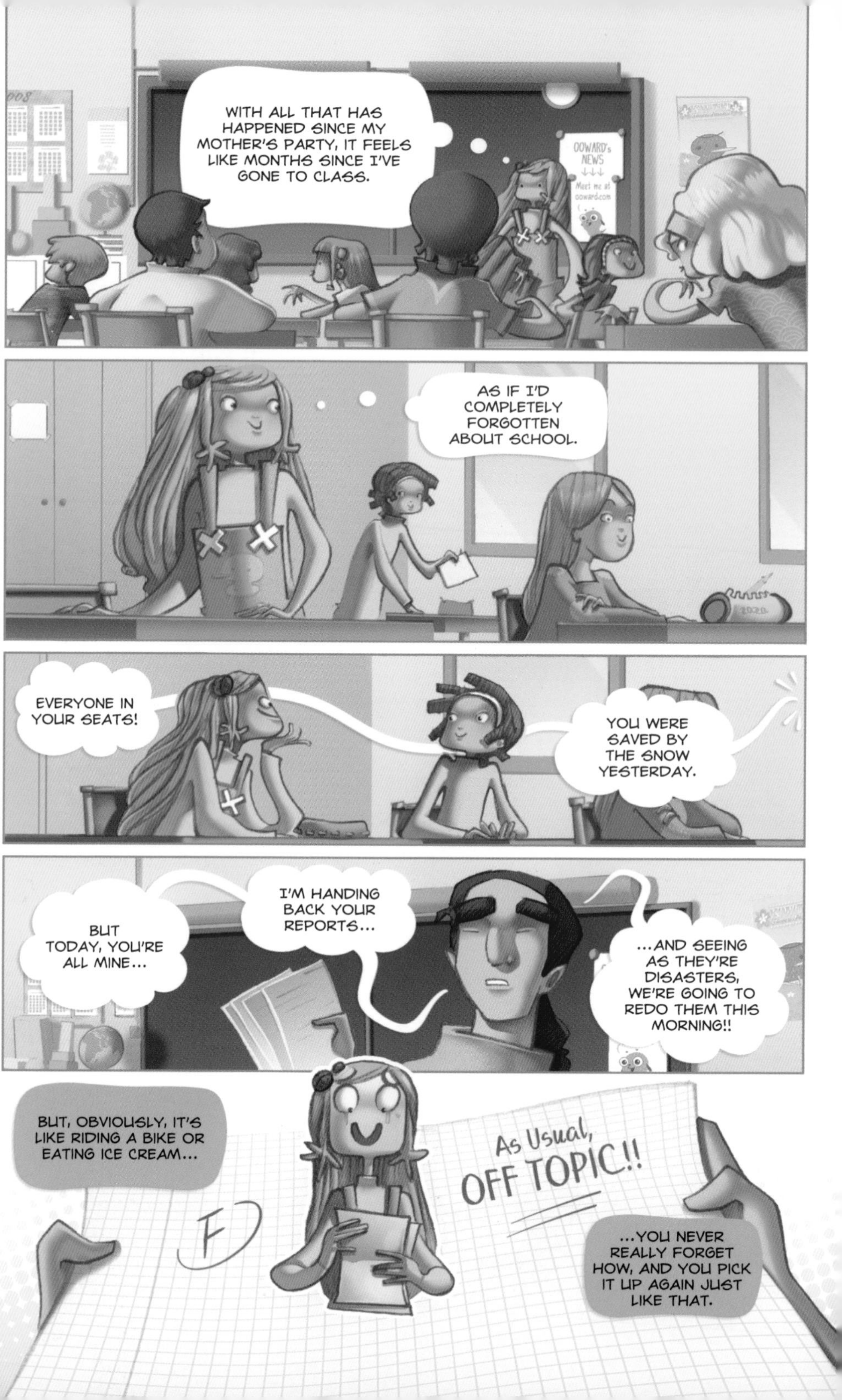
WITH ALL THAT HAS HAPPENED SINCE MY MOTHER'S PARTY, IT FEELS LIKE MONTHS SINCE I'VE GONE TO CLASS.
OOWARD's NEWS
Meet me at ooward.com
AS IF I'D COMPLETELY FORGOTTEN ABOUT SCHOOL.
EVERYONE IN YOUR SEATS!
YOU WERE SAVED BY THE SNOW YESTERDAY.
BUT TODAY, YOU'RE ALL MINE...
I'M HANDING BACK YOUR REPORTS...
...AND SEEING AS THEY'RE DISASTERS, WE'RE GOING TO REDO THEM THIS MORNING!!
BUT, OBVIOUSLY, IT'S LIKE RIDING A BIKE OR EATING ICE CREAM...
F
As Usual, OFF TOPIC!!
...YOU NEVER REALLY FORGET HOW, AND YOU PICK IT UP AGAIN JUST LIKE THAT.

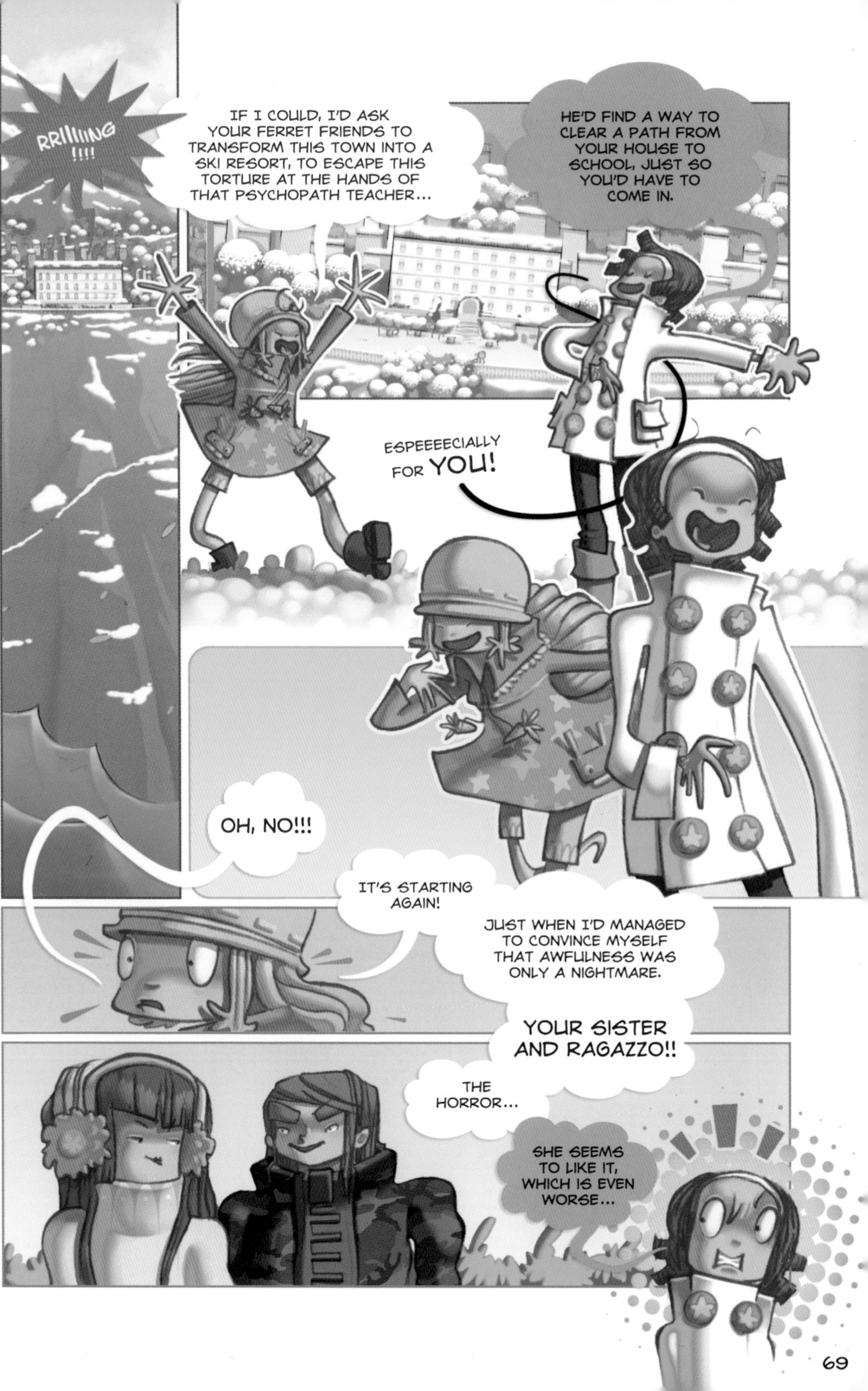
RRIIIIING !!!!
IF I COULD, I'D ASK YOUR FERRET FRIENDS TO TRANSFORM THIS TOWN INTO A SKI RESORT, TO ESCAPE THIS TORTURE AT THE HANDS OF THAT PSYCHOPATH TEACHER...
HE'D FIND A WAY TO CLEAR A PATH FROM YOUR HOUSE TO SCHOOL, JUST SO YOU'D HAVE TO COME IN.
ESPEEEECIALLY FOR YOU!
OH, NO!!!
IT'S STARTING AGAIN!
JUST WHEN I'D MANAGED TO CONVINCE MYSELF THAT AWFULNESS WAS ONLY A NIGHTMARE.
YOUR SISTER AND RAGAZZO!!
THE HORROR...
SHE SEEMS TO LIKE IT, WHICH IS EVEN WORSE...

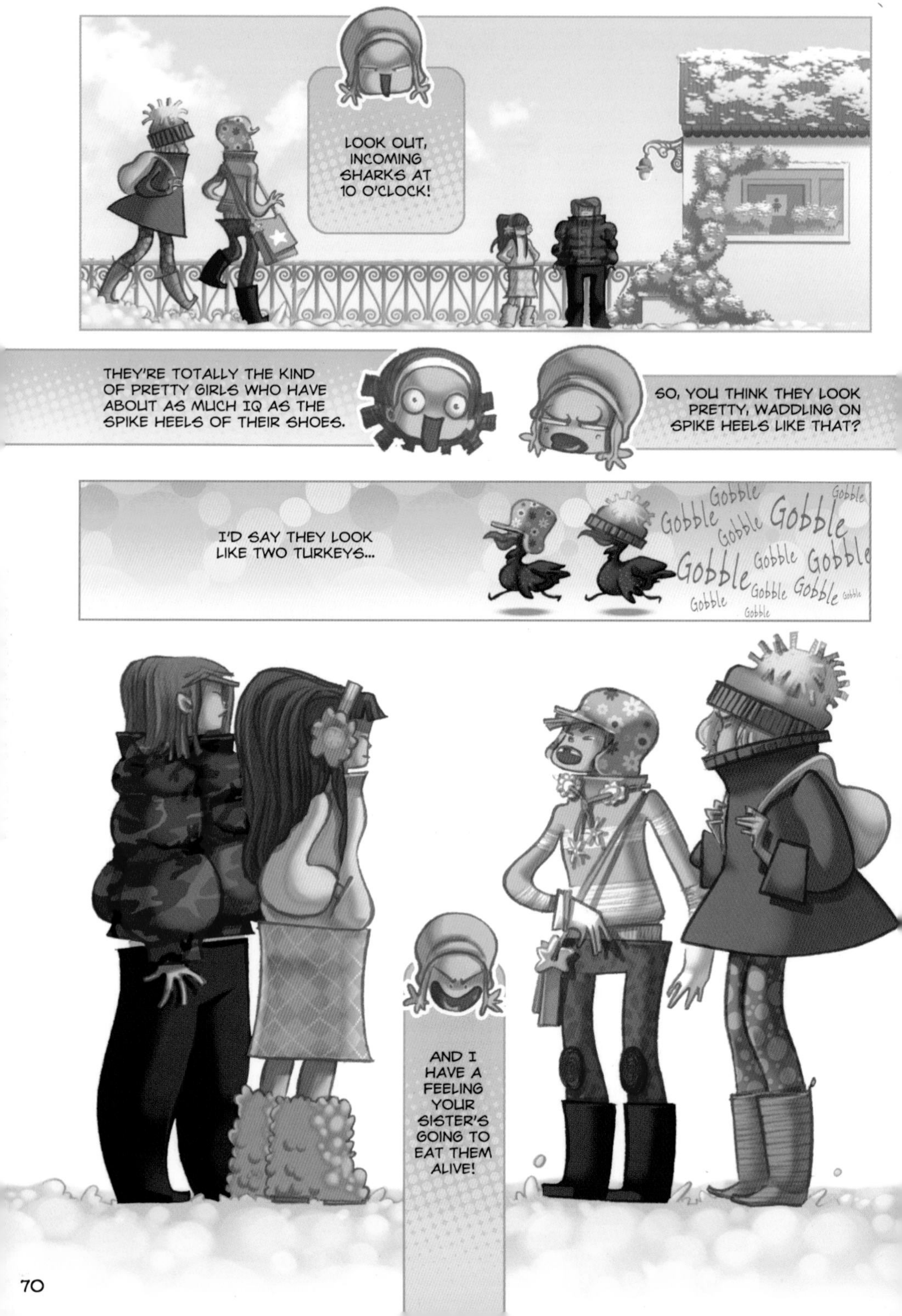

LOOK OUT, INCOMING SHARKS AT 10 O'CLOCK!
THEY'RE TOTALLY THE KIND OF PRETTY GIRLS WHO HAVE ABOUT AS MUCH IQ AS THE SPIKE HEELS OF THEIR SHOES.
SO, YOU THINK THEY LOOK PRETTY, WADDLING ON SPIKE HEELS LIKE THAT?
I'D SAY THEY LOOK LIKE TWO TURKEYS...
Gobble Gobble Gobble Gobble Gobble Gobble Gobble Gobble Gobble Gobble Gobble Gobble
AND I HAVE A FEELING YOUR SISTER'S GOING TO EAT THEM ALIVE!

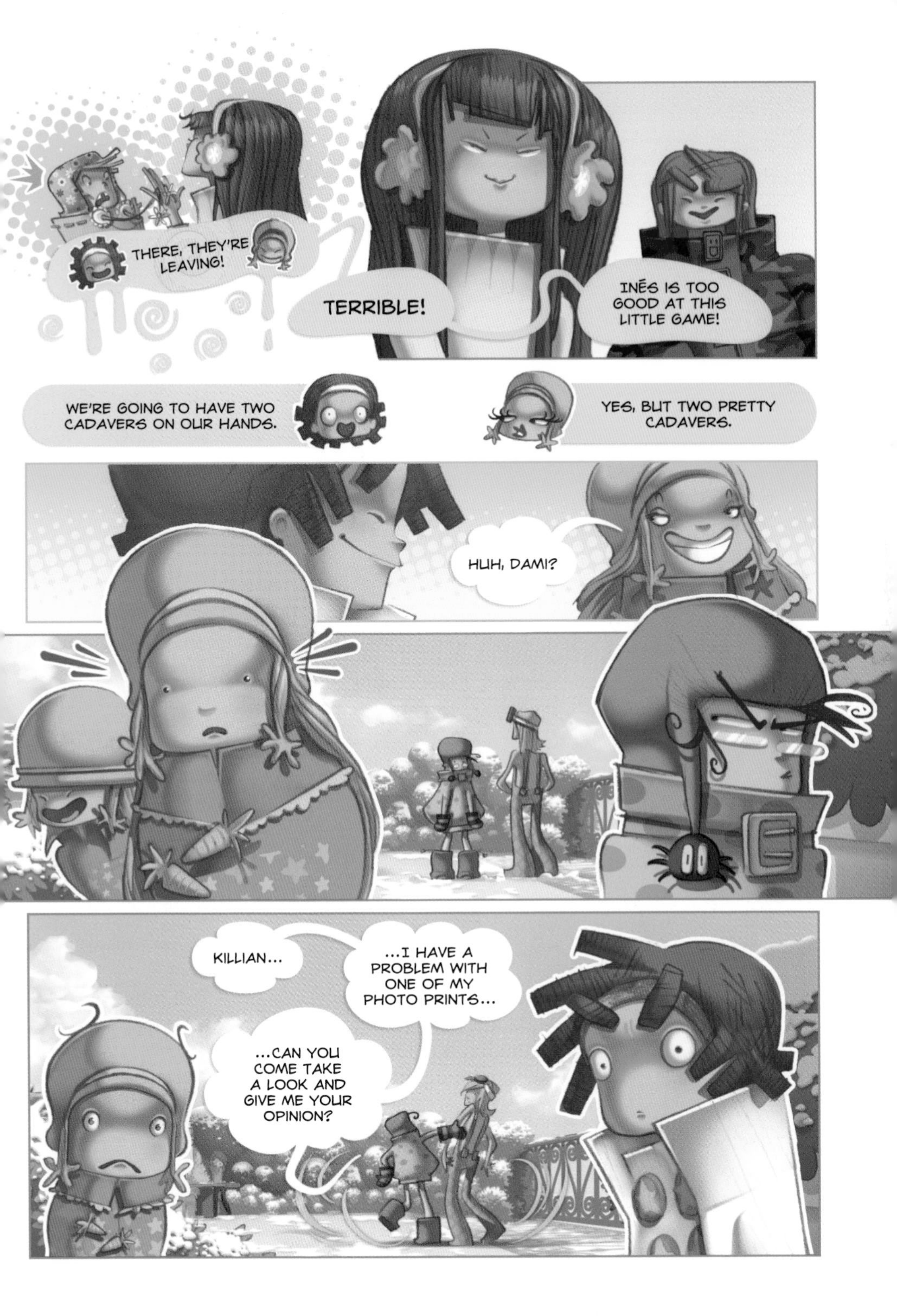
THERE, THEY'RE LEAVING!
TERRIBLE!
INÉS IS TOO GOOD AT THIS LITTLE GAME!
WE'RE GOING TO HAVE TWO CADAVERS ON OUR HANDS.
YES, BUT TWO PRETTY CADAVERS.
HUH, DAMI?
KILLIAN...
...I HAVE A PROBLEM WITH ONE OF MY PHOTO PRINTS...
...CAN YOU COME TAKE A LOOK AND GIVE ME YOUR OPINION?

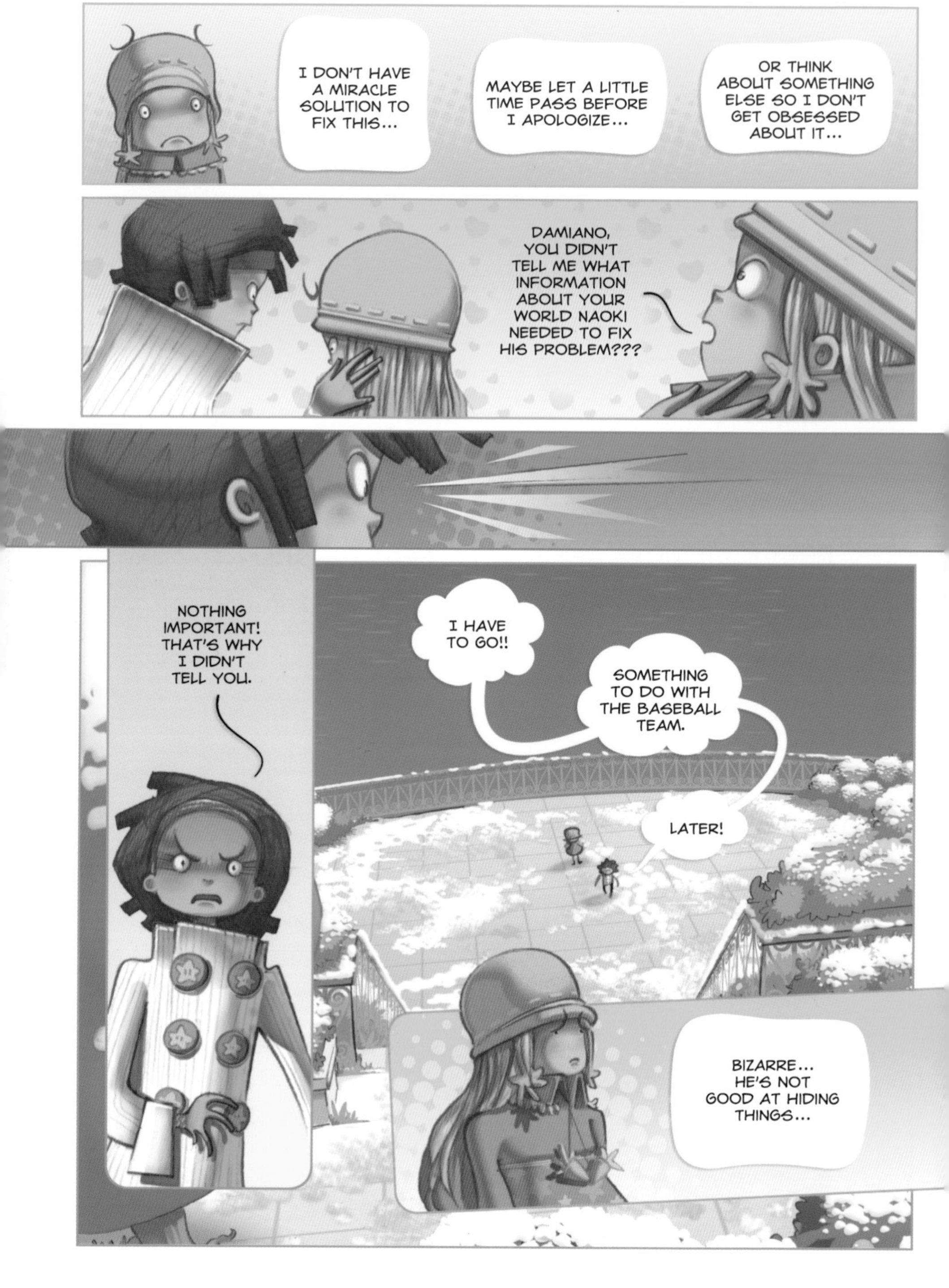
I DON'T HAVE A MIRACLE SOLUTION TO FIX THIS...
MAYBE LET A LITTLE TIME PASS BEFORE I APOLOGIZE...
OR THINK ABOUT SOMETHING ELSE SO I DON'T GET OBSESSED ABOUT IT...
DAMIANO, YOU DIDN'T TELL ME WHAT INFORMATION ABOUT YOUR WORLD NAOKI NEEDED TO FIX HIS PROBLEM???
NOTHING IMPORTANT! THAT'S WHY I DIDN'T TELL YOU.
I HAVE TO GO!!
SOMETHING TO DO WITH THE BASEBALL TEAM.
LATER!
BIZARRE... HE'S NOT GOOD AT HIDING THINGS...

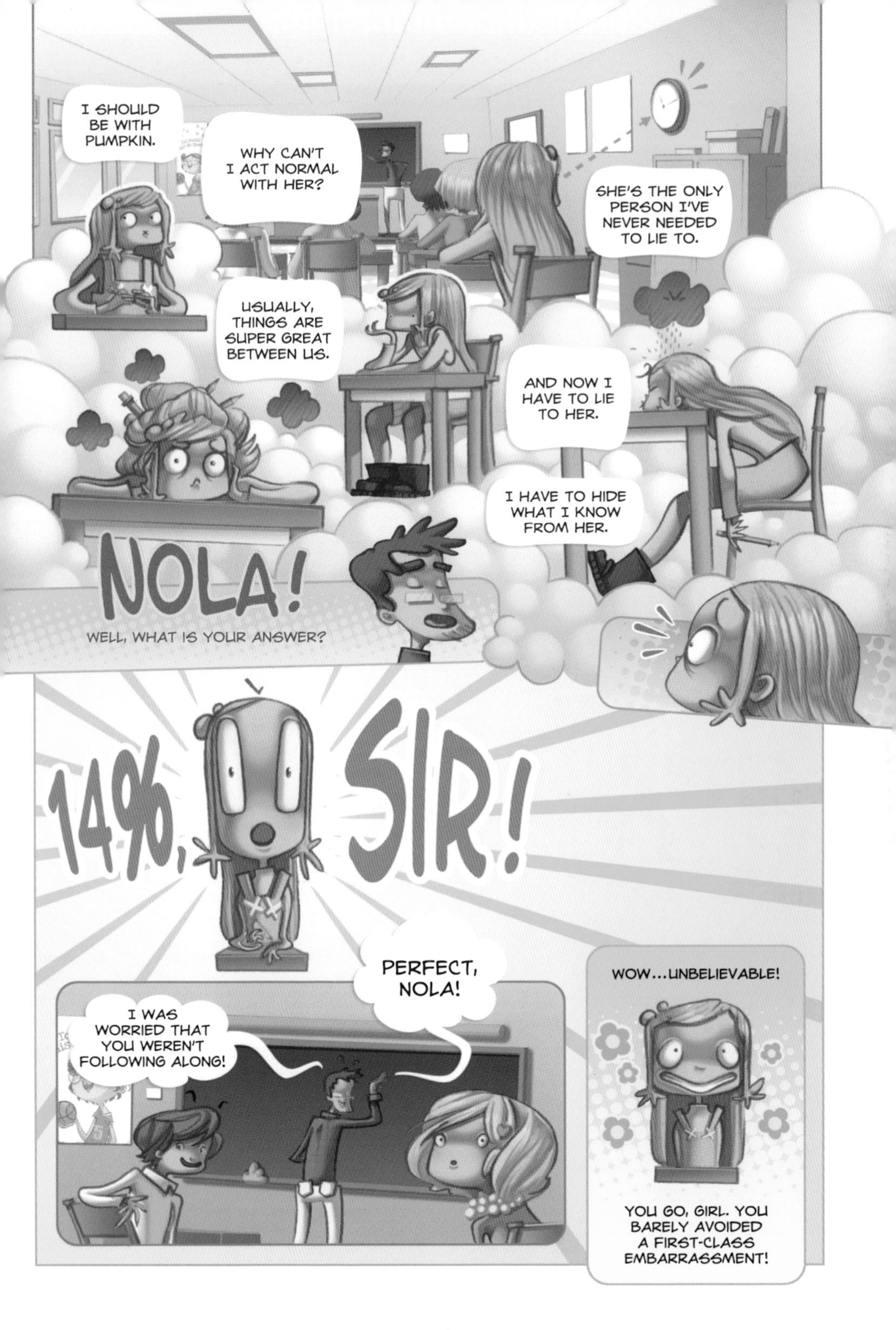

I SHOULD BE WITH PUMPKIN.
WHY CAN'T I ACT NORMAL WITH HER?
SHE'S THE ONLY PERSON I'VE NEVER NEEDED TO LIE TO.
USUALLY, THINGS ARE SUPER GREAT BETWEEN US.
AND NOW I HAVE TO LIE TO HER.
I HAVE TO HIDE WHAT I KNOW FROM HER.
NOLA!
WELL, WHAT IS YOUR ANSWER?
1496, SIR!
PERFECT, NOLA!
I WAS WORRIED THAT YOU WEREN'T FOLLOWING ALONG!
WOW...UNBELIEVABLE!
YOU GO, GIRL. YOU BARELY AVOIDED A FIRST-CLASS EMBARRASSMENT!

WHEN THE NORMAL COURSE OF THINGS IS INSIDE OUT...

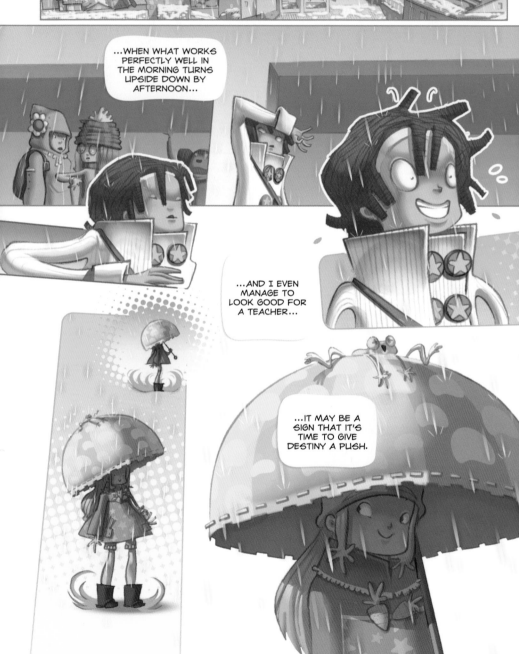

...WHEN WHAT WORKS PERFECTLY WELL IN THE MORNING TURNS UPSIDE DOWN BY AFTERNOON...

...AND I EVEN MANAGE TO LOOK GOOD FOR A TEACHER...

...IT MAY BE A SIGN THAT IT'S TIME TO GIVE DESTINY A PUSH.

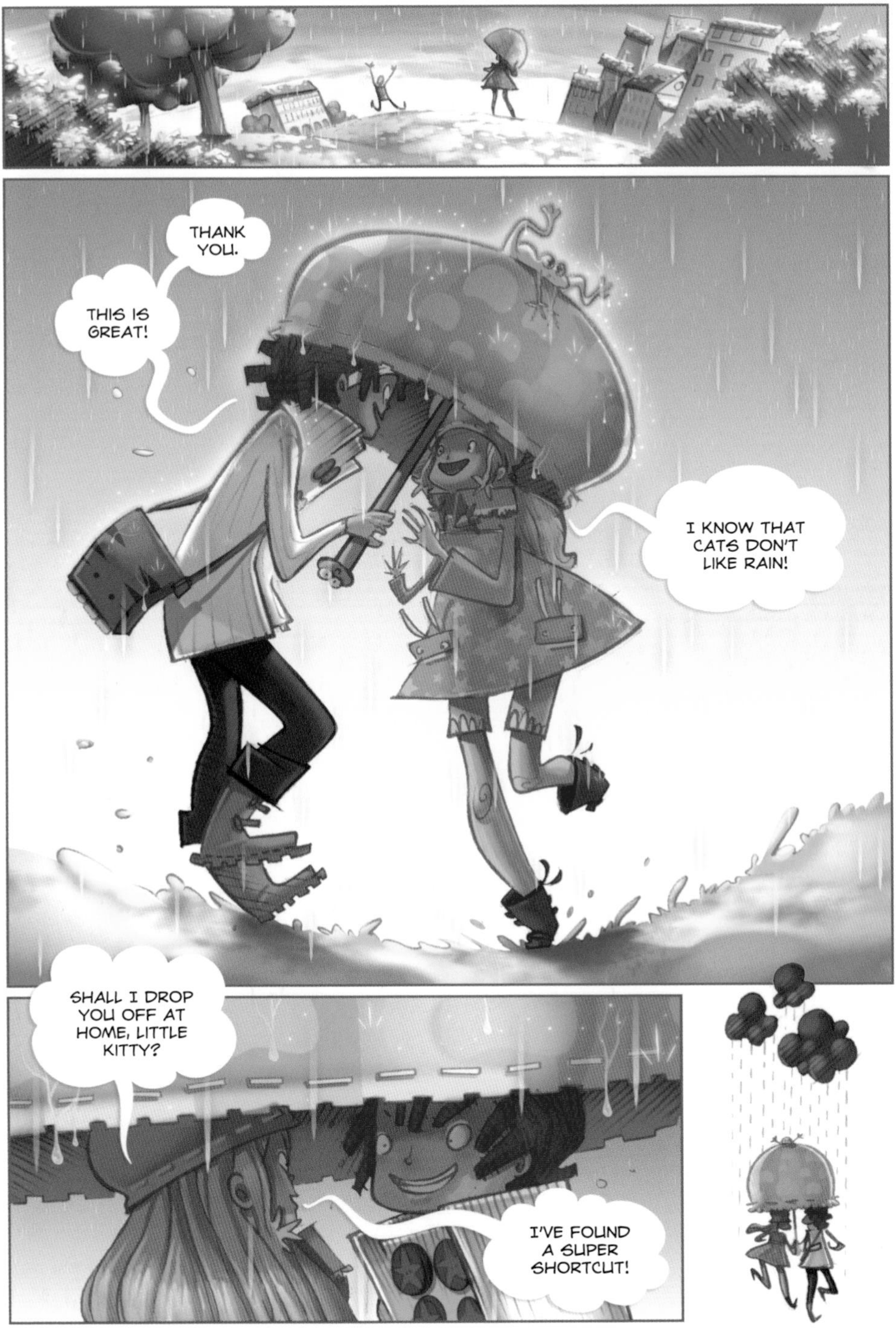
THANK YOU.
THIS IS GREAT!
I KNOW THAT CATS DON'T LIKE RAIN!
SHALL I DROP YOU OFF AT HOME, LITTLE KITTY?
I'VE FOUND A SUPER SHORTCUT!

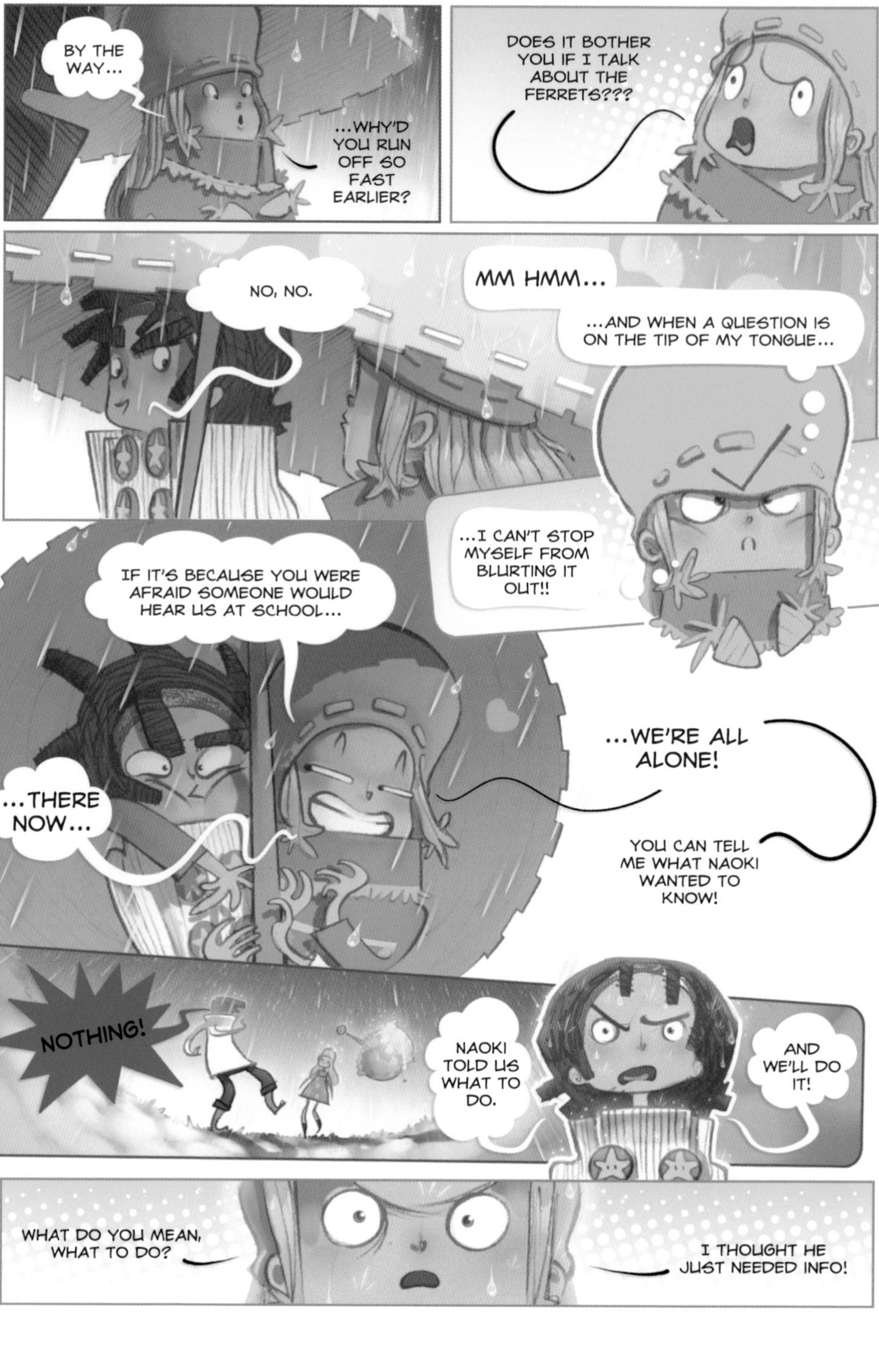
BY THE WAY...
...WHY'D YOU RUN OFF SO FAST EARLIER?
DOES IT BOTHER YOU IF I TALK ABOUT THE FERRETS???
NO, NO.
MM HMM...
...AND WHEN A QUESTION IS ON THE TIP OF MY TONGUE...
...I CAN'T STOP MYSELF FROM BLURTING IT OUT!!
IF IT'S BECAUSE YOU WERE AFRAID SOMEONE WOULD HEAR US AT SCHOOL...
...THERE NOW...
...WE'RE ALL ALONE!
YOU CAN TELL ME WHAT NAOKI WANTED TO KNOW!
NOTHING!
NAOKI TOLD US WHAT TO DO.
AND WE'LL DO IT!
WHAT DO YOU MEAN, WHAT TO DO?
I THOUGHT HE JUST NEEDED INFO!

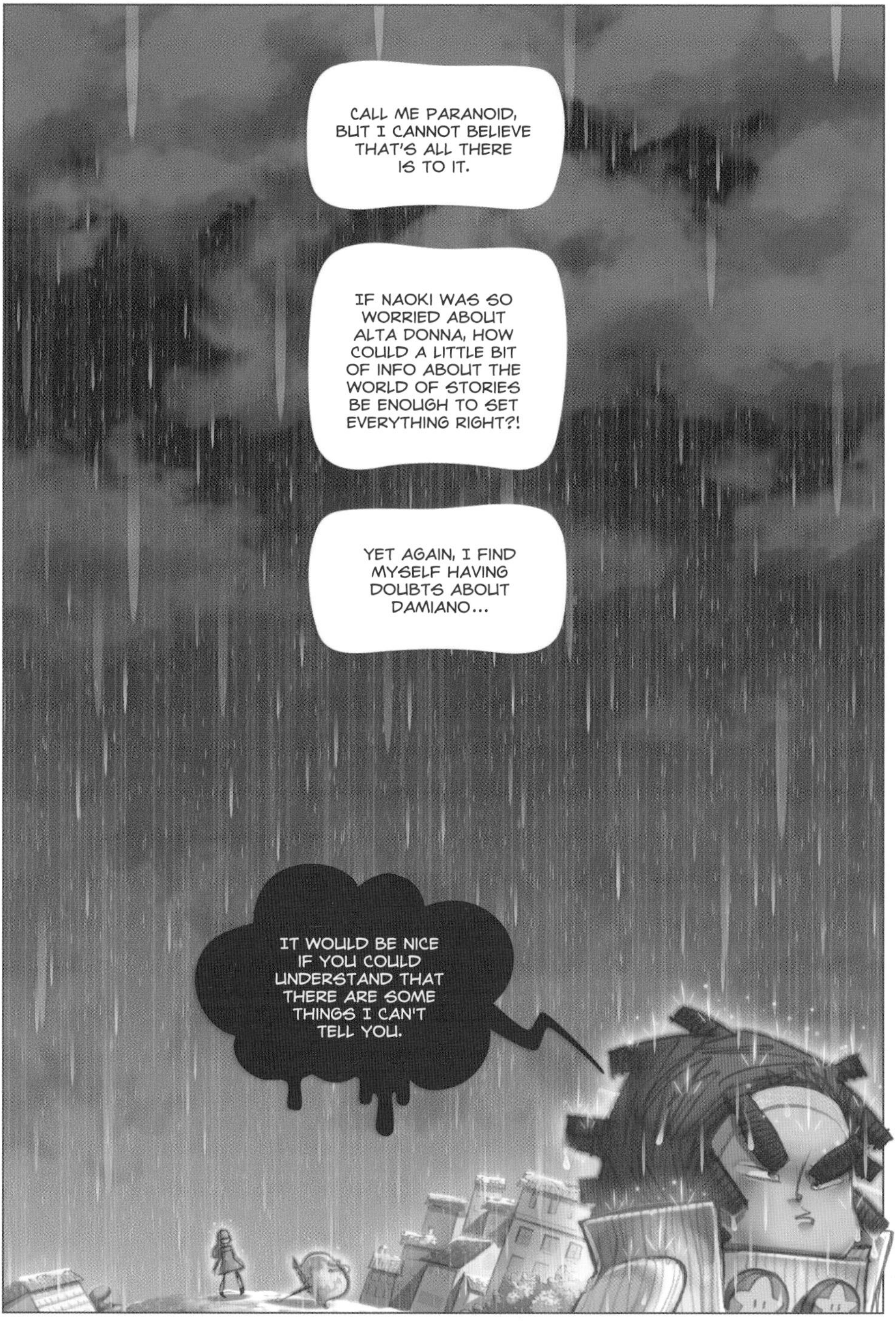
CALL ME PARANOID, BUT I CANNOT BELIEVE THAT'S ALL THERE IS TO IT.
IF NAOKI WAS SO WORRIED ABOUT ALTA DONNA, HOW COULD A LITTLE BIT OF INFO ABOUT THE WORLD OF STORIES BE ENOUGH TO SET EVERYTHING RIGHT?!
YET AGAIN, I FIND MYSELF HAVING DOUBTS ABOUT DAMIANO...
IT WOULD BE NICE IF YOU COULD UNDERSTAND THAT THERE ARE SOME THINGS I CAN'T TELL YOU.

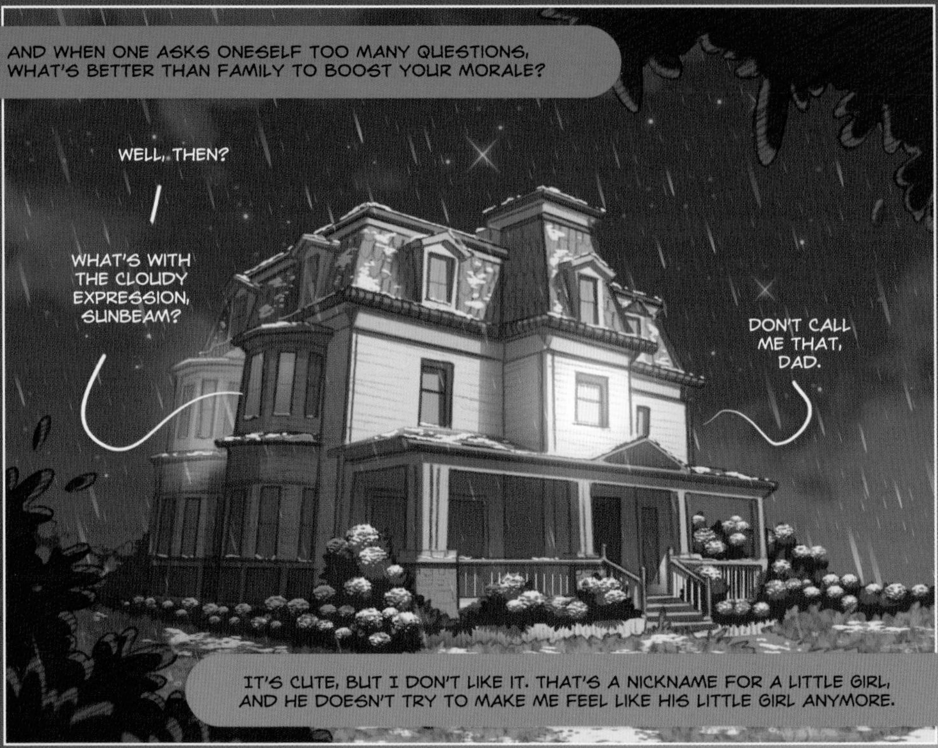
AND WHEN ONE ASKS ONESELF TOO MANY QUESTIONS, WHAT'S BETTER THAN FAMILY TO BOOST YOUR MORALE?
WELL, THEN?
WHAT'S WITH THE CLOUDY EXPRESSION, SUNBEAM?
DON'T CALL ME THAT, DAD.
IT'S CUTE, BUT I DON'T LIKE IT. THAT'S A NICKNAME FOR A LITTLE GIRL, AND HE DOESN'T TRY TO MAKE ME FEEL LIKE HIS LITTLE GIRL ANYMORE.

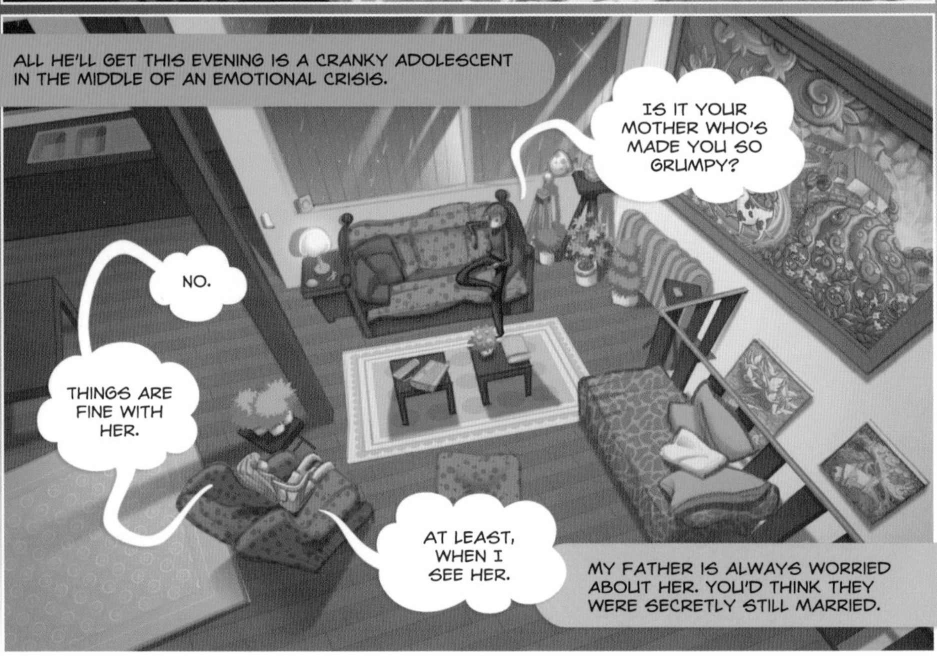
ALL HE'LL GET THIS EVENING IS A CRANKY ADOLESCENT IN THE MIDDLE OF AN EMOTIONAL CRISIS.
IS IT YOUR MOTHER WHO'S MADE YOU SO GRUMPY?
NO.
THINGS ARE FINE WITH HER.
AT LEAST, WHEN I SEE HER.
MY FATHER IS ALWAYS WORRIED ABOUT HER. YOU'D THINK THEY WERE SECRETLY STILL MARRIED.

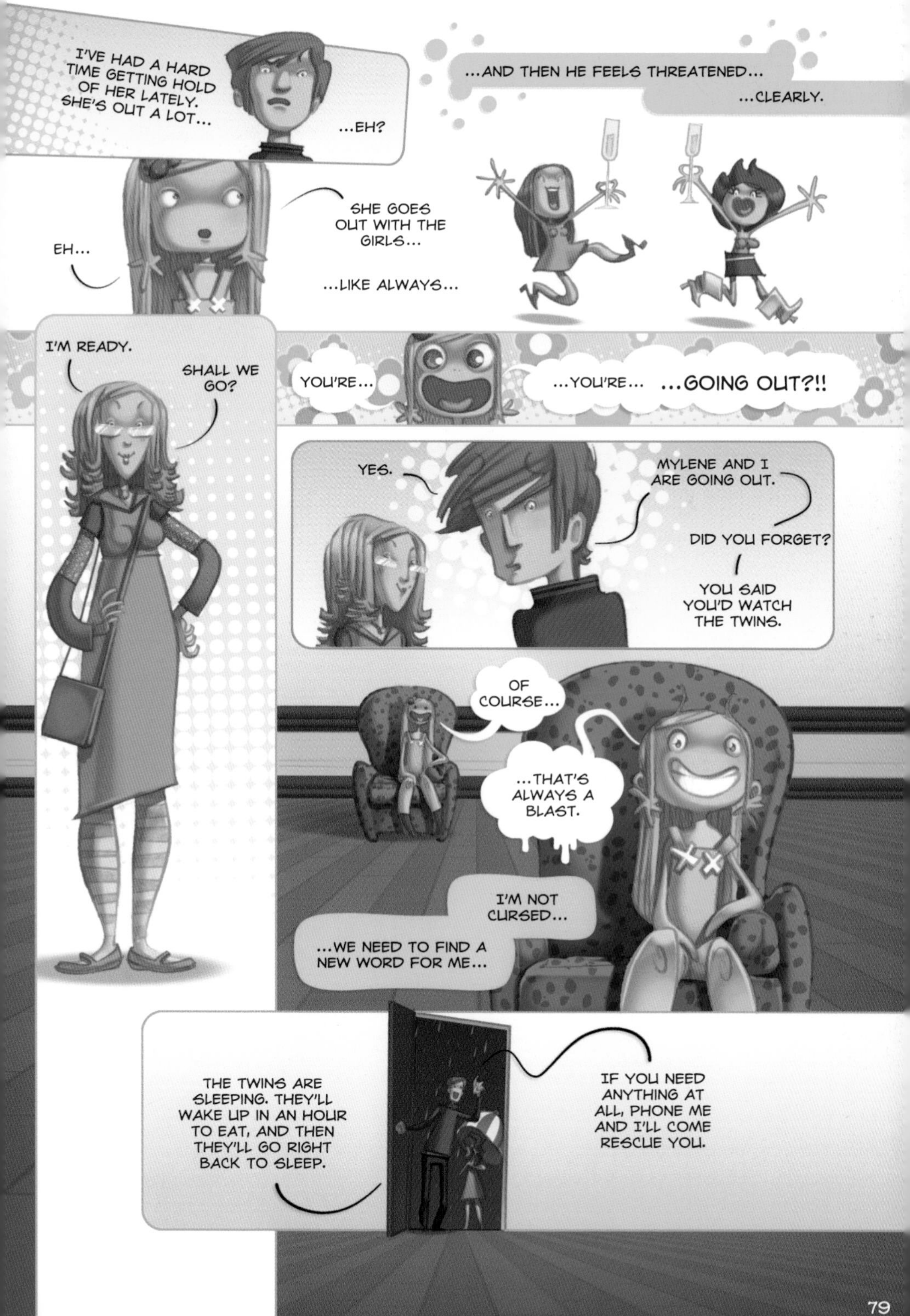

I'VE HAD A HARD TIME GETTING HOLD OF HER LATELY. SHE'S OUT A LOT...
...EH?
EH...
SHE GOES OUT WITH THE GIRLS...
...LIKE ALWAYS...
...AND THEN HE FEELS THREATENED...
...CLEARLY.
I'M READY.
SHALL WE GO?
YOU'RE...
...YOU'RE...
...GOING OUT?!!
YES.
MYLENE AND I ARE GOING OUT.
DID YOU FORGET?
YOU SAID YOU'D WATCH THE TWINS.
OF COURSE...
...THAT'S ALWAYS A BLAST.
I'M NOT CURSED...
...WE NEED TO FIND A NEW WORD FOR ME...
THE TWINS ARE SLEEPING. THEY'LL WAKE UP IN AN HOUR TO EAT, AND THEN THEY'LL GO RIGHT BACK TO SLEEP.
IF YOU NEED ANYTHING AT ALL, PHONE ME AND I'LL COME RESCUE YOU.

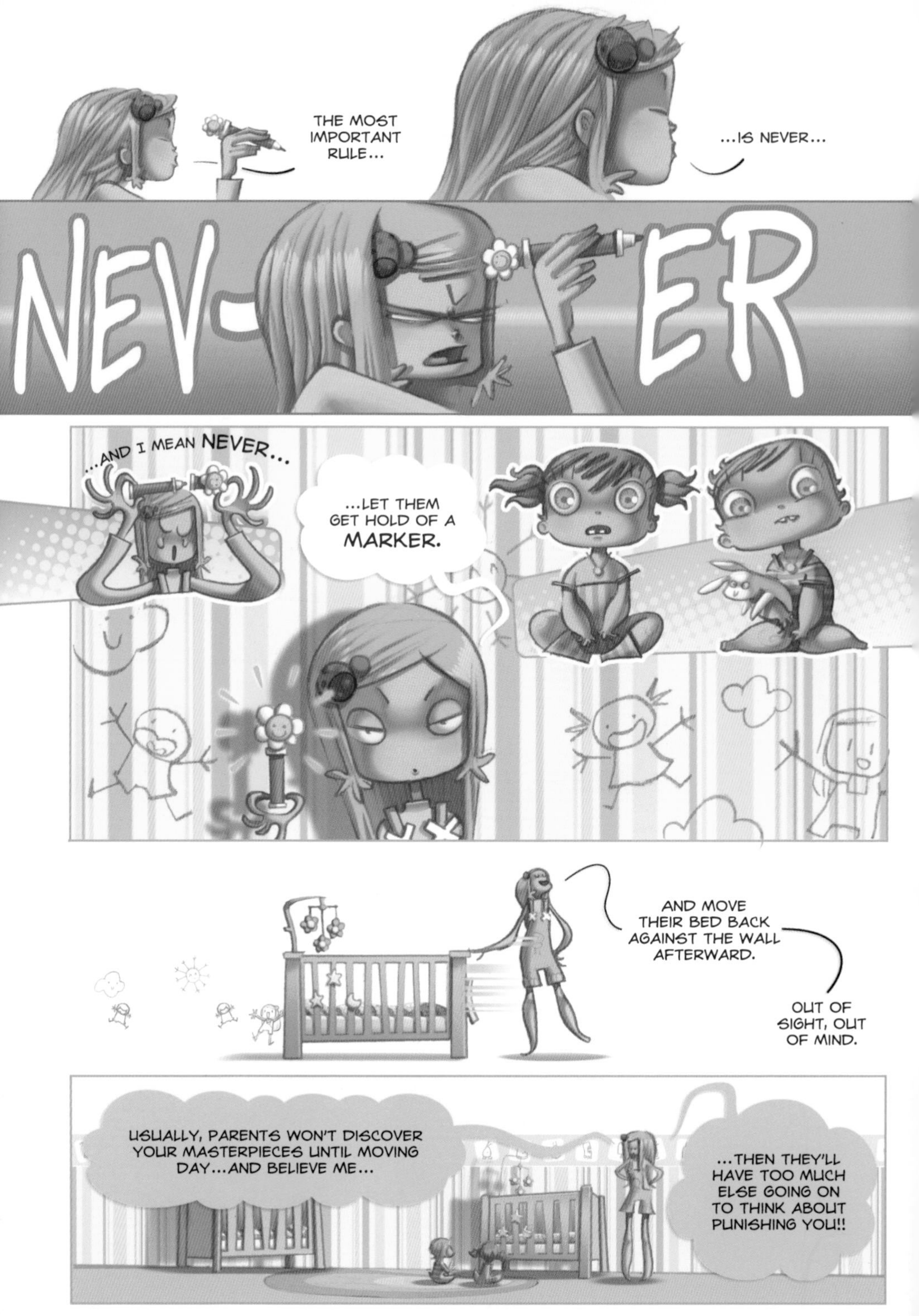
THE MOST IMPORTANT RULE...
...IS NEVER...
NEV-ER
...AND I MEAN NEVER...
...LET THEM GET HOLD OF A MARKER.
AND MOVE THEIR BED BACK AGAINST THE WALL AFTERWARD.
OUT OF SIGHT, OUT OF MIND.
USUALLY, PARENTS WON'T DISCOVER YOUR MASTERPIECES UNTIL MOVING DAY...AND BELIEVE ME...
...THEN THEY'LL HAVE TOO MUCH ELSE GOING ON TO THINK ABOUT PUNISHING YOU!!

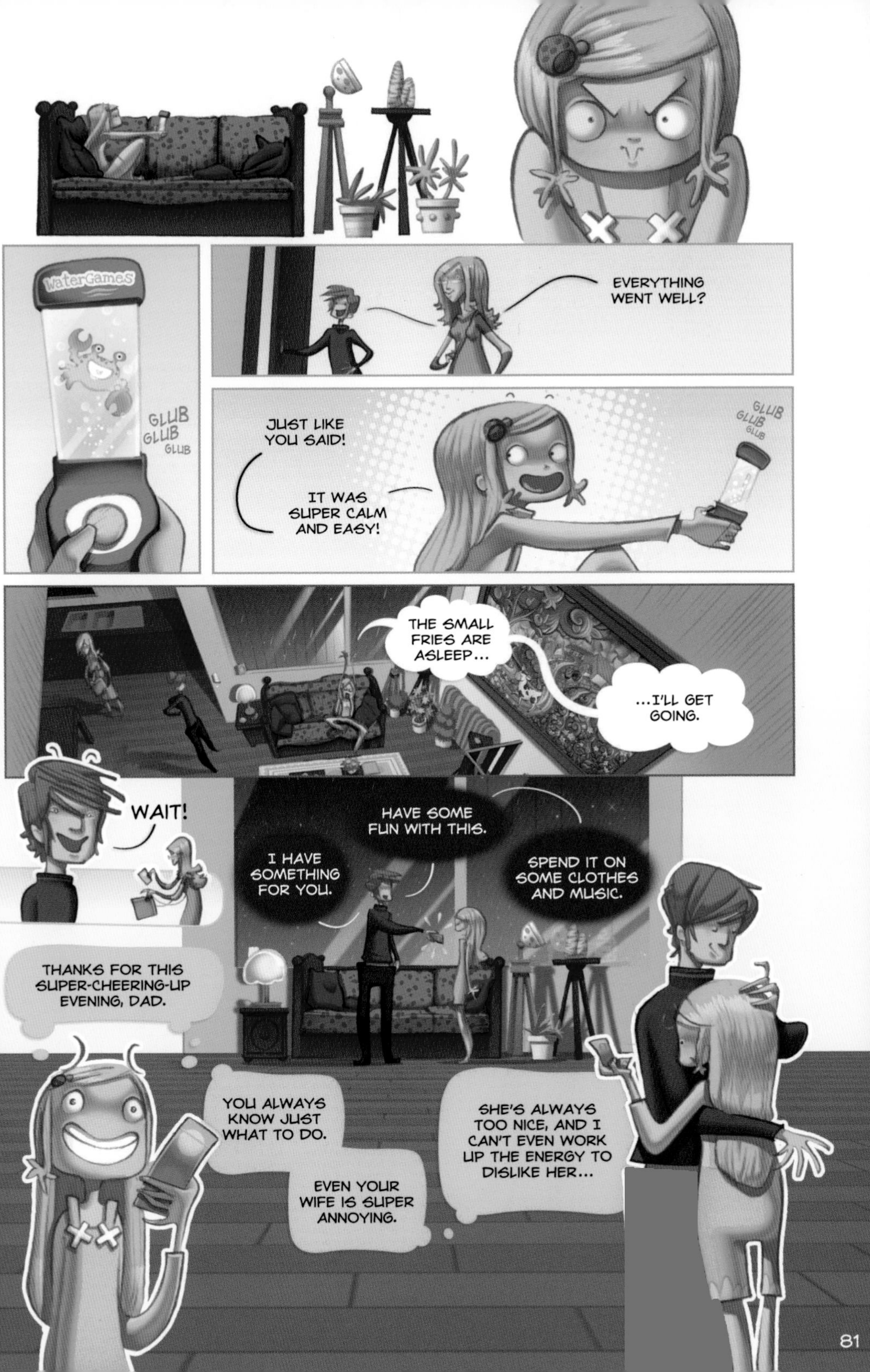
EVERYTHING WENT WELL?
WaterGames
GLUB GLUB GLUB
JUST LIKE YOU SAID!
IT WAS SUPER CALM AND EASY!
GLUB GLUB GLUB
THE SMALL FRIES ARE ASLEEP…
…I'LL GET GOING.
WAIT!
I HAVE SOMETHING FOR YOU.
HAVE SOME FUN WITH THIS.
SPEND IT ON SOME CLOTHES AND MUSIC.
THANKS FOR THIS SUPER-CHEERING-UP EVENING, DAD.
YOU ALWAYS KNOW JUST WHAT TO DO.
EVEN YOUR WIFE IS SUPER ANNOYING.
SHE'S ALWAYS TOO NICE, AND I CAN'T EVEN WORK UP THE ENERGY TO DISLIKE HER…

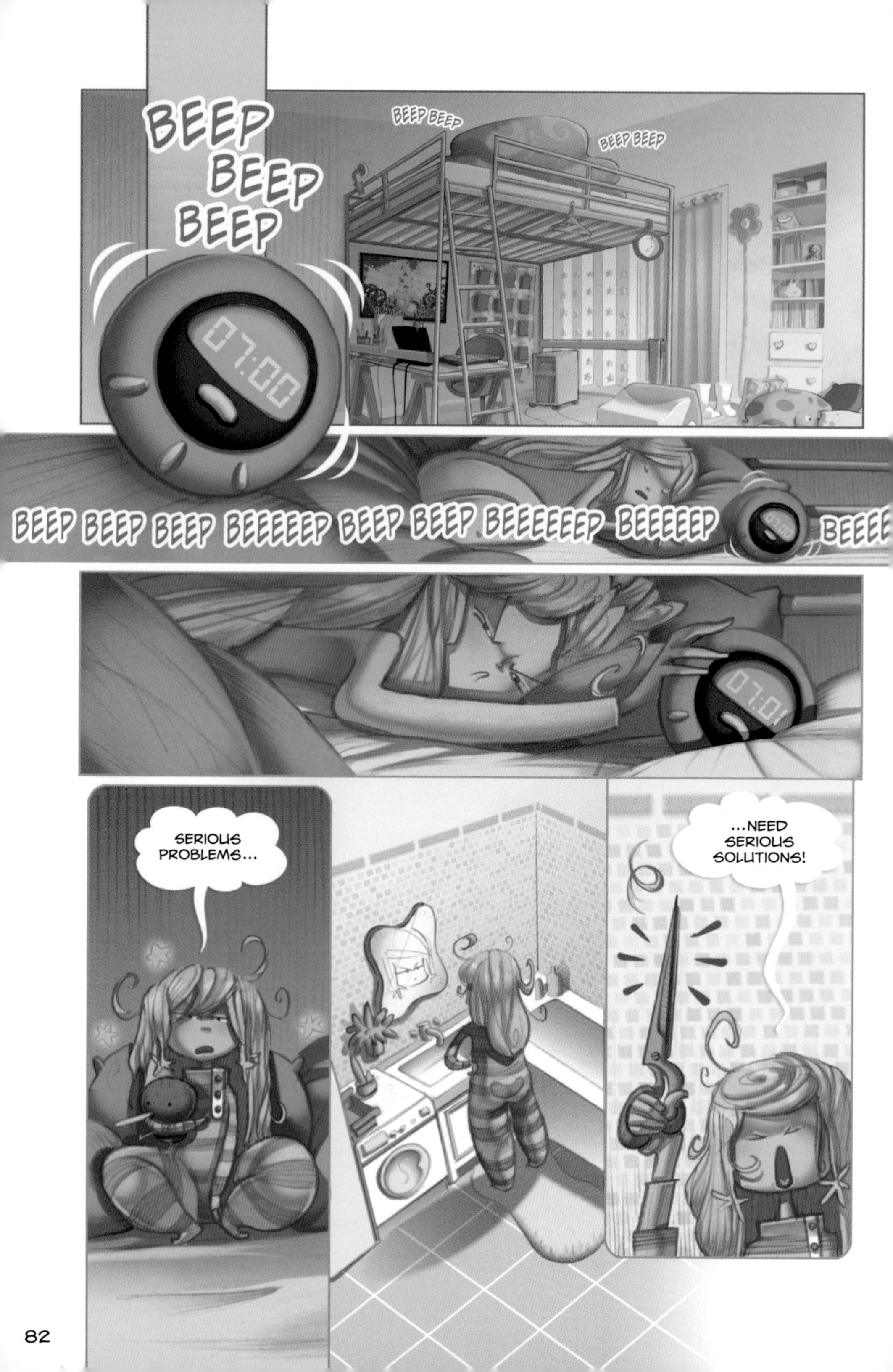
BEEP
BEEP
BEEP
BEEP BEEP
BEEP BEEP
07:00
BEEP BEEP BEEP BEEEEEP BEEP BEEP BEEEEEEP BEEEEEP
BEEEE
07:01
SERIOUS PROBLEMS...
...NEED SERIOUS SOLUTIONS!

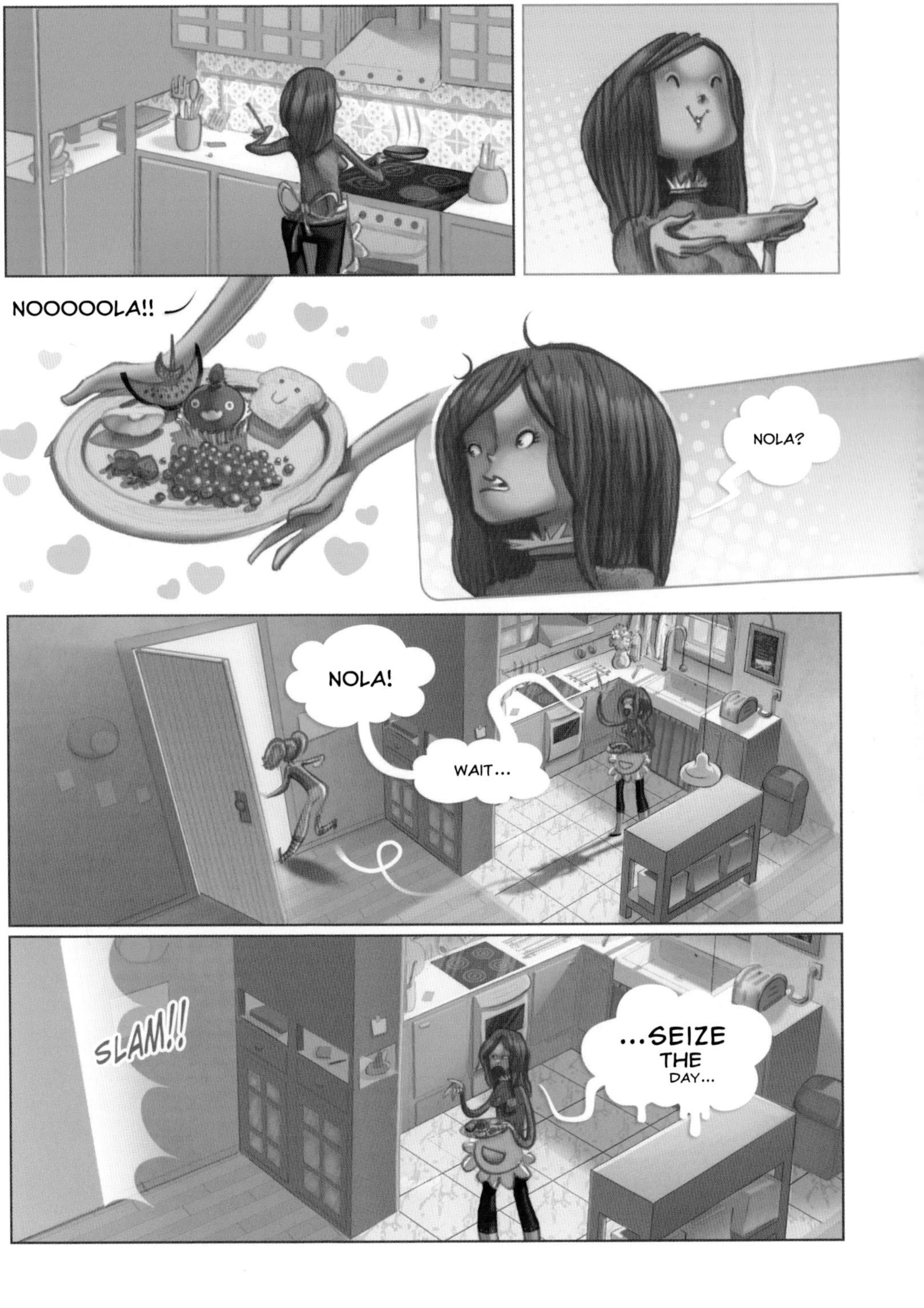
NOOOOOLA!!
NOLA?
NOLA!
WAIT...
SLAM!!
...SEIZE THE DAY...

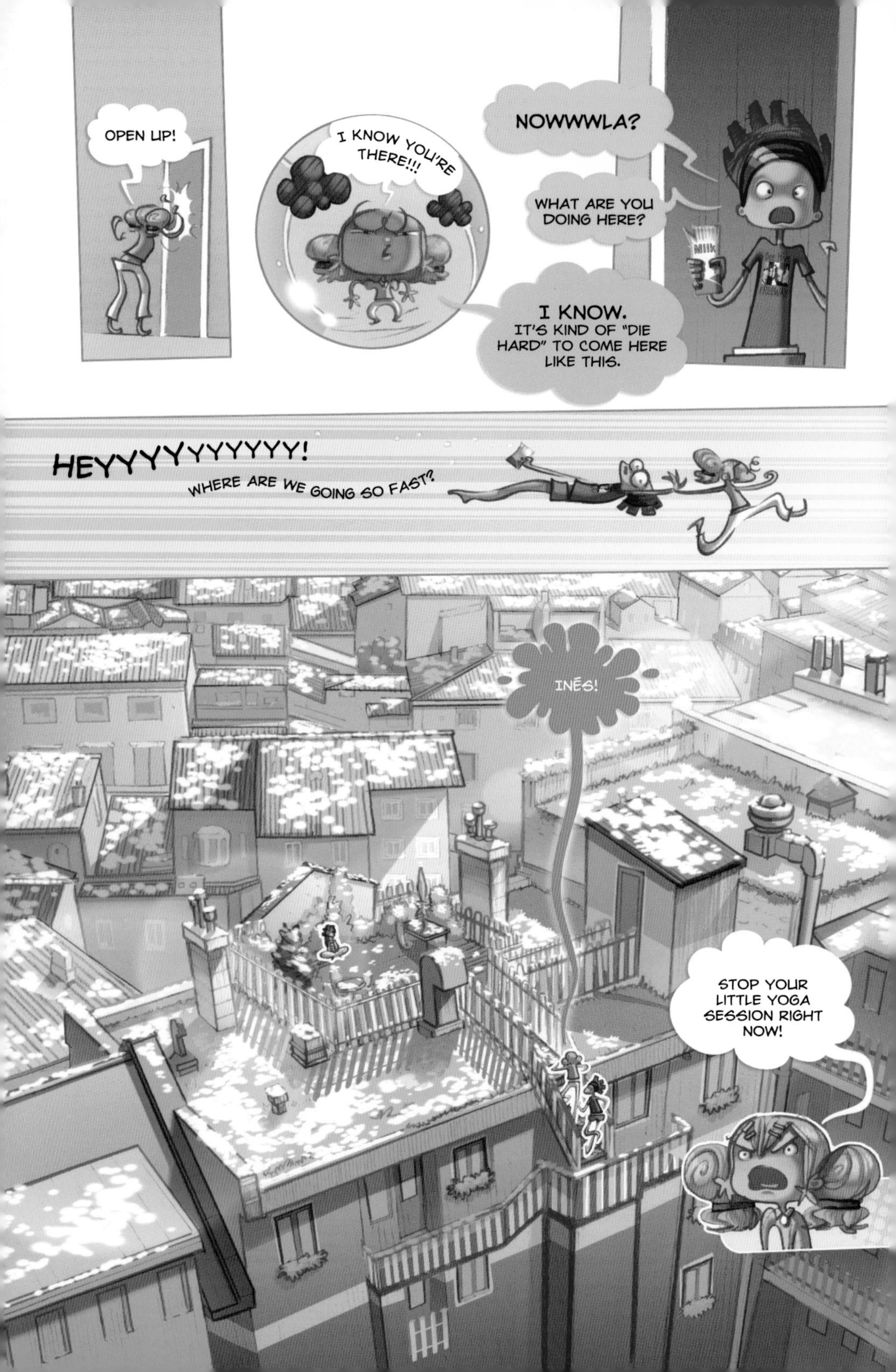
OPEN UP!
I KNOW YOU'RE THERE!!!
NOWWWLA?
WHAT ARE YOU DOING HERE?
I KNOW. IT'S KIND OF "DIE HARD" TO COME HERE LIKE THIS.
HEYYYYYYYYYY!
WHERE ARE WE GOING SO FAST?
INÈS!
STOP YOUR LITTLE YOGA SESSION RIGHT NOW!

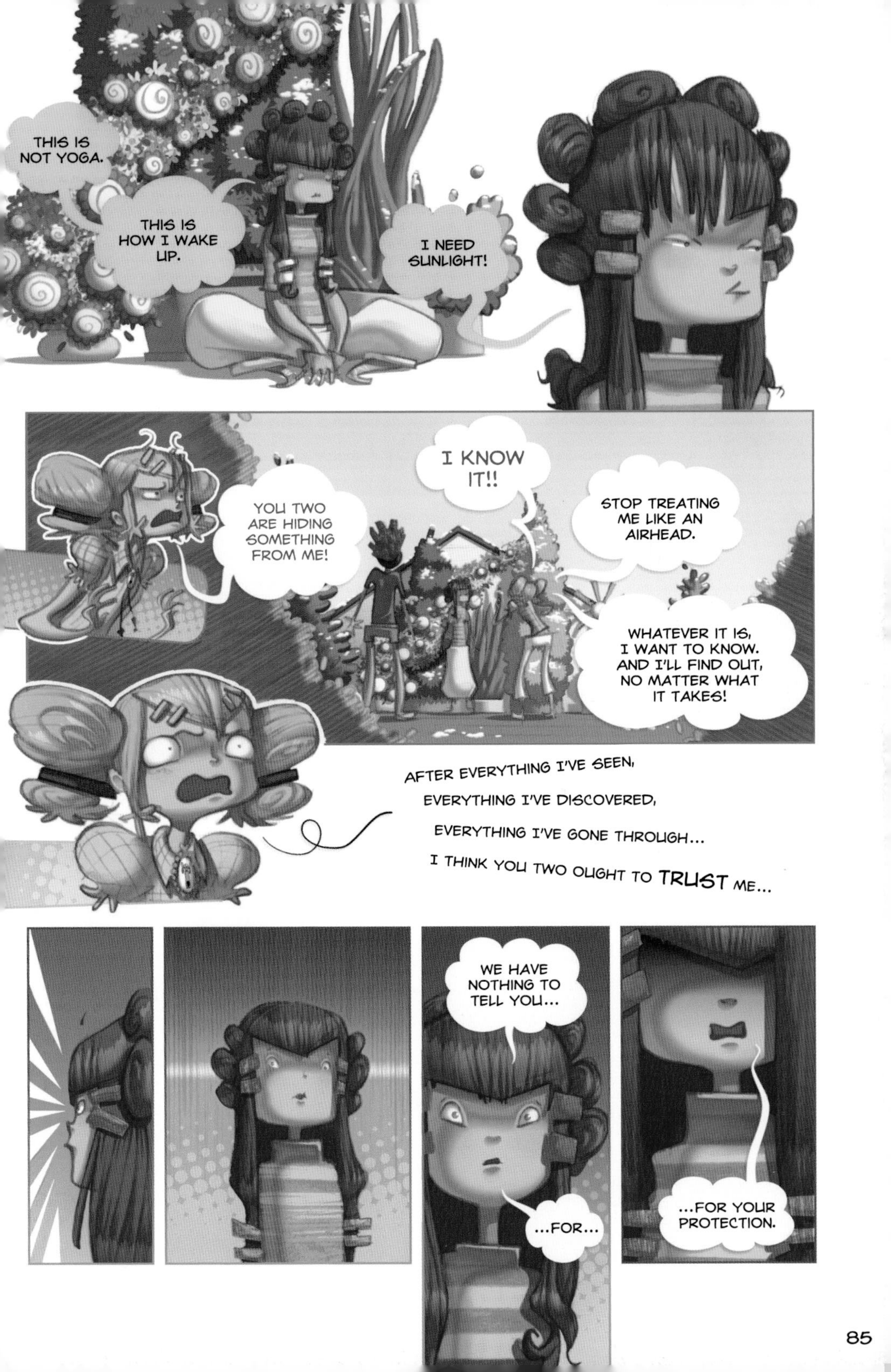

THIS IS NOT YOGA.
THIS IS HOW I WAKE UP.
I NEED SUNLIGHT!
YOU TWO ARE HIDING SOMETHING FROM ME!
I KNOW IT!!
STOP TREATING ME LIKE AN AIRHEAD.
WHATEVER IT IS, I WANT TO KNOW. AND I'LL FIND OUT, NO MATTER WHAT IT TAKES!
AFTER EVERYTHING I'VE SEEN,
EVERYTHING I'VE DISCOVERED,
EVERYTHING I'VE GONE THROUGH...
I THINK YOU TWO OUGHT TO TRUST ME...
WE HAVE NOTHING TO TELL YOU...
...FOR...
...FOR YOUR PROTECTION.

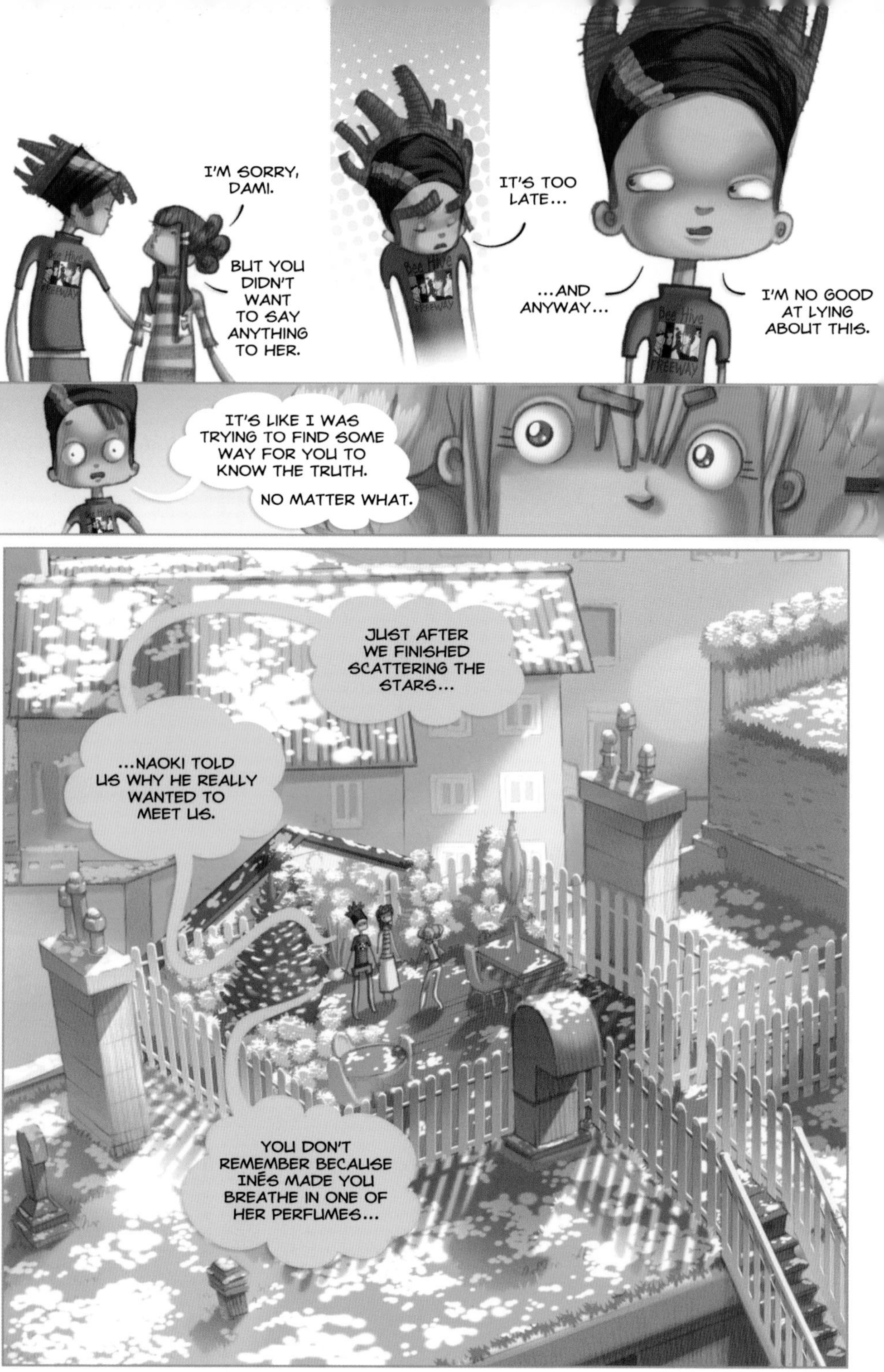
I'M SORRY, DAMI.
BUT YOU DIDN'T WANT TO SAY ANYTHING TO HER.
IT'S TOO LATE...
...AND ANYWAY...
I'M NO GOOD AT LYING ABOUT THIS.
IT'S LIKE I WAS TRYING TO FIND SOME WAY FOR YOU TO KNOW THE TRUTH.
NO MATTER WHAT.
JUST AFTER WE FINISHED SCATTERING THE STARS...
...NAOKI TOLD US WHY HE REALLY WANTED TO MEET US.
YOU DON'T REMEMBER BECAUSE INÉS MADE YOU BREATHE IN ONE OF HER PERFUMES...

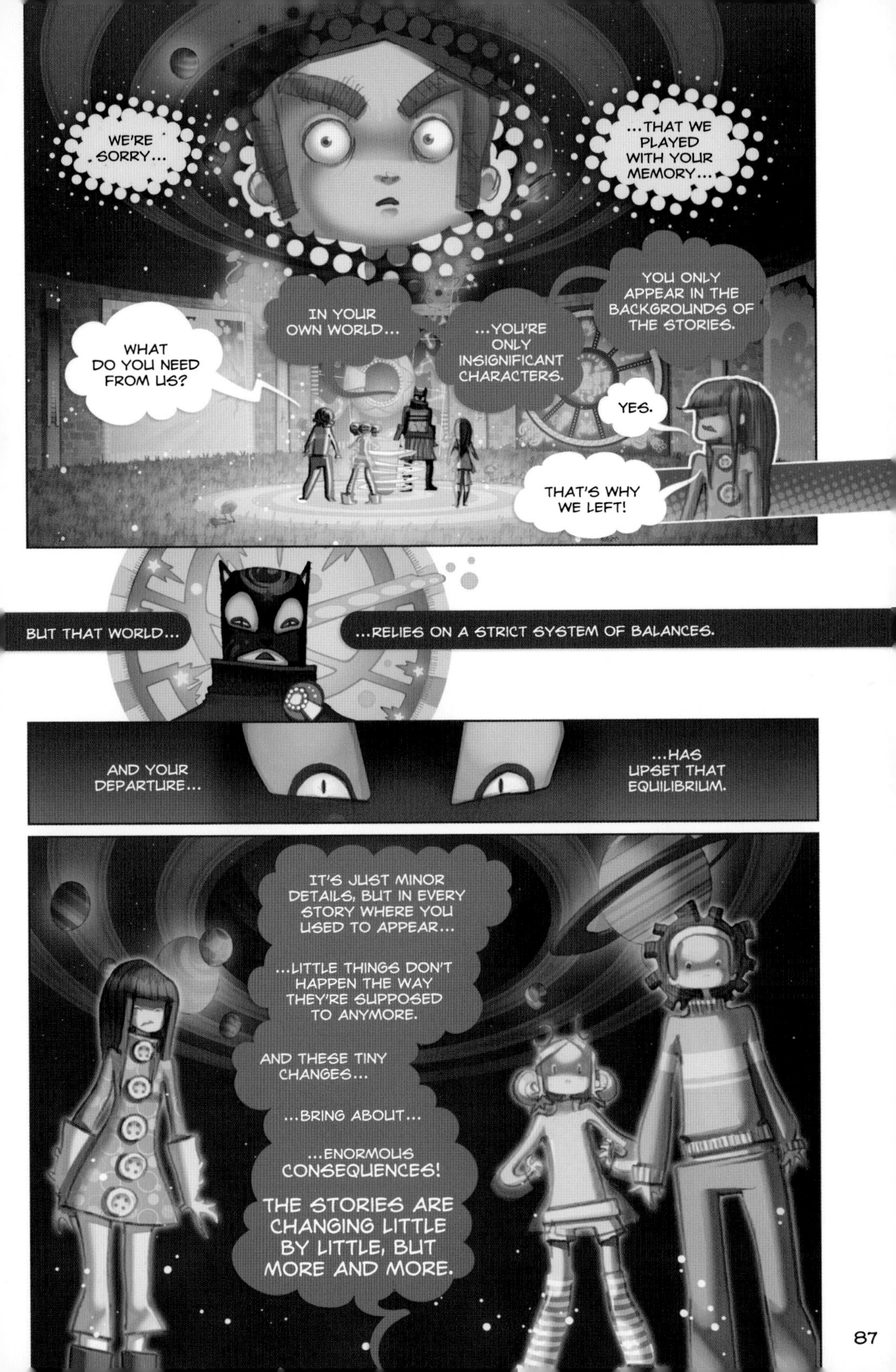
WE'RE SORRY...
...THAT WE PLAYED WITH YOUR MEMORY...
WHAT DO YOU NEED FROM US?
IN YOUR OWN WORLD...
...YOU'RE ONLY INSIGNIFICANT CHARACTERS.
YOU ONLY APPEAR IN THE BACKGROUNDS OF THE STORIES.
YES.
THAT'S WHY WE LEFT!
BUT THAT WORLD...
...RELIES ON A STRICT SYSTEM OF BALANCES.
AND YOUR DEPARTURE...
...HAS UPSET THAT EQUILIBRIUM.
IT'S JUST MINOR DETAILS, BUT IN EVERY STORY WHERE YOU USED TO APPEAR...
...LITTLE THINGS DON'T HAPPEN THE WAY THEY'RE SUPPOSED TO ANYMORE.
AND THESE TINY CHANGES...
...BRING ABOUT...
...ENORMOUS CONSEQUENCES!
THE STORIES ARE CHANGING LITTLE BY LITTLE, BUT MORE AND MORE.

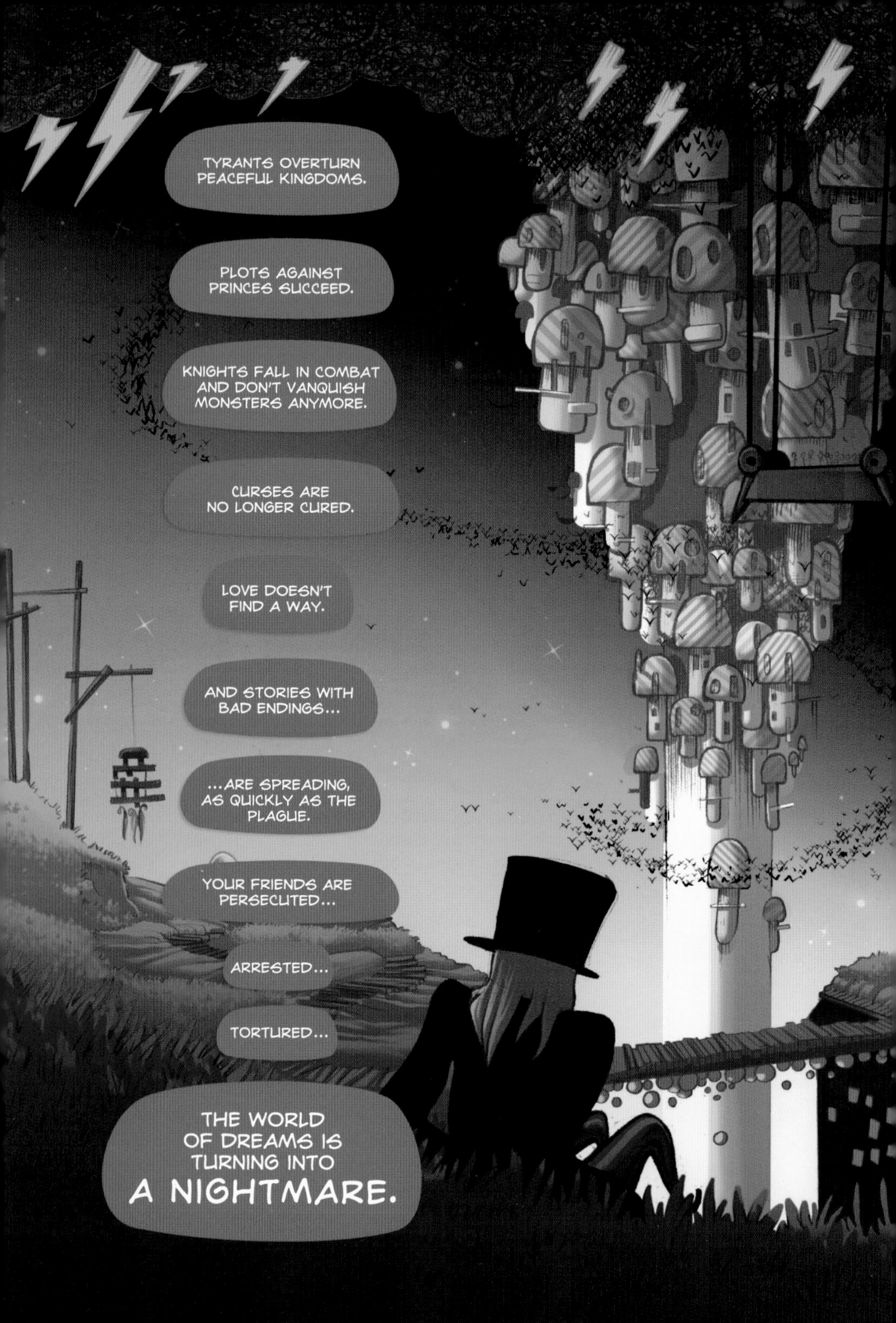
TYRANTS OVERTURN PEACEFUL KINGDOMS.
PLOTS AGAINST PRINCES SUCCEED.
KNIGHTS FALL IN COMBAT AND DON'T VANQUISH MONSTERS ANYMORE.
CURSES ARE NO LONGER CURED.
LOVE DOESN'T FIND A WAY.
AND STORIES WITH BAD ENDINGS...
...ARE SPREADING, AS QUICKLY AS THE PLAGUE.
YOUR FRIENDS ARE PERSECUTED...
ARRESTED...
TORTURED...
THE WORLD OF DREAMS IS TURNING INTO A NIGHTMARE.

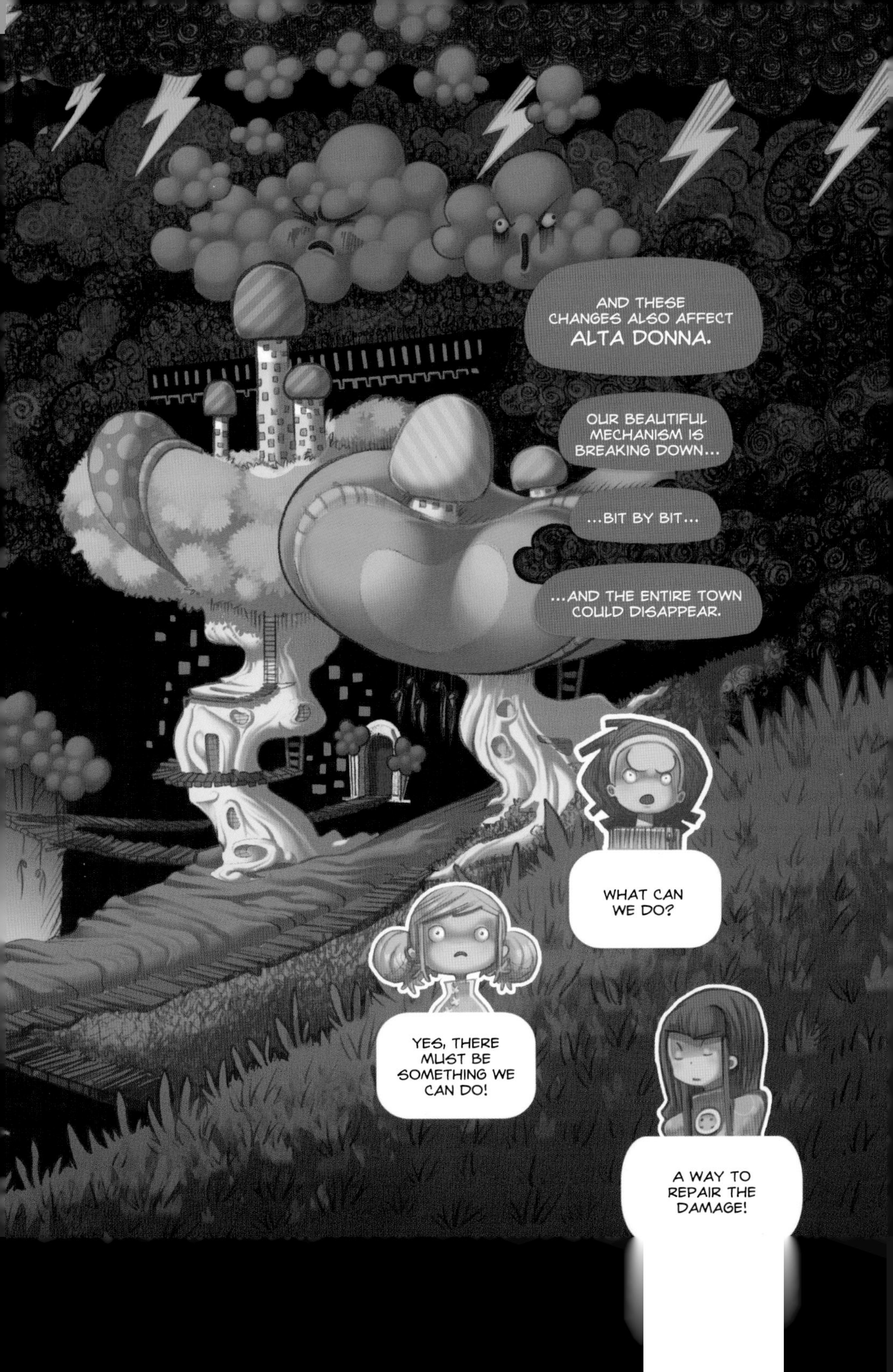
AND THESE CHANGES ALSO AFFECT ALTA DONNA.
OUR BEAUTIFUL MECHANISM IS BREAKING DOWN...
...BIT BY BIT...
...AND THE ENTIRE TOWN COULD DISAPPEAR.
WHAT CAN WE DO?
YES, THERE MUST BE SOMETHING WE CAN DO!
A WAY TO REPAIR THE DAMAGE!

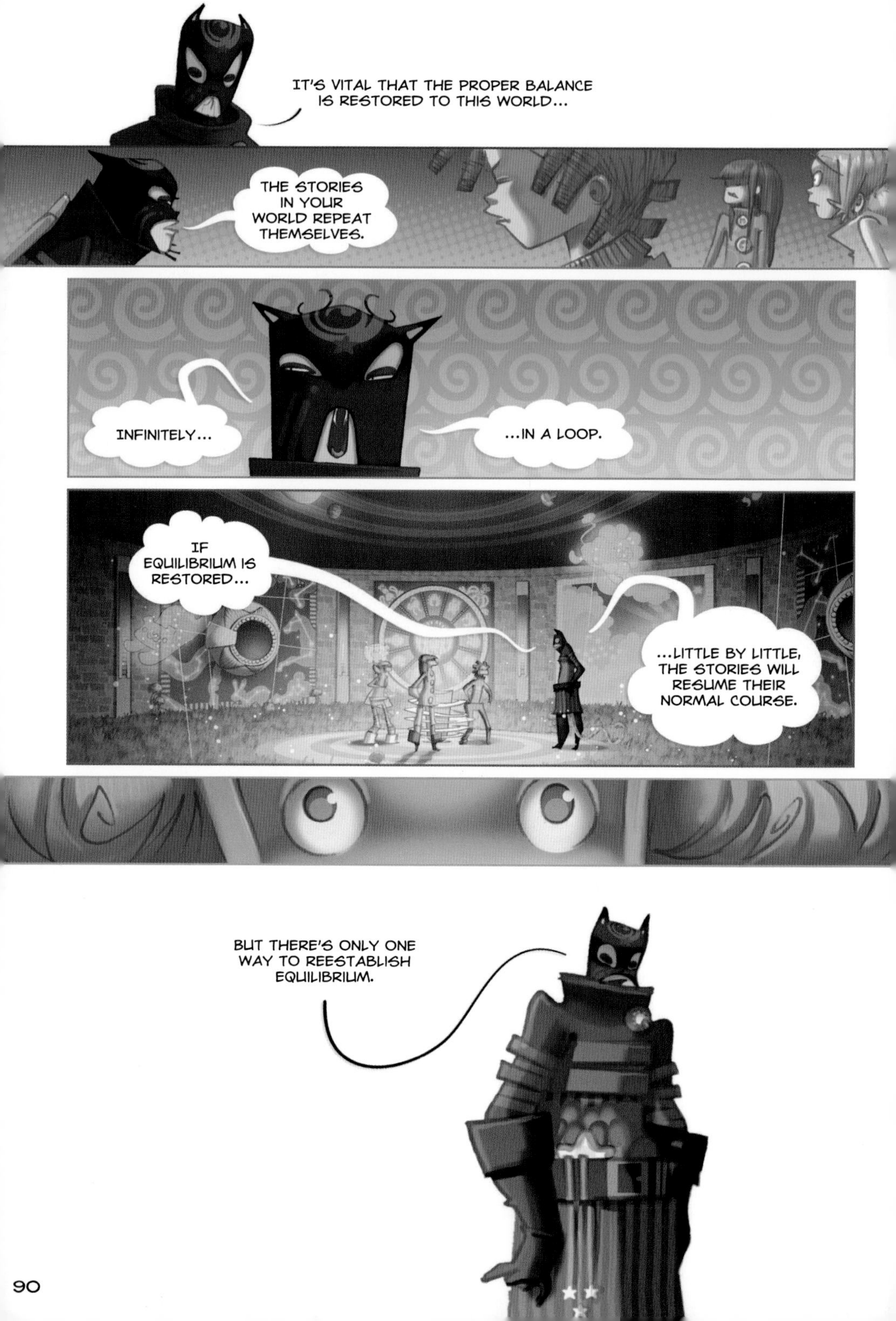
IT'S VITAL THAT THE PROPER BALANCE IS RESTORED TO THIS WORLD...
THE STORIES IN YOUR WORLD REPEAT THEMSELVES.
INFINITELY...
...IN A LOOP.
IF EQUILIBRIUM IS RESTORED...
...LITTLE BY LITTLE, THE STORIES WILL RESUME THEIR NORMAL COURSE.
BUT THERE'S ONLY ONE WAY TO REESTABLISH EQUILIBRIUM.

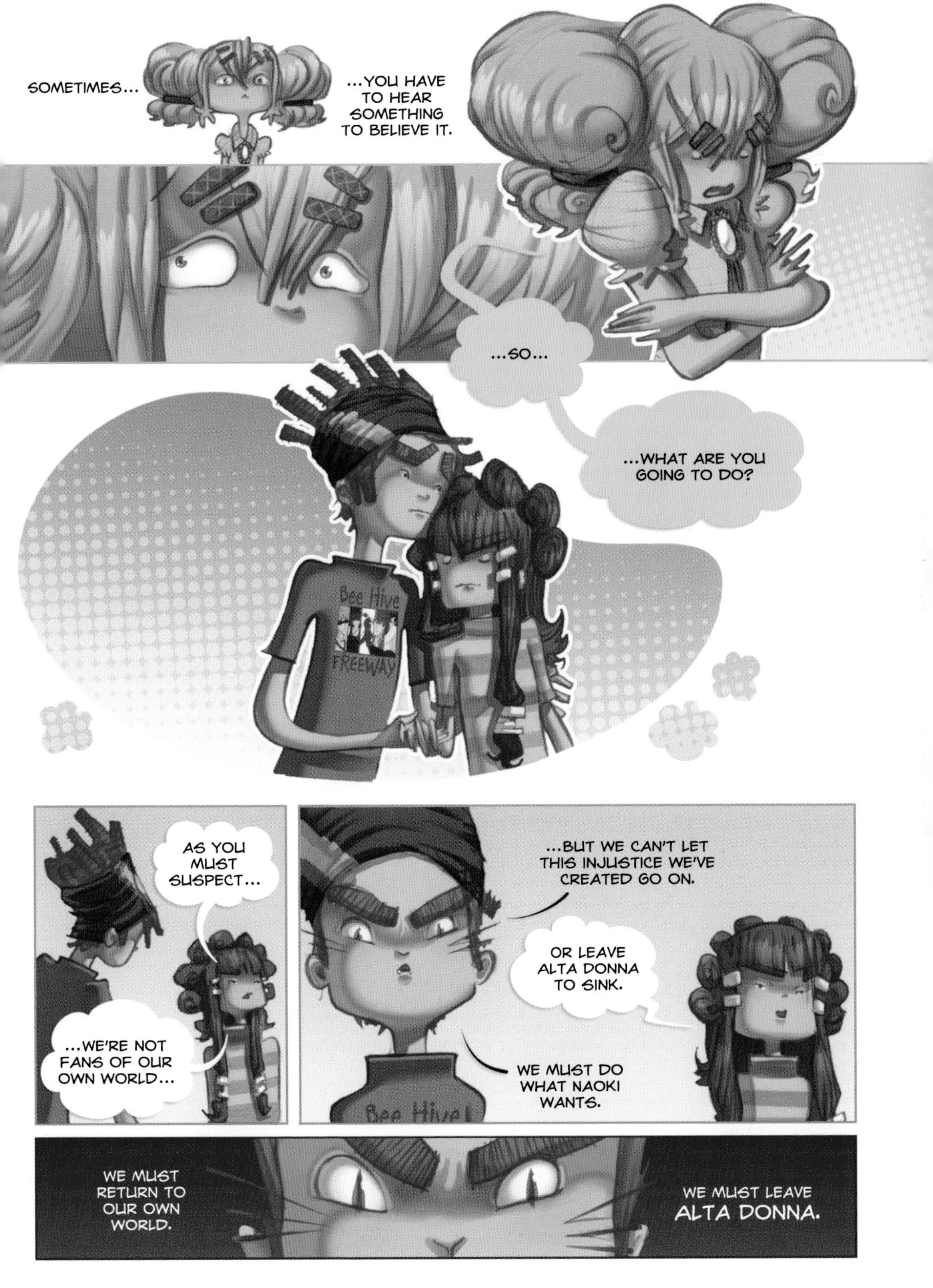
SOMETIMES...
...YOU HAVE TO HEAR SOMETHING TO BELIEVE IT.
...SO...
...WHAT ARE YOU GOING TO DO?
Bee Hive
FREEWAY
AS YOU MUST SUSPECT...
...WE'RE NOT FANS OF OUR OWN WORLD...
...BUT WE CAN'T LET THIS INJUSTICE WE'VE CREATED GO ON.
OR LEAVE ALTA DONNA TO SINK.
WE MUST DO WHAT NAOKI WANTS.
Bee Hive
WE MUST RETURN TO OUR OWN WORLD.
WE MUST LEAVE ALTA DONNA.

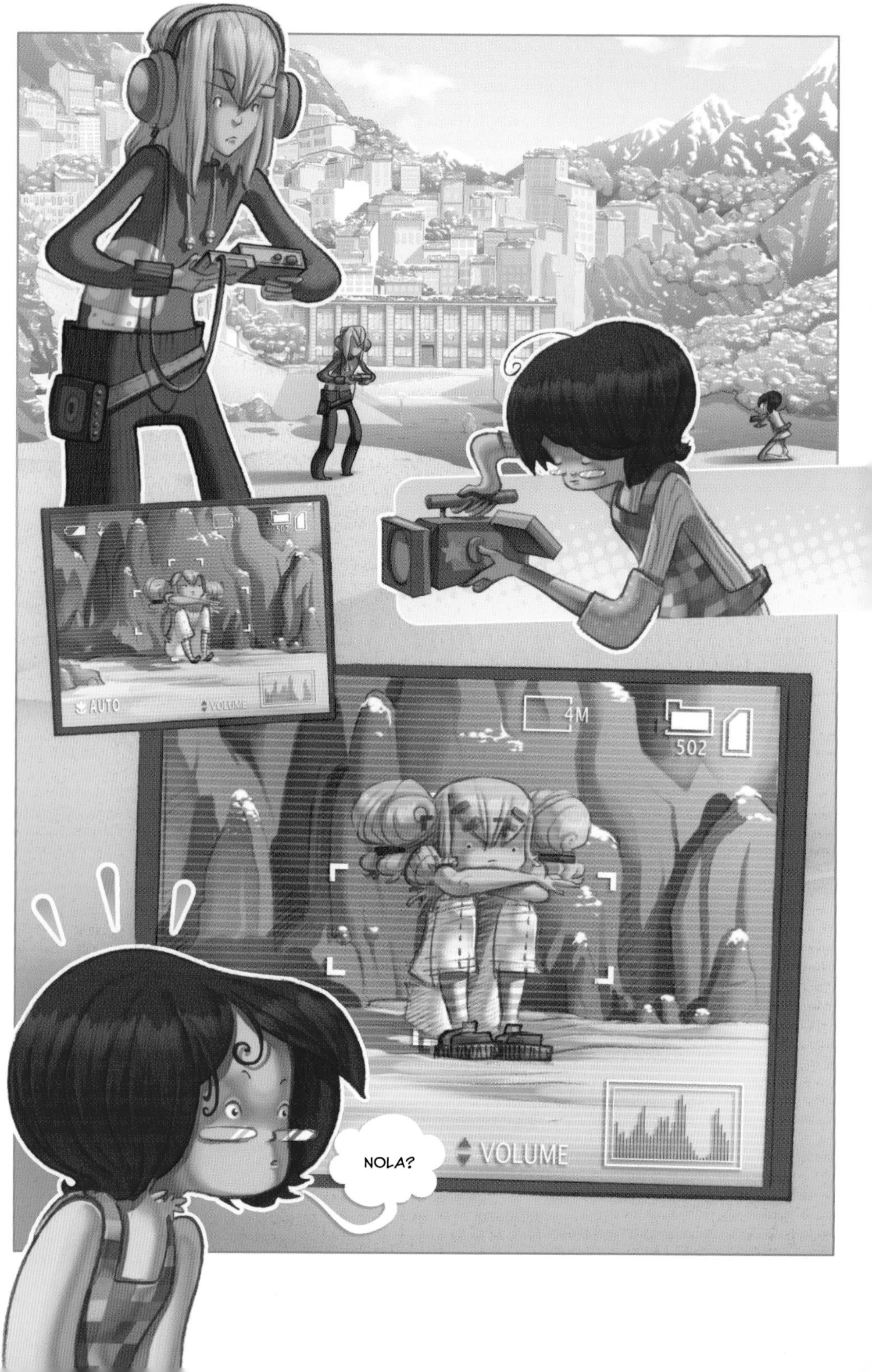
4M
502
AUTO
VOLUME
4M
502
VOLUME
NOLA?

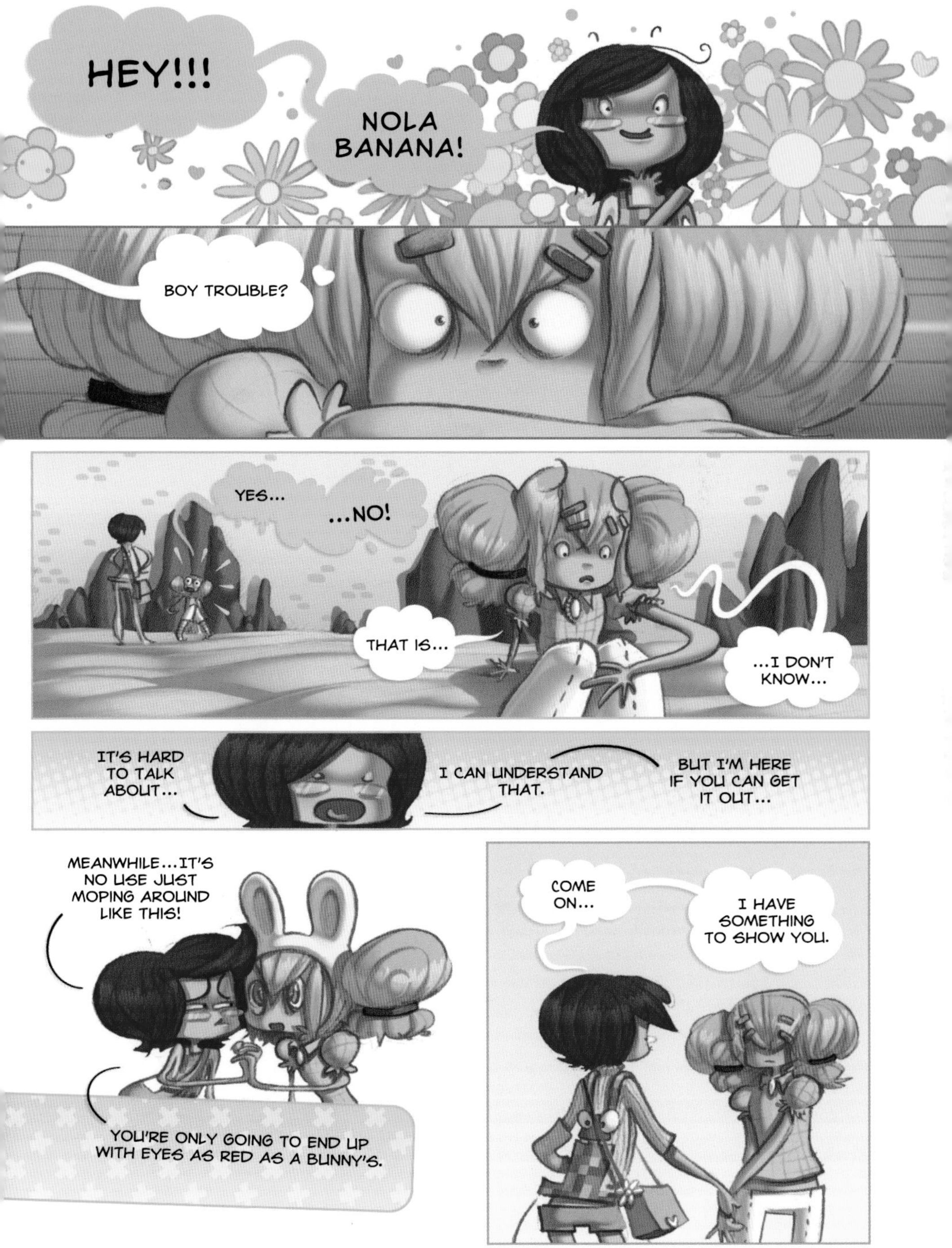
HEY!!!
NOLA BANANA!
BOY TROUBLE?
YES...
...NO!
THAT IS...
...I DON'T KNOW...
IT'S HARD TO TALK ABOUT...
I CAN UNDERSTAND THAT.
BUT I'M HERE IF YOU CAN GET IT OUT...
MEANWHILE...IT'S NO USE JUST MOPING AROUND LIKE THIS!
YOU'RE ONLY GOING TO END UP WITH EYES AS RED AS A BUNNY'S.
COME ON...
I HAVE SOMETHING TO SHOW YOU.

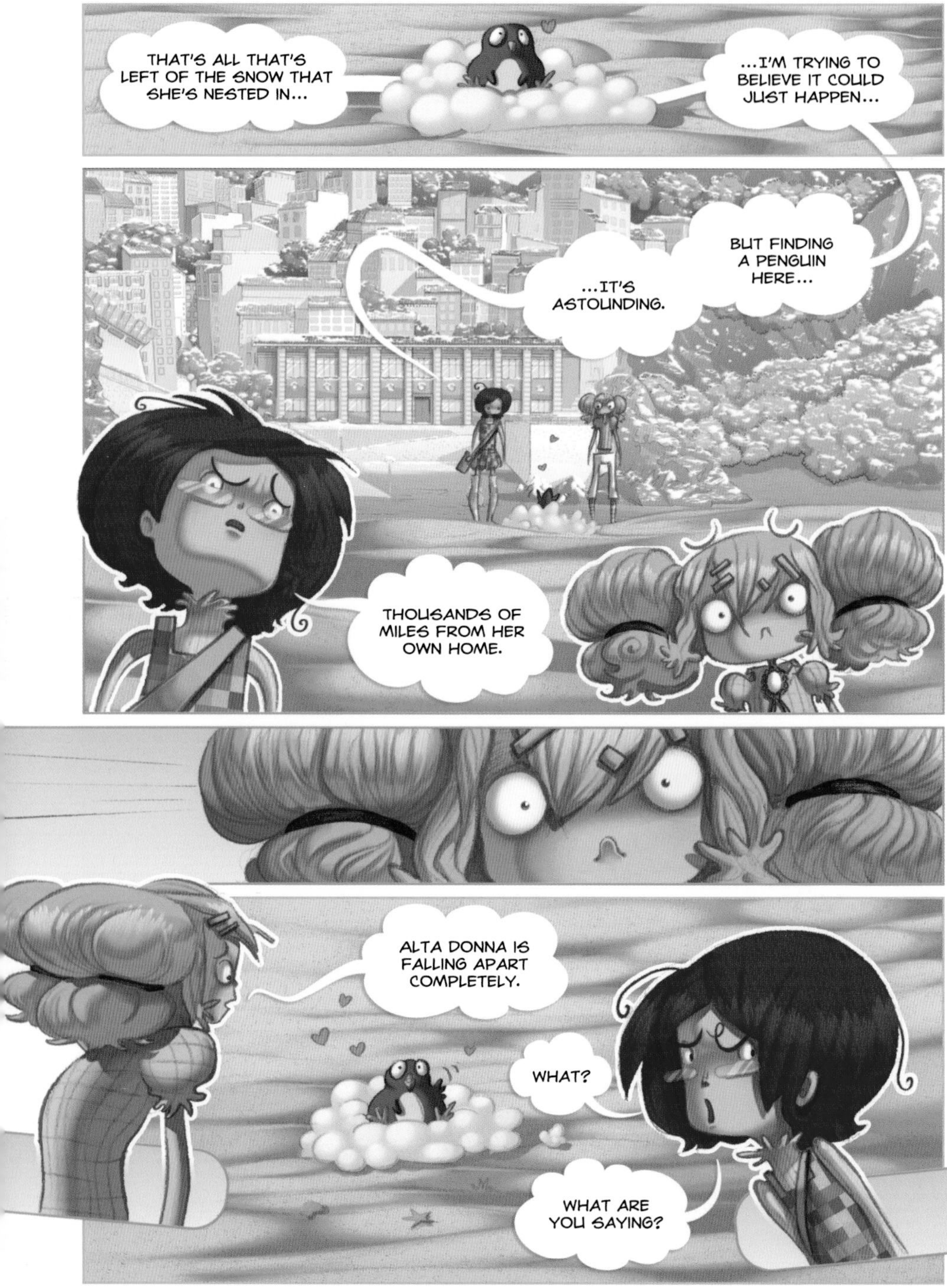
THAT'S ALL THAT'S LEFT OF THE SNOW THAT SHE'S NESTED IN...
...I'M TRYING TO BELIEVE IT COULD JUST HAPPEN...
BUT FINDING A PENGUIN HERE...
...IT'S ASTOUNDING.
THOUSANDS OF MILES FROM HER OWN HOME.
ALTA DONNA IS FALLING APART COMPLETELY.
WHAT?
WHAT ARE YOU SAYING?

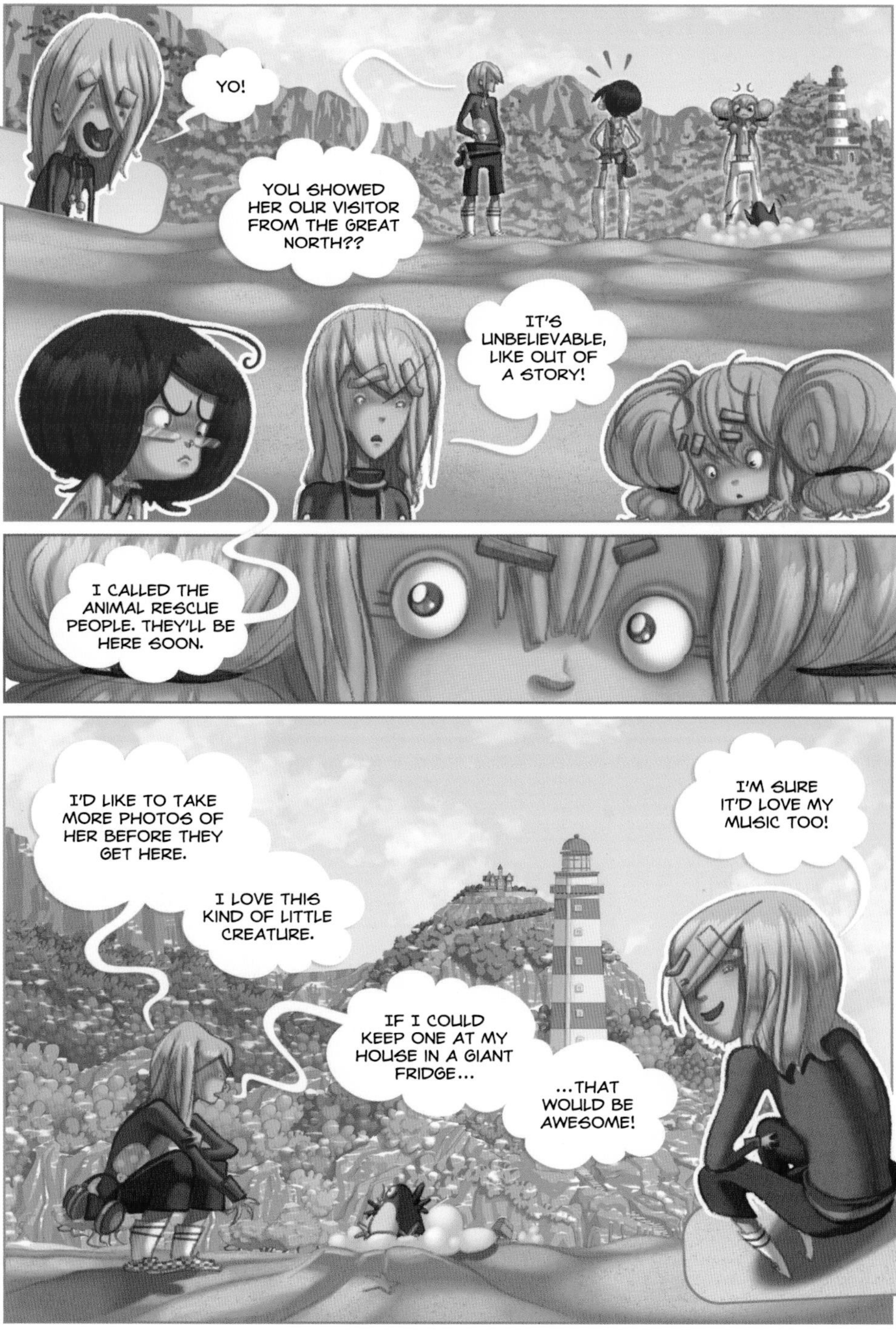
YO!
YOU SHOWED HER OUR VISITOR FROM THE GREAT NORTH??
IT'S UNBELIEVABLE, LIKE OUT OF A STORY!
I CALLED THE ANIMAL RESCUE PEOPLE. THEY'LL BE HERE SOON.
I'D LIKE TO TAKE MORE PHOTOS OF HER BEFORE THEY GET HERE.
I LOVE THIS KIND OF LITTLE CREATURE.
I'M SURE IT'D LOVE MY MUSIC TOO!
IF I COULD KEEP ONE AT MY HOUSE IN A GIANT FRIDGE...
...THAT WOULD BE AWESOME!

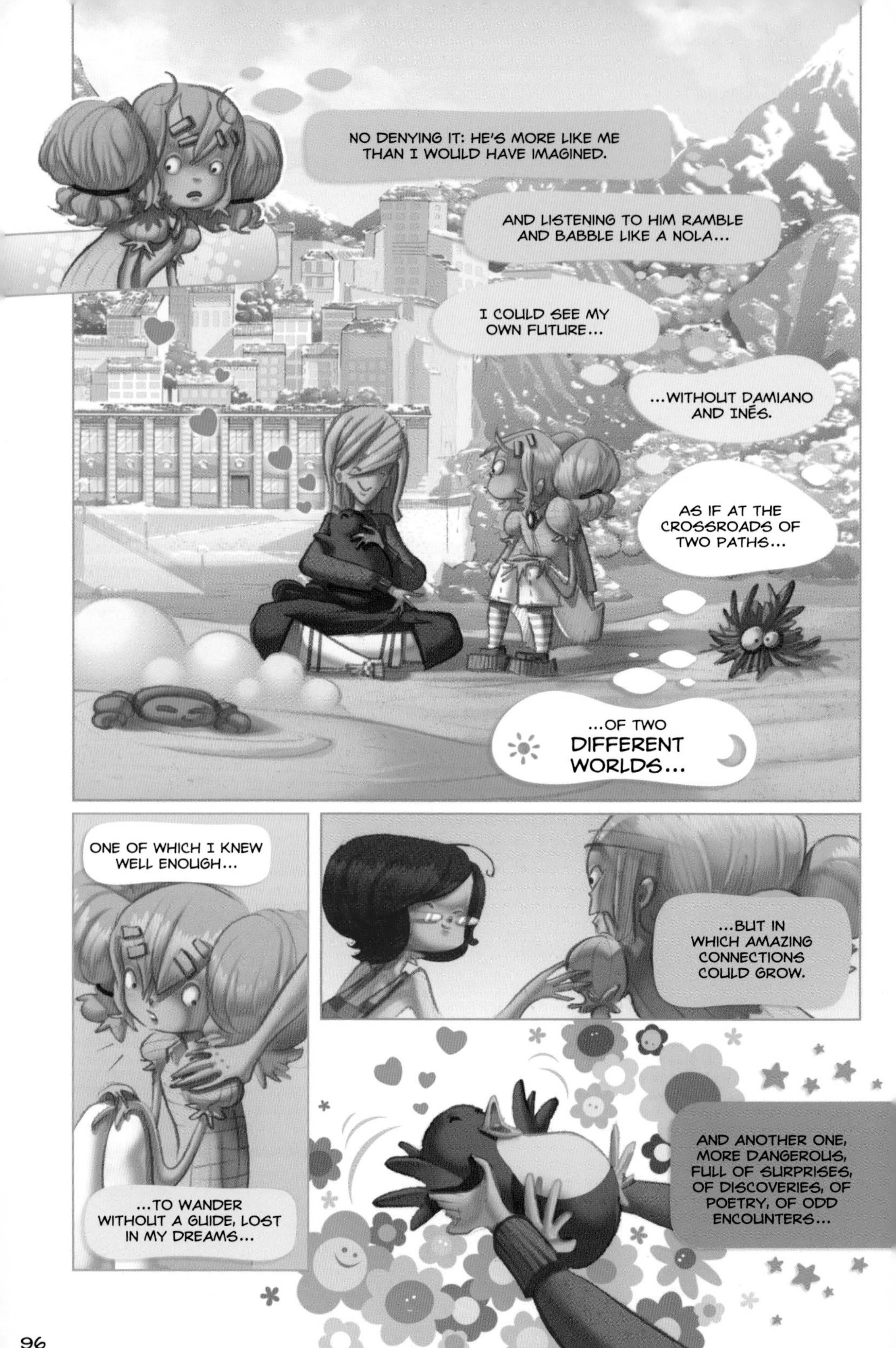
NO DENYING IT: HE'S MORE LIKE ME THAN I WOULD HAVE IMAGINED.
AND LISTENING TO HIM RAMBLE AND BABBLE LIKE A NOLA...
I COULD SEE MY OWN FUTURE...
...WITHOUT DAMIANO AND INÉS.
AS IF AT THE CROSSROADS OF TWO PATHS...
...OF TWO DIFFERENT WORLDS...
ONE OF WHICH I KNEW WELL ENOUGH...
...TO WANDER WITHOUT A GUIDE, LOST IN MY DREAMS...
...BUT IN WHICH AMAZING CONNECTIONS COULD GROW.
AND ANOTHER ONE, MORE DANGEROUS, FULL OF SURPRISES, OF DISCOVERIES, OF POETRY, OF ODD ENCOUNTERS...

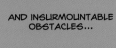

AND INSURMOUNTABLE OBSTACLES...

...EVEN FOR A DREAMER LIKE ME.

I DON'T KNOW WHAT'S ON YOUR MIND TODAY, KIDDO...

...BUT IT SEEMS LIKE SOMETHING TOO HEAVY TO CARRY AROUND.

EVEN FOR A DREAMER LIKE YOU.

PUMP...

...CAN I TALK TO YOU...?

AND I TOLD HER EVERYTHING...

...IN SPITE OF ALL MY PROMISES...

...THE PLEDGES TO KEEP THE SECRET.

YOU CAN'T JUST MAKE UP A BEST FRIEND...

...ESPECIALLY FOR A DREAMER LIKE ME.

SOME THINGS HURT HEARTS TOO MUCH AND LOOSEN TONGUES.

I BELIEVE THAT FRIENDSHIP CAN SOMETIMES SURVIVE A SMALL BETRAYAL THAT CAN'T BE AVOIDED, A SECRET THAT HAS TO BE TOLD.

IF THERE WAS ONE PERSON WHO'D BELIEVE ME AND HELP ME...

ESPECIALLY IF YOU DO IT BECAUSE YOU'RE LOOKING FOR A HELPING HAND.

...IT WAS PUMPKIN.

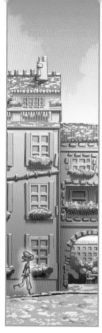

GOOD MORNING, SUNSHINE.

YOU JUST MISSED YOUR FATHER.

DID HE COME TO CHECK ON THE DAMAGE?

WHAT DAMAGE?

HE SENSED A THREAT FROM THE NEW BOYFRIEND.

HE CAME TO SEE IF YOU'D MADE BREAKFAST FOR ONE...

...OR FOR TWO...

DON'T TALK NONSENSE, NOLA.

INSTEAD, TELL ME WHAT'S GOT YOU OUT OF BED AT DAWN ON A SATURDAY.

IF YOU TELL ME WHAT KEPT YOU FROM GOING TO WORK AT DAWN ON A SATURDAY.

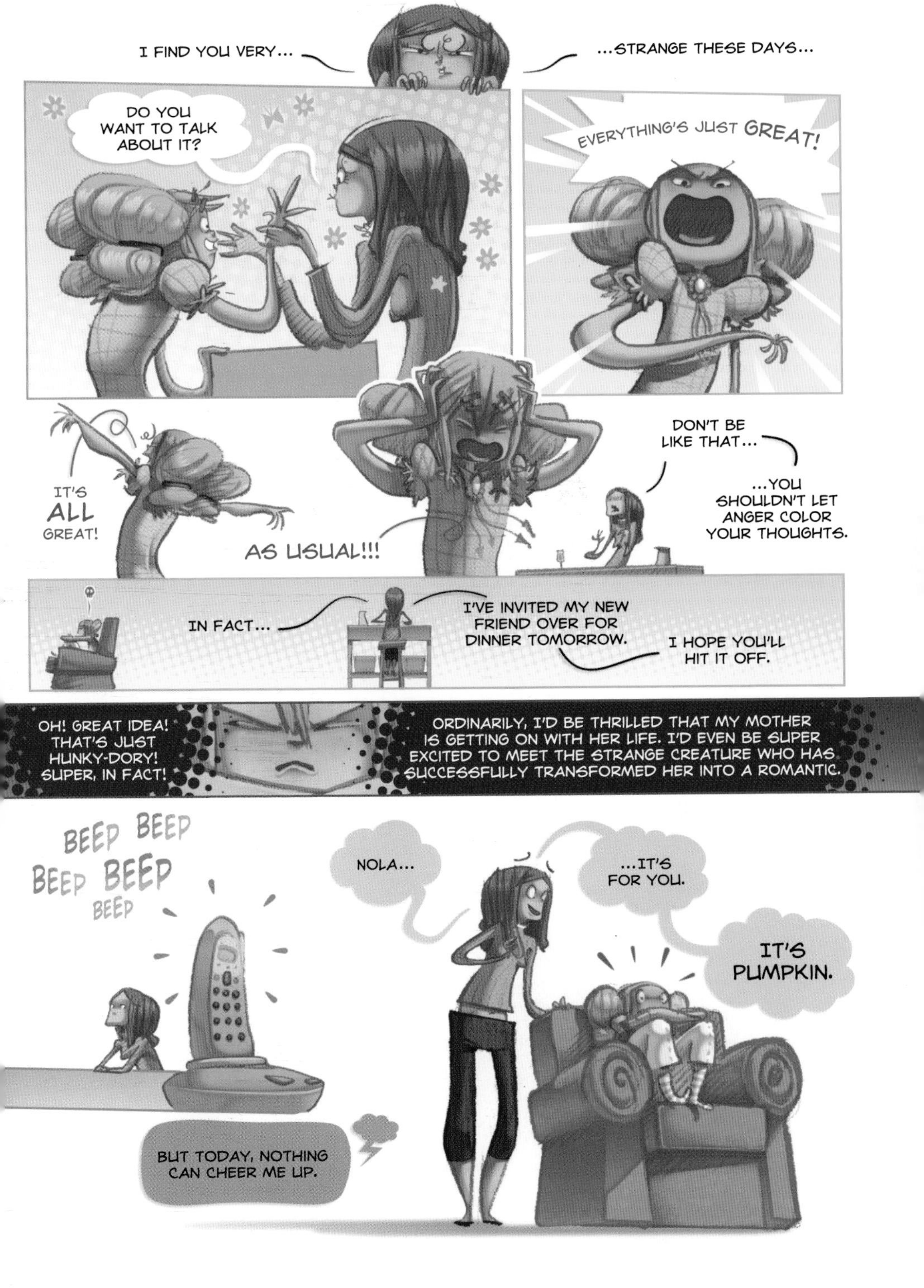
I FIND YOU VERY...
...STRANGE THESE DAYS...
DO YOU WANT TO TALK ABOUT IT?
EVERYTHING'S JUST GREAT!
IT'S ALL GREAT!
AS USUAL!!!
DON'T BE LIKE THAT...
...YOU SHOULDN'T LET ANGER COLOR YOUR THOUGHTS.
IN FACT...
I'VE INVITED MY NEW FRIEND OVER FOR DINNER TOMORROW.
I HOPE YOU'LL HIT IT OFF.
OH! GREAT IDEA! THAT'S JUST HUNKY-DORY! SUPER, IN FACT!
ORDINARILY, I'D BE THRILLED THAT MY MOTHER IS GETTING ON WITH HER LIFE. I'D EVEN BE SUPER EXCITED TO MEET THE STRANGE CREATURE WHO HAS SUCCESSFULLY TRANSFORMED HER INTO A ROMANTIC.
BEEP BEEP
BEEP BEEP
BEEP
NOLA...
...IT'S FOR YOU.
IT'S SUPER PUMPKIN.
BUT TODAY, NOTHING CAN CHEER ME UP.

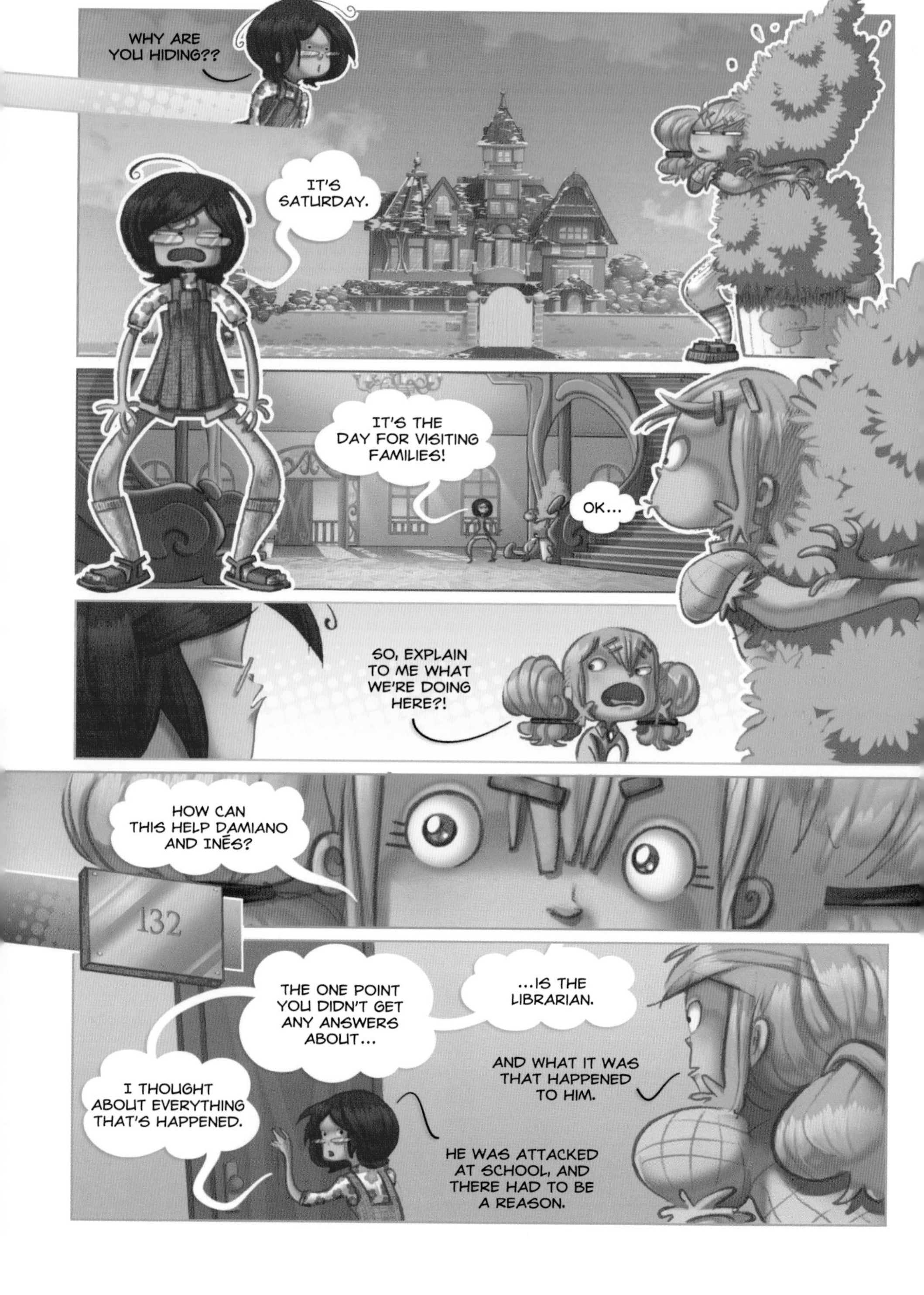
WHY ARE YOU HIDING??
IT'S SATURDAY.
IT'S THE DAY FOR VISITING FAMILIES!
OK...
SO, EXPLAIN TO ME WHAT WE'RE DOING HERE?!
HOW CAN THIS HELP DAMIANO AND INÉS?
132
I THOUGHT ABOUT EVERYTHING THAT'S HAPPENED.
THE ONE POINT YOU DIDN'T GET ANY ANSWERS ABOUT...
...IS THE LIBRARIAN.
AND WHAT IT WAS THAT HAPPENED TO HIM.
HE WAS ATTACKED AT SCHOOL, AND THERE HAD TO BE A REASON.

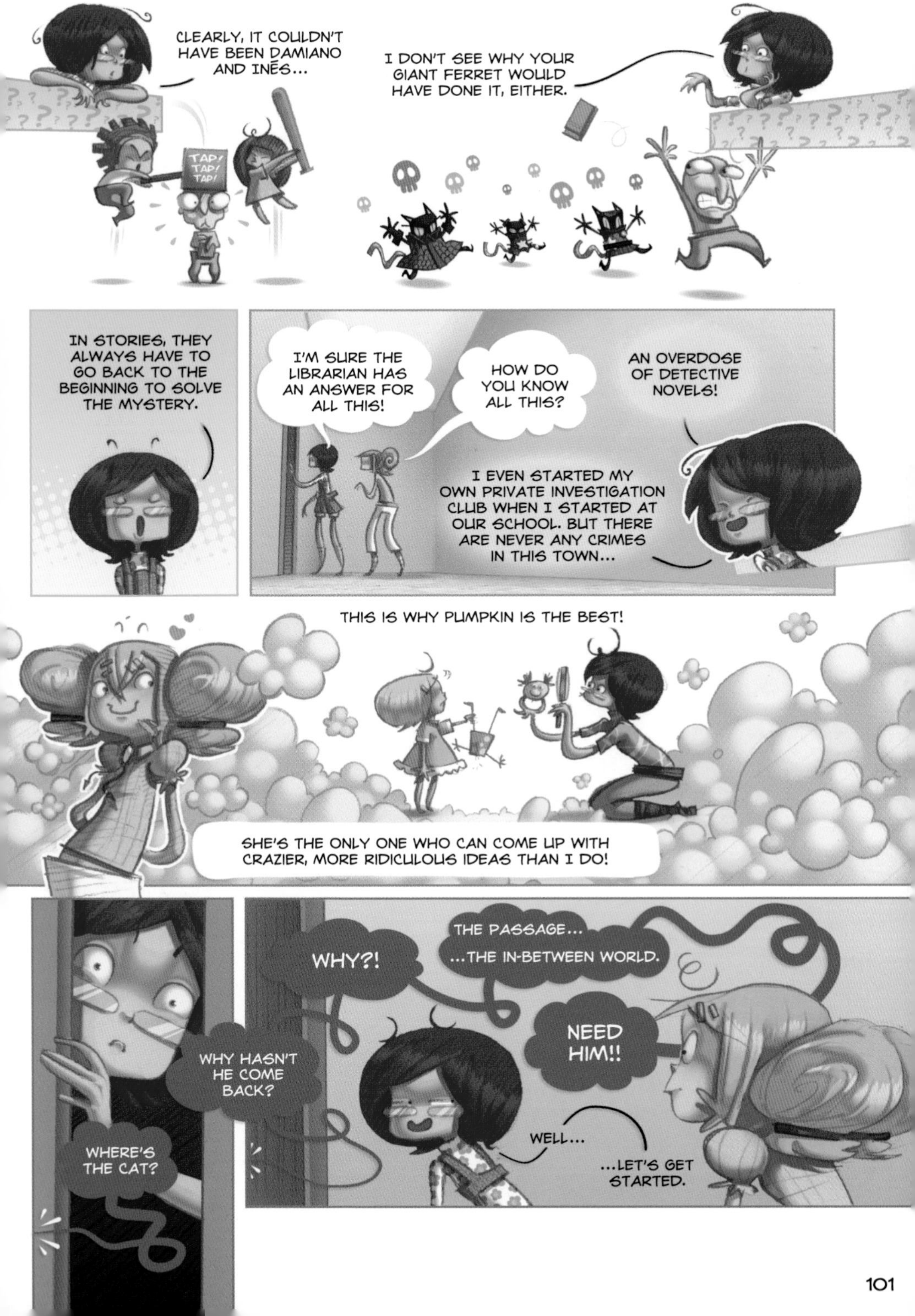
CLEARLY, IT COULDN'T HAVE BEEN DAMIANO AND INÉS...
TAP! TAP! TAP!
I DON'T SEE WHY YOUR GIANT FERRET WOULD HAVE DONE IT, EITHER.
IN STORIES, THEY ALWAYS HAVE TO GO BACK TO THE BEGINNING TO SOLVE THE MYSTERY.
I'M SURE THE LIBRARIAN HAS AN ANSWER FOR ALL THIS!
HOW DO YOU KNOW ALL THIS?
AN OVERDOSE OF DETECTIVE NOVELS!
I EVEN STARTED MY OWN PRIVATE INVESTIGATION CLUB WHEN I STARTED AT OUR SCHOOL. BUT THERE ARE NEVER ANY CRIMES IN THIS TOWN...
THIS IS WHY PUMPKIN IS THE BEST!
SHE'S THE ONLY ONE WHO CAN COME UP WITH CRAZIER, MORE RIDICULOUS IDEAS THAN I DO!
WHY HASN'T HE COME BACK?
WHERE'S THE CAT?
WHY?!
THE PASSAGE...
...THE IN-BETWEEN WORLD.
NEED HIM!!
WELL...
...LET'S GET STARTED.

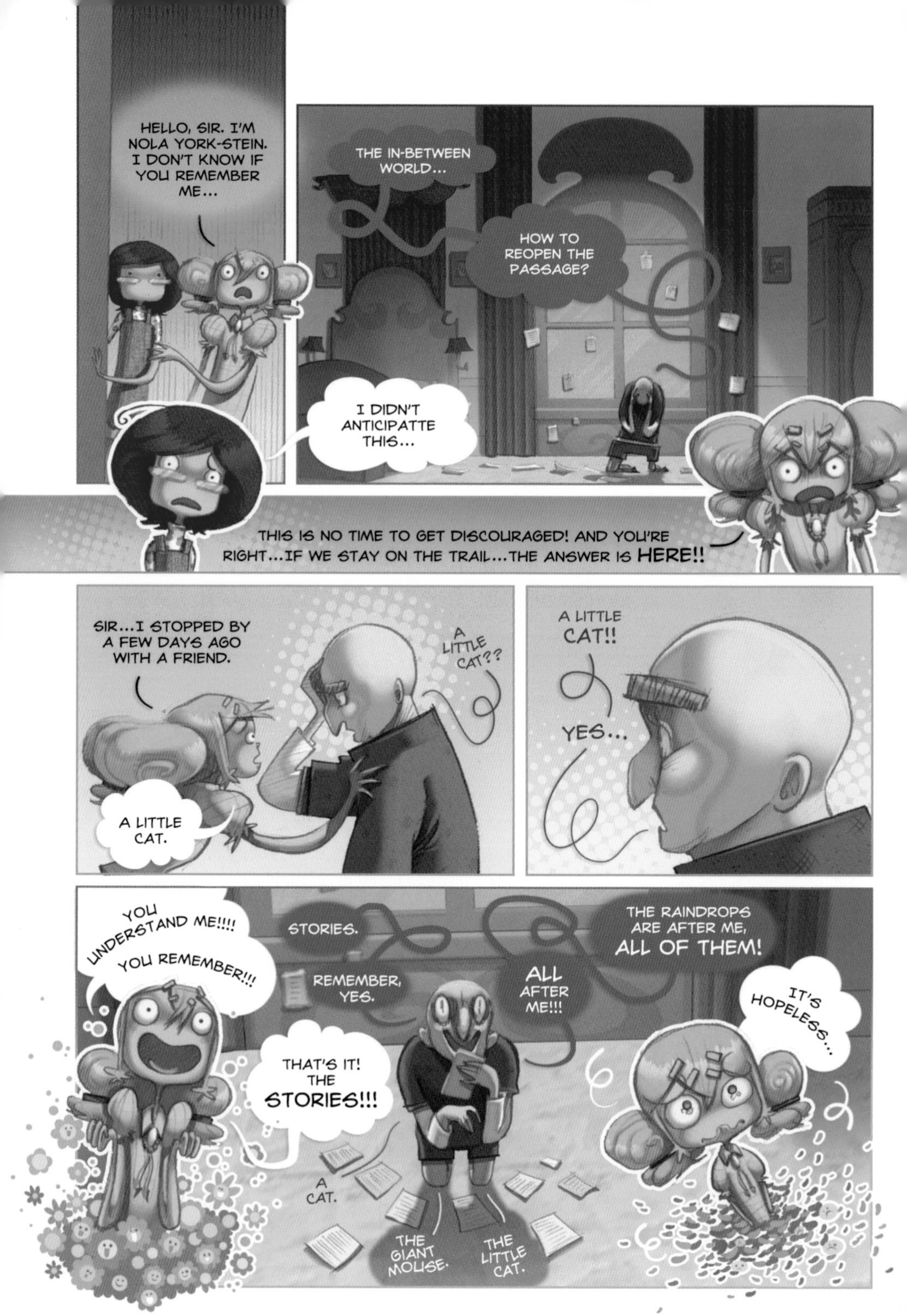
HELLO, SIR. I'M NOLA YORK-STEIN. I DON'T KNOW IF YOU REMEMBER ME...
THE IN-BETWEEN WORLD...
HOW TO REOPEN THE PASSAGE?
I DIDN'T ANTICIPATTE THIS...
THIS IS NO TIME TO GET DISCOURAGED! AND YOU'RE RIGHT...IF WE STAY ON THE TRAIL...THE ANSWER IS HERE!!
SIR...I STOPPED BY A FEW DAYS AGO WITH A FRIEND.
A LITTLE CAT.
A LITTLE CAT??
A LITTLE CAT!!
YES...
YOU UNDERSTAND ME!!!!
YOU REMEMBER!!!
STORIES.
REMEMBER, YES.
THE RAINDROPS ARE AFTER ME, ALL OF THEM!
ALL AFTER ME!!!
IT'S HOPELESS...
THAT'S IT! THE STORIES!!!
A CAT.
THE GIANT MOUSE.
THE LITTLE CAT.

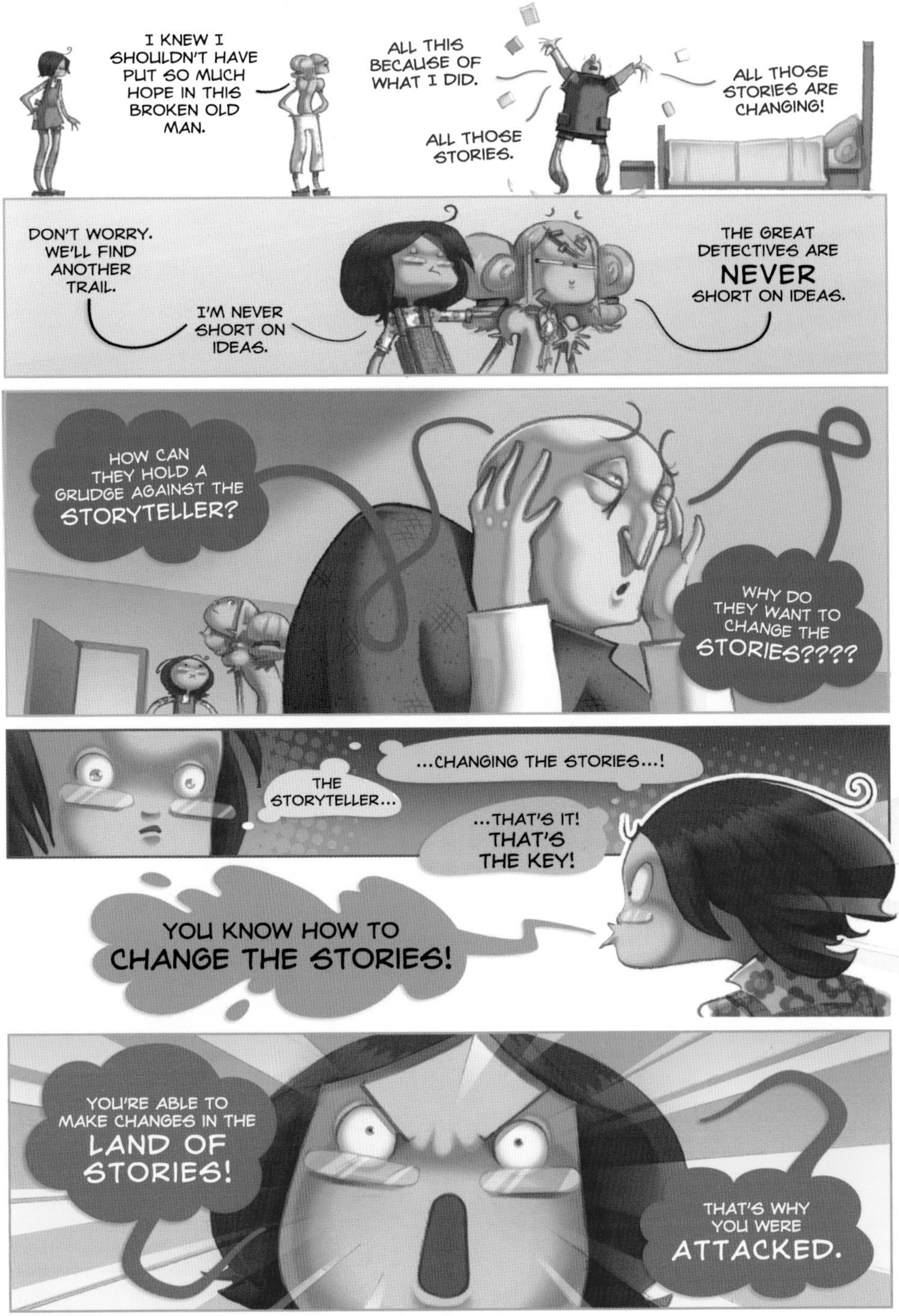
I KNEW I SHOULDN'T HAVE PUT SO MUCH HOPE IN THIS BROKEN OLD MAN.
ALL THIS BECAUSE OF WHAT I DID.
ALL THOSE STORIES.
ALL THOSE STORIES ARE CHANGING!
DON'T WORRY. WE'LL FIND ANOTHER TRAIL.
I'M NEVER SHORT ON IDEAS.
THE GREAT DETECTIVES ARE NEVER SHORT ON IDEAS.
HOW CAN THEY HOLD A GRUDGE AGAINST THE STORYTELLER?
WHY DO THEY WANT TO CHANGE THE STORIES????
THE STORYTELLER...
...CHANGING THE STORIES...!
...THAT'S IT! THAT'S THE KEY!
YOU KNOW HOW TO CHANGE THE STORIES!
YOU'RE ABLE TO MAKE CHANGES IN THE LAND OF STORIES!
THAT'S WHY YOU WERE ATTACKED.

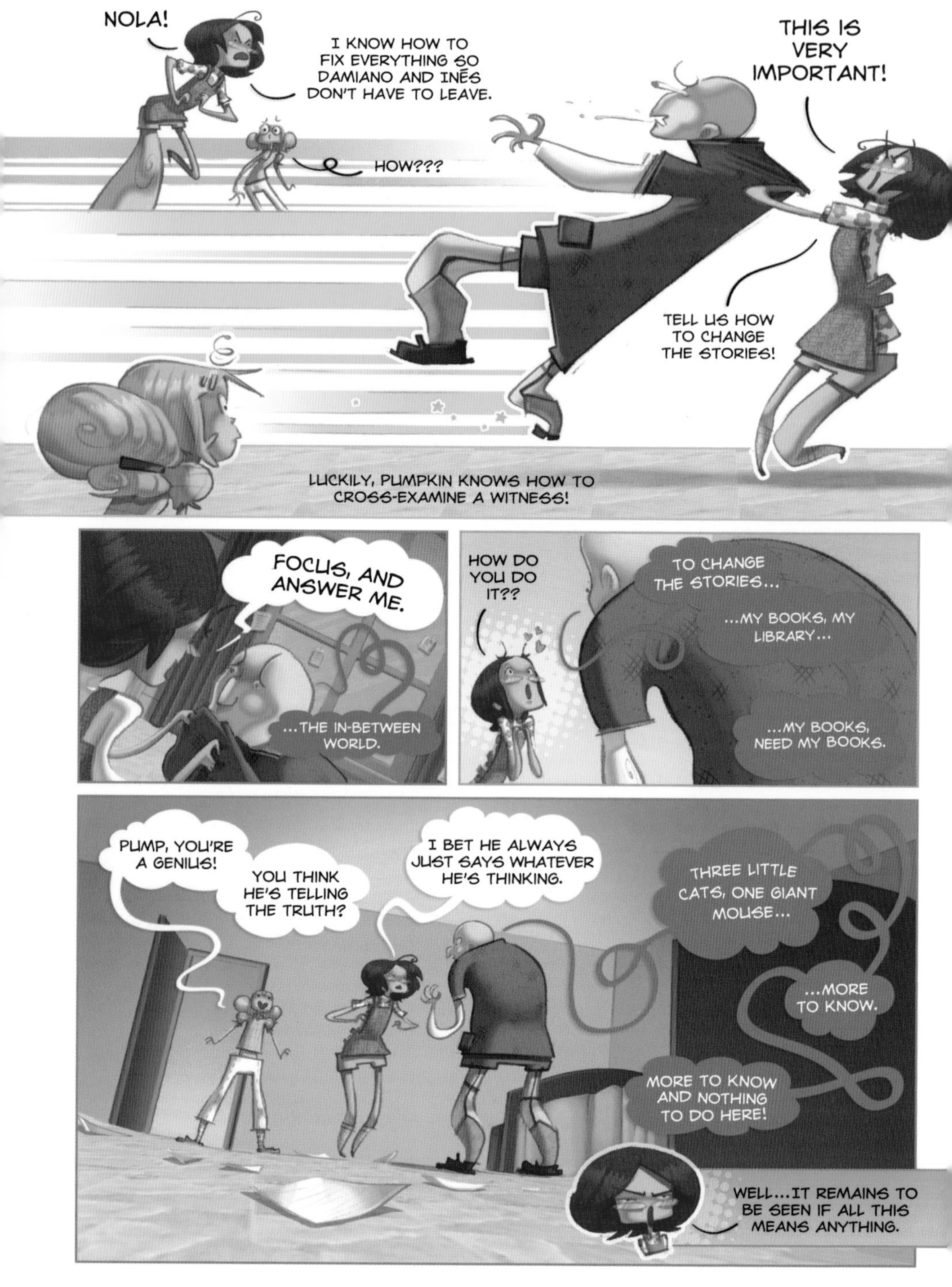
NOLA!
I KNOW HOW TO FIX EVERYTHING SO DAMIANO AND INÉS DON'T HAVE TO LEAVE.
HOW???
THIS IS VERY IMPORTANT!
TELL US HOW TO CHANGE THE STORIES!
LUCKILY, PUMPKIN KNOWS HOW TO CROSS-EXAMINE A WITNESS!
FOCUS, AND ANSWER ME.
...THE IN-BETWEEN WORLD.
HOW DO YOU DO IT??
TO CHANGE THE STORIES...
...MY BOOKS, MY LIBRARY...
...MY BOOKS, NEED MY BOOKS.
PUMP, YOU'RE A GENIUS!
YOU THINK HE'S TELLING THE TRUTH?
I BET HE ALWAYS JUST SAYS WHATEVER HE'S THINKING.
THREE LITTLE CATS, ONE GIANT MOUSE...
...MORE TO KNOW.
MORE TO KNOW AND NOTHING TO DO HERE!
WELL...IT REMAINS TO BE SEEN IF ALL THIS MEANS ANYTHING.

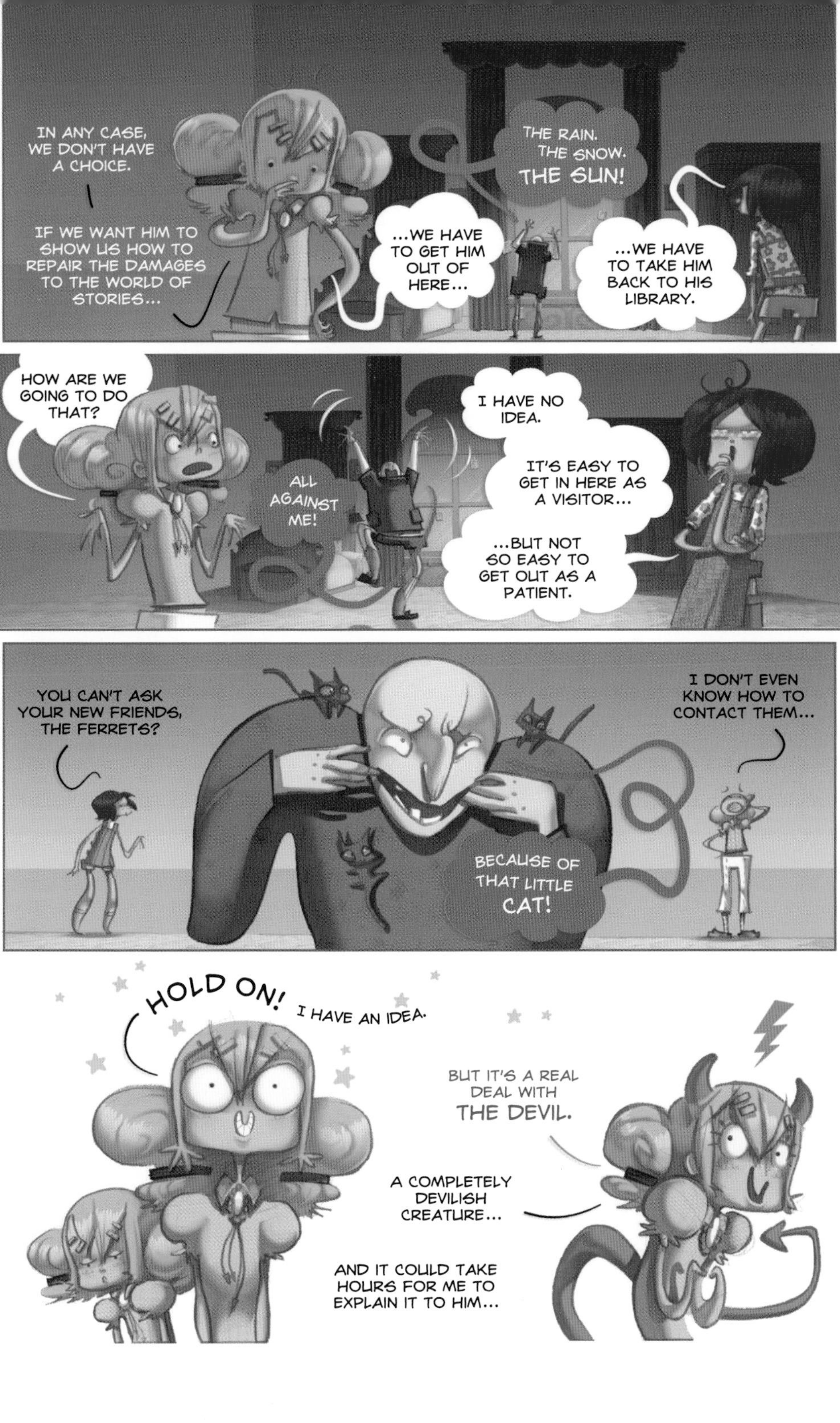

IN ANY CASE, WE DON'T HAVE A CHOICE.
IF WE WANT HIM TO SHOW US HOW TO REPAIR THE DAMAGES TO THE WORLD OF STORIES...
...WE HAVE TO GET HIM OUT OF HERE...
THE RAIN. THE SNOW. THE SUN!
...WE HAVE TO TAKE HIM BACK TO HIS LIBRARY.
HOW ARE WE GOING TO DO THAT?
ALL AGAINST ME!
I HAVE NO IDEA.
IT'S EASY TO GET IN HERE AS A VISITOR...
...BUT NOT SO EASY TO GET OUT AS A PATIENT.
YOU CAN'T ASK YOUR NEW FRIENDS, THE FERRETS?
I DON'T EVEN KNOW HOW TO CONTACT THEM...
BECAUSE OF THAT LITTLE CAT!
HOLD ON! I HAVE AN IDEA.
BUT IT'S A REAL DEAL WITH THE DEVIL.
A COMPLETELY DEVILISH CREATURE...
AND IT COULD TAKE HOURS FOR ME TO EXPLAIN IT TO HIM...

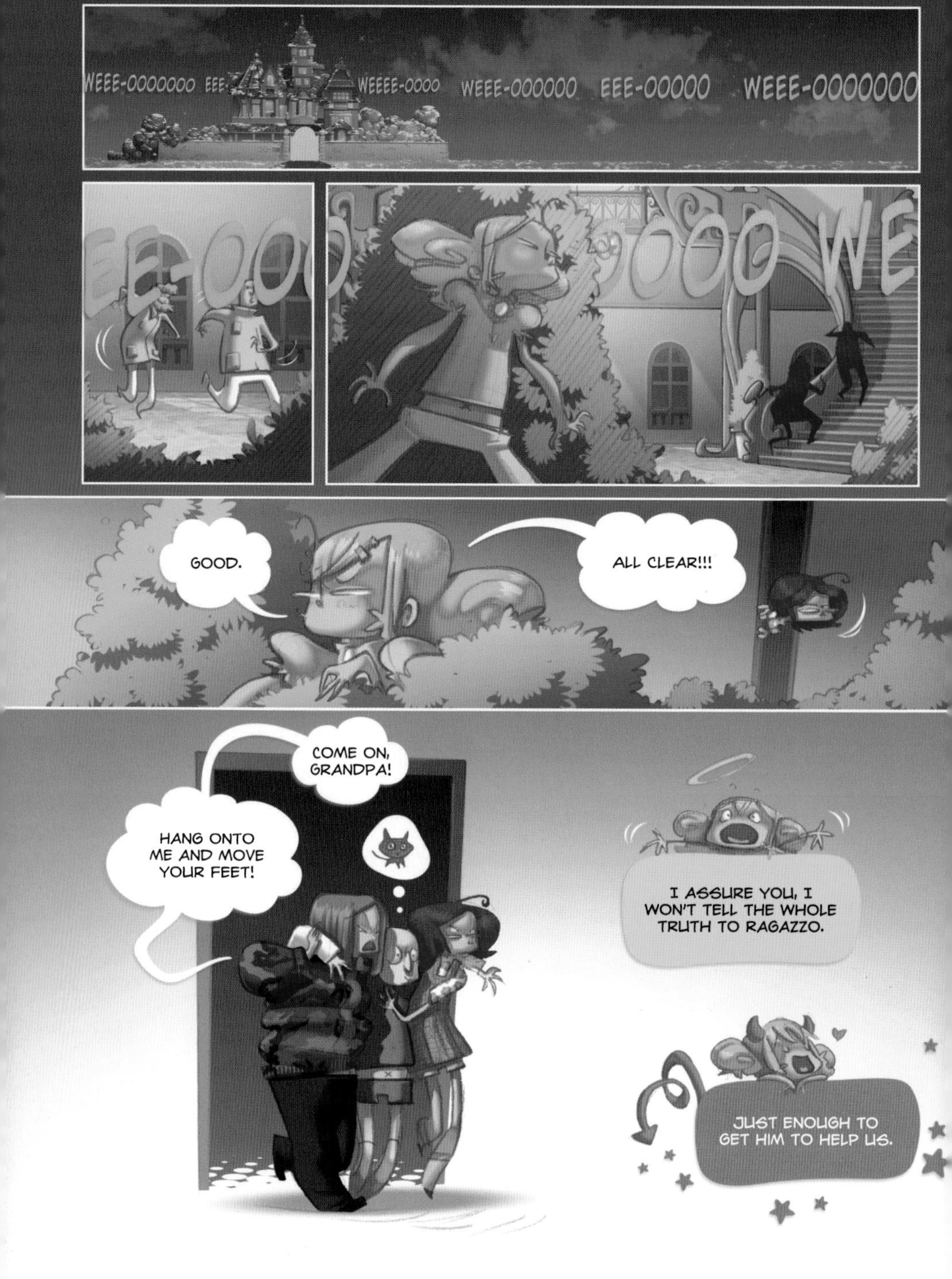
WEEE-OOOOOOO EEE WEEEE-OOOO WEEE-OOOOOO EEE-OOOOO WEEE-OOOOOOO
EE-OOO
OOOO WE
GOOD.
ALL CLEAR!!!
COME ON, GRANDPA!
HANG ONTO ME AND MOVE YOUR FEET!
I ASSURE YOU, I WON'T TELL THE WHOLE TRUTH TO RAGAZZO.
JUST ENOUGH TO GET HIM TO HELP US.

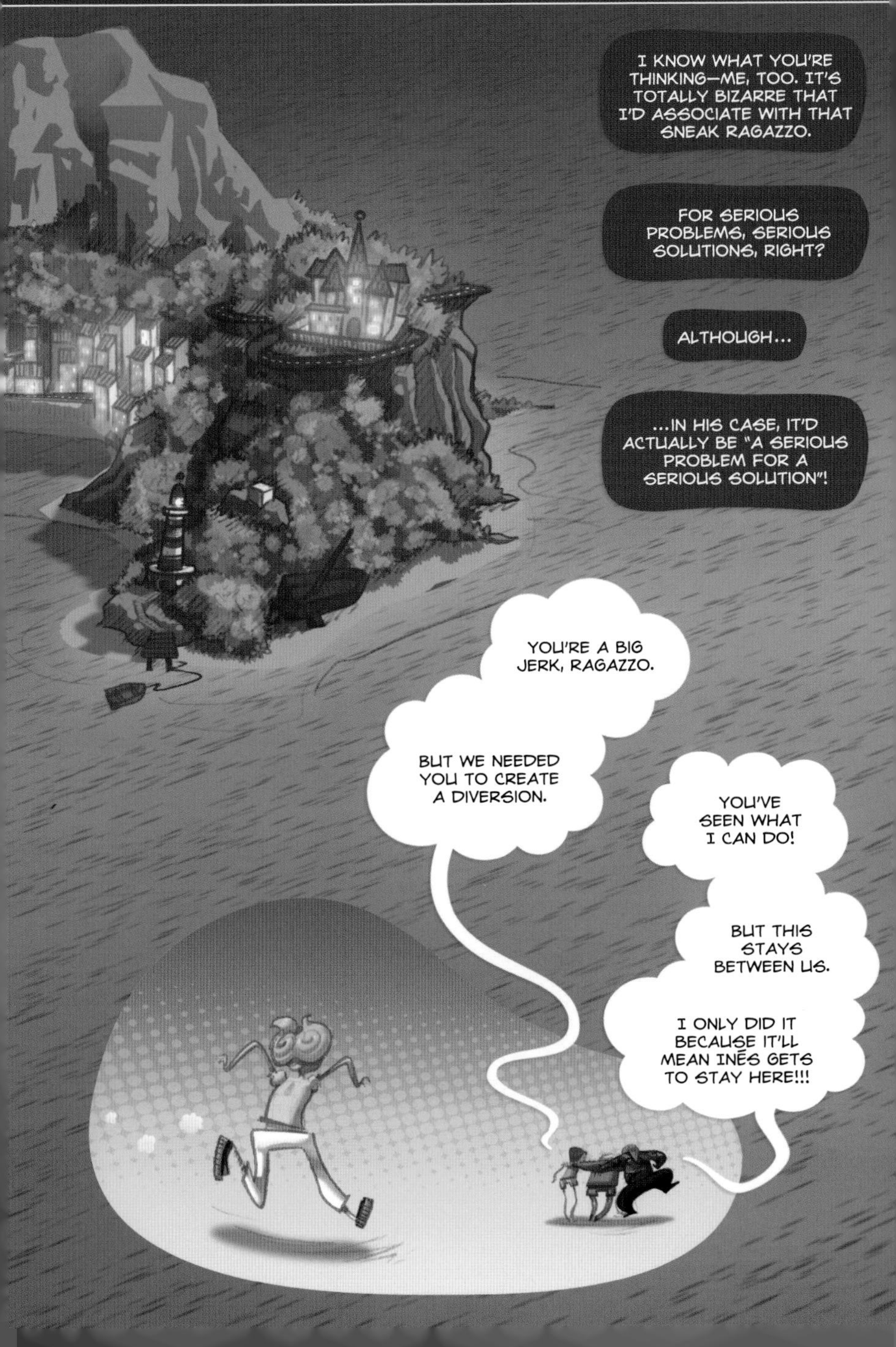
I KNOW WHAT YOU'RE THINKING—ME, TOO. IT'S TOTALLY BIZARRE THAT I'D ASSOCIATE WITH THAT SNEAK RAGAZZO.
FOR SERIOUS PROBLEMS, SERIOUS SOLUTIONS, RIGHT?
ALTHOUGH...
...IN HIS CASE, IT'D ACTUALLY BE "A SERIOUS PROBLEM FOR A SERIOUS SOLUTION"!
YOU'RE A BIG JERK, RAGAZZO.
BUT WE NEEDED YOU TO CREATE A DIVERSION.
YOU'VE SEEN WHAT I CAN DO!
BUT THIS STAYS BETWEEN US.
I ONLY DID IT BECAUSE IT'LL MEAN INÉS GETS TO STAY HERE!!!

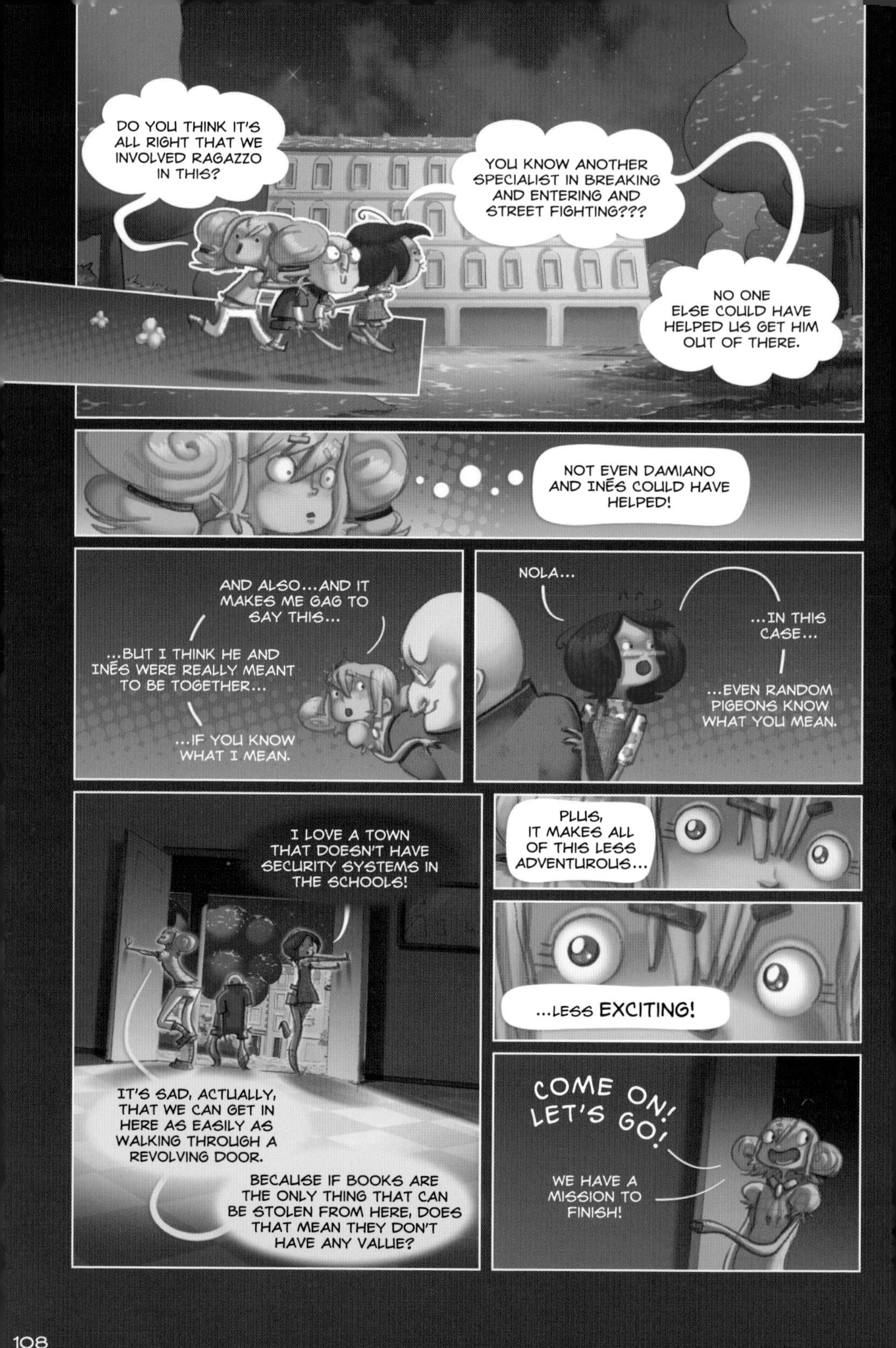

DO YOU THINK IT'S ALL RIGHT THAT WE INVOLVED RAGAZZO IN THIS?
YOU KNOW ANOTHER SPECIALIST IN BREAKING AND ENTERING AND STREET FIGHTING???
NO ONE ELSE COULD HAVE HELPED US GET HIM OUT OF THERE.
NOT EVEN DAMIANO AND INÉS COULD HAVE HELPED!
AND ALSO...AND IT MAKES ME GAG TO SAY THIS...
...BUT I THINK HE AND INÉS WERE REALLY MEANT TO BE TOGETHER...
...IF YOU KNOW WHAT I MEAN.
NOLA...
...IN THIS CASE...
...EVEN RANDOM PIGEONS KNOW WHAT YOU MEAN.
I LOVE A TOWN THAT DOESN'T HAVE SECURITY SYSTEMS IN THE SCHOOLS!
IT'S SAD, ACTUALLY, THAT WE CAN GET IN HERE AS EASILY AS WALKING THROUGH A REVOLVING DOOR.
BECAUSE IF BOOKS ARE THE ONLY THING THAT CAN BE STOLEN FROM HERE, DOES THAT MEAN THEY DON'T HAVE ANY VALUE?
PLUS, IT MAKES ALL OF THIS LESS ADVENTUROUS...
...LESS EXCITING!
COME ON! LET'S GO!
WE HAVE A MISSION TO FINISH!

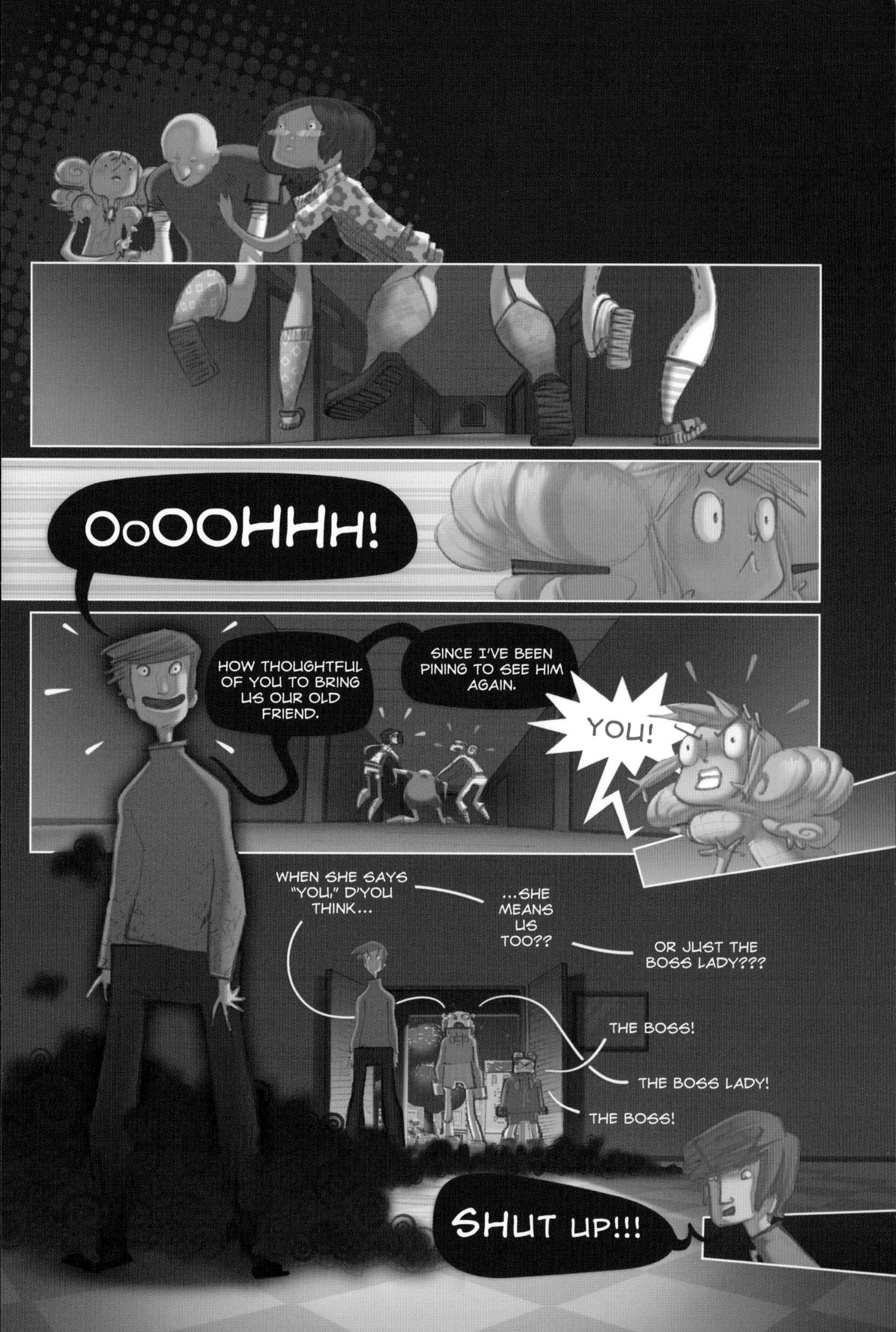
OoOOHHH!
HOW THOUGHTFUL OF YOU TO BRING US OUR OLD FRIEND.
SINCE I'VE BEEN PINING TO SEE HIM AGAIN.
YOU!
WHEN SHE SAYS "YOU," D'YOU THINK...
...SHE MEANS US TOO??
OR JUST THE BOSS LADY???
THE BOSS!
THE BOSS LADY!
THE BOSS!
SHUT UP!!!

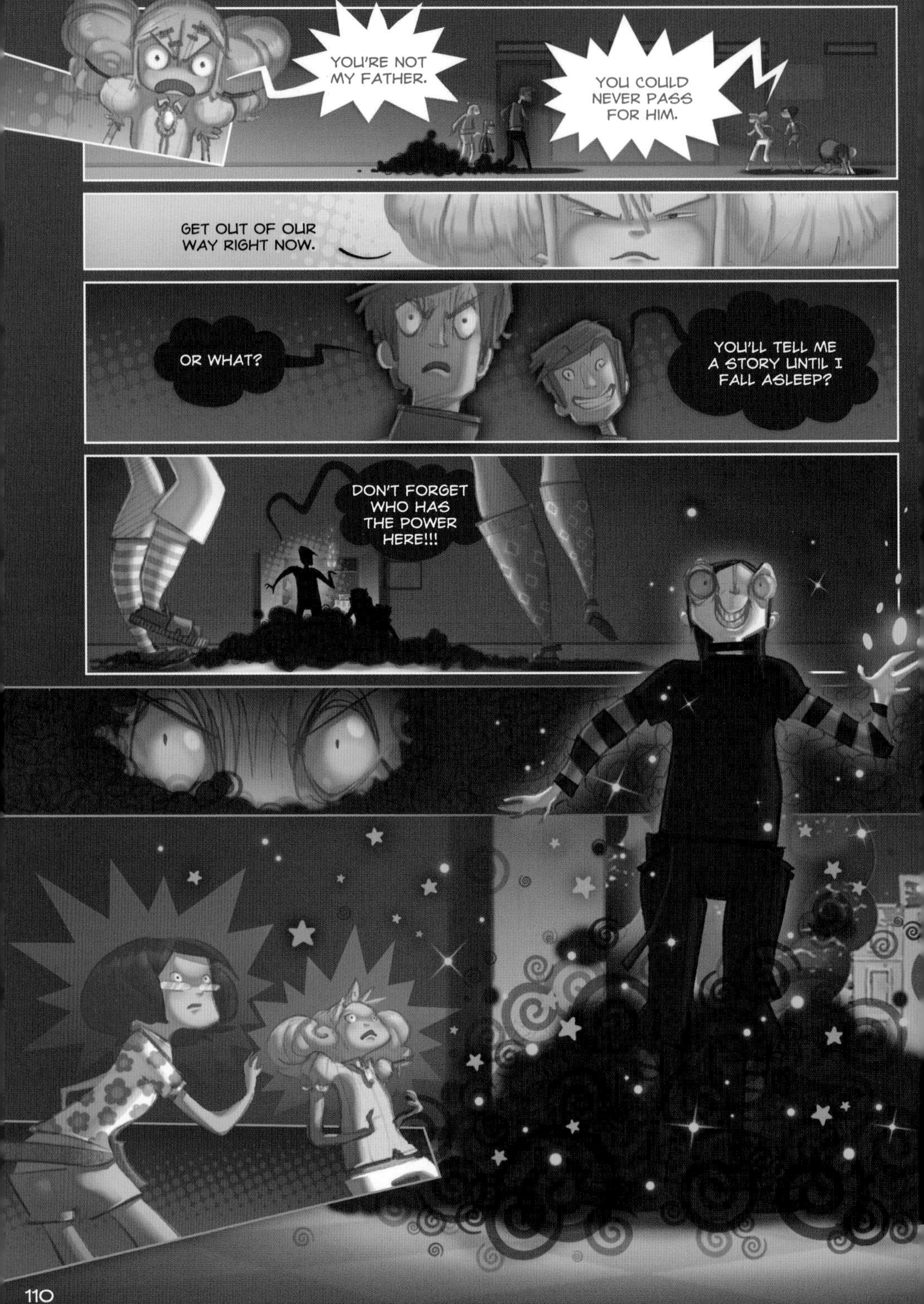

YOU'RE NOT MY FATHER.
YOU COULD NEVER PASS FOR HIM.
GET OUT OF OUR WAY RIGHT NOW.
OR WHAT?
YOU'LL TELL ME A STORY UNTIL I FALL ASLEEP?
DON'T FORGET WHO HAS THE POWER HERE!!!

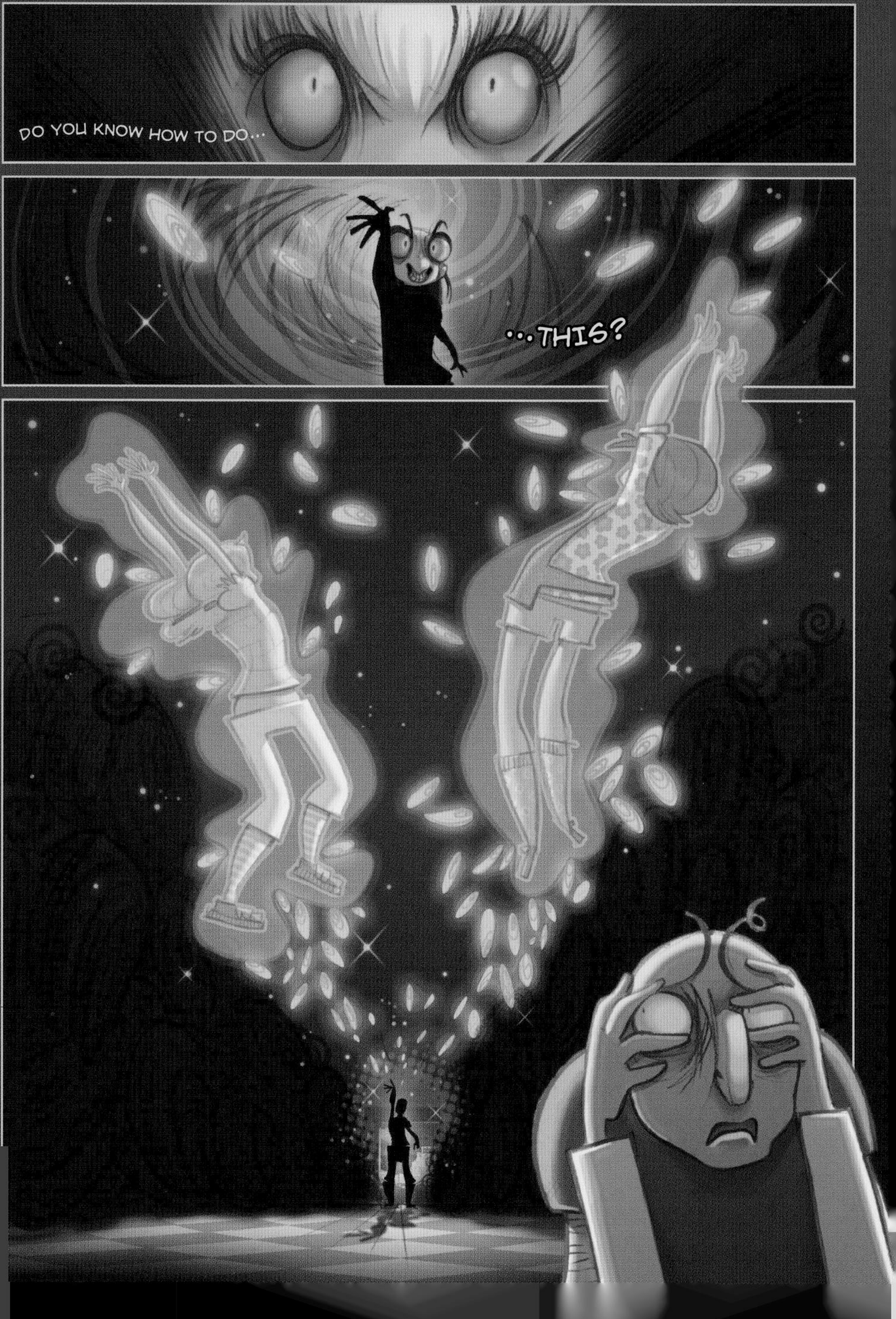
DO YOU KNOW HOW TO DO...
...THIS?

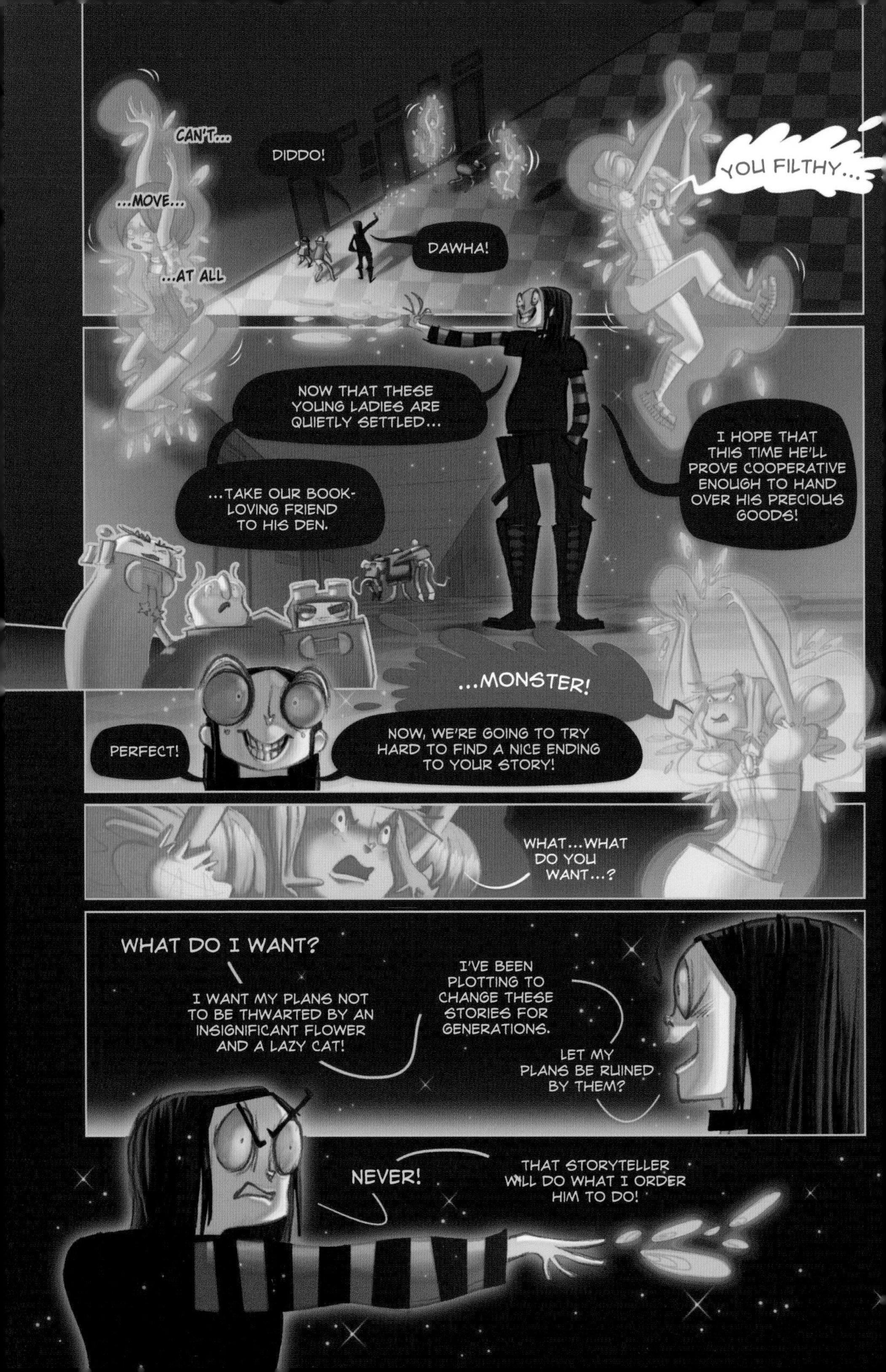
CAN'T...
...MOVE...
...AT ALL
DIDDO!
DAWHA!
YOU FILTHY...
NOW THAT THESE YOUNG LADIES ARE QUIETLY SETTLED...
...TAKE OUR BOOK-LOVING FRIEND TO HIS DEN.
I HOPE THAT THIS TIME HE'LL PROVE COOPERATIVE ENOUGH TO HAND OVER HIS PRECIOUS GOODS!
...MONSTER!
PERFECT!
NOW, WE'RE GOING TO TRY HARD TO FIND A NICE ENDING TO YOUR STORY!
WHAT...WHAT DO YOU WANT...?
WHAT DO I WANT?
I WANT MY PLANS NOT TO BE THWARTED BY AN INSIGNIFICANT FLOWER AND A LAZY CAT!
I'VE BEEN PLOTTING TO CHANGE THESE STORIES FOR GENERATIONS.
LET MY PLANS BE RUINED BY THEM?
NEVER!
THAT STORYTELLER WILL DO WHAT I ORDER HIM TO DO!

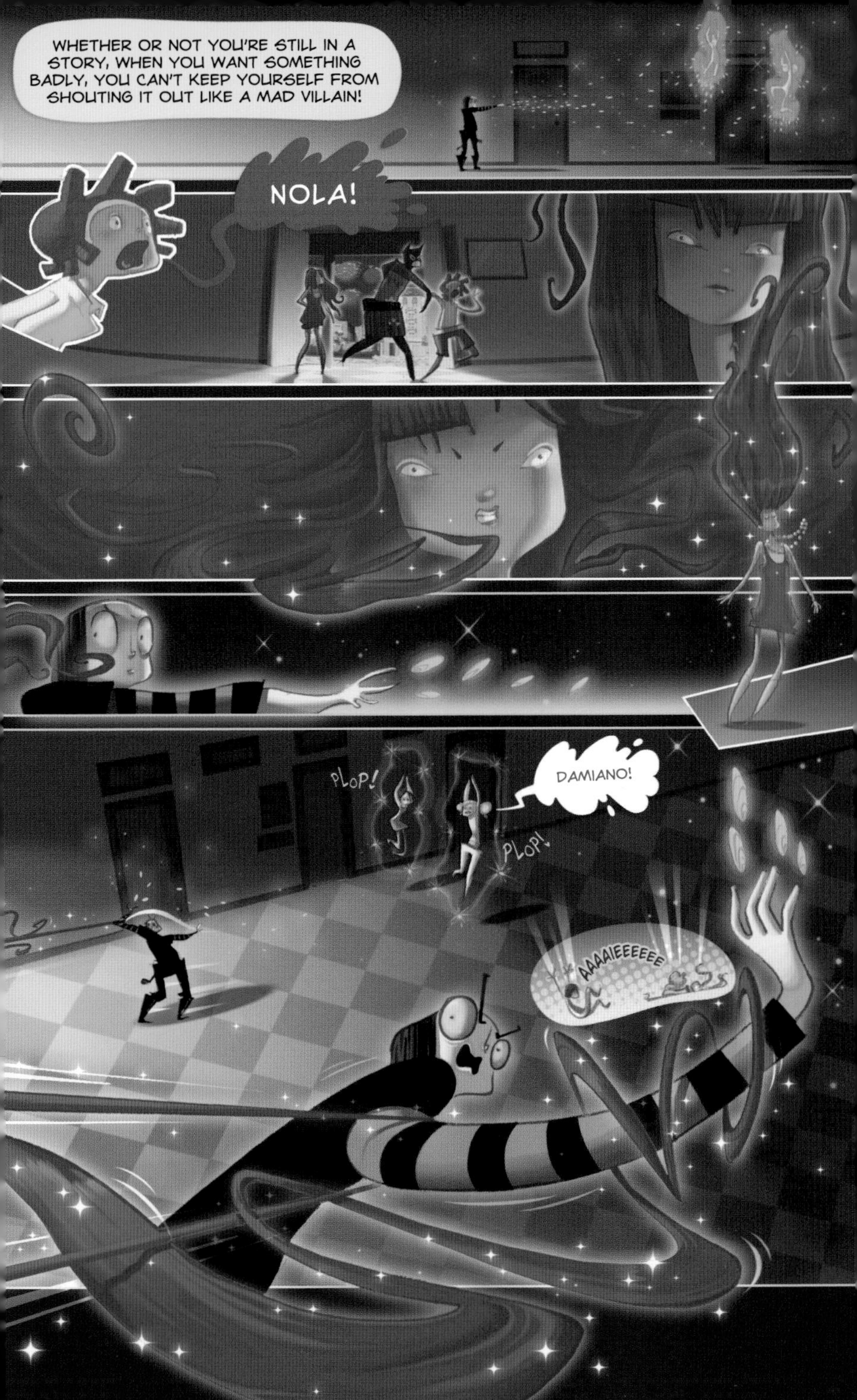
WHETHER OR NOT YOU'RE STILL IN A STORY, WHEN YOU WANT SOMETHING BADLY, YOU CAN'T KEEP YOURSELF FROM SHOUTING IT OUT LIKE A MAD VILLAIN!
NOLA!
PLOP!
DAMIANO!
PLOP!
AAAAIEEEEEE

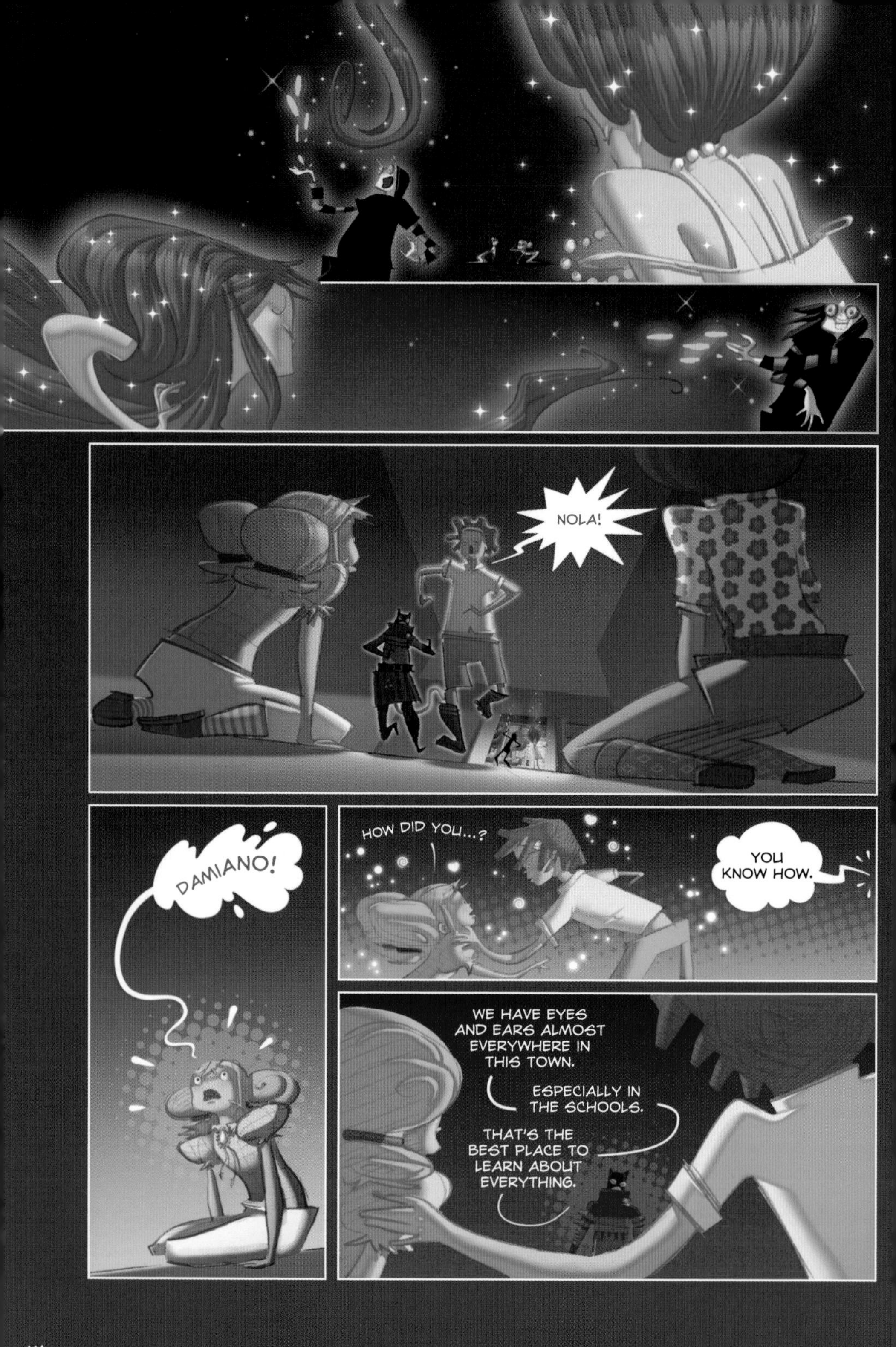
NOLA!
DAMIANO!
HOW DID YOU...?
YOU KNOW HOW.
WE HAVE EYES AND EARS ALMOST EVERYWHERE IN THIS TOWN.
ESPECIALLY IN THE SCHOOLS.
THAT'S THE BEST PLACE TO LEARN ABOUT EVERYTHING.

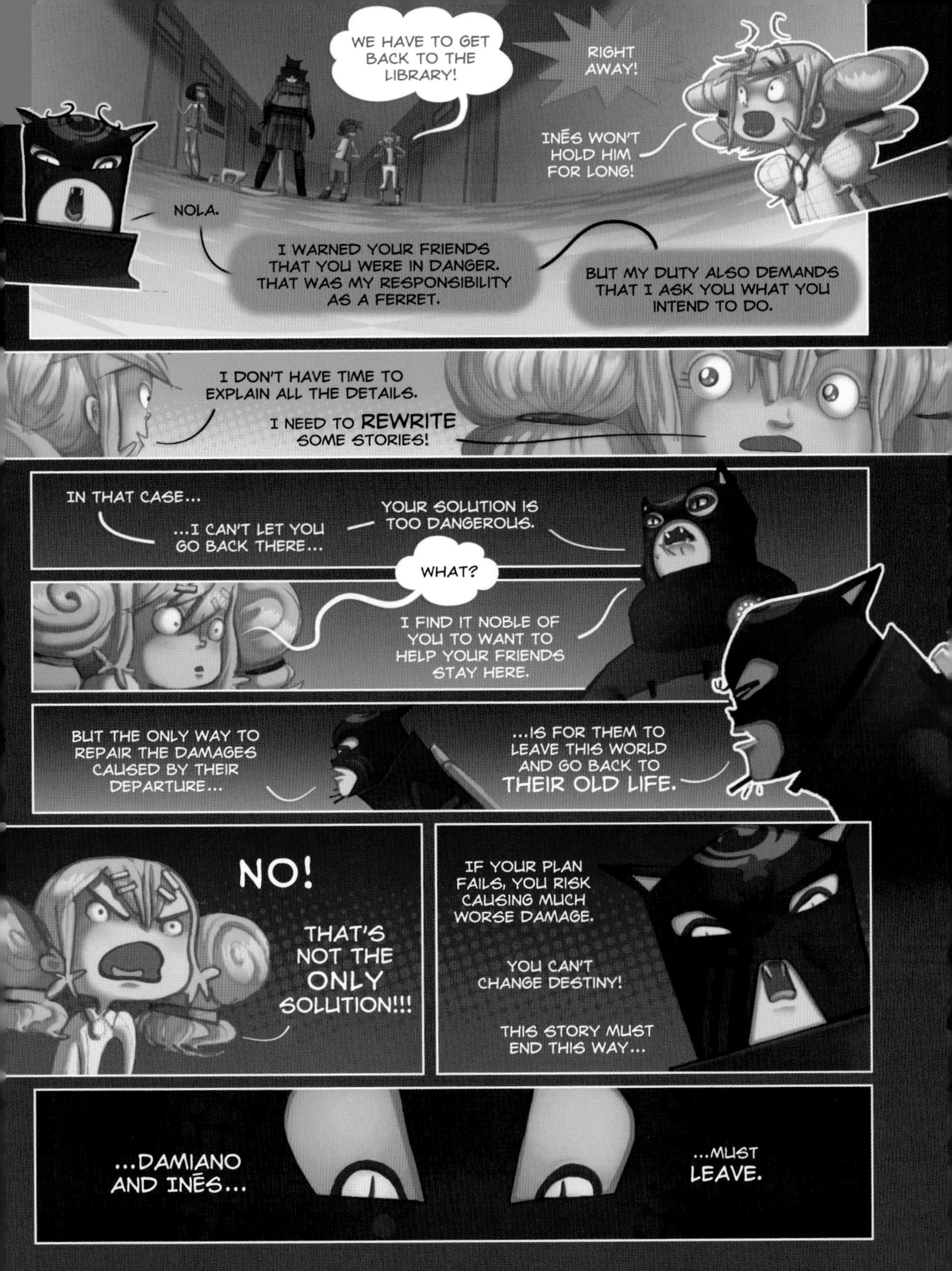
WE HAVE TO GET BACK TO THE LIBRARY!
RIGHT AWAY!
INÉS WON'T HOLD HIM FOR LONG!
NOLA.
I WARNED YOUR FRIENDS THAT YOU WERE IN DANGER. THAT WAS MY RESPONSIBILITY AS A FERRET.
BUT MY DUTY ALSO DEMANDS THAT I ASK YOU WHAT YOU INTEND TO DO.
I DON'T HAVE TIME TO EXPLAIN ALL THE DETAILS.
I NEED TO REWRITE SOME STORIES!
IN THAT CASE...
...I CAN'T LET YOU GO BACK THERE...
YOUR SOLUTION IS TOO DANGEROUS.
WHAT?
I FIND IT NOBLE OF YOU TO WANT TO HELP YOUR FRIENDS STAY HERE.
BUT THE ONLY WAY TO REPAIR THE DAMAGES CAUSED BY THEIR DEPARTURE...
...IS FOR THEM TO LEAVE THIS WORLD AND GO BACK TO THEIR OLD LIFE.
NO!
THAT'S NOT THE ONLY SOLUTION!!!
IF YOUR PLAN FAILS, YOU RISK CAUSING MUCH WORSE DAMAGE.
YOU CAN'T CHANGE DESTINY!
THIS STORY MUST END THIS WAY...
...DAMIANO AND INÉS...
...MUST LEAVE.

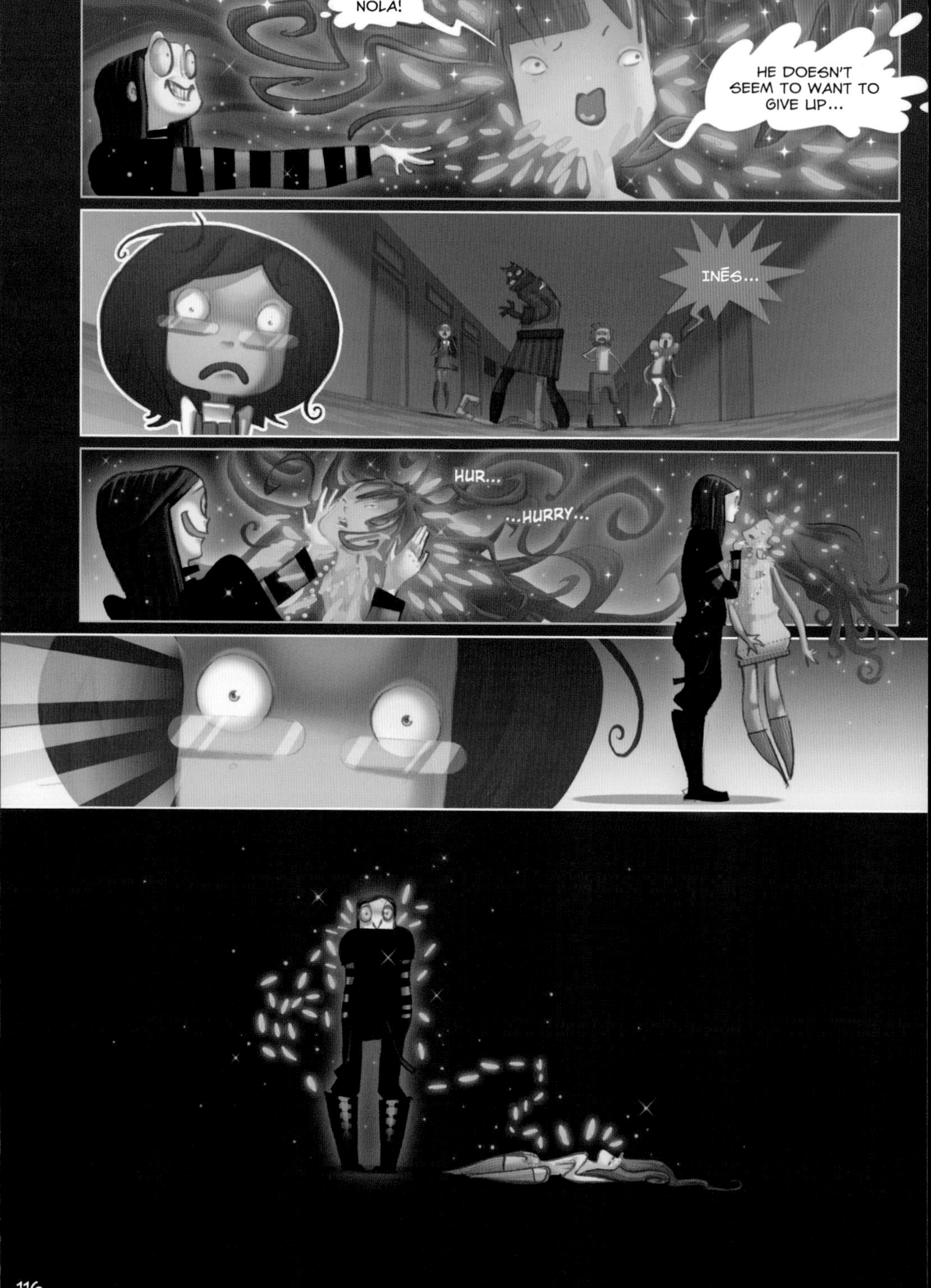
NOLA!
HE DOESN'T SEEM TO WANT TO GIVE UP...
INÉS...
HUR...
...HURRY...

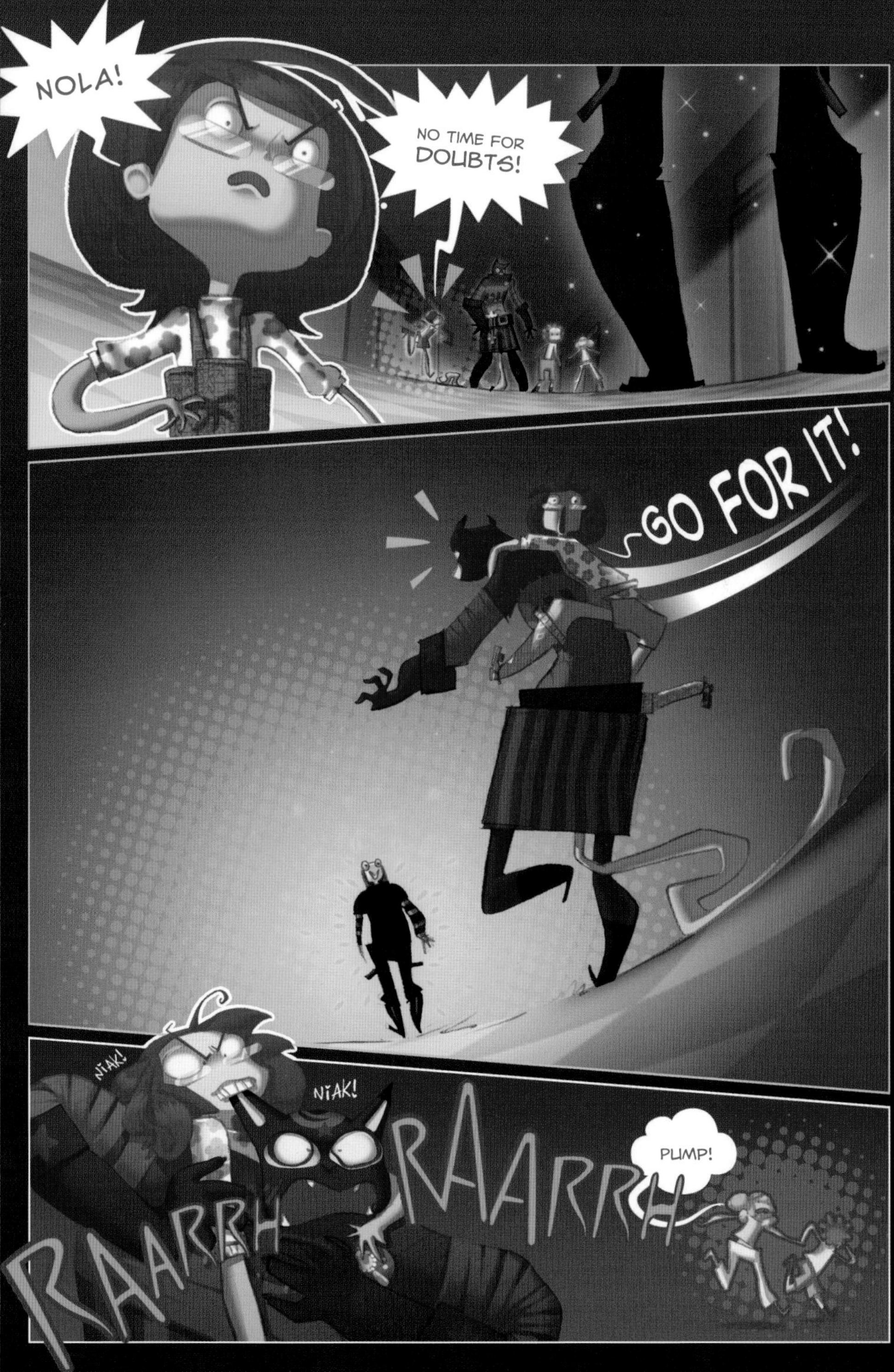

NOLA!
NO TIME FOR DOUBTS!
GO FOR IT!
NIAK!
NIAK!
RAARRH
RAARRH
PUMP!

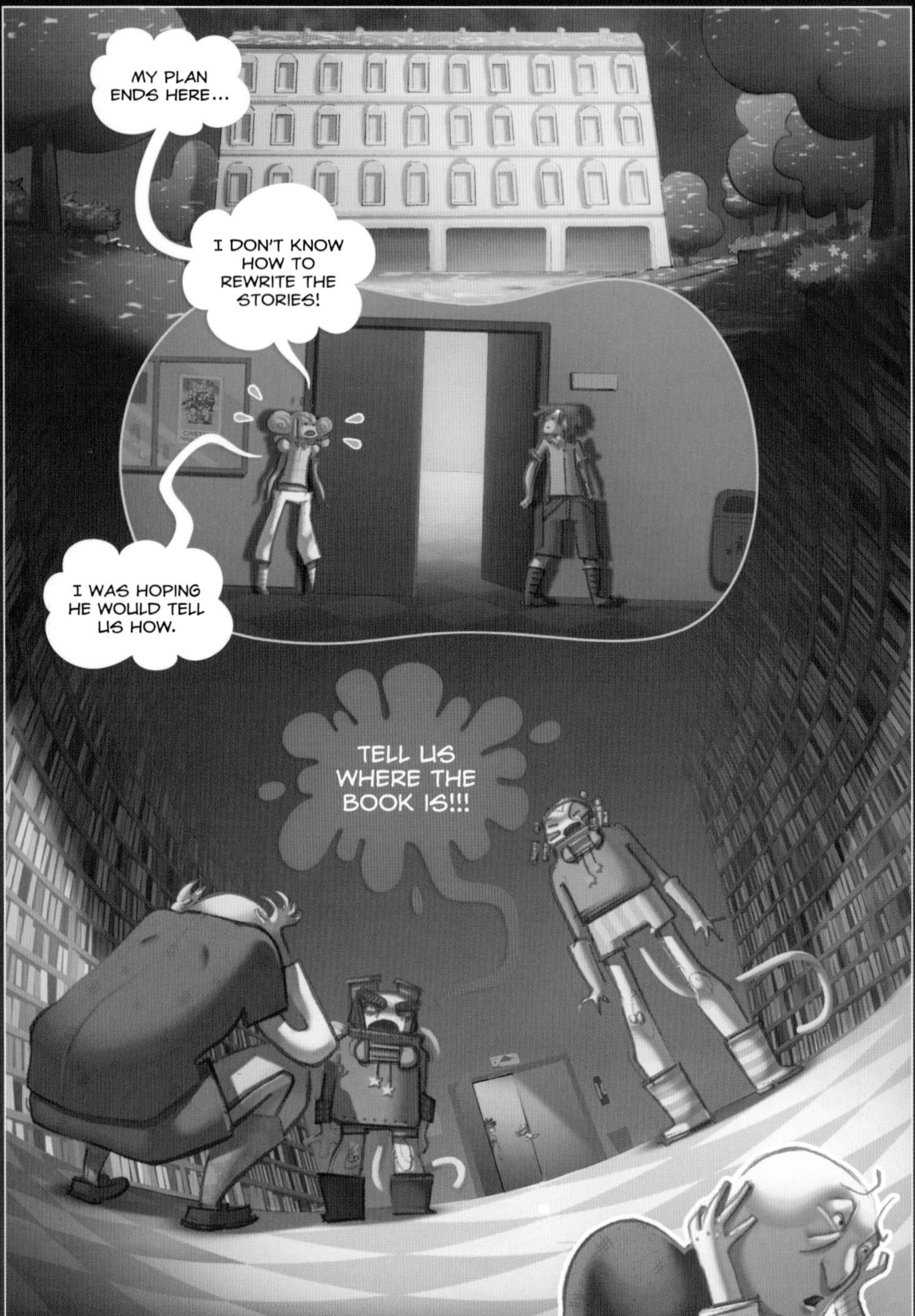
MY PLAN ENDS HERE...
I DON'T KNOW HOW TO REWRITE THE STORIES!
I WAS HOPING HE WOULD TELL US HOW.
TELL US WHERE THE BOOK IS!!!

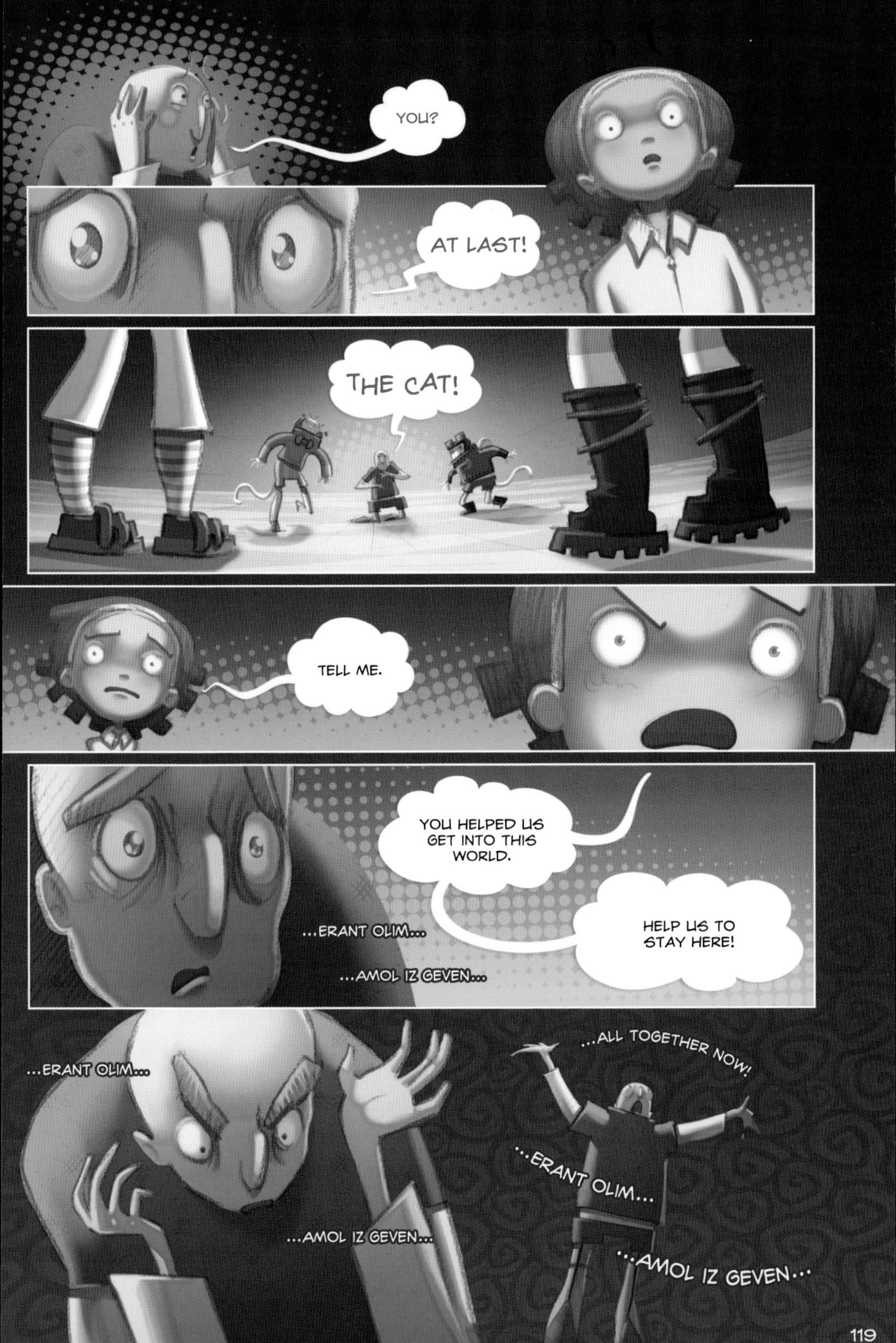
YOU?
AT LAST!
THE CAT!
TELL ME.
YOU HELPED US GET INTO THIS WORLD.
HELP US TO STAY HERE!
...ERANT OLIM...
...AMOL IZ GEVEN...
...ERANT OLIM...
...AMOL IZ GEVEN...
...ALL TOGETHER NOW!
...ERANT OLIM...
...AMOL IZ GEVEN...

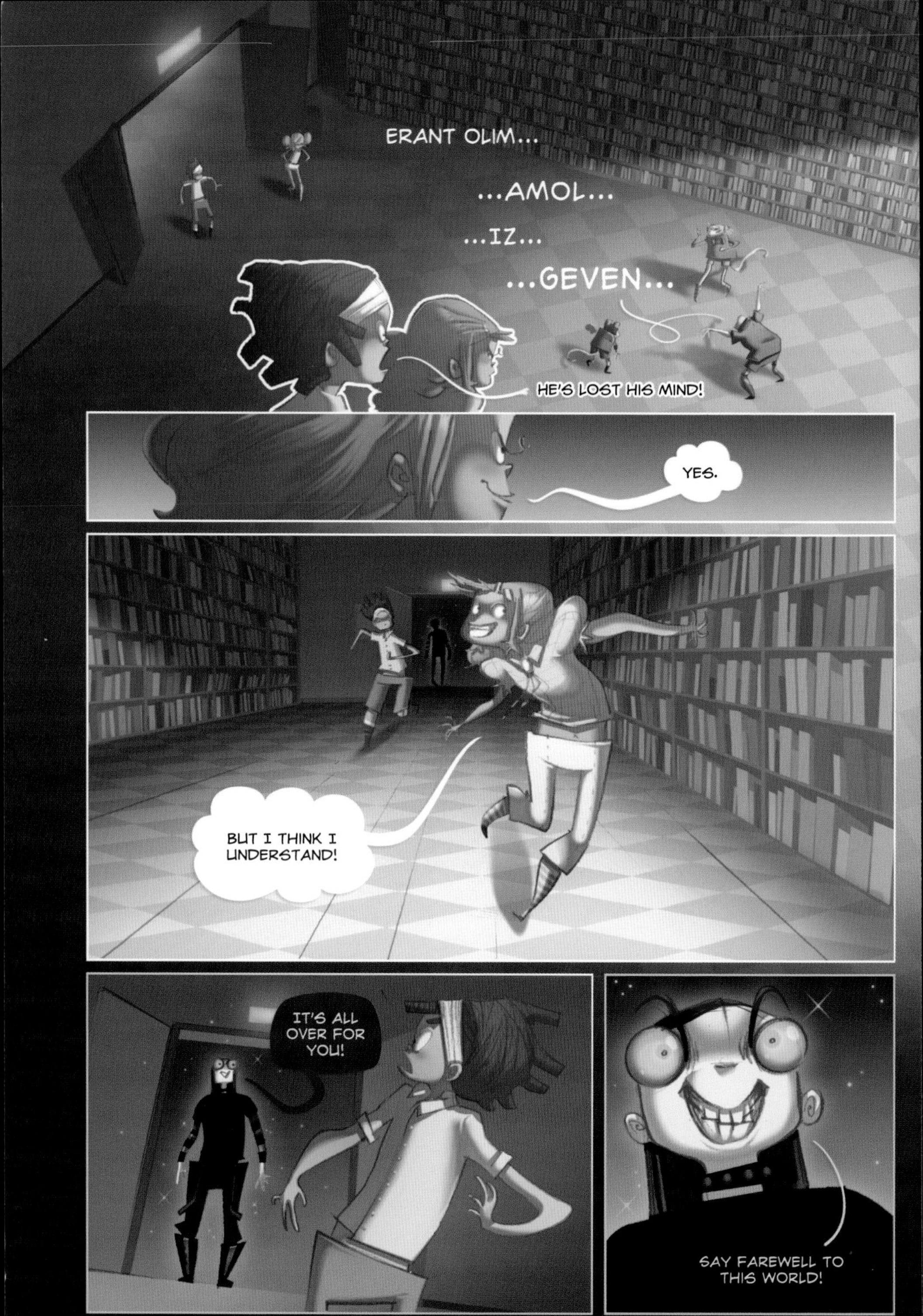
ERANT OLIM...
...AMOL...
...IZ...
...GEVEN...
HE'S LOST HIS MIND!
YES.
BUT I THINK I UNDERSTAND!
IT'S ALL OVER FOR YOU!
SAY FAREWELL TO THIS WORLD!

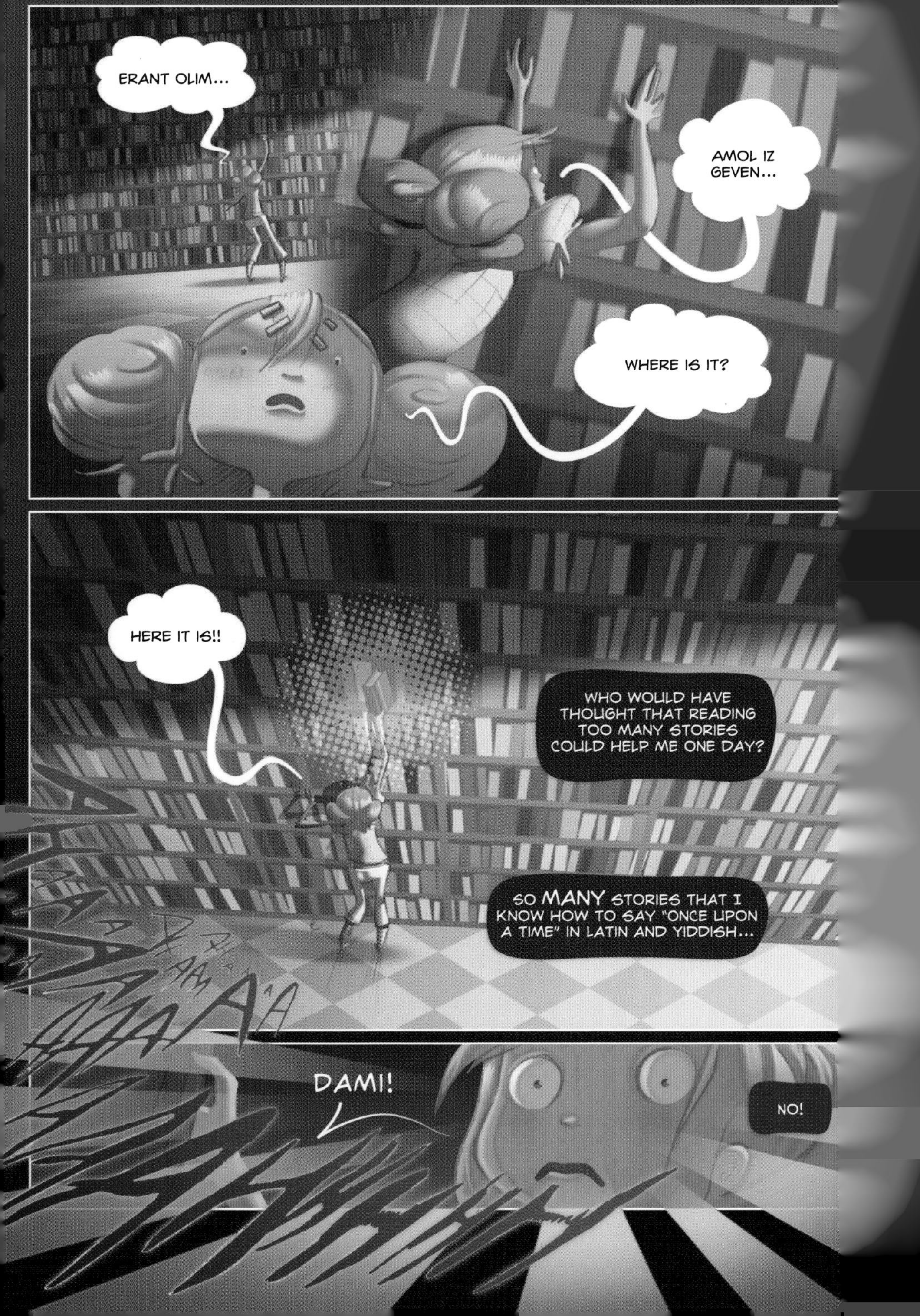
ERANT OLIM...
AMOL IZ GEVEN...
WHERE IS IT?
HERE IT IS!!
WHO WOULD HAVE THOUGHT THAT READING TOO MANY STORIES COULD HELP ME ONE DAY?
SO MANY STORIES THAT I KNOW HOW TO SAY "ONCE UPON A TIME" IN LATIN AND YIDDISH...
DAMI!
NO!

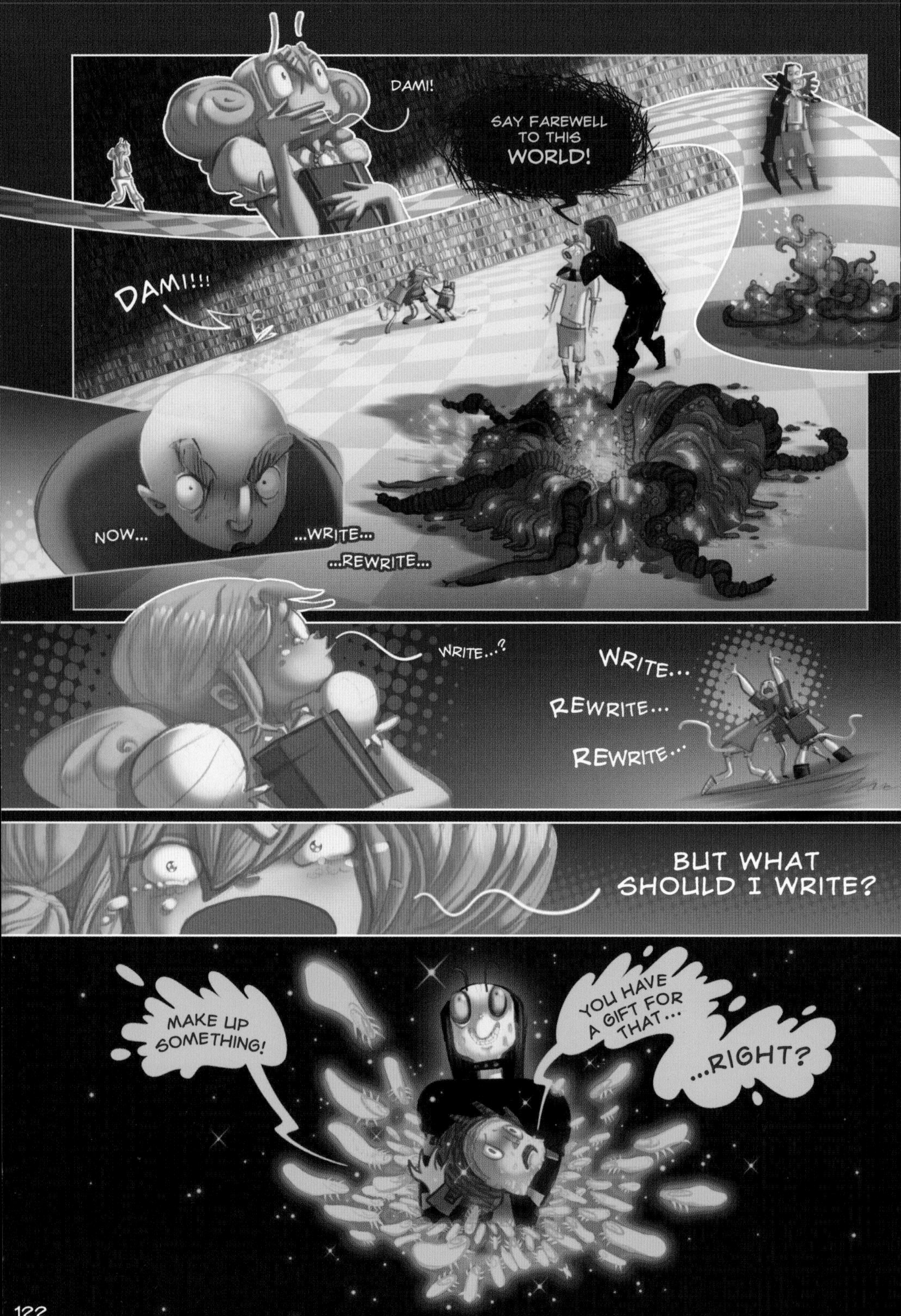
!!
DAMI!
SAY FAREWELL TO THIS WORLD!
DAMI!!!
NOW...
...WRITE...
...REWRITE...
WRITE...?
WRITE...
REWRITE...
REWRITE...
BUT WHAT SHOULD I WRITE?
MAKE UP SOMETHING!
YOU HAVE A GIFT FOR THAT...
...RIGHT?

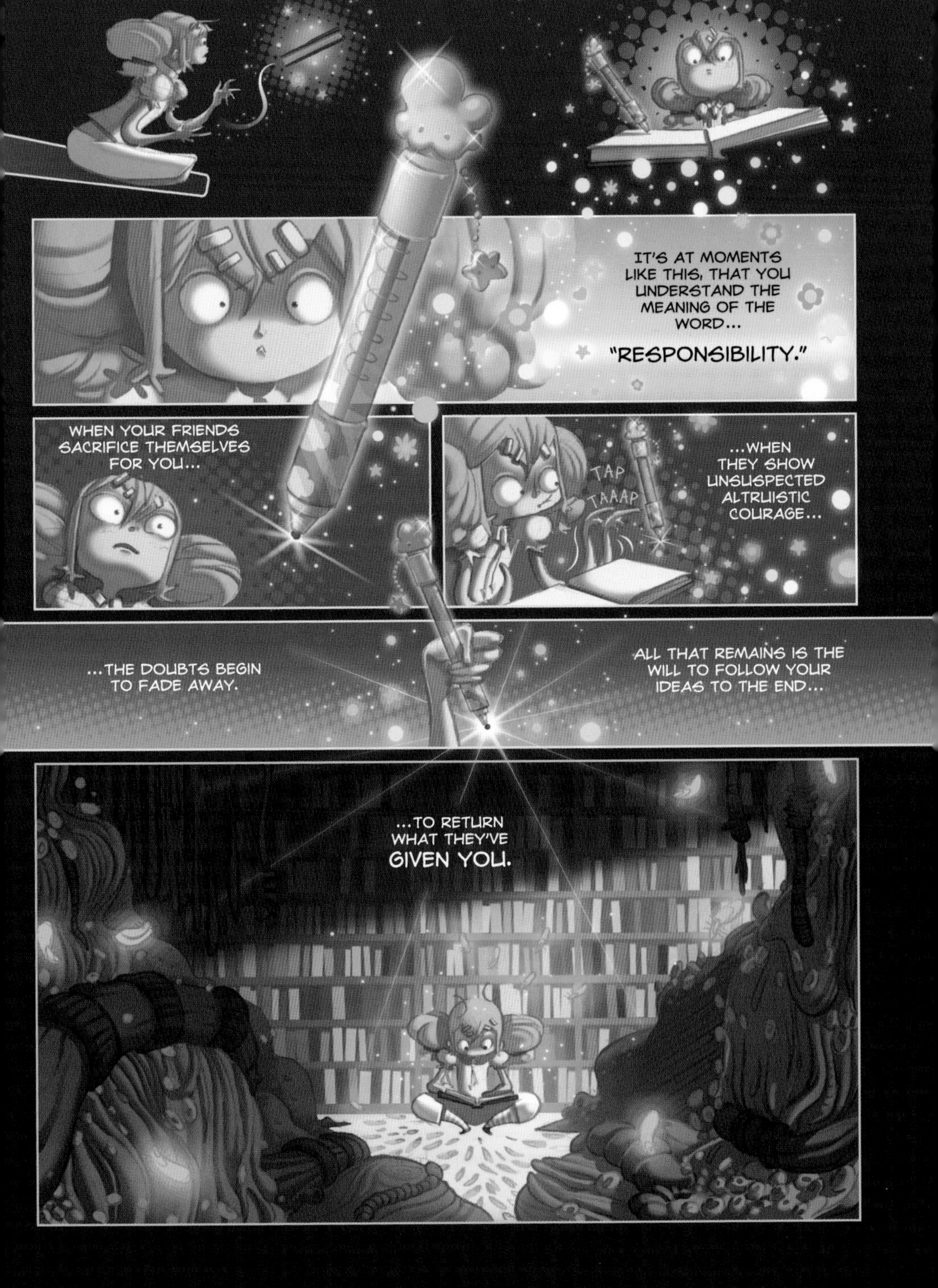

IT'S AT MOMENTS LIKE THIS, THAT YOU UNDERSTAND THE MEANING OF THE WORD...
"RESPONSIBILITY."
WHEN YOUR FRIENDS SACRIFICE THEMSELVES FOR YOU...
TAP
TAAAP
...WHEN THEY SHOW UNSUSPECTED ALTRUISTIC COURAGE...
...THE DOUBTS BEGIN TO FADE AWAY.
ALL THAT REMAINS IS THE WILL TO FOLLOW YOUR IDEAS TO THE END...
...TO RETURN WHAT THEY'VE GIVEN YOU.

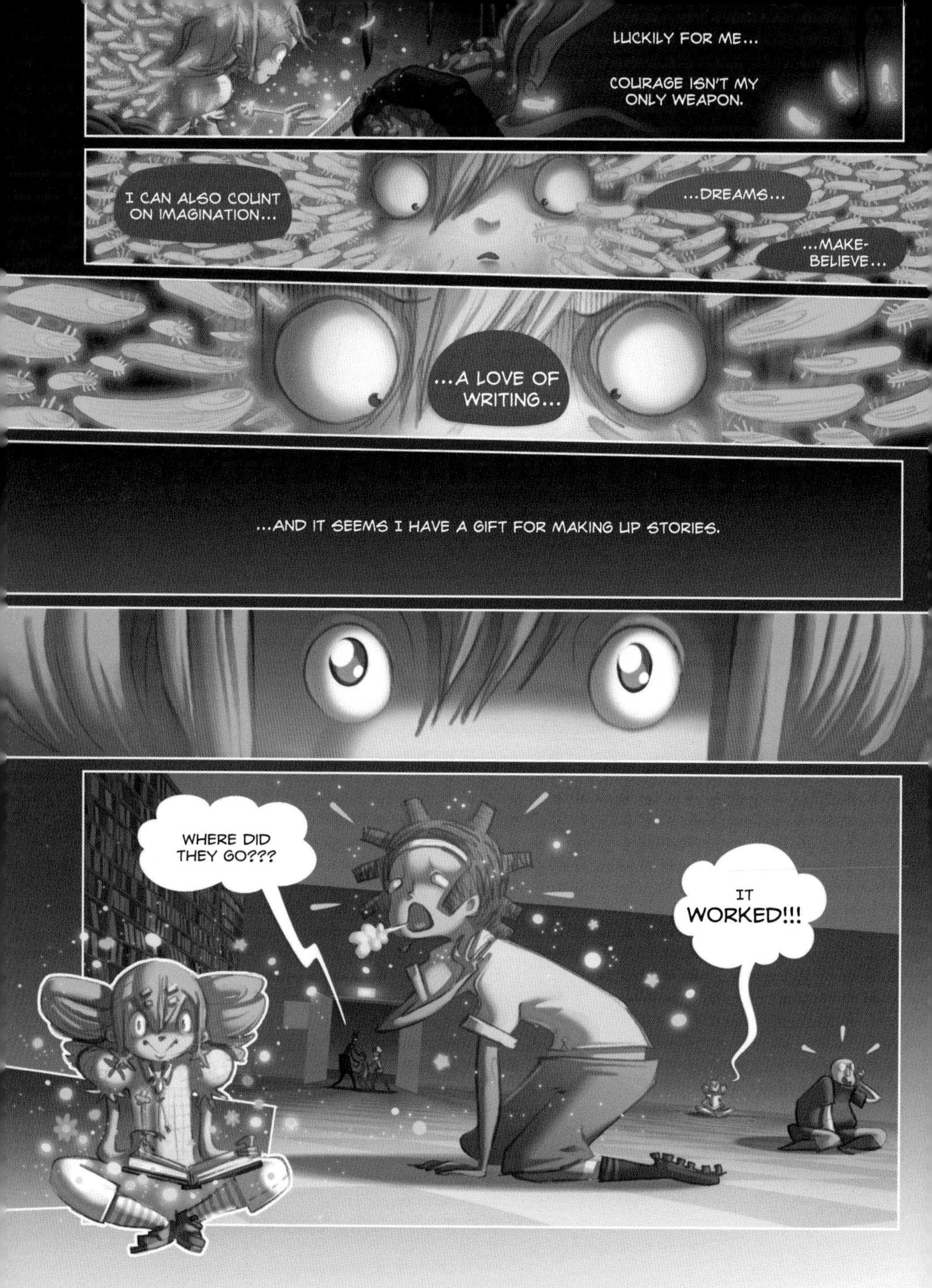
LUCKILY FOR ME...
COURAGE ISN'T MY ONLY WEAPON.
I CAN ALSO COUNT ON IMAGINATION...
...DREAMS...
...MAKE-BELIEVE...
...A LOVE OF WRITING...
...AND IT SEEMS I HAVE A GIFT FOR MAKING UP STORIES.
WHERE DID THEY GO???
IT WORKED!!!

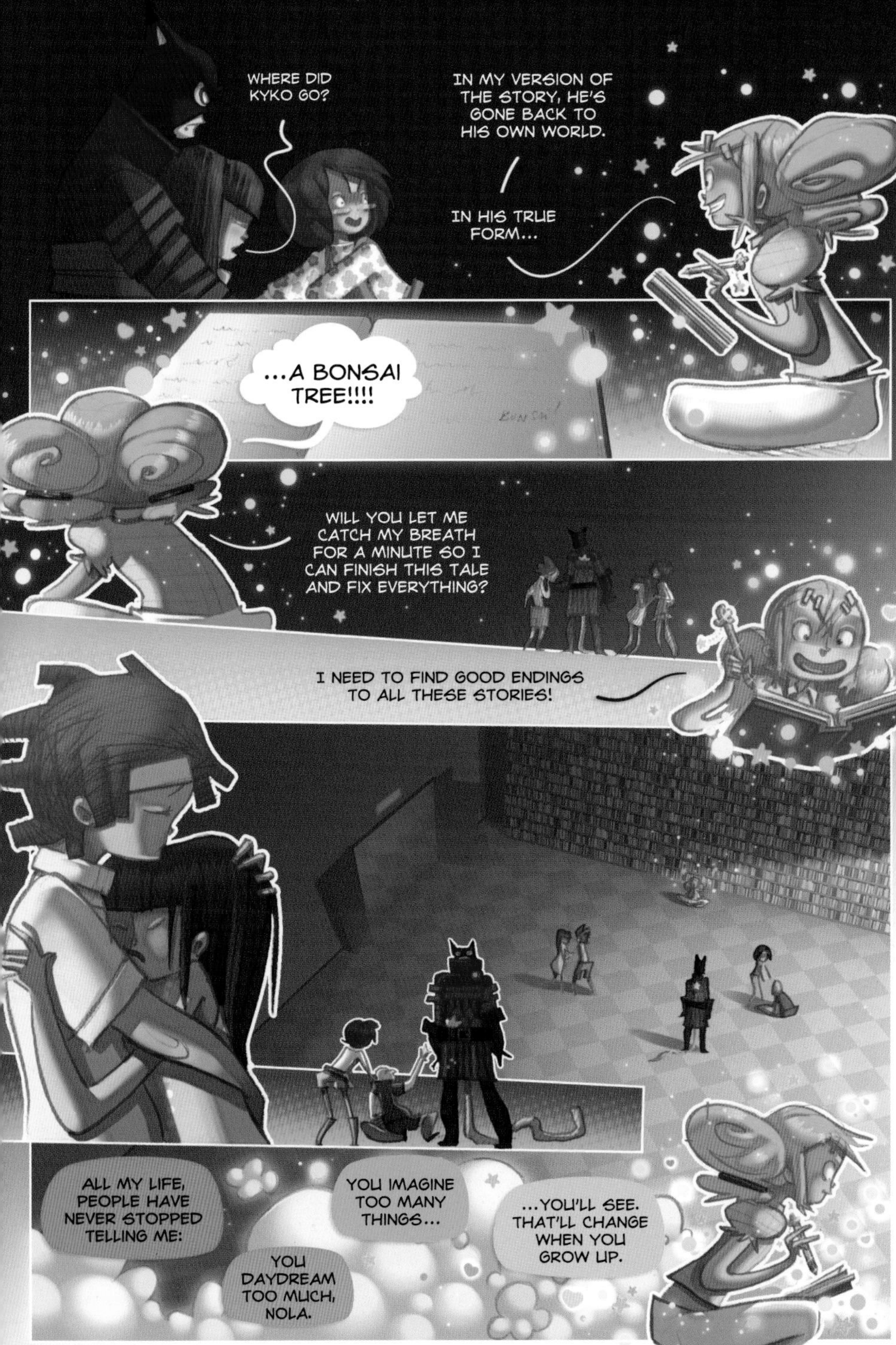
WHERE DID KYKO GO?
IN MY VERSION OF THE STORY, HE'S GONE BACK TO HIS OWN WORLD.
IN HIS TRUE FORM...
...A BONSAI TREE!!!!
WILL YOU LET ME CATCH MY BREATH FOR A MINUTE SO I CAN FINISH THIS TALE AND FIX EVERYTHING?
I NEED TO FIND GOOD ENDINGS TO ALL THESE STORIES!
ALL MY LIFE, PEOPLE HAVE NEVER STOPPED TELLING ME:
YOU DAYDREAM TOO MUCH, NOLA.
YOU IMAGINE TOO MANY THINGS...
...YOU'LL SEE. THAT'LL CHANGE WHEN YOU GROW UP.

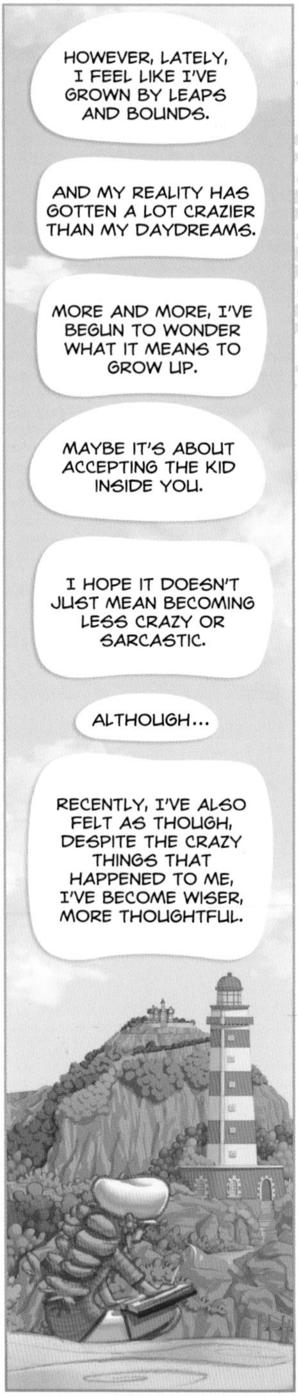
HOWEVER, LATELY, I FEEL LIKE I'VE GROWN BY LEAPS AND BOUNDS.
AND MY REALITY HAS GOTTEN A LOT CRAZIER THAN MY DAYDREAMS.
MORE AND MORE, I'VE BEGUN TO WONDER WHAT IT MEANS TO GROW UP.
MAYBE IT'S ABOUT ACCEPTING THE KID INSIDE YOU.
I HOPE IT DOESN'T JUST MEAN BECOMING LESS CRAZY OR SARCASTIC.
ALTHOUGH...
RECENTLY, I'VE ALSO FELT AS THOUGH, DESPITE THE CRAZY THINGS THAT HAPPENED TO ME, I'VE BECOME WISER, MORE THOUGHTFUL.

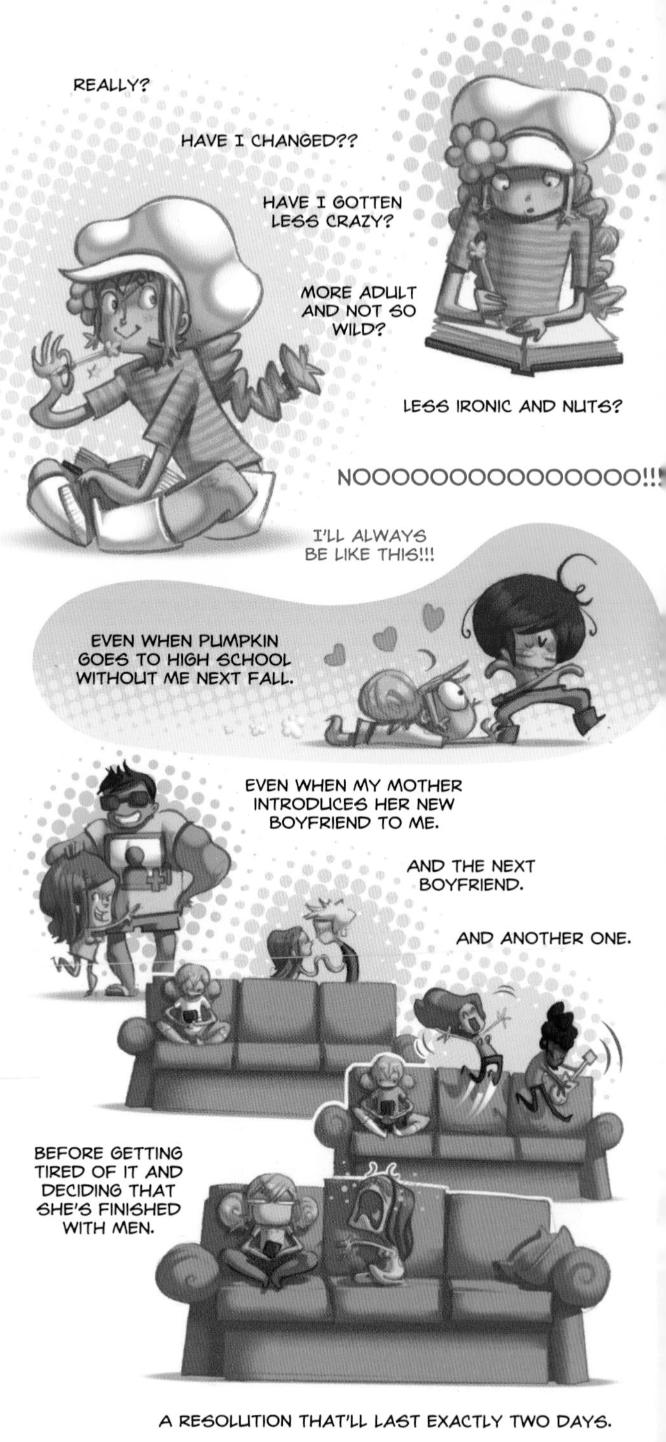
REALLY?
HAVE I CHANGED??
HAVE I GOTTEN LESS CRAZY?
MORE ADULT AND NOT SO WILD?
LESS IRONIC AND NUTS?
NOOOOOOOOOOOOOOO!!!
I'LL ALWAYS BE LIKE THIS!!!
EVEN WHEN PUMPKIN GOES TO HIGH SCHOOL WITHOUT ME NEXT FALL.
EVEN WHEN MY MOTHER INTRODUCES HER NEW BOYFRIEND TO ME.
AND THE NEXT BOYFRIEND.
AND ANOTHER ONE.
BEFORE GETTING TIRED OF IT AND DECIDING THAT SHE'S FINISHED WITH MEN.
A RESOLUTION THAT'LL LAST EXACTLY TWO DAYS.

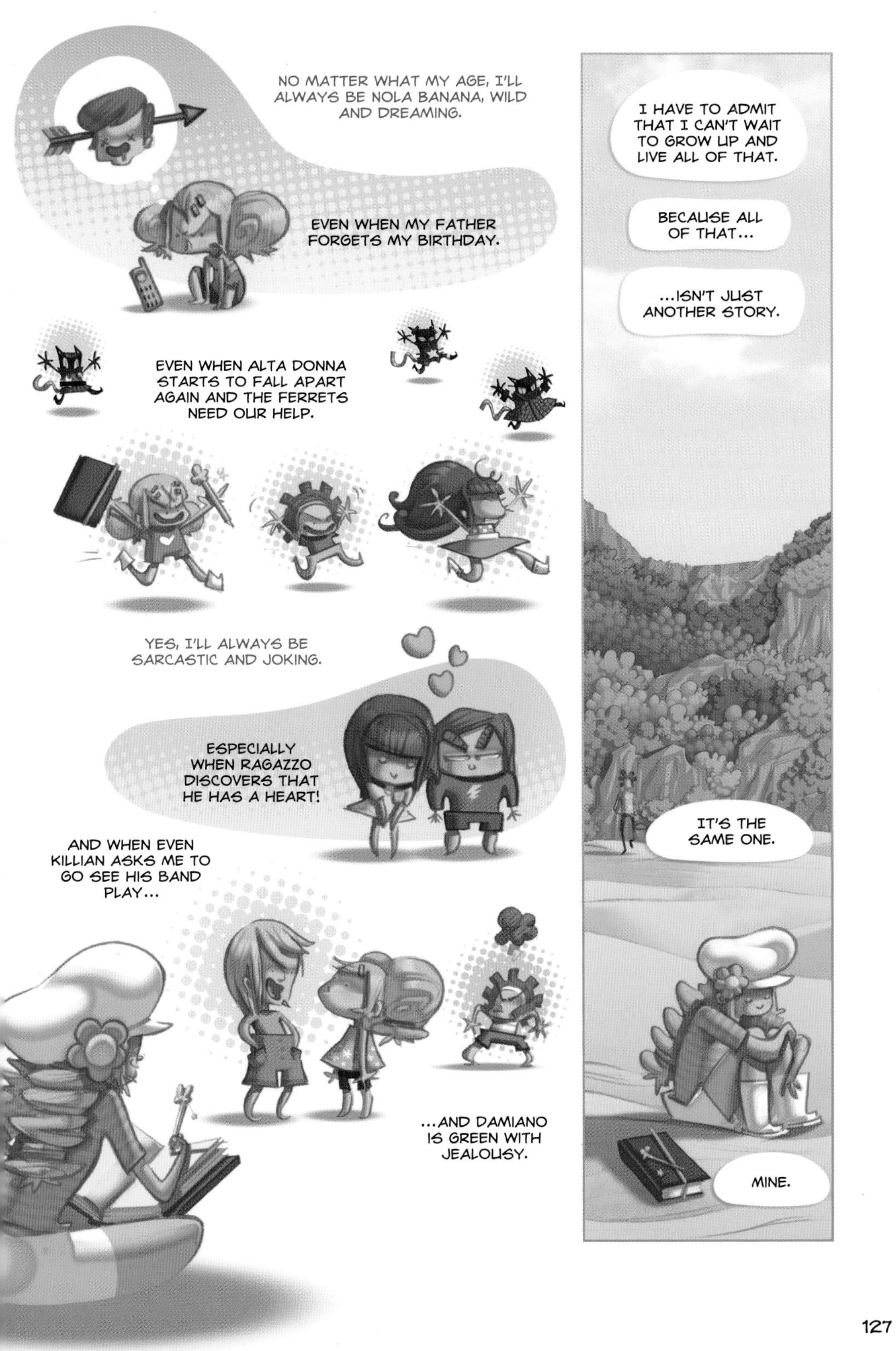
NO MATTER WHAT MY AGE, I'LL ALWAYS BE NOLA BANANA, WILD AND DREAMING.
EVEN WHEN MY FATHER FORGETS MY BIRTHDAY.
EVEN WHEN ALTA DONNA STARTS TO FALL APART AGAIN AND THE FERRETS NEED OUR HELP.
YES, I'LL ALWAYS BE SARCASTIC AND JOKING.
ESPECIALLY WHEN RAGAZZO DISCOVERS THAT HE HAS A HEART!
AND WHEN EVEN KILLIAN ASKS ME TO GO SEE HIS BAND PLAY...
...AND DAMIANO IS GREEN WITH JEALOUSY.
I HAVE TO ADMIT THAT I CAN'T WAIT TO GROW UP AND LIVE ALL OF THAT.
BECAUSE ALL OF THAT...
...ISN'T JUST ANOTHER STORY.
IT'S THE SAME ONE.
MINE.

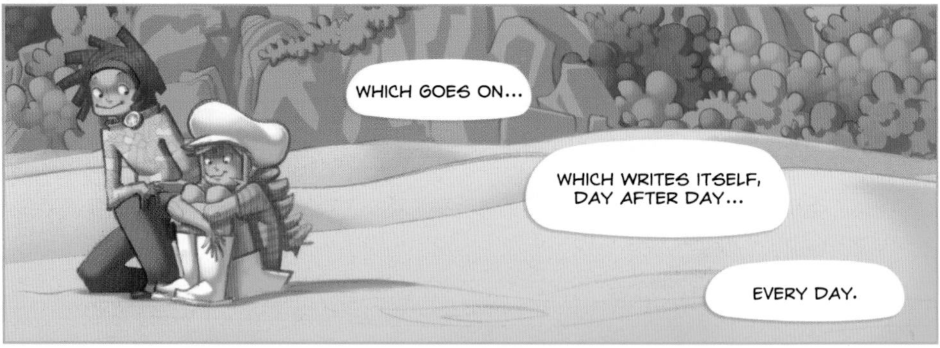
WHICH GOES ON...
WHICH WRITES ITSELF, DAY AFTER DAY...
EVERY DAY.

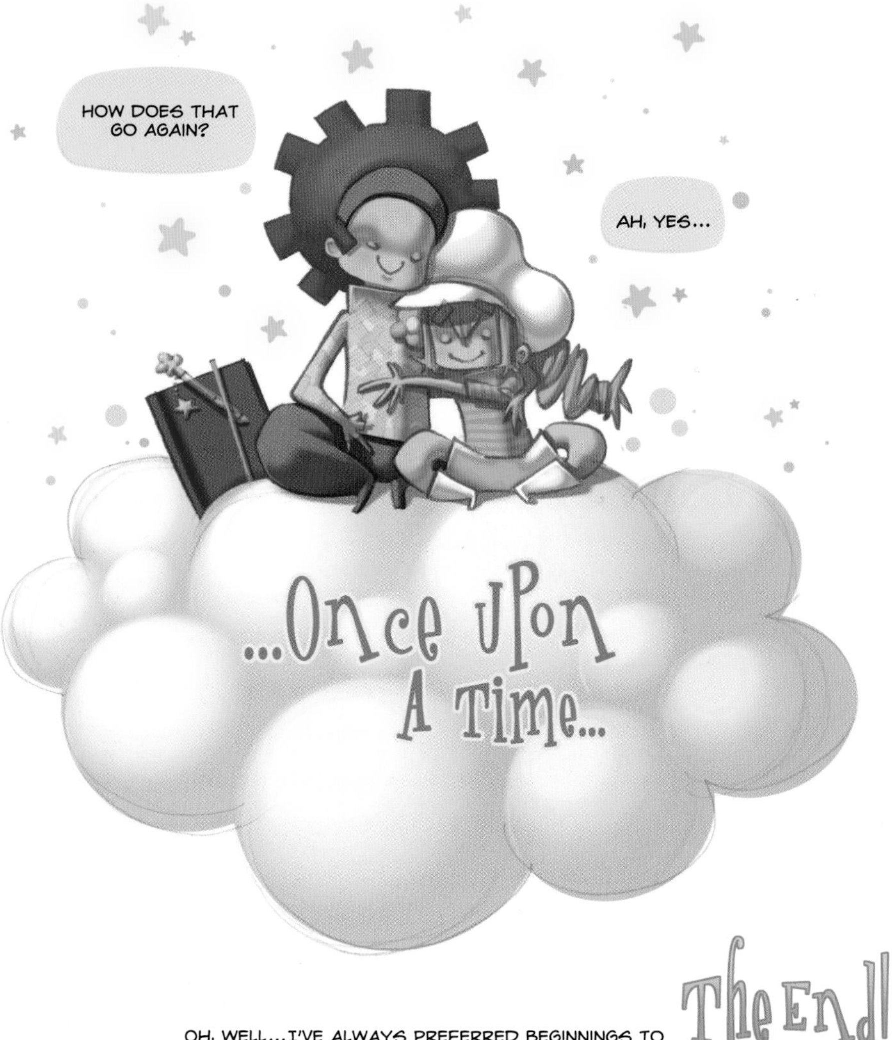
HOW DOES THAT GO AGAIN?
AH, YES...
...Once upon A Time...
OH, WELL...I'VE ALWAYS PREFERRED BEGINNINGS TO The End!